darkmatters

darkmatters

a novel   PAUL M. LEVITT

University of New Mexico Press
Albuquerque

Library of Congress Cataloging-in-Publication Data

Levitt, Paul M.

Dark matters : a novel / Paul M. Levitt.—1st ed.

p. cm.

ISBN 0-8263-3034-7 (cloth : alk. paper)

1. Triangles (Interpersonal relations)—Fiction.

2. Women labor union members—Fiction.

3. Anti-communist movements—Fiction.

4. College students—Fiction.

5. Boulder (Colo.)—Fiction. I. Title.

PS3612.E935D37 2004

813'.54—dc22

2003026964

Printed and bound in the USA by Thomson-Shore, Inc.

Set in Janson Text 10/14.2

Display type set in Gill Sans Condensed

Design and composition: Robyn Mundy

Production: Maya Allen-Gallegos

To Nancy Levitt

Acknowledgments

If, as Tennessee Williams says, life is all memory except for the present moment, then I am especially indebted to those who are the source of my memories: Marty Litman, who found through classical music the means to survive in a world inhospitable to his physical imperfections; Morris Judd, who lost his teaching position at the University of Colorado because of McCarthyism and yet never relinquished his belief in the goodness of people; my wife, Nancy Levitt, whose spirit runs through a great deal of this story; and my parents, Benjamin and Jeanette Levitt, whose remembrances of times past have always excited my imagination.

A book, though, is more than the past remembered in the present. It also rests on the labors of others, like librarians and colleagues. To these people I am also indebted: Elissa Guralnick, who read the manuscript numerous times and made invaluable suggestions about tone and form; Nancy Mann, who once again has lent her brilliant editorial skills to improve one of my manuscripts; Margot Brauchli, who let me glimpse some of her southern family's skeletons; Josef Michl, who served as my Czech translator and fact finder; and by no means least of all the editor of the University of New Mexico Press, Luther Wilson, a man of integrity and high purpose.

Note: Since this book was written, the University of Colorado has released the secret FBI report that cost several decent people their jobs. The release of the report, after fifty years, was owing to the courage of Clint Talbott, journalist extraordinaire, and the former editor/publisher of the *The Daily Camera* newspaper, Colleen Conant.

Marty

Not everyone has enjoyed my disadvantages. My mother, fifty at my birth, spent her childhood in a Polish shtetl, where she acquired the habits she passed on to me. So I, feeling at least two hundred years old, treat evolution and the evil eye as equal engines of change. Schooled in both superstition and science, I am often in error but rarely in doubt.

My father, who sailed in steerage from Lithuania to America, owned a small store, Bartelman's Grocery, in a seedy part of Detroit. We lived upstairs among mismatched furniture and tasteless knickknacks, assailed by the pungent smells that rose from the large wooden barrels downstairs holding herring and pickles in brine. My father expressed his love of his new country not by parading or flying a flag, but by collecting patriotic souvenirs: a music box that played "The Star Spangled Banner" and a cast metal model of the Washington monument, as well as one of the Empire State building; a glass paperweight, embedded with a scene of the White House that snowed when shaken; and his favorite, a tin wind-up toy of Uncle Sam that walked and smartly saluted. From our living-room window I watched the American hurlyburly, but owing to temporal lobe epilepsy, which caused visual distortions, I never took part, and was schooled at home by a rabbi who also taught me Kabbalah. Until my mother's death, she crippled me with love. Refusing to let me fend for myself, she tied my shoes till I turned twelve, kept me from rough and tumble street play, forbade bicycles as dangerous (I still don't know how to ride one), and discouraged me from using my hands, which to this day are sweaty, soft appendages that can do little more than open a book, put a record on the turntable, and, of course, hunt and peck on the typewriter.

darkmatters
LEVITT

Having little to occupy my childhood, I read a great deal, acquiring an ear for the rhythms of language, and a command of subjects that qualified me to attend a first-rate private college. But my mother, who began each day by giving her husband and son their marching orders, refused to let me matriculate out of sight of the family. Her only concession to my desire to leave Detroit was to send me to the University of Colorado, where my sister and brother-in-law, who had moved to Greeley, could keep an eye on me. When I expressed an interest in studying music, she asked rhetorically who would run my father's grocery store. I could study business. Even my father, who from time to time secretly took my side, had to agree. A knowledge of commerce would make our store prosper or at least, if it failed, as it subsequently did with the untimely death of my dad, would enable me to find work elsewhere. Fortunately, I took night courses in literature and composition that helped me gain employment at a major Los Angeles post office writing reports for "Mail Recovery."

Now almost forty, after years of psychoanalysis, paid for by a friend, I have come to accept my modest position and my imperfections, finding solace in the Kabbalah. I am consoled and challenged by seeking to apprehend in material objects God's emanations. Since I believe that every word holds a recondite meaning, I have made the arcana of language my particular hobby. But words, as the Kabbalah contends, are but the vestments of feelings and ideas, and woe to him who takes the vestment for the real. Surely David had this in mind when he said: "Open Thou mine eyes, that I may behold wondrous things out of Thy law" (Psalms 119:18). I, like him, wish to see what lies hidden under the cloak of words.

Even at the Mail Recovery room, I pore over envelopes that cannot be delivered for one reason or another: no forwarding address, indecipherable handwriting, incorrect number or street, no city or state. I spend untold hours trying to make sense of the imperfect codes that lie before me like a spiritual enigma. Sadly, my failures can be seen in the thousands of letters that languish in our dead-letter bin.

At the end of a year, we read and destroy them. I cannot describe the sadness of discovering the tokens of affection and need that have miscarried: a wedding band intended for some finger forlornly awaiting its purchase, a check meant to relieve a son's misery, an apology sent to repair a misunderstanding, a get-well card. On errands of life, these letters sped to death.

I grieve over the thousand varied emotions, sympathies, and expressions that go to make up correspondence, all those countless attempts at communication between persons that we convert into lifeless, meaningless trash. All reduced to permanent silence. When I think about the untold stories committed to the shredder and imagine how I would feel if my own letter miscarried, I feel an overwhelming urge to seek other employment. (In fact, I have asked my supervisor, Werner Henker, for a transfer to the passport department.) The Egyptian character of the post-office masonry doesn't help, weighing upon me with its gloom and inducing in me thoughts of mummified pharaohs, lords of all the hieroglyphics. Lives rest on hope, the hope that tomorrow our pain and penury will disappear and the world will be restored to the Edenic state where once perfection reigned. Through prayer, the language of hope, I convey to the Deity my wish to leave behind the tedium of reports and the frustration of trying to decipher failed missives. When I declined Mr Henker's offer to become his amanuensis—I thanked him but said I would prefer not to—I made clear that the repetitive nature of my heartbreaking labors was exacerbating my solitary life.

A retiring sort, I appear to Mr. Henker as the opposite of a companionate colleague who has an occasional drink with the gang and guffaws at jokes about "going postal." He regards my aloofness as an accusation that he and the other office workers are unfit to be my friends. But I prefer my own company, finding pleasure in reading and listening to music. The thought of writing a book would never have crossed my mind but for the delivery to my home of a large footlocker. The trunk and a sealed envelope had come from a New Jersey public administrator assigned to probate Ben Cohen's will. The man had informed me some weeks before that I would be receiving both. Ben, having died without any known relatives and virtually broke, had left behind a request that his papers and books come to me. Opening the envelope, I found a brief note. "Dear Marty, Some reminders of times gone by. Keep the books, but for the rest, read and enjoy—then destroy. Adios, Ben."

My eyes teared, and I decided to delay exploring his possessions. My sister and I having disposed of my parents' remnants, I did not relish the thought of once again picking through the bones of memory. Belongings are like texts; each tells a story.

When I put down Ben's note, I listened to a record of *Così fan tutte* to assuage my sorrow; and as I sat there, I could hear in Mozart's music Ben's

darkmatters LEVITT

voice and all the others. I could hear the youthful arias of our past, though the material substance of them had already vanished like a dream. Ignoring my initial impulse, I opened the footlocker and rustled through the contents: books, letters, postcards, newspaper articles (Ben was a journalist), polemics, some finished, some not. In a notebook, I discovered a manuscript titled "Dark Matters," and shortly realized that Ben had begun a novella about his college days and beyond. Probably to distance himself from the material, he wrote in the third person. I wept to see that I held a central place in the story, and on the instant decided to take the liberty of adding my own voice—to honor the memory of my dearest friend.

As a religious man, I pray at the outset of journeys. So now, before exploring my own feelings and the hidden truths of Ben's life, I pray that I can sing the Lord's song in a strange land, and that my right hand will not forget its cunning.

*   *   *   *

Ben's arrival in Brackett Hall at the start of the new term in January came as a disagreeable surprise to my tormentors. Ty Handsel and his fraternity brothers had amused themselves since my matriculation in September by short-sheeting my bed, putting rodents in my room, hiding my clothes while I showered, and occasionally, if they could gain access to the kitchen, knocking on my door and throwing a pie in my face. My short stature and pudgy appearance, as well as my thick lips and broad nose, furnished a rich source of ridicule. In the fall semester, unable to pass chemistry, Ty had changed his major from pharmacy to business. We shared an accounting class, which confounded him as much as had organic compounds. Ben had recently been discharged from the Army, where he had served in the Korean war and had been wounded in the head, an injury that required the insertion of a metal plate at the back of his skull. He had been admitted to the University of Colorado on the G.I. Bill as a graduate student majoring in labor economics and labor history in the Department of Economics, which paid him a modest sum to grade papers and conduct a discussion session for Professor Zumbrat's large lecture class. As a graduate student, having finished a B.A. degree at Amherst followed by a stint in the service, he would normally have been living off campus, not in a dorm. But since

darkmatters
LEVITT

he entered in mid-year with rentals scarce, and since Brackett Hall had a vacancy, the housing office assigned him to a place there. His room, a few doors from mine, stood next to the residential advisor's. Ben and the RA never got along. They fought over rules. Ben hated them; the RA, devoid of imagination, had no other guide.

We met when I heard someone in the hall singing, "The Kingdo-om of this world is be-e-come the Kingdom of our Lord." Given the fraternity louts and country hicks resident in the dormitory, I knew it had to be a stranger. Cracking my door, I saw a tall, thin fellow with curly black hair, Levis (at the time, unfashionable) riding jauntily low on his hips and underneath his white dress shirt a red tank top. Instead of shoes, he wore low-class Keds. Though I'd learned to keep my musical tastes to myself, I blurted out, "The Hallelujah chorus!" My forwardness I ascribed to my surprise at hearing a dorm rat singing anything other than "The Tennessee Waltz," or "Rag Mop," or "Good Night, Irene."

He pointed a finger at me. "From?"

"Handel's *Messiah*. I have an LP with the Luton Choral Society, Thomas Beecham conducting. Want to hear it?"

"Beecham, I'm told, has a coruscating wit. Perhaps that's why his orchestra plays so well."

"Coruscating! You must love words. So do I. Beecham's a redoubtable presence."

"A leviathan."

And the word games continued . . . until Prague.

The moment he entered my room, loneliness fled. From that day forth, he became my friend and protector, meting out prompt retribution to anyone who picked on me. The first time he bloodied Ty's nose occurred just outside the cafeteria, where Ben and I had taken every meal together during the first week of school. Ty brushed past me and, looking back, said: "I see, Marty, you have a—girlfriend." Ben grabbed him by the shoulder and with one punch sent him sprawling, his nose flooding blood. (If Ben's response seems greater than the provocation, I confess that I had primed him with tales of Ty's tyrannies.)

The second and last time took place in the dorm. Ty had barged into my room unannounced, grabbed my accounting work sheets—the assignment for that week—and walked out. Having failed to do the homework, he intended to copy from me. I yelled at him to return the papers, but he

darkmatters
LEVITT

just laughed. Ben, on the phone in the hall at the time, dropped the receiver and said: "Give 'em back!"

Ty asked truculently, "Who's going to make me?" and foolishly shoved Ben out of his way, with the result that Ben struck him full face with an elbow, a blow that not only broke Ty's nose and blackened his eyes for several weeks, but also got Ben expelled from Brackett Hall. Put on probation as well, he would have left school had I not pleaded with him that his absence made me vulnerable to Ty's vengeful malice. Lying on the floor, Ty had sworn that his "brothers" would get me; and although Ben had replied that he'd call out his Army buddies to scrape up Ty and his frat friends, I knew if Ben left, I was defenseless.

"You sure leveled him," I said pleased as punch. "He never saw it coming. For that matter, neither did I."

Ben shrugged. "Army training. It's now instinctive."

Ben

Raised on stories of revolution and want, on tales of persecution and pogroms, Ben Cohen imbibes his parents' hatred of injustice and their dream of a better world through socialism. What he never feels is his parents' embrace, because they reserve their passions for politics. In particular, they despise Czar Nicholas Romanov, whose death they celebrate, and the Cossacks, who periodically raid their defenseless village. Invariably it is a Saturday. Killing Jews at prayer in the small synagogue gives them special pleasure. From time to time, they steal a child, whom they school in Christianity. Kidnapped in his tenth year, Ben's father lives among his kidnappers long enough to distrust religion and ride a horse like a Cossack, lessons that he passes on to Ben. The Cohen family eventually raises enough money to ransom their son. Of course, Czar Nicholas countenances these raids and kidnappings, earning the undying odium of the Cohens. Ben's uncle, in fact, spends several years in Siberia for blowing up a bridge. Although born in America twelve years after the 1917 revolution, Ben too loathes the murdered Nicholas. Like his father, who has fought the White Russians, he believes that the revolution has turned out a tyrant and improved the lot of the peasants.

At the end of the first world war, the country lies in ruins. The Baron de Hirsch Fund helps relocate Jewish families in Argentina and Cuba, also in Canada and the U.S., with the proviso that the immigrants till the few acres allotted them. His parents come through Ellis Island and farm for several years in southern New Jersey. There Ben is born and learns to ride. The family speaks Russian and Yiddish at home. Though his mother learns some English, his father treats "Americanese" as a barbarism, perhaps

darkmatters

because he also speaks French, a language that he associates with refinement and elegance. Ben's one-room schoolhouse, lacking Russian rigor, earns his parents' contempt. In search of a more cosmopolitan school, they move to Brooklyn, to Sheepshead Bay. His mother runs a small dry-goods store, which she has bought from a distant cousin. Ben helps behind the counter, translating. His father, overjoyed at leaving farm work, settles into the life of an ash manufacturer, smoking ceaselessly as he reads Russian and French novels. Although he misses riding horses, he replaces the equestrian art with Yiddish vaudeville, which he attends at least twice a week. He arrives for the matinee and stays for the evening performance. Ben's mother does all the work.

When Ben isn't helping at the store or studying, he haunts Coney Island. Surf Avenue cuts Coney in half. On one side stands the amusement park, on the other, a row of restaurants owned mostly by Italians, some of them Mafia. Occasionally Ben runs errands for them. Life on the streets provides its own education. But a scholarship to Amherst lands him among ideas and in a society unlike his own. Majoring in history and economics, he writes a senior thesis on the labor standoff between Samuel Gompers and President Grover Cleveland. Ever after, he takes for his motto Gompers's reply to the frustrated president, who had asked Gompers what the union wanted. Gompers said "More!"

In college he dates girls from Mount Holyoke and Smith, finding them for the most part spoiled by wealth and blind to the needs of those who cook their food and sweep out their dorms. One strikingly pretty young woman catches his fancy. She is a sophomore, he a senior. They date. He takes sensuous pleasure in her appearance, though he thinks her willful. Brought up to be ornamental, she can hardly blame herself for failing to serve any practical purpose. Ben never intends to love her, merely to unspoil her and to assault her child-like mind, through shock or through shame. But to his amazement, he finds himself drawn precisely to her upper-class manners and excesses—and wealth. By a strange alchemy, her willfulness increases her erotic appeal and commands his impulse to love. Like a tonic chord, he keeps returning. They see each other that summer, in Cape May, New Jersey, where thoughts of her consume him so thoroughly that he actually looks forward to his stint in the Army to escape her thralldom.

After a serious occipital wound, he leaves the army with a purple heart and accepts a mid-year offer from the Department of Economics at the

darkmatters LEVITT

University of Colorado to pursue a Master of Arts degree. Driving from Brooklyn to Boulder, with all his belongings stashed in his oft-painted DeSoto, he arrives on a cold, clear January day, only to find that the small town has no vacancies. Seoul has given him a taste for the rose water scent of young, eager women, and for Asian cuisine; but the dorm forbids women guests and serves execrable meals. Another problem soon surfaces: he acquires a protégé who can barely put one foot in front of the other without tripping. While walking to his room, singing "The Hallelujah chorus," he attracts the attention of Martin Bartelman, who invites him into his room to listen to Handel's *Messiah*. Marty is studying business, but his heart belongs to classical music. During the magisterial choruses, Marty dabs his eyes. Ben is reminded of Howard Rosenfeld, no more than ten, who attended Sabbath services at his local shul in Brooklyn. When the men stood to say the Kaddish, Howard always rose and, with tears running down his face, recited a prayer for his mother, who had died from a botched appendectomy.

One fraternity boy in particular picks on Marty. Ty Handsel comes from Minnesota wealth and looks Nordic: blonde, tall, creamy skin, finely chiseled features. Marty, in contrast, has dark hair, a wide soft nose, and a perpetual five o'clock shadow. Short and uncoordinated, he laughs too loudly and suffers from some glandular condition that causes him to perspire continually, especially the palms of his hands. His familiarity with good music puts him at odds not only with the dorm boys but also with most of America. So too does his passion for books and words. Ben warns Ty to lay off the pranks and leave Marty alone. But Ty, like many other bullies, torments his victim in order to entertain his friends, who would be disappointed if he stopped. Ty makes the mistake of goading Ben, who hits him. The housing authority puts Ben on probation for fighting, though Ty receives only a verbal reprimand. One evening, he grabs Marty's homework and refuses to return it. Ben and Ty fight. The administrator in charge of housing, having little room to negotiate under the rules, severs Ben's contract with the dorm and returns the money owed him.

Expelled from Brackett Hall, Ben rents a log cabin in Eldorado Springs, an old mining town five miles west of Boulder, situated at the foot of a mountain canyon on a river. An old woman who lives in Denver had formerly used the cabin on weekends during the summer. But now, disabled by age and illness, she is glad to receive the rent. An honorable woman, she warns him that the well is dry; but he says that he can solve the problem, which he does by purchasing a hundred feet of garden hose, running it from the pump-house motor to the river below the house, and extracting the City of Louisville's water for free. To stymie the river inspector, who periodically tours the waterway looking for poachers, he removes the hose from the stream every morning and replaces it every evening. Lacking a hot water heater, he uses the men's gym at school for showers and, on those days when it's closed, steals into one of the men's dormitories. Foolishly, he showers one day at Brackett Hall and runs into the RA. Marty hears the altercation and dashes in to say that Ben has come to visit him.

In the future, he bathes in the basement of the Clare Small gym, a dark and dingy cluster of lockers surrounding a tiled stall with a broken shower head. He studies at the cabin or in the library. The economics department gives him an office, really a bullpen that he shares with five other graduate students. One of them, a Czech exchange student, is the daughter of an official in her country's communist government. Hence she is both privileged and sympathetic to socialism. Dana Reháková dresses fashionably in western clothes and speaks several languages, among them Russian and a flawed English. They have in common an interest in politics and a tongue that they can speak when they wish to shut others out. A tall, slim woman, she has straight creamy hair that she keeps cropped, and small child-like hands. She could pass for a teenager, but in fact she is twenty-six and holds a degree from Charles University in Prague. Her clothes reek of nicotine, as does the bullpen where she usually spends her days, grading papers and voraciously devouring cigarette smoke.

"Why American students write so bad?" she asks Ben. "They know one language only. You will think they could learn it. They write like I speak, terrible."

"What brings you here? It's a state university. With your connections you could have gone to Harvard or Yale."

"In Denver my sister lives."

They will resume this conversation, but not until weeks later.

Marty

From virtually the first day that we met, Ben had talked about the need to supplement his G.I. Bill and graduate-student stipend. His own tastes were modest, but I gathered he had other expenses, considerable ones. That's why I couldn't understand his insistence on finding work as a hasher at the large colonial sorority house just west of the campus. Sororities paid in food—three meals a day—not money. And besides, Ben had begun to make purchases with twenties instead of counting out ones. Something didn't add up. My experience with Kabbalah should have made me see behind the symbol to the real. The lure of the sorority, I finally realized, had nothing to do with saving on meals or working with Jessie, the wonderful cook who gave the boys extra portions for the holiday periods; it had to do with Clarissa Stanton. That I took so long to guess owed more to my own unfamiliarity with these new symbols than to the absence of clues.

Although the house had filled all its positions for hashers and house-boys, Ben dropped in daily on Jessie to ask if she needed a substitute or an additional hand. As luck would have it, one of the hashers got roaring drunk and wrapped his car around a tree, an accident that landed him in plaster for two months. His ill fortune opened the door for Ben, who received a warm welcome from Jessie but a cool one from the other hashers, who rightly guessed that the name Cohen was Jewish. The ringleader, Ron Johnson, worshipped Senator McCarthy and belonged to some whites-only group in Wyoming. He, too, had served in the Korean War, and he refused to abide any liberal opinions, particularly ones arguing that the North and South Korean governments were equally corrupt. These disagreements led Ben to make copies of the Bill of Rights, which he carried

darkmatters
LEVITT

with him and freely distributed during disputes of this kind. Ron washed dishes. Ben served and collected them. One Sunday, Ron pushed a pile of china from the sink to the floor and blamed the breakage on Ben. Matters went from bad to worse when he learned of Ben and Clarissa's closeness. Having designs of his own on this wealthy Kentucky debutante, Ron, who had boxed in the service, challenged Ben to a fight. As Jessie told the story, Ben asked if he had a choice of weapons. But Ron, failing to see the drift of the question, said:

"Fists, man, fists! That's what we fight with."

"No, Ron," said Ben. "You're the challenger. I'm the challenged. In sporting circles, the person who is challenged gets to choose the weapons. And I pick Thompson submachine guns."

Utterly nonplussed, Ron began cursing everything from Jersey to Jerusalem, concluding with the declaration that Ben was a coward.

Jessie feared a titanic collision. Ben's face darkened and Ron sneered. But the fight fizzled when hasher Mike Dillingham, who had an atrophied leg from polio, remarked:

"You got it wrong, Ron. Cunning ain't cowardice."

Ron, whom I subsequently met at a party in the sorority house, looked more pitiable than fearsome. A bad imitation of Humphrey Bogart, he aped the five o'clock shadow, the cigarette dangling from a corner of the mouth, the wet lips, the semi-slurred speech, and the name "Honey" that Bogey gave to every woman he met. I mention Ron the reprehensible for only one reason: he contributed to the Kentucky fiasco.

The first time I visited Ben at the sorority house, I met both Clarissa and Abby—and saw for myself what he had been saying about the cretinism rampant among their sorority sisters. A young woman sat at the piano. Another, seated on one of the numerous living-room couches, asked, "What are you playing?" and just as the piano player replied "Claire de Lune," another girl entered the room and said with some surprise, "Claire de Lune? Is she a new pledge? I've never met her."

Ben, wearing a white serving jacket, came through the swinging doors of the dining room and took me into the shining aluminum kitchen, where Jessie, a hard-boiled, wrinkled, cigarette-smoking old woman, stuck out a gnarled hand.

"Any friend of Ben's . . ." she said, and broke off.

"Do you live far from here?" I asked, not skilled in the art of small talk.

"Far enough away so as I can get a drink. Louisville. Christ, don't you hate these goddamned dry towns?"

In the 1950s, Boulder was dry/blue. The town ended at 28th street, and on Sundays all the bars, as well as the stores, closed. Restaurants could serve 3.2 beer, a poor substitute for the real thing. Even the few liquor stores on the outskirts of town observed Sunday shutdown, so most of us went to Denver to buy the hard stuff at Harry Hoffman's. We'd load up the car, and on the way home the booze in the bottles piped a gurgling tune. My favorite restaurant, Roger's Kitchen, located on Pearl Street in a yellow house, and owned by a black couple, served the best fried chicken and honey-dipped biscuits I've ever tasted—and didn't mind if a customer showed up with a flask or with a bottle discreetly tucked away in a bag.

Ben suggested we take our dates to dinner at Roger's. When they finally appeared, Clarissa, wearing a white cashmere sweater and a grey Tyrolean jacket, came down the long staircase, followed by Abby, in a sorority sweatshirt, playing lady in waiting to Princess Radiance. Clarissa walked with the lissome turned out step of a ballet dancer. Slender, small, and for her size surprisingly buxom, she dressed principally in white, as I came to discover, perhaps to complement her pale skin and flaxen hair, or to provide a striking contrast to her dark eyes, which shone alternately with affection and danger.

Before Ben could introduce us, Clarissa walked straight up to me and extended her hand.

"You're Martin Bartelman. Shalom! I understand Detroit is your home. I'm Clarissa Stanton, Lexington is mine."

Ben had obviously told her I was Jewish, which explained the "Shalom," but what struck me then and still makes me chuckle was her ambiguous "Lexington is mine." It didn't take me long to realize that she didn't just live there, she reigned.

A baseball fan, Clarissa immediately engaged me in conversation about the Detroit Tigers and Hank Greenberg. From the outset, we had one thing in common: we both hated the New York Yankees. In no time, she had me eating out of her hand. Her dark eyes and expressive mouth made her appear shamefully wanton; and she used both in the service of her will. Combining southern charm with a fierce spirit, she almost always got her way. When guile didn't work, she resorted to guts. She embodied, as I slowly realized, a truly formidable force.

Clarissa's roommate, Abby Hedley, from Boston, was a cow-eyed butterball. She bulged from her fat red cheeks to her bouncy derrière. Good-humored and lively, she loved gossip and would go to any lengths to obtain it, including reading Clarissa's diary. A splendid athlete, she could thwack a tennis ball with the force of a man and ski down expert slopes like a racer. Everything I could not do, she accomplished with ease. A passionate and sentimental girl who never failed to cry at the sappiest movies, she taught me to see the humor in my own defects and those of others. A home economics major, she had no more interest in ideas than a pig does in Latin. But she soldiered on in school, never complaining about her C grades or her burnt jam tarts. I grew to care for her exceedingly, even though we had absolutely nothing in common.

The suggestion that we all go to Roger's for dinner was warmly received, even by Abby, who had been teamed with me as a twosome. My heart thumped. Abby, virtually my first date, took me by the arm as we went out the door. Ben had an old, blue, four-door DeSoto jalopy with a sun visor. We piled in and, since Ben's gas tank needle never hovered much above empty, headed for a sparse stand of trees north of Canyon Blvd., between 13th and 14th, to a hand-driven pump that took only quarters. Even the gas stations closed on Sundays. Among us we managed four quarters, which easily gave us enough petrol to reach the restaurant and, road conditions permitting, the Chautauqua gazebo, where we planned to roast marshmallows over an open fire.

Earlier in the day it had begun to snow, reason enough to wear a heavy overcoat and sweater. But even Roger's in winter could be uncomfortably cold. As we pulled up, I noticed a garish fuchsia Cadillac parked at the curb. Two tables stood occupied, one by an elderly couple sharing a crossword puzzle, and the other by two men lost in conversation. I surmised that the Cadillac belonged to the men. Ben paused and whispered that maybe we ought to try the Flagstaff House, a small restaurant on the mountainside west of Boulder. But Clarissa observed that we couldn't get up the steep road without chains, and that would take longer than she wanted to wait, exclaiming: "I'm starved!"

The owner, at Ben's request, seated us at a distant table. As we sorted ourselves out, I noticed that Ben made a point of sitting with his back to the men. Clarissa asked was something wrong. He hunched over the table and mumbled:

"I know one of them . . . a real talker. He'll drive you nuts."

Naturally, I took note of the two men. A short, muscular fellow, wearing a T-shirt faced our way. I could see that he had bad spiky teeth. Although balding, he looked to be only in his late twenties. The other fellow, a little younger, wore a one-button-roll blue jacket, with a yellow silk tie no more than an inch wide. I observed that he had suede shoes, hardly the footwear for winter weather. Unlike his companion, he had hair, styled in a crew cut, and a paunch, jowls, and a midnight shadow.

"Which?" asked Clarissa.

"The guy with his back to me."

She seemed to want to pursue the matter, but other people entered the restaurant and Ben changed the subject, talking about the recent disclosure that FBI agents had been roaming the campus to identify professors suspected of communist sympathies. Three people, two in the Department of Philosophy, including a professor of mine, and one in the Department of Chemistry, had been singled out. The campus buzzed with the question: what would the president do?

darkmatters
LEVITT

Ben

Over lunch, Dana discloses that her sister has married a Marine corporal stationed at the American Embassy in Prague.

"She marries him in order to emigrate, I think."

"A marriage of convenience."

"Aren't all? Both people, they barter for something they want."

"So much for passion."

Ben suspects that what he has just heard is not entirely true. The children of Czech government officials think twice about leaving the country lest they bring suspicion down on their parents. Perhaps her sister has left for other reasons. And what of Dana?

They discuss the memorandum that the graduate students have just received from the chairman. It says that in all likelihood, teaching assistants, like faculty, will have to sign a loyalty oath.

"I'd rather pack it in than sign," says Ben.

"You mean you would quit?"

"Why not? If I'm going to sell my soul it's not going to be for an assistantship."

"I see nothing wrong that a person declares his loyalty."

"You of all people! Dana, they want to prevent us from teaching what they call subversive ideas, like socialism."

"My government doesn't want for us to teach capitalism. Change just the 'isms,' you'll see . . . our countries are pretty alike. Both, how do you say, squash dissent. Both put in jail the disloyal. Both call the other ism traitorous. You have Senator McCarthy, we do too. Not in your country, not in mine, no freedom of thought."

darkmatters LEVITT

"Surely, Dana, you'd have to agree that we enjoy a great deal more free-dom than you do."

"Under capitalism, you are free to starve. So people are stealing to feed themselves. The good thing is the police, unless they think you are bad man, don't follow you. Under socialism, we have enough to eat. We have no hungry robbing us. No hungry bribed with bread. But against arrest we have no one protecting us. To tell you truth, I think if people has to choose between living with hunger or harassment, most will the last choose."

"I would prefer to live under a government that both feeds its people and leaves them alone."

"Who wouldn't! Do you know such a place?"

Their conversation drifts back to the loyalty oath and Dana asks him what he knows about the university president. "Not enough" would be an honest reply.

"Rodney Stoneham is no scholar. He's a lawyer, a Republican, and tied to the downtown Denver Republican lawyers and the state legislature. They put him in office."

"Sounds like Czechoslovakia. I tell you: we are the same."

"He's said to have some managerial skills."

"The apparatchiks also. Be glad you have a president who defends you."

Ben has heard, though he does not tell Dana, that the president's public statements in support of academic freedom are not to be trusted. It is alleged that in private, Stoneham has been acceding to legislative and regential pressure for a witch hunt, and that it was he who invited the FBI onto campus. In fact, the faculty has scheduled a meeting to discuss the proposed firing of three faculty members, and the current campus climate of fear and intimidation.

Ben remarks that his political science professor, Harold Ermine, has dedicated several classes to a discussion of the "Red Scare," and goes on to explain that Ermine, a Jew who fled from Germany, has experienced mass hysteria and likens it to a rapacious beast. "Now that three C.U. profes-sors have been named, he is doing all that he can to enlighten his students and colleagues about the dangers that attend the suppression of ideas."

Dana, strangely quiet, looks perturbed. She fingers the buttons on her jacket and shifts her watchband. Ben waits.

"Ermine?"

"Yes."

"How do you know President Stoneham is now a friend with the FBI?"

"I didn't say that, you just did."

"That's what I hear. But how can one prove it?"

"Good question."

"Any ideas?"

"Officials come and go. Secretaries have ears. Letters arrive. Calls are made and received."

"My father, once in Washington he met Rodney Stoneham. I can't believe he deceives his faculty."

"Your father must be a good judge of character."

"He is, and a kind man. Without him helping me, I will not be in Boulder."

A student arrives, a chirpy one. Ben remembers a Korean whore with a smoky voice.

Marty

Abby asked me if I liked basketball. She clearly enjoyed attending the games. When I told her that I was allergic to sports, she insisted:

"Oh, you must go with me. You'll love it."

Having a good time seemed her sole preoccupation; but her idea and mine of what constituted a good time did not accord (except for one thing, which did not happen until a month later).

Looking at Ben, who had said almost nothing, Clarissa asked: "Something wrong?"

"I may be asked to sign a loyalty oath."

"What's the big deal? Just sign it."

"What does loyalty mean?"

Clarissa laughed. "It means having eyes only for me."

"Faculty who refuse to sign will be called communists."

"Not everyone who's charged with being a communist is innocent, you know."

"Innocent of what? Being a communist is no crime."

Clarissa treated Ben's response as a personal slight. "I hate them!"

"For what? Where in the laws of this country does it say that membership in the Communist Party is a crime?"

"Do you know what my family would say if they could hear you?"

"You do, Clarissa, have a right to your own opinions, you know."

This reproach stung her.

"They want to burn our churches and overthrow our government."

"That's what the FBI says."

"And they ought to know!"

"A lot of people joined the party in the thirties because of the Depression. They believed that communism offered a better world than bread lines and soup kitchens. They wanted a fairer distribution of wealth. They meant well."

"Meant well, my eye. Dishonest and devious is more like it."

"Was it dishonest and devious when the communists defended Negroes from lynchings . . . when they mobilized hunger marches during the Depression . . . when they organized coal miners and sharecroppers and farm workers?"

"All for their own selfish purposes."

"Let's say you're right. Let's say the communists had ulterior motives. Does that make their defense of the desperate less important?"

Clarissa's dark eyes flashed menacingly. I could see her steeling herself for an argument.

"They foment revolutions and strikes; they kill innocent people; they rob the rich, they—"

"Our country foments revolutions all over the world to preserve its interests. When our own workers go on strike for a better wage, the rich owners bring in thugs to beat them up and even kill them. If being a communist means opposing these sorts of things, I'm all for being a communist."

Abby's attitude was ho-hum, but Clarissa now had a full head of steam.

"I don't believe you mean that!"

"Then you don't know me."

"You a communist . . . *au contraire*!"

What she meant, of course, was that she would never consort with one.

Ben related some of the social advances in Europe that had originated with left-wing parties, and recounted America's opposition to social security and the eight-hour working day. Lacking the information to rebut Ben's greater knowledge of U.S. labor history and the distribution of wealth in America, she stood at a disadvantage. He could talk knowledgeably for hours about anarchists and strikes, and about people like Sacco and Vanzetti, and about his intended thesis on the 1911 Triangle Shirtwaist Company fire, in which 146 people (mostly young women) had died because the bosses had locked the factory exits. She, a foreign language and literature major, repeatedly muttered *merde*. Her affection for Ben warred with her anger. Which impulse would get the upper hand remained to be seen. Although Clarissa's good manners never failed her, at least not in my presence, I felt certain that any concessions she made to Ben would come at a price.

darkmatters
LEVITT

Ben

The chirpy student wants to know why Ben gave her a D on her essay. Professor Zumbrat, who likes to leaven his lectures with literary quotations, had cited Emile Zola. The student has attributed the words to Zelda, the wife of F. Scott Fitzgerald. Ben tries to explain. The young woman needs a few extra points so that she can raise her grade to a C-. He points out that "conspicuous consumption" is not, as she has indicated in her paper, "just another way of saying a person is fat," though he can see the metaphorical possibilities of the student's response. He tries to humor her and says, falsely, that one student thought the phrase meant a bad case of tuberculosis. She fails to laugh. He realizes that she probably doesn't know that consumption is a synonym for TB. Miffed, she presses him to see intelligence in her obtuseness. He explains what it means to consume wealth lavishly and not for reasons of utility. She replies, "Well, that's just your opinion."

What the student means, of course, is that her opinion and Ben's have equal weight. She, like a great many students, confuses the political guarantee that she has a right to her opinion with the correctness of it. When he points out that some opinions are more informed than others, she seems confused. So he asks her: "Would you seek advice about heart disease from a gardener or a cardiologist? Conversely, would you seek advice about weeds from a cardiologist or a gardener?"

She defeats him. "I haven't got a heart problem and I live in an apartment."

Dana, sitting across from him, suppresses a laugh.

The student stands and Ben realizes that the sorority pin on the girl's sweater identifies one of the richest houses on campus. She leaves in a huff.

darkmatters
LEVITT

"Will you sign, yes?"

Dana's question forces him to rearrange his mind. He reflects and replies: "You're teaching here as well. Exchange students are not exempted from the oath. Hell, you're all the more dangerous, coming from a foreign country."

"I'll of course sign. It doesn't matter to me."

Why should it matter to him? Spies and bomb throwers would readily sign—to cover their tracks. Is he just angry at being asked to kiss the ring of the pontiff, when the church knows full well that he's a loyal son of the faith? No, he decides that forced loyalty petrifies opinion.

"It's a means of enforcing conformity."

"Ben, I come from a country where a way of life is dreary sameness. But we get full stomachs and free care in hospital. A bargain, I think. Be practical. Tell yourself all the good things you get for making your signature."

"I'd sign in a minute if it meant an end to hunger and medical costs. But I get nothing in return."

"You get keeping your job."

"At the price of my silence."

"It's the same in socialist countries. I told you . . . your country and mine have a great much in common."

"I don't disagree, Dana, but the fact remains your father has a government post and you live well because of it. How many Czech students get to come to America?"

"I'll buy your lunch."

He leaves a message for Clarissa that he can't meet her, that he has to grade papers. He and Dana walk to the Hill and order soup and salad at the large cafeteria next to Kinsley's clothing store. Clarissa and Abby appear. They whisper and leave. Dana sees Ben's discomfort and asks him about Clarissa.

He explains that he met her in Massachusetts and followed her to Colorado.

"On occasion I used the Smith College library. She came in one day, accompanied by a snooty professor. I stood thumbing through the very card-catalogue drawer they wanted. The prof knew me for a visitor—Smith's a girl's school—so he asked me to step aside. I did. Clarissa looked ashamed. The professor pointed out some book to her and left. I said nothing, but she muttered: 'He thinks he shits roses and pisses cologne.' Now how many coeds would say something like that? Not many, I can tell you, particularly not many dressed in argyle knee socks and matching skirt and sweater. We had a few library dates before I asked her out to dinner. She must have thought we'd drive into Boston and eat at a classy restaurant. Instead, I took her to a small town called Athol, a favorite burg of mine, and we devoured steamed clams from cardboard buckets. She liked the place. I think it was the first date where she really slummed."

Dana pats her mouth with a napkin. "Ask me for steamed clams. I'll love it as a feast, especially here in the, how do you say, wild west."

Even though, as always, he finds himself magnetically drawn to the feminine, Ben does not want to encourage Dana's interest. Entangled with Clarissa, he still feels guilty about Yumi.

He first meets Yumi in a bar and lets her drive him around Seoul on the back of her Lambretta. She says that if he moves off the base, she will cook for him and "be better than a wife." From her previous soldier-lover, she has learned a great deal of English. He likes her gentle ways and receives permission to live with her. They rent a small house, which she selects, on a hillside in the west of Seoul. When his regiment moves north, she follows. Lodging in a nearby village, she waits each day for him to leave camp, to come to her, to love her, to take her back to New York. The North Korean assault that forces the Americans to withdraw from Osan leaves her stranded behind. Yumi's family, through an interpreter, asks him what happened to their daughter. He can barely bring himself to say that he doesn't know, an admission that leads Yumi's mother to tell him he deserves to die. For months after, he contemplates suicide, volunteering for the dangerous assignment that nearly costs him his life.

darkmatters
LEVITT

Marty

Just when I thought we had buried the body, Abby of all people asked Ben why, feeling as he did about communism, he had fought in Korea.

"I enlisted because all my fellow students had college deferments. Have you ever noticed that it's the poor and disadvantaged who fight America's wars? In England, young men from the upper classes regard it as an honor to fight for their country. But here, the wealthiest kids are exempt, one way or another."

"Just wondering," said Abby indifferently, and reached into her purse for a Kleenex.

Ben wanted to expand on the English idea of war and honor, but Clarissa cut him short by quoting from Wilfred Owen, a favorite poet of his.

"'The old lie: *Dulce et decorum est/ Pro patria mori.*' So much for honor," said Clarissa.

Abby asked for a translation.

"Sweet and fitting it is to die for the fatherland," said Clarissa. "It comes from Horace and is meant ironically."

I had guessed right: Clarissa would not be overmastered. Ben probably regretted showing us the war poems of Owen and Sassoon and others: he'd only given Clarissa an extra arrow for her quiver. Thank goodness, Abby asked "Who's Horace?" and Mrs. Rogers requested our dinner orders. That ended the chill, but unfortunately ushered in further tensions. Clarissa and Abby started talking about the sorority meals and Jessie's cooking, both of which they found superb but judged rather dear, given their monthly dues.

darkmatters
LEVITT

"I wouldn't be surprised if it's all the food Jessie sends home with the hashers that drives up the cost," said Clarissa, with just the slightest edge to her voice.

I began to have the feeling that Ben and Clarissa had argued earlier, because she seemed determined to maintain her annoyance. Ben ignored most disagreements, but if they touched upon labor and wages, his gag response never failed. He immediately shot back, "We get paid in food. It comes to crap in dollars. If your sorority sisters feel that we're inflating their dues, they ought to work in the kitchen for a day."

As I soon discovered, whenever Ben blunted Clarissa's barbs by comparing the privileged life of the sorority girls to that of the average working stiff, she never replied. I asked him what he thought she was thinking. His answer still lingers, "She's probably thinking, 'How could he ever fit into my family?'"

Abby excused herself to make a call. We could catch snatches of her conversation from the small cloakroom that housed the phone.

"I can't. Not tonight. I told you, I'm with Clarissa."

To spare me any embarrassment, Clarissa interpreted.

"She was supposed to study tonight with Trudy. Abby is *so* forgetful."

Of course I knew better. If Abby had forgotten, she would have phrased her excuse differently. Nobody says, "Not tonight," after previously agreeing to meet that same night. I would have expected her to say, "I know, but something came up," or words to that effect. Mind you, it didn't really matter. This was my first date with her. She owed me nothing. If she had a boyfriend—and why shouldn't she—I understood. She was doing Clarissa a favor by going out with me. When she returned to the table, Clarissa, not wishing to be caught in a lie, said, "I told Marty you forgot about your study date with Trudy tonight."

Abby looked like a trapped hare. Her eyes darted toward me and back to Clarissa. Trying to raise a laugh—wit has never been my strong point— I said, "I hope I haven't got you in trouble with your *steady* date. You can always tell him that I'm just a tag-along. No threat. Just safe Marty Bartelman."

You could see that Abby wanted to come clean; but if she did, she would stamp Clarissa as a liar. Instead, Abby launched into a transparent story about her previous boyfriend being so possessive that she had to account for all her time away from him. I didn't know whether to laugh or sympathize.

darkmatters
LEVITT

Next she started gushing about a party at the Delt fraternity house. "You simply must go!" Although Ben pointed out that he and I were not members, she said, "Oh, it doesn't matter. The president of the fraternity is a good friend of mine, Brian Hazelwood, and if I ask him I just know it'll be okay."

But of course, Ben and I were not just non-Delts, we were independents.

When I first arrived at the university, two classmates had asked me to join their Jewish fraternity. Not believing in those kinds of organizations—in the early 1950s they were all segregated and elitist—I said no and the two fellows subsequently cut me dead.

Nevertheless, now Clarissa enthusiastically chimed in, insisting we *had* to go—all of us. Ben gave me a doleful glance and mumbled something in Russian.

"I hate it when I can't understand you," said Clarissa, only half seriously.

"I can't believe who's talking, Mademoiselle Paris herself!"

Abby, who had recently been to Paris, began to complain about the French. "No matter what I say, they say *Comment*? Is that true of Russians, too?" she asked Ben.

"Most of them don't speak French," said Ben, looking like a naughty gnome.

"You know what I mean." Ben would have continued his teasing had she not shifted the subject. "How come your family came to the United States . . . why did they leave?"

He seemed pleased by her interest. "The first world war left the country devastated. A Jewish agency helped relocate families in Argentina and Cuba, also in Canada and the U.S. My parents came through Ellis Island and eventually settled in Brooklyn."

"Do your folks speak English?"

"Russian and Yiddish at home. In her store, my mother speaks a little English. I used to help her behind the counter, translating."

"What does your dad do?"

"He smokes cigarettes."

Abby, not a little surprised at this statement, said incredulously, "You mean, he doesn't work?"

"He reads all day or attends Yiddish vaudeville. My mother supports him."

Ben's brief narrative left Abby breathless. She had just been given a privileged glimpse into a world she never knew existed. Her appetite whetted, she wanted more. So Ben told her about his uncle's imprisonment and his father's efforts on behalf of the Bolsheviks. He also revealed that two cousins had been blinded by mustard gas in the Great War. Abby couldn't stop asking questions. She gazed at Ben longingly—and Clarissa stared at her piercingly.

"Where is your mother's store?"

"Near Coney Island. A good location, actually, because she gets business from the amusement park and beach crowd, and sometimes the local Mafia."

"Mafia!" Abby squealed, vicariously tasting the delicious danger.

"I used to make deliveries for them. In return, they gave me a season pass for the Cyclone roller coaster and the other rides."

"You worked for the Mafia!" she said in awe of the word and, at that moment, madly in love with Ben.

"I just ran errands. No rough stuff. Most of those guys, if they walked in here right now, would look just like your normal family man, except maybe for their loud suits. They really loved their kids. The only time I ever ran into trouble was when I criticized one of them for working as a strikebreaker. He said that in his line of work you never asked those kinds of questions, and told me to mind my own business, which I did. But it taught me a useful lesson. The rich have no qualms about hiring hoods to protect their financial interests."

This statement gave Clarissa a chance to redirect the discussion from Ben to herself. Clearly miffed at Abby's panting interest in Ben's background, she remarked that she had been to Coney with her aunt, riding the bumper cars and even trying the parachute jump, but not the roller coaster. Ben asked her if she had stopped at any of the fortune-telling booths, and she shook her head no.

"I used to go regularly. They all said the same thing: that I would take a long trip and meet a beautiful woman."

"Well, she wasn't wrong," said Clarissa, fondly and possessively. "You went to Korea and you know me!"

I wondered about that word "know," well aware of its biblical meaning. My rabbinic tutor had not neglected those lessons.

"What was the worst thing that ever happened to you in Korea?" asked Abby excitedly.

"Must we?" replied Clarissa, visibly annoyed.

Ben crossed his arms on his chest and sat staring off into space, as if trying to summon a difficult memory. I hoped he would take Clarissa's cue and say nothing.

"Much of the fighting took place in the mountains. To get our wounded from the hills to the camp, we had strung a cable with a harness. Periodically, the North Koreans would train their 76mm cannon at the injured guy being lowered on the cable. But from a mile away, it was a one in a million shot. A friend of mine, Walter Simon, a funny kid with a strong Newark accent— he pronounced tall, tawwl, and sofa, sofer—well, he took some shrapnel in the legs. We put him into the harness and sent him down. A shot rang out and I saw Walter slump. When I got back to camp, they had already zipped him into a body bag. I kneeled and opened it. The shell had passed through the soft tissue without exploding. His stomach and chest—" Ben began to catch in the throat and his eyes misted over. "Were gone."

His sobs cut him short. Clarissa hugged him and Abby began to cry. My mouth went dry. Gulping water, first my glass and then, without thinking, Abby's, I reached across the table and patted his hand. Some evening, I thought. It began in a snowstorm, proceeded to an argument, and had now provoked tears. Shortly, Ben said he felt all right and pulled out a flask, from which he drank liberally.

"I think I can use some of that," said Abby, speaking for all of us, as we passed the flask around until we had emptied it. Abby held it upside down. A last drop spilled into her spoon, which she licked.

"Here, let me," said a voice. The fellow with the one-button roll jacket, whom Ben had turned his back to, held out a silver flask. "Ain't you gonna introduce me to your friends, Benny? Nice broads." But before Ben could reply, he put the flask on the table, slid over a chair, and sat between Ben and Abby, who courteously inquired:

"What about your friend?"

"Aw, he don't like company. He ain't like me, sociable."

"This," Ben reluctantly said, "Is Inky Miller," but failed to introduce us to him.

Inky smiled broadly. "Glad to meet yous. Ben and me, we're old pals. We know each other from Brooklyn . . . Surf Avenue."

"We liked to ride the Cyclone together," Ben said defensively.

"Yeah, that was some ride. Say, stop me if I'm wrong. But yous guys are all in college. Right?" Without waiting for an answer, he continued. "Did ya ever read *The Amboy Dukes*? Great stuff!" He chuckled and vacantly remarked, "She was a real blonde."

"Never did," said Clarissa coldly.

He pulled out a crumpled box of cigars. "You mind if I light up an Old Goldie?" No one spoke. "They taste like rope dipped in goat's piss, but they're the smoke of the Yankees. Yuh musta heard Mel Allen on the radio saying, 'It's an old goldie!' when one of the Yanks hit the ball outta the park."

"I'm a Cardinal fan," said Clarissa acidly.

"Does that mean you do or you don't mind if I light up?"

Clarissa turned away. "It doesn't matter to me."

Hearing no objections, he lit the stinking stogie and sat there reeking from cheap cologne and cigar smoke.

Clarissa returned her gaze to Inky. I thought her eyes would eviscerate him.

Oblivious to the uncomfortable silence, he puffed on his cigar and rocked in his chair, as if *davening*.

"Benny, you'll never guess who I saw in this restaurant," Inky said reverently, "Lefty Lewant! Remember Lefty? He did two years at Leavenworth. What a guy, Lefty! He was passin' through on his way to Frisco. Did ya ever notice how people from Frisco hate when you call the place Frisco? They want you to say San Francisco. Like it mattered. Jesus, some people!"

I had never seen Ben so uncomfortable.

"Good talking to you, Inky."

"Hey, I didn't finish tellin' you about Lefty."

"Maybe some other time, Inky. We're having a private dinner."

Momentarily, Inky grimaced, but the broad smile quickly returned. "Ya gotta hear this, Benny. I told him, I mean Lefty, not to tie the knot again until he got a divorce. But he got greedy. One rich dame after another. They sent him up for bigamy. Turns out he had three wives. And wouldn't you know it, two of 'em met at a bingo game. Great game, bingo! I never play it myself. I prefer a sure thing."

Inky had a way of moving from one subject to another without transitions. He rambled on a bit longer until he suddenly turned to Ben. "I never asked you: whatcha studying?"

The construction of that sentence gave me pause. It sounded as if Ben and Inky had seen each other since Brooklyn.

Clarissa, nervously turning a sapphire ring on her finger, looked ready to bolt. Inky apparently noticed, because he suddenly rose.

"Nice meeting yous. If you want a hot tip, bet against the point spread in the Colorado-Bradley game." He smiled, leaned over, and took his flask. "Like I said, Benny, nice chicks."

With that enigmatic statement, Inky returned to his table. Ben's war story already forgotten, Clarissa turned to him disgustedly. "Would you kindly explain *that*?"

"He saved my life in Korea."

I didn't know whether to laugh or believe him. Clarissa's skepticism could be read in her face. But Abby, with bosom bouncing and eyes aglow, pursued his statement.

"What happened?!"

"Let's save it for another day. This one's been hard enough."

Dinner conversation amounted to a few abbreviated banalities. No one could summon the energy to pursue any more arguments or stories—or lies. We all knew what our behavior betokened. The evening smoldered, even though Abby tried to fan the dying embers.

"Anyone for marshmallows?"

In the back of the car, we had left a bag of them with four metal skewers that the women had brought from the sorority house.

"It'll be cozy under the gazebo, with the snow coming down." Abby pushed on. "We've got blankets, and cigarettes, and . . ."

"I have a headache," said Clarissa dryly. "I'd like to go home."

We spun and skidded our way west on Pearl Street, turned south on Broadway, and prayed that we could make it up the hill just north of the campus. Ben said that given all the cars spinning and stuck on the hill, we would need a good running start. Gunning it on Broadway and going about fifty, he swerved through the stalled cars as if racing a slalom. Never stopping for the light on University, he turned right, made a U-turn and stopped the car in front of the house. Whether Ben's madcap driving had refocused her mind or whether she felt genuinely concerned, Clarissa inquired:

"How will you get back to Eldorado Springs?"

"Slowly."

We saw the girls to the door. Ben and Clarissa embraced. I noticed he trembled. Abby and I shook hands and exchanged a few bantering words. As we walked away, she called:

"Remember, a fool and his money are soon partying."

For some reason, Ben bridled.

The women entered the house, and I asked him if he knew the name of the fellow she'd phoned from the restaurant.

"Brian Hazelwood. Rich as old Henry Ford and just as bigoted. He's a spoiled kid . . . drives a foreign car. She'll eventually dump him. He's even sillier than her."

"You and Clarissa argued today, didn't you?"

Ben turned to me pained. "I changed our lunch date. She's used to men who dance her tune and, for love of her, lead apes in hell. But I refuse."

When we reached the car, I jumped in. Then it came to me: *The Taming of the Shrew*. Ben waited a few minutes in the falling snow for the light in Clarissa's room, which faced the street, to come on. It never did. Even so, he waved to the darkened window. As we pulled away, I saw Abby's room, next door to Clarissa's, suddenly ablaze with light. I had no trouble imagining the two bosom friends engaged in a surly tête-à-tête.

Marty

The incongruity of it: on Thursday night, the faculty and staff held a meeting in the university theatre to protest President Stoneham's acquiescence to a campus witch hunt and the imposition of a loyalty oath; and on Saturday night, the Delt fraternity house gave a party, riotous with rum and ribaldry. Ben and I went to both, though on reflection I feel that he might have avoided considerable travail had we at least missed the first.

darkmatters
LEVITT

Ben

For weeks the newspapers have been editorializing that the C.U. campus has to be cleansed of all communist influence. *The Denver Post*, among the worst rabble-rousers, publishes scabrous articles that all but invite the FBI, the Army, and all available spy hunters to descend on Boulder. The letters to the editor, except for a courageous few, drip with venom. A state senator from Lamar loudly and frequently praises Senator Joseph McCarthy's "patriotic service" to the country. A local liquor store owner with the apt name of John Q. Publik wants to storm the campus and "get all those Reds." He is not alone. The American Legion, of course, pitches in, as well as most of the other fraternal organizations, including the Greek ones on campus. The atmosphere feels like a dry electrical summer storm, with lightning periodically illuminating the night sky. An attack is followed by deceptive calm, only to be followed by yet another outbreak. The three professors under investigation must feel vulnerable to lynching. Ben observes wryly that the two Jews among them will probably be accused of child murder. He is convinced that the country and community, gripped by a terrible fever, have returned to the Middle Ages. Faith has supplanted facts. Anyone touched by communism has consorted with the Devil. The attractiveness of this faith comes from its simplicity. All America's ills can be ascribed to communism. And what especially appeals to those who believe in witches is the ease with which they can be identified and punished. It takes only one person saying: "He's a communist." Nothing more. If the accused objects, a committee of superpatriots subjects him to an inquisition. Silence means certain guilt, and self-exculpations merely prove communist cunning. Ben feels that he has an insight into what Giordano

darkmatters
LEVITT

Bruno and other heretics must have endured. The witch hunters have no taste for accuracy or history, no patience with logical arguments; they have found a divining rod that can identify the malefactors and, like all people in search of a political panacea or a silver bullet to slay the great Satan, they cling irrationally to their belief, belligerently blind to the complexity of human thought.

Outsiders gravitate to Boulder. Right-wing groups drive through town shouting obscenities. The Veterans of Foreign Wars, in military dress, protest the outrages occurring in the foreign town of Boulder. Mine-Mill Local 890 from Bayard, New Mexico, currently striking, sends representatives to support the professors. Students take sides. The more conservative ones begin to audit the classes of professors they regard as suspect (most of the faculty) and send reports to the senator from Lamar. Although the student vigilantes don't know Marx from Maimonides, that doesn't stop them from passing judgment about their professors' loyalty and competence and behaving no better than the big brothers they abhor in the Soviet Union. Protesters grow fearful, and the faculty are losing the will to resist. Even Zumbrat has become timid about testing ideas in the give-and-take of the classroom. Ben wonders, will the professors let ignorance muffle dissent? State universities all over the country are suffering the same fate. The civil compact between communities and colleges collapses as the former adopt reactionary shibboleths and direct "their" universities to pay obeisance to a faith unamenable to proof.

The three professors, all past members of the Communist Party, have been given bogus reasons for their threatened dismissals, ranging from poor teaching to a lack of collegiality. In the manner of all unimaginative people, the state legislators decide that communism can be extirpated with a rule: a loyalty oath. The C.U. Board of Regents supinely announces that it will "employ no person, in any capacity whatsoever, who is a member of or otherwise affiliated with any organization, group, society, or other association which advocates, encourages, abets, or teaches, by written or spoken word, the duty, necessity or propriety of, or has among its objectives or purposes, changing the form of government of the United States or the State of Colorado by any means other than those prescribed by the respective laws and constitutions thereof." The long-winded document merely says "Observe the laws of the country." Its real intent—to discourage professors from introducing controversial ideas into the classroom—

darkmatters
LEVITT

succeeds at the cost of dividing the university. Even the local school board directs teachers to inculcate into students "patriotism," whatever that means. Ben puts no store in such directives, persuaded that morality comes from conscience or even self-interest, but never from a law. Communists all over America are gladly signing loyalty oaths because the oaths give them protective covering.

Ben has decided not to sign. He will attend the meeting called to protest the imposition of a loyalty oath.

darkmatters
LEVITT

Marty

The weather boded ill. Dark clouds from the west scudded over the mountains and a sleety snow came in slants. The few street lamps on Broadway cast a dim light, and an occasional car clattered by with its rear wheels sporting chains. The scene had an Edward Hopper feel to it. Ben had volunteered to check faculty and press credentials at the door, a position that enabled him to admit me. The theatre, the venue for the meeting, had a balcony with two doors. Ben policed one of them. All those who tried to enter the meeting without passes, and whom Ben turned away, behaved graciously, except for John Q. Publik. He claimed that he spoke for—you guessed it!—the citizens of Boulder.

"When did they elect you to represent them?" Ben asked.

"I have lived here my whole life. The rest of you are just carpetbaggers."

It didn't strike me that Mr. Publik had answered Ben's question, but in his own mind, his longstanding roots in the community qualified him to speak for all.

"No permission, no admission," said Ben.

Mr. Publik grew querulous: "Haven't I seen you in my store?"

"In the past maybe, but not in the future. I promise."

Turned away, Mr. Publik swore that he would take his complaints to the papers and the governor.

By 7:30, the main floor and balcony overflowed. The theatre smelled of wet wool and felt, from all the damp overcoats and brimmed hats that the men arrived wearing. The crowd, mostly male (in those days, C.U. women faculty could be counted on two hands), either stored their toppers

darkmatters
LEVIT

under their chairs or held them on their laps. During the meeting some of the men held up their hats and shook them in support of a point.

The president and his V.P., Farkus Doleman, briskly swept down the aisle. The V.P., a dyspeptic, cadaverous stiff in a suit too short in the arms, had often displeased the faculty, who called him Fartus. While Stoneham worked the crowd, stopping to greet different professors and slapping still others on the back, Doleman self-confidently strode to the stage—bare except for one chair and a podium—moved his index finger back and forth, presumably counting the president's backers. Standing at the rear of the balcony, Ben and I could guess people's thoughts only by reading their body language. From the start I felt it would be more melee than meeting: I saw more shaking of fists than shaking of heads.

Doleman spoke first. "As we all know, the nation is watching us, just as they watched the proceedings at Berkeley. If we pass the test, it will be for one reason, President Stoneham. He alone has the administrative skills and personal qualities to see us through this storm."

I wasn't sure which test he had in mind, but I did understand that for some faculty, this meeting represented a test of President Stoneham's integrity. We all knew that the he had those qualities that college presidents must have to succeed. A great shmoozer and football fan, he could press flesh with the best, an asset, as I've discovered from Mr. Henker, far more important than intelligence; a first-rate mind spawns original ideas, and therefore disaffects the sequacious.

Introducing Rodney the Round as "our greatly esteemed President Stoneham," a salutation that elicited hearty applause, Doleman settled his bag of bones into the chair. Lifting his rotund self up the steps of the stage, Stoneham patted his thinning, vaselined hair, gave a great hawk, grasped the podium, and began.

Ben

Ben thinks of his father, who reluctantly left a land and a language he loved. His mother had said that the war-torn country would take decades to recover, and that given the uncertainties in Russia, America glittered golden and promising. His father has failed to adjust. When Ben scolds him for escaping into books and nicotine, his father tells him to live in his skin for one day to see what it feels like. "The wearer knows," he admonishes, "where the shoe pinches." As Ben watches Stoneham, he makes a conscious effort to meld with the man, to climb into his head and think his thoughts, to become him.

darkmatters
LEVITT

Ben/Stoneham

A packed house. The votes, do we have them? All those telephone calls to rally support. A splotch of red in the sea of dark overcoats: Mabel Vancey's hat. Everyone knows and loves Mabel. A full professor. The only woman we have at that rank. They'd listen to her if she talked. Making them understand the tugs and pulls at work in the background, and yet framing the struggle as a matter of principle, not personalities, that's what's needed. But I'm damned if I do and damned if I don't. What I think hardly matters. The institution is what counts. If the FBI takes over, the decision will be out of my hands. Better I should decide. Condor stays. I hired him. The other two . . . well, why shouldn't they go if they've been indoctrinating their students? Don't look rattled. Be firm.

Wait for quiet and then begin. "Ladies and gentlemen, I shall not mince words. I have had to make some very difficult decisions, and if at some points I have yielded to pressure it is because I am endeavoring to save the institution from worse dangers."

Cheering. Hold up a hand. How satisfying to have friends who approve of my administration and trust me. See! Howard Smythe and Clifford Cleasby and others smiling. They know I represent their best interests.

"Right on, Rodney!"

"Yes!"

"Well said!"

If Ermine sides with me, my critics will quickly decamp. But even if they complain, they can't say I haven't honored the faculty. I see Schmidt and Collins and Walker and Dennis, all recipients of presidential awards. And loyal Doleman, of course. Always faithful, smiling, perhaps thinking

darkmatters
LEVITT

of his public pronouncement: "Cut the few and save the U." Do I dare use that expression? No, it will sound as if I'm prejudging their cases. The instructors . . . they will support me. It's in their best interests, what with tenure down the road. Hell, it's for the good of us all, or almost all, if the legislature perceives us as having no truck with communism. Almost the very words of the Denver Downtown Republican Club. Damn, they even got personal in the newspapers, warning me to rein in the reds. Let *them* try it. Faculty. Cantankerous bastards! One wrong step and we can kiss next year's budget goodbye.

"Although universities are often more advanced in their thinking than the general population"—pause for effect—"we receive our support from the voters, the legislature in particular. We do ourselves a disservice to get out too far in front of public opinion. Note that I am not taking issue with free thought, but with radical thought."

Clapping . . . also fidgeting. A sign of impatience. There will be resistance. But at least they've not missed the point. Call on Professor Polder-Pitton. I know some call him a sourpuss, but he'll find the prospect of a straitened budget unsettling. French professors always do.

"Rights, rights, we all want our rights. But the rights of the individual must take a backseat to the greater good."

Splendid choice. Polder-Pitton has got the meeting off on the right foot.

"We must think of our academic community and its welfare." Wonderful! Polder-Pitton is continuing. "If to save the orchard, we have to prune a branch, so be it."

"Here, here!"

"How in the hell"—it's Joe Klein—"did an academic community became an orchard within two sentences? Jesus, can't you see that false accusations put everyone at risk?"

Joe Klein, that frail dwarf, if only his terrible smoker's cough would kill him! Christ, look at the number of hands. Let Tabard speak. He's a supporter. Supporter. Jockstrap. The Department of Linguistics always has the balls to back you.

"Let us think of triage, and remember the word's origins. It began with French wool growers in the eighteenth century, but its most illuminating use comes from eighteenth century coffee bean growers, who sorted their beans according to best, middling, and broken. The last category came to be known as 'triage coffee.' In war, we attend to the most seriously wounded first, which is how most of understand the word today."

Damn it! You've called on the wrong man. He's ready to defend the three as the most needy of all.

"Therefore to protect the best and the middling, we must sell off our 'triage coffee.'"

A friendly conclusion, but his analogy would test the interpretive powers of Solomon.

Klein is snarling. "Sell out! he means."

Shouting from the balcony. Only one sentence is intelligible: "I have never heard more addled reasoning in my whole life."

"Who is that?" Farkus better have a few words with him. His comment has roiled the crowd. I can feel the impatience. Troublemakers are spoiling for a fight. Just remember: keep tempers from flaring, but also make your position clear.

"I have repeatedly said that the university as a state agency has a definite responsibility to sustain the institutions of democracy through its teaching and research. But Communist Party membership is not compatible with democracy and provides indisputable evidence that a teacher with communist ties is incapable of performing his job without influence."

"Right!"

"Absolutely!"

Thank goodness for friends—and debtors. Call on Ermine. He of all people will have to weigh in on your side. As always he is dressed impeccably: a grey pin-striped suit, with a light blue shirt and a silver tie.

"Are you saying . . ."

Undoubtedly he will ask for a clarification.

". . . that membership in the Communist Party, whether ten years ago or now, renders a chemist incapable of imparting to his students a knowledge of atoms?"

The reference is to Professor Stanley Fine. Perhaps now would be a good time to talk about disloyal scientists and the Manhattan project. No, let Augustine Silica reply. A lousy speaker . . . but he is the Chairman of Chemistry. That ought to carry some weight.

"Augustine!"

Funny how his head resembles a watermelon.

"Professor Fine has a poor working relationship with his colleagues and of late has been fomenting trouble."

"I don't understand—" Is Harold interrupting or has Silica finished? I'm counting on Harold. "—Professor Fine has been working in Paris the last two years."

Silica is shaking his head disapprovingly. "He writes us letters complaining that our research doesn't even rise to the mediocre. His lack of collegiality has become legendary."

"*Is* the department's work any good? Where does it rank in the country?"

Not Joe Klein again! Indefatigable! A constant thorn in my side. If only I could remove him!

Silica sputters: "I'm doing all that I can to improve a weak department. Just, just because Professor Fine has been awarded a Guggenheim fellowship gives him no right to act high and mighty."

"What about Judson Meyer?"

Klein again, mentioning the one man I have made up my mind to dismiss.

"You reported that he's a pedestrian teacher . . . your very word, pedestrian . . . and yet our department ranked him tops among the four instructors we recently hired."

Judson Meyer. A maverick. Always standing on principle. Trained in classics as well as philosophy. His students praise his wit and his warmth. He prides himself on teaching students how to make distinctions. Although he'd never believe it, I have from time to time directed a few pre-law students to enroll in his class. But he . . . it's not yet time to tell the faculty what I know. Just keep to the script.

"His progress toward the degree is too slow."

"It's a buyer's market!"

Who's the good soul who said that? Peter Spada! Be sure to send him a note of thanks.

"He's finished his Ph.D. written and oral exams," Klein is hoarsely replying, "and is currently writing his thesis."

The meeting is getting out of hand. People are speaking without being recognized. My chest hurts. Where are my pills? No, don't be popping them here.

Professor Cuisse, from Physical Education, is complaining: "He seems to have it in for our students. He gives them all low grades."

"Maybe they deserve them," says Klein, lighting a cigarette and immediately coughing.

darkmatters LEVITT

"How do you expect a kid to learn if he's always getting D's? It's demoralizing."

Sharing a joke about grades with the faculty might win some support. Wait. Judge their temper. Damn, I've missed the moment.

"Meyer's just an untenured instructor." Professor Knox is speaking; he too is on my side. "In my department, instructors serve at the will of the administration." Knox is looking at you. Nod in agreement. "What's the issue? Meyer is not a regular faculty member . . ."

"And therefore without rights!" Professor Ermine says ironically. "Academic freedom is like any freedom. It is meaningless unless everyone has it. If the untenured don't have the same rights as the tenured, we are like a society half free and half slave."

In the second row, I see that fidgety speech professor whose name I can never remember. An ally, call on him.

"Professor Ermine," he protests, "you sound like a Marxist, "turning one class against another."

Professor Samuels wants to speak. Yes, he will support you. A conservative with an admirable record of having opposed communist oppression in Europe, he is also a distinguished political scientist.

"The test for any free nation," he says, "is to welcome all opinions, even those that would extinguish our freedom. But put yourself in the president's place. He's in an impossible situation, given the legislature. They have drawn a line in the sand. It tries a man's soul to know whether to step over it."

Yes! Send him a thank-you note, too. His is the right analogy, a religious one.

"In the case of our three instructors," he continues, "I fail to see why we can't reappoint them and see if they meet the university's test for fairness. If we find them closed-minded, we can dismiss them."

Hearty applause. Forget the note. Without realizing it, Samuels has compromised you. He doesn't see that to cut the few will save the U. With Samuels and Ermine on the other side, my position is weakening. Why didn't Doleman set out some water . . . how would he like to have a mouth full of feathers? The heat in here is unbearable. My underarms and the front of my shirt, drenched. I don't want the faculty to see me sweating. Keep your jacket on, Rodney, even though others are removing theirs.

"What about Professor Samuel's sound proposal?"

Ermine has directed his question at me. He has support among the faculty. Don't say something you'll regret. You don't approve of conducting personnel matters in public. If Judson goes . . . it will ease the pressure. Besides, he's not a team player.

"Judson Meyer," I say his name as if I find it slightly distasteful, "has refused to answer pertinent questions."

The storm is closer, closer.

Joe Klein jumps to his feet and ferociously brays: "So the complaints about his teaching and insufficient progress toward the degree were bogus. The real issue is Meyer's refusal to tell you and your hirelings what you want to know."

Documents. Always have documents. The letter. Read the letter. You are perspiring badly. Before matters get worse, read the letter. "I have here a letter from Judson Meyer." Remove it from your vest pocket carefully so as not to let them see your sweaty shirt.

Dear President Stoneham,

> *I should like to bring to your attention an occurrence in connection with the current investigation of the faculty.*
>
> *On Tuesday, I was interviewed by two FBI agents known to you. During our conversation these gentlemen raised questions which, for reasons of principle, I concluded that I must decline to answer. I indicated that the questions asked were not relevant when viewed in relation to the tradition of academic freedom of the profession and particularly in relation to the tradition of academic freedom at the University of Colorado, the members of whose faculty have heretofore enjoyed an atmosphere of freedom unsurpassed at any other institution with which I am acquainted. I further pointed out that their questions were inconsistent with the requirement of the academic community for the maintenance of a framework of democratic values for the free association of scholars in their unhampered pursuit of truth. Finally, I stated that their questions were not in keeping with the spirit and intent of the democratic principles explicitly formulated in the Bill or Rights.*
>
> *I discussed these reasons with the FBI agents and expressed my concern for the principles involved. Because of my concern and in the*

interest of clarity, I am writing to you. If you would like to talk to me about this matter, I shall be glad to confer with you.

Sincerely yours,
Judson A. Meyer
Department of Philosophy

"So you see"—Now drive home the point, but all the while exercise restraint—"Judson refuses to cooperate."

Harold's on his feet. After all you've done for him!

"Surely, President Stoneham," Ermine is looking at me pleadingly, "given your courageous behavior in the past, you would defend a person's right to keep his political affiliations and personal thoughts to himself. We all know how Senator McCarthy and his friends behave. They ask if you are or ever were a communist. If you say no, and they have different information, they cite you for perjury. If you say yes, they demand that you name everyone you've ever seen at a meeting, all of your friends. If you forget any names, that too is perjury. Let us not conduct ourselves in this vile manner."

The heat in this damn place is killing me. Dare I mop my brow and neck? Will it be an admission of weakness? Forget the hankie. "I have prepared a statement."

Why delay? It's foolhardy. Harold has rebuked *you*, his friend, his benefactor. Well, let him pay the price. Two can play at this game. They will say Ermine forced the president's hand.

"I had hoped that we could all have agreed on these matters." Breathe deeply. My face feels florid. I don't want them to sense my rage. An administrator must stay calm, whatever the provocation. "But since we cannot agree, I must, in my capacity as president, speak for the well-being of the institution."

Hesitate. Let them take in the effect. Yes, they're listening. What's that circling my head? A large winter fly? Chase it away? No, mustn't give the impression that you're waving dismissively at the faculty. A droll joke might mitigate their anger—a "fly in one's soup"? But what if they take it as condescending facetiousness? No, now's not the time. Damn mustache. It's tickling my lip. Smooth it with your thumb and index finger. That's better. Maintain your bearing. Try to look presidential.

darkmatters
LEVITT

"It is customary to say that a man's political views have no relationship to his place as a teacher in a university. When we say this, I think we mean such political views as are compatible with the very essence of a free society. There is certainly a wide range of political ideas that properly fall within that definition. But unfortunately, there are today political views that are fundamentally destructive of a free society, views that are not consonant with the freedom of inquiry. If political views held by a university teacher are of that kind, then it becomes our obligation to concern ourselves about them. Such views would in the long run be destructive of a university as a center of independent thought. The holders of such views often masquerade, whether they know it or not, under the aegis of freedom, while in reality they are devoted to intolerance."

Silence. I'll bet they think the Downtown Club has drafted the speech. You can see it in their faces. Contemptuous! Ah, applause.

"Exactly!"

"Yes!"

"Amen!"

What a relief! Some at least agree. Will the others notice that by reading Meyer's letter and introducing my own opinion, I have compromised my judicial impartiality? Klein will say, "You have bared the white bone of your baseness," a favorite phrase of his. My opinion, though, has given a few of them pause.

The twitchy speech professor makes a motion: "The assembly accept by acclamation the president's position."

With that opening, my friends can now weigh in.

"I always thought the price of liberty was protecting distasteful ideas. Tasteful ones need no protection."

Heads turn. Damn it! Who *is* that young man in the balcony? Others are mystified, too.

"He looks familiar, but I can't place him."

"Is he on the faculty?"

What's this? Ermine . . . marching down the center aisle of the theatre, mounting the stage, requesting a word with the faculty. I can say nothing. A hush. All eyes on him.

"Few would disagree that loyalty implies that one will not seek to overthrow the government by illegal means. But when a person is required to demonstrate his loyalty through betrayal, this way lies madness. If we are all now to be judged for the sins of our youth, and if the oath of loyalty you support is retroactive, then I say, President Stoneham, there is sufficient ground for censuring *you* and your administration."

Riotous shouting. Accusations. Finger pointing. Of all those in your debt . . . that Harold Ermine would do this thing! I hired him, saved him when he and his family fled Germany. That *he* should suggest that I be censured! Talk about loyalty . . . a traitor. Restrain yourself, Rodney, don't lose control.

"You of all people!"

Damn, I wanted to sound ill-used, but it came out as bluster. Ermine is quivering with emotion, and yet he speaks with disciplined passion.

"I decry the FBI's presence on campus as a witch hunt. Universities can remain vital only if non conformists are protected, as the young man in the balcony observed."

Harold is preempting the high moral ground, speaking of his escape from the Nazis, regretting that I, I who made possible his professorship in America, am now behaving like those who drove him from Germany. He's leaving the stage, thank god! Rancorous confusion. I need to say something to counter his emotional appeal. I would just love to say: cut the few and save the U. But I can't. Agree with your opponent . . . always a good ploy.

"Membership in a university faculty should not and must not divorce anyone from his fundamental rights as a citizen. The free expression of political views is the very essence of a free society."

Joe Klein is waving his hat and rasping: "Apparently you do not believe that membership in the Communist Party constitutes an exercise of political freedom. It saddens me to say you seem to have forgotten what the essence of a free society is."

Booing. The irascible bastard! I should deplore the booing, but I won't. I'll let my supporters express their contempt. But Ermine has struck the more telling blow, and the faculty will never reproach him, given his experiences with the Nazis.

Horace Heaume, from French, is twisting his fedora in rage and taking my side. "I've had enough of all the shilly-shallying. We know that Condor is a commie. He admitted it. I say fire him and the others, and let's take the oath."

"Hear, hear!"

"Yes!"

"Let's cut our losses and move on!"

No, no, keep Condor on! If he's fired, I'll look like a jackass. I recruited him. Cut the two and save the U.

The tumult is dying down. A good sign. Call on friendly speakers. But you can't ignore the chairman of philosophy, Edward Mackison. Two of the three instructors come from his department. With philosophers you never know. He studies eastern religions and non-violence; he's bound to say mushy things.

"I would remind my colleagues that Professor Condor has tenure, a contract that all faculty should be loath to abrogate. The decision to fire a teacher should rest with the department, not with the president or some FBI investigators brought to the campus. I would further remind my colleagues that the loyalty oath is a political test that guarantees neither loyalty nor academic competence."

Surprisingly unsentimental. A good mind, not to be underestimated. Maybe he can be brought over to my side.

Professor Heaume is arguing with those around him. Good, he will not be rebutted. "I, for one, am willing to surrender a small part of my autonomy, *vis-à-vis* the state, in order to preserve a large part. I say it's worth the money."

At least I can still count on the French department!

"We're talking about morality, not cash," Joe Klein growls.

"I must demur," says Professor Barbute, "because—"

"Lionel, spare us your Rotary speech about the morality of money!"

How dare that pinko economist interrupt. I've never liked Milford Garner. His candor and feistiness may appeal to the faculty, but I wish I could add his name to the list. And Joe Klein's! Milford had better take care. His classroom practice of challenging students to consider the imperfections of all economic systems, including capitalism, has not gone unnoticed. Some would like to see him dismissed. Undoubtedly he will defend the three professors, and go on about academic freedom. He always does.

"It is *your* job, President Stoneham, to protect the faculty from outside interference," says Garner. "We all know the rules and the laws. We don't need a president to recite them. We need a president to defend us from their pernicious stupidity."

A ripple of ovation, but not thunderous. All to the good. You can tell that the faculty want the nastiness over so they can get back to their labs and the library. It's late. Point to the clock. Just several more minutes. The air has become pungent. This place reeks with smoke and sweat. Still a few fierce tempers shredding the debate. Use their impatience. The clock. Indicate your wish to end the proceedings. Christ, not another! Dean Johann Van Zandt. Slight. Soft-spoken. How can I ignore his raised hand? Although he commands enormous respect for his fairness toward faculty, he serves at my will. I hope he remembers.

"Yes, Dean Van Zandt?"

"President Stoneham, I wish merely to observe that no institution can face the future with hope unless it can look upon its past with pride. I should not like to leave this meeting until we know your decision on the three faculty and whether you will insist on the imposition of the oath."

Avoid this decision. Rendering a judgment in public makes it intractable. You need wriggling room.

Milford Garner is protesting. "We have yet to resolve the issue of censure."

Damn him! He is trying to push me over the line. Stay calm. I can see that a majority of those seated here clearly have mixed feelings: wishing to preserve academic freedom, but feeling compromised by the left-leaning faculty. Avoid a vote at all costs. The response to Milford is less than robust. Seize the moment and point emphatically at the clock. Yes! My friends are putting on their coats. Most of the faculty have no stomach for a fight. The usual malcontents are mumbling, saying I'm cutting the meeting short. The idea of censure is quietly dying. I nod at Doleman, my trusted right-hand man. He takes my cue and asks the faculty to applaud me. Most clap, some don't. Make a mental note of the conspicuous abstainers. Hold your head up. Leave the stage with dignity. Farkus will do the dirty work. He relishes it.

darkmatters
LEVITT

Marty

As Stoneham lumbered off the stage and exited through a side door of the theatre, Doleman peremptorily announced that in the coming weeks everyone, from pipe fitters to professors, would be required to sign the loyalty oath, and that as good Americans the C.U. faculty ought to be proud to honor their flag.

The irrepressible Joe Klein, puffing on a cigarette and wheezing like a faulty bellows, leapt to his feet to get in one last lick.

"Where the hell you been all night? Haven't you heard what we've said? An oath abridges our freedom. It's telling us we can't say certain things, or belong to such-and-such group, or read a particular book. You and the president are insulting the very flag you're hiding behind. That flag was created by revolutionaries, by dissenters, by dangerous men."

"And you're one of them!" someone shouted, only partially jesting.

Doleman replied coldly: "Anyone who fails to sign the oath will be fired."

The meeting adjourned.

A more fractious assembly I had never attended. I couldn't imagine how some of these people could remain on speaking terms with one another. I remembered a cousin of mine who had escaped the German death camps because a kindly neighbor hid her. How many of these men would have done the same? Those who argued that retaining the three men would invite the legislature to cut the university budget struck me as blind to the implications of their acceding to a suffocating conformity. And those who said that they had full confidence in the president to handle the matter—meaning: don't bother us, we don't want to get involved—made me wish that for one day they could be pariahs, with numbers tattooed on their arms, seeking succor from people just like themselves.

Ben and I made the mistake of lingering in the theatre lobby to talk to a few professors. Doleman, finding us in colloquy, demanded that Ben and I identify ourselves and our relationship to the university. At first, Ben refused, but when I spoke up he must have felt compromised, because he followed suit. As some drunken kids in the campus quadrangle caterwauled "Good Night, Irene," we sloshed through the snow to the Hill. A few people peeled off to grab a bite at a greasy spoon called the Fishbowl. The rest—most of whom supported the three professors—trooped into Tulagi's, a 3.2 beer hall. At the bar, Ben got into an argument with the son of a regent, who complained that he had taken Milford Garner's class and been required to read Karl Marx.

"Did you ever read this?" Ben asked, handing him one of his many copies of the Bill of Rights.

"What is it?"

"A revolutionary document that might just change your life."

"What are you, a pinko?"

"Listen, punk, while you were playing golf at your daddy's country club, I was ducking bullets in Korea."

The kid immediately shut up.

Ben always said that the one advantage to his having fought in Korea was that it gave him the moral edge in arguments with right wingers, most of whom had never served.

Shortly, Judson Meyer showed up at Tulagi's. We elbowed our way to his table and listened as he talked about the legal costs of defending his good name and keeping his job. Ben and several other students volunteered to raise money for his defense. Broke and timid, I had nothing to offer but my typewriter. Ben said that he would help compose the solicitation letter and work on a fact sheet that we agreed to distribute. Except for the one tattered copy I still own, I don't suppose any other exists. It reads: "Many students and faculty joined the Communist Party convinced that when the fascist powers intervened in the Spanish Civil War, a second world war was imminent. The Party promised peace but not through appeasement. Revolted by the policies of Chamberlain and Daladier, they felt that collective sanctions of the type then being urged by the Communist Party

darkmatters
LEVITT

might prevent a war." The sheet ends with a plea: "Let us not forget the political mood and warring temper of the 1930s."

I had been a young child in the '30s; I knew only from books the strikes, the marches, the political assassinations, the mob violence, and the flirtation of influential people, like William Randolph Hearst, with fascism. Not until Prague did I discover that the party to which so many had flocked in the hope of a better world was no better than Senator Joseph McCarthy and his ilk.

Ben

Abby escorts Clarissa, Marty, and Ben to the Delt party. Entry, by invita-
tion only, takes the form of a handsome card designed to look like a bottle
of Chivas Regal scotch, with an explanation of how to knock on the door:
three fast raps, pause, and two fast raps. She has prevailed upon Brian
Hazelwood to give her three extras. The fraternity house, done up like a
speakeasy, includes a fake front door containing a slide that the bouncer
opens upon hearing the required knocks. Advised to dress in 1920s style,
the women wear flapper flimsies with fringe. A used clothing store fixes up
Marty and Ben with some knickers, which they call plus fours. Ben also
buys a benny and a rough tweed jacket.

Inside, blue light bathes dozens of tables, covered with red and white
checkered tablecloths, and a bar. To one side, a small ragtime band plays
on a portable stage, where later a master of ceremonies will tell jokes, dance,
and play the saxophone. A portion of the hardwood floor, set aside for dancing, has been waxed. Someone spills his drink, which beads like little blis-
ters. The ceiling glows with phosphorescent stars and a crescent moon. A
"woman greeter," imitating Texas Guinan, says "Hello, suckers!" and seats
us close to the stage. Almost immediately, Clarissa and Ben take to the
dance floor and cut quite a rug. Other couples notice and give them room
as they perform the Charleston, the Black Bottom, and the Texas Tommy.
While Abby and Marty and the others watch, Ben devours Clarissa. Her
diaphanous white dress, with its blue sash belted around the hips, accentuates her slim figure. She contrasts with the rouged and mascaraed young
women who hold out their cigarettes for their dates to jump up and light:
sedentary young women already beginning to thicken, with their fat arms,

spreading hips, puffed up faces, and double chins. Ben knows that Clarissa's beauty will wane gracefully, and never permit him to rest. Her face and figure please him aesthetically, like the Modigliani woman that he always returns to see in the Museum of Modern Art: a white flower on a slender stem against an opaque background. Her beautiful hands move toward him. He takes them and turns her. She glides back to him, as if connected by an invisible cord. The luminous blackness of her eyes excites him. In the hot, perfumed air, he feels passion aswarm like bright-hued butterflies. She presses close to him. He whispers.

"You know, you must know, how much I love you. I can't tell you why, or what it is. It just is. I love you."

Her eyes brighten, as if inviting him into her thoughts. She shapes her mouth for a kiss. He bends down. Her lips seem to melt in his mouth. For an instant, her tongue grazes his and teasingly withdraws. But her eyes remain clear, unflinching. He knows what that look means: her body will succumb but never her spirit. In his heart, he experiences a vague disappointment.

He remembers Yumi teaching him to love. That first night, he loses all control as she kisses the length of his body and her dove-like hand gently takes his penis into her mouth. Slowly, over the weeks, she teaches him to restrain himself and savor the subtlety of her tongue and her sweet-sucking mouth. From her he learns to give labial pleasures, tonguing her pinkness, up, down, and around. Her febrile body pulsates and sweats in response, becoming ever more insistent. When he enters her, her arms enfold him like wings; she opens, and together they rise and soar, as he is held fast in her mysterious wetness. She unfailingly senses the moment his mind no longer has command of his body, and pulls him into her all the harder; and then he cries out, entering into a free fall, like the start of a parachute jump.

With Clarissa, it is different. She restrains herself; she says it fuels fantasy and heightens the pleasure. Reluctant to overstep the bounds of conventional sexuality, she encourages him to ravish and guide her. If he told her that another woman has taught him how to give pleasure, she would be terribly hurt. But where does she think his lovemaking comes from, a book? Not likely. He is teaching her things western girls rarely know. Now an acolyte, she will, he trusts, eventually become a priestess of Eros. Were Clarissa to marry someone else, would she bestow upon him what she has learned in Ben's bed? At least not at first. Modesty would demand the reliable missionary position.

"Should we try something new?" she says. And they swing into the Staircase, a step they've often hoofed at the Timber Tavern to while away a slow evening. They are now alone on the dance floor, the cynosure of this provincial world.

Marty

Abby couldn't take her eyes off them. She had never seen Ben and Clarissa strut their stuff. I tried small talk, but I could see that imagination had carried her onto the dance floor and into Ben's arms. I slurped, having unconsciously drained off my drink. Abby quit her sorcerer's dream, and we fell into conversation about our two friends. Though Ben had told me about his family background, he never talked about Clarissa. Abby, an inveterate gossip, related all, even the intimate secrets of friends.

Clarissa Stanton came from Lexington, known for its old wealth, southern traditions, and racehorsey culture. She had attended a preparatory girl's school in Virginia, where her father had dropped her off with the admonition, "Now, I don't want you getting any ideas." But she did.

Somewhere Clarissa's mother had graduated from a finishing school and had acquired a smattering of French, which she passed on to her daughter. Playing the sprite, Clarissa would wave a hand at her sorority sisters or Ben and declare, *Allez-vous-en*: away with you, begone. But more often she could be heard saying *au contraire*, as she sweetly and intractably demurred.

Although she looked like a child next to many of her sorority sisters, she had the precocity that comes from debutante balls and the street smarts that come from a familiarity with the demi monde. Her family moved in the horsey set—her father published a newspaper—but she had preferred the company of his reporters, often following them from one seedy story to another. Her mother thought that her exposure to wild men would make her unsuited for marriage. She complained that Clarissa had never been a girl, but rather, since the age of eight, a woman. I suspect that Mrs. Stanton was right.

According to Abby, she and Clarissa had first met in their freshman year at Smith, where they remained until transferring together to the University of Colorado. Ben, two years older than Clarissa, had regularly dated her while he was at Amherst, which is just a short distance from Smith. Abby said that although they cared a great deal for one another, Ben's egalitarian feelings and Clarissa's parents lay behind their wartime separation.

Once, when Clarissa feared she was pregnant, she confided to Abby that she and Ben were lovers. Her fears, however, turned out to be unwarranted. Here Abby digressed, telling me the story of a friend from her hometown who had spent weeks trying to discover an abortionist. The man she eventually found knew no more about gynecology than a blind man about color. In his darkness, he butchered her and she died. Abby started to cry. I reached over and took her hands in mine, and hoped that I would never have to scrounge for a doctor to scrape an embryo from the womb of my lover. In Detroit, an abortionist lived across the street from our store. I used to see a parade of young women go in upright and come out bent over, holding their guts. My parents pretended not to see. But I somehow knew that many of those women ended up dead or sterile for life. My rabbinic tutor had inveighed against abortion, but with Talmudic wisdom had observed that if a woman makes such a decision, the medical means ought to be available. Coat hangers, he said, were no substitute for humane laws.

"Bitchin' dancers, those two," said a young man who came up to Abby and me.

"Marty, I'd like you to meet Brian Hazelwood. Brian, this is Marty Bartelman."

We shook hands and he joined us, as we watched Ben and Clarissa swing into yet another step. Brian, deeply tanned, made me think he had just returned from Bermuda, but in fact, he said, his color had come from a sun lamp. When I complimented his tux, which fit like a tailor's truth, he proudly explained that he had purchased it in London. A weight lifter, he wore a pinky ring, a ruby, that looked as if he'd been feeding it steroids. I'm often reminded of Brian by my neighbor's teenage sons, who share his passion for "hard bods" and for exercise, provided it's not mental.

"She's a real looker, just like you said, Abby," referring of course to Clarissa.

"Keep your eyes to yourself. The lady's already taken."

darkmatters LEVITT

"Who's the guy?"

"Ben Cohen. I told you he would be Clarissa's date."

"And who's yours, Marty?"

"I don't have one. I'm just here to watch."

"Well, just wait a few minutes. I know a sexy Theta whose boyfriend will be drunk as a coon in under two minutes. I'll introduce you."

"I'm fine where I am. Thanks, anyway."

With other couples nerving themselves to resume dancing, Abby and Brian swept out on the floor, she nimble and quick, he strong and gymnastic. They couldn't compete with Ben and Clarissa, but they ran a respectable second. Everyone else was a two-stepping klutz.

A pretty brunette, with a kite-shaped sorority pin bearing the initials KAT, plopped down at the table. Mildly drunk, she vaguely said, "Would you believe, he's already blotto. That boy has got a problem." She giggled. "But don't we all?"

I suspected that this was Brian's Theta. She introduced herself as Helen.

"Spelled h-e-l-l-i-o-n," she laughed. "Wanna dance?"

"Not my thing."

"What is?"

"Books, opera, chamber music."

"Geez, an egghead!"

"Not really."

"Dya ever hear of *The Great Gatsby*?"

"Yes. I've read it."

"Guess what?"

"What?"

"I had to give a report, but didn't know squat. So I asked one of our hashers—Pablo's his name—what to say. He told me to sling the crap that the book wasn't about Gatsby, but about the narrator, Nick Carraway. Did you ever hear anything so dumb?" I would have disagreed had she not continued. "The funny thing is . . . the teacher gave me an A. Now whatta you think of that?"

"Maybe your friend Pablo was right."

"Get serious!"

"Or maybe your professor finds you attractive."

"You think so? Yeah, he probably does," she giggled. "He's really just a graduate student . . . and to tell ya the truth he did ask me out."

"Let me guess: you accepted."

"Hey, why not? Besides, he was cute." She giggled. "Say, I don't recognize you. Are you a Delt?"

"No."

"I didn't think so. You're not wearing a Delt pin or blazer. So what are you?"

I could have said a student, a business major, a Jew, a resident of Detroit. But I knew what she meant, so I answered: "Unaffiliated."

"A GDI!" she exclaimed aghast.

The initials stood for "God Damned Independent" and, in some quarters, excited praise, not opprobrium.

"How could you?!" she exclaimed, as if I had just mugged my mother. "I couldn't stand to be an independent. It would be *so* boring . . . without the parties and all. I'd rather be dead."

At the table to my right, two couples had engaged themselves in a discussion about beer.

"Schlitz, man, you can't beat it."

The other fellow replied: "You ever had Pabst Blue Ribbon? It makes all the other American beers taste like piss."

"I like anything that isn't 3.2," said one of the girls.

"My father," said the other girl, "swears by Budweiser. But then he grew up in St. Louis."

At a table behind me, another profound discussion was in full swing: about virginity.

Girl: "I certainly am!"

Boy: "You can't be serious."

Girl: "I don't believe in it till marriage."

Boy: "Not even if you love the guy."

Girl: "If he loves me, he ought to be willing to wait."

Boy: "This isn't 1900."

Girl: "Then find yourself another date."

Boy: "Maybe I will."

With that declaration, the fellow stood up and wandered off. The woman just sat there tapping her fingers on her beer stein.

The brunette, having difficulty keeping her eyes open, declared that she needed to make "a johnny stop," weaved across the room, and disappeared in the crowd.

darkmatters
LEVITT

A guy and three gals sat down at the vacant table to my left. One of them, Brenda Oates, I knew from my Italian Renaissance history course. She always wore a butterfly pin on her right shoulder, and must have owned dozens of them because I never saw her wear the same one twice. The pin aptly corresponded to her butterfly mind. She flitted from one subject to another, talking in a stream of associations.

The fellow said: "You'll never guess what I heard today. Some Negroes are forming their own fraternity. Christ, what next: hog maws and chitterlings on the school menu?"

Brenda took her cue. "We used to have a Negro cook, Jemima. I never liked that name, you know. My favorite is Darlene. A cousin of mine had that name: Darlene Densmor. She acted in a movie. But she retired, you know. My dad says that as soon as he retires he's going to take me canoeing in Acadia State Park. That's in Canada. Did you know that they speak two languages up there? English and French. God, I really hate my French class! The other day, the other kids in that class laughed at me when the professor said he knew children this high"—she held her hand about two feet above the floor—"who could speak French fluently. 'Well, of course, they can,' I said, 'they're probably French.' I really thought I'd like to visit France, but not any more. They all speak French there."

A short time later, the musicians took a break and our dancing friends returned.

"Bitchin' party, isn't it?" Brian asked, looking at me. But fortunately he continued, relieving me of the need to reply. "What do you guys think about CCNY and LIU and the point shaving? I hear that Bradley and Kentucky are also involved."

Never having participated in sports, I knew little about them. I wasn't even sure that I knew the meaning of point shaving, though I remembered Inky mentioning it.

"You'll have to explain what it means, Brian. I have no idea."

"Every day the papers list the point spread . . . the odds the gamblers are giving. For example, they'll say Syracuse will beat Iona by ten points or more. If Syracuse beats them by less than ten, or if Iona wins, anyone who bet against the point spread wins. So gamblers go to the players and say, 'Hey listen, kid, I'm not asking you to throw the game. I'm just asking you to win by less than the point spread. If you do, there's a lot of dough in it for you.'"

Even I could figure out the implications. Players on the take would have to miss shots deliberately, or slow up the game, or lose the ball, or do whatever it took to keep the score down.

"I bet," said Brian, "it's a communist plot."

"What makes you think so?" Ben asked.

"College basketball in America is like a religion. The Reds are atheists. They would do anything to run down our religion."

Clarissa told Brian that she found his comments "off the wall." "No matter how much we love sports, sports and religion are not the same thing."

"I still think it's a plot."

"Well," said Ben ironically, "we know that they're everywhere. In government, universities, under the bed, right here at this table. Hell," Ben continued, "a friend of mine got a 'D' on a Latin exam, and I'm sure it's part of a communist conspiracy."

From Brian's expression, I guessed he was entertaining the possibility that Ben actually meant what he said. "Really? Well, we know there's three of them on the campus right now. So you think your friend's Latin professor is also one?"

Ben reached across the table and touched Brian on the hand. "Don't worry, fellow, I hear the guy's too pixilated to be a Red."

"Huh?!"

Brian, unfamiliar with the word, couldn't determine whether Ben was being critical of the professor or the Reds. "I don't know why we don't just drop an atomic bomb on Russia and get rid of the problem. My father says that Russian Jews caused the revolution there." He paused and smiled guiltily at Ben and me. "Cohen and Bartelman . . . they're Jewish names, aren't they?" He turned to Abby for help, but she averted her eyes. "Well, you know what I mean. I can tell you guys aren't that kind."

"What kind?" said Ben.

Clarissa, wishing to avoid a nasty scene, interposed: "Ignore Ben, he just loves an argument. If you say no, he'll say yes. He delights in playing the gadfly. I ought to know."

Brian devoured Clarissa with a suitor's eyes. "If you were my girlfriend, I'd never say no to you."

Abby blurted: "Like hell!"

But Brian strangely added: "For her, yes."

The table fell silent, as each of us, I suppose, wrestled with the import of Brian's statement.

"Oh, never mind," he said, standing up, "come on, let's all get knee-walking drunk," and he departed.

"Where's his family from," asked Ben, "besides hunger?"

"His father's with some chemical company in Delaware," said Abby. "I think he's a tax lawyer."

"That's a laugh," said Ben humorlessly. "Guys like him are hired to find loopholes in the law—or to create them—so that corporations escape paying taxes."

"His mother comes from old Virginia money. They keep a boat on Chesapeake Bay. The damn thing's so big it sleeps about ten people."

Suddenly the band struck up a musical introduction and the emcee, a short, thin, black-haired guy, with irregular teeth and sloping eyes, stepped out of the crowd and onto the stage. He introduced himself as Ed Lowry. In his initial routine, he played the saxophone and engaged in some eccentric dancing, à la Joe Frisco. At the conclusion, he ushered in his two sidekicks, Florrie and Larry. Florrie, no taller than four and a half feet, wore a bathrobe. Larry, a tall, handsome, well dressed man, had slicked-down hair parted in the middle. Ed warmed up the audience with a few jokes.

"Will someone please call out a number, and I will guess what it is."

Some drunken Delt actually yelled "thirty-three." Lowry paused and then repeated it. The kid seemed impressed.

"You know, I used to go with a girl with a wooden leg, but I broke it off."

A few people groaned, but not Abby, who gave out with a good-hearted laugh.

"A man never gets into trouble chasing women. It's after they're caught that the trouble begins."

He went on in this vein for several minutes, finally introducing the skit that he and his friends had come to perform.

"The last time we did this act," he said, "people actually cried, cried for their money back. No, that's a bit of an exaggeration. What happened was . . . the people laughed so hard they fell right out of their chairs. I don't want anybody to get hurt here, so fellows, open your vests, loosen your belt, sit back, and relax. Girls . . . just do the best that you can."

Abby found that joke worth a whoop and a holler. She clearly enjoyed this old-fashioned humor. Brian assumed a slightly pained expression. I suspected that coming from a strait-laced family, he found her response a little too enthusiastic. The emcee asked that the love seat be moved from a corner of the room to the stage, and exited. Florrie disrobed disclosing underneath a mouth-watering negligee. Larry removed his jacket, which he threw off to one side, and put on house slippers. The two of them sat down and passionately embraced. From off-stage a door slammed.

Larry: (*Startled*) Who's that?

Florrie: Just my husband. Don't worry, he's open-minded. He understands these things.

Larry: I certainly hope so

Florrie: Darling! This is so heavenly.

Larry: Wonderful. (*They kiss. He breaks free of the embrace*) Are you sure it's all right?

Florrie: You have absolutely nothing to worry about. George is a very modern husband. We never interfere with each other.

Larry: Never interfere with each other? (*She nods*) I'm sure glad to hear that. (*He passionately embraces her*) Darling!

(*Off-stage noise. He tries to break off the embrace. She restrains him reassuringly. Ed, playing George the husband, enters carrying a lunch box*)

George: (*Cheerfully*) Good evening, dear.

Florrie: Hello, George, you're early tonight.

George: Dinner ready?

Florrie: I didn't have time. You'll find the can opener on the sink.

George: I see. (*Crosses to center*) By the way, have my shirts come back from the laundry?

Florrie: Oh, I forgot to send them out.

George: Forget it. I can wear this shirt for another two weeks. (*He crosses to left of stage*) Have you seen my slippers anywhere?

Florrie: (*Pointing to her lover's feet*) He's wearing them. Do you mind?

Husband: It's quite all right. I have to find the can opener. (*He exits*)

Larry: He is modern, isn't he?

darkmatters
LEVITT

Florrie: (*As they embrace*) You see, I told you we had nothing to worry about.

(*As the lovemaking becomes intense, the husband reenters, carrying a jacket over his arm*)

George: (*Tapping the lover on the shoulder*) Pardon me! (*The lover looks up*) Is this your jacket?

Larry: (*Looking at jacket*) Yes, it is.

(*The husband pulls out a gun and shoots the lover. The wife screams*)

George: (*Holding up the jacket to the audience*): No fraternity emblem. He must be a GDI!

The Delt house rocked with laughter, and Brian, overcome with merriment, fell off his chair. The people at the adjoining tables, already wildly amused, laughed uncontrollably when Brian did his dive. I thought that Abby would explode from delight. She bounced in her chair, clapped, and slapped her sides. Clarissa chuckled, whether at the skit or at Brian's behavior I couldn't say. Ben and I looked at each other uneasily. After the place quieted down, the emcee turned to Florrie and said, "What shall we do next?" She replied: "I'll spin a coin. If it's heads, we'll drink; if it's tails, we'll dance; and if it stands on edge, we'll send everyone home to study." The place broke up.

darkmatters
LEVITT

Ben

The following week, Ben receives a summons to appear before the University Disciplinary Committee (UDC), composed of four students—one from each class—and V.P. Farkus Doleman, who presides over the hearing. The twofold charge: assault and battery against Ty Handsel, and the distribution of Marxist literature. Since Marty was present at the fights with Ty, he attends as a witness. The proceedings take place in a first-floor conference room of the new Glen Miller Memorial Center. Ben, of course, knows one of his accusers, Ty, but has no idea about the identity of the other.

Doleman begins with a reference to Marty's attendance at the protest meeting in the theatre.

"You knew the meeting was open only to faculty and teaching assistants, and yet you misrepresented your friend here in order to obtain entry for him to a meeting that specifically forbade undergraduates and staff. Your record indicates that you have been expelled from Brackett Hall and are currently on probation. If the current charges prove true, you will be expelled. Let us begin with the first charge, assault and battery."

Doleman asks the recording secretary to bring in Ty Handsel, who ignores Ben's presence and recounts, with some embarrassment (which pleases Marty), the thrashings he had received at Ben's hands.

"Did you provoke him?" says one of the students.

"All I did was tease Marty a little. You know, harmless stuff."

Marty jumps in and recounts what Ty calls harmless. Most of the pranks merely elicit snickers from the students on the committee, but when he talks about Ty's grabbing his homework, the mood swings in Ben's favor.

darkmatters
LEVITT

Doleman, who clearly wants to see Ben get the boot, addresses him. "Is it not true that you served in the Army?"

"Yes, I fought in Korea."

"Ah, fought! The very word that I want to discuss. The Army trained you to fight, by which I mean, you were taught how to kill."

"I believe that's the point of a war—to kill the enemy."

"You realize, Mr. Cohen, that if a professional prizefighter strikes someone not trained in fighting, he can be jailed for assault with a deadly weapon: his fists. Did you know that, Mr. Cohen?"

"Yes. The Army warned us about misdirecting our training."

"But you did."

"Against a bully."

A second student asks: "Why didn't you just report him?"

"I could have. Marty could have as well. But we thought that it would just make things worse for Marty."

"How?"

"Guerilla warfare. It's insidious. I've seen it firsthand. So I chose to put an end to the harassment immediately—which I did."

"Ah!" says a delighted Doleman, "you don't deny the charge?"

"No."

Marty tries to defend Ben by describing the worthlessness he felt when Ty and his friends hounded him, and his fear at opening the door or turning a corner. "Frankly, I felt terrified."

Ty just laughs. Ben shoots him a glance that says: if you want to step outside right now, I'm ready. The others see Ben's expression as well. Marty fears that Ben will shortly be out on the street.

After a few more questions, Ty leaves, and Doleman turns the committee's attention to the second charge: the distribution of Marxist literature. Again the recording secretary leaves the room. She returns with the regent's son, the one who had argued with Ben at Tulagi's.

"Please," says Doleman, "tell Mr. Cohen what you wrote to the committee."

The kid repeats—accurately—his encounter with Ben at the bar. He recounts talking about his class in economics and his suspicions regarding Professor Milford Garner's loyalty to this country. Ben, he remarks, had disagreed with him "in a very aggressive manner" and had handed him something to read.

"He told me to read this." He removes from his briefcase the single sheet of paper that Ben had given him. "I read it carefully and even showed it to my father. As you know, he's one of the regents of this university. We both agreed it was subversive, nothing but communist propaganda. But you already know all about it because I sent you a copy with my complaint."

"Yes," says Doleman, "we received a copy and distributed it to the committee." The recording secretary, taking her cue, produces the document and hands it to Fartus, who passes it to Ben and asks:

"Do you recognize this document?"

"I certainly do."

"Then you admit you gave it to Mr. Lawrence?"

"Yes."

"Are you aware of the campus rule against distributing literature deemed subversive?"

"I am."

"Have you anything further to say before the UDC retires to make a decision?"

"One thing. That piece of paper, which educated people call the Bill of Rights, guarantees the American people freedom of speech, assembly, and worship. In some quarters it is recognized as the first ten amendments to the U.S. Constitution."

You can feel the committee's shock suck the air out of the room. Their embarrassment palpably fills the vacuum. Ben returns the document to Doleman, who studies it closely, probably for the first time. The students, who, Ben suspects, have been influenced by the prez's flunky, study their own copies. The plaintiff, now bilious, speaks up.

"My father . . . well, he really didn't read it closely. I mean . . . I just ran it past him."

Ben admires the jerk for defending his father, but he has no doubt that Regent Lawrence wouldn't know the Bill of Rights from the Gettysburg Address, nor would most of the other regents. As Ben's accuser makes a quick exit, Doleman requests Ben and Marty to wait in the hall while he and the students deliberate.

"May I see it?" Marty asks.

Ben hands him a copy.

"I can guess why the others fell for it. The paper has no title. It simply lists, in abridged form, ten rights."

Ben puckishly admits the omission is deliberate. "It smokes out the patriotic know-nothings."

In under five minutes, the committee clears him of all charges, though they warn him against fighting.

As the two friends leave the hearing, Ben murmurs, "It all depends on the issue."

Ben

Ben knocks and enters Marty's room to find him lazily listening to a Beethoven sonata and making plans for his spring break. Ben has in tow a fellow with thick eyeglasses and a rolled cigarette dangling from the corner of his mouth whom he introduces as Joe Riley.

"Good view of the other dorms from here. I don't suppose very much escapes your attention," Joe says enigmatically.

"I was lucky to get this room. It's close to the bathroom."

"Joe's a senior in political science," Ben adds.

"Think it'll last as long as *Rag Mop*?" Joe cracks, referring to the Beethoven.

They all laugh.

Ben and Joe are raising money for the three professors, and have decided to attend a meeting in Denver of the Mine, Mill, and Smelter Workers Union to ask them for help. The year before, the union had been drummed out of the Congress of Industrial Organizations (CIO) for alleged communist ties. Mine-Mill's colorful history includes its direct descent from the Western Federation of Miners, a radical union of hardrock miners who had helped found the Industrial Workers of the World (IWW), the "Wobblies," famous for their socialistic ideas. At the time, Mine-Mill and a New Jersey-based zinc corporation are engaged in a fierce strike, subsequently made famous by the film *Salt of the Earth*, written and produced by directors, actors, and writers blacklisted in Hollywood because of their leftist politics. The strike centers in the small mining town of Hanover, New Mexico, in the Pinos Altos mountains. Having begun in October 1950, it pits Local 890, almost all of whom are

darkmatters
LEVITT

Hispanic, against a corporation in no mood to make concessions to "spics."

Mine-Mill has an important office in Denver, a city friendly to labor unions. Joe's parents have close ties to the union, serving in some political capacity, though Ben never learns exactly what. Ben asks Marty if he'd like to join them, and he says yes. Had Ben waited until the sonata ended, as he wanted to do, he would never have met Esperanza. They climb into Ben's DeSoto parked in front of Brackett Hall, and drive over to Broadway and east to the Boulder-Denver toll road. As they pass the stables on the north side of the road, Ben remarks that he and Clarissa have recently gone riding. Joe, who clearly regards the equestrian arts as an expression of conspicuous laziness on the part of the rich, inquires how Ben can afford the fees.

"Clarissa pays."

Joe, who has met her, asks sardonically, "You mean, she doesn't stable her own horse there? I'm amazed."

"She does," replies Ben sheepishly. "Two horses, in fact. She rides one; I ride the other."

Marty expresses surprise. "I knew that your father had taught you all about horses and riding, but I had no idea that you and Clarissa regularly rode together."

"We follow the foothills, west of here, to Devil's Thumb and take the canyon right up to the talus scree run. The country up there smells of pine needles and wet earth. It's a far cry from Brooklyn."

"Who's better?" Joe mumbles roguishly.

"Better?"

"Rider."

"She's much the better jumper, as you might expect. But when it comes to racing or running a horse through timber, I think she'd agree that I have her there."

At the Broomfield exit, Ben slows down, throws a quarter into the toll basket, and continues on to Denver. The long stretches of empty, rolling fields have a light covering of snow, broken only by the brown stalks of last year's growth and an occasional for-sale sign: a hundred dollars an acre.

Ben, who has been thinking about the meeting in the university theatre, observes, "I disagree with everything Stoneham stands for, but I can appreciate his predicament."

Joe snarls. "I can't. He's an asshole!"

darkmatters
LEVITT

"Come on, Joe, what do you expect him to do: give up his friends and his family? They're all steeped in GOP politics. Besides a wife, he's married to a way of living. His habits and manners and dress and speech have all been forged by his politics. And you want him to be born again? Forget it! Would you throw over everything . . . lose the company and respect of your spouse and buddies . . . to uphold a principle? Christ, most people would renounce the Bill of Rights for five dollars more in their paycheck."

"Any pal of mine who opposed freedom of thought and association would quickly be no pal." Joe's Irish face reddens and his testiness increases. "I'll tell you who Stoneham's friends are: sixty-year-old fraternity boys, knickered golf geezers, snake-oil merchants, corporate shills, bible beaters, swamp salesmen, windbags. To satisfy them, he's trampling the rights of three decent men—and blackening the name of the university. So spare me the sentimental shit. When Stoneham took the job, he should have known it involved more than sitting in a box with his friends at a football game."

Ben feels, as he often does, that Joe's socialist principles are more heartfelt than his own. He says nothing until he tells Joe, who has lit a Pall Mall, to blow the smoke out the window. Joe pays no attention. The unease becomes palpable. To break it, Marty reverts to the word game that he and Ben have frequently played.

"Lavation!"

"Comes from the verb to lave, to wash."

"Gerful!"

"Don't know it."

"It means changeable."

"Glossolalia."

"Nonsensical talk, gibberish."

Joe angrily flicks his cigarette out the window. "Gibberish! That's what you two guys are full of. For Christ's sake, who the hell do you think is ever going to understand you if you use words like that? Not everyone has the time to sit around and read a dictionary. Some people work from early to late. So just can it!"

Ben drives into a run-down area, not far from Four Points, and parks in front of a dull, yellow house, surrounded by a rotting wood fence. Joe directs him to "take a gander across the street. Those guys standing next to the Buick are FBI."

Marty, obviously scared, lapses into a whisper. "How do you know?"

"Trust me. J. Edgar's boys come to our house so often, you'd think we were pals. You can spot 'em a mile off. Short haircut and clean shaven. Always wear dark suits and ties with white shirts. Polished wing-tips. Their dress code."

"What should we do?" a troubled Marty asks.

"Just wave to them and say hello, to let them know that we know."

Joe takes his own advice, but Marty and Ben turn their backs on the men. The broken slats in the fence and dandelion lawn remind Ben of a farm in Carmel, New Jersey, owned by a hermit who wears long underwear in summer.

They climb outdoor stairs to the second floor and enter a rundown apartment. The green velour living-room furniture has pads or tape over the cushions to protect the sitters from the broken springs. A skinny fellow with a wispy chin beard tells them to make themselves comfortable and hands out bottles of Rainier ale. Ben's sofa seat threatens to break its bonds and castrate him. A man in cowboy boots and belted Levis stands next to the front window, scanning the street. Ben worries that the two FBI agents will enter the house; when they do not, he wonders what they hope to achieve by remaining outside. About seven or eight people have preceded them and three or four more arrive shortly thereafter, among them Esperanza Morales, a stunning woman in her mid-twenties with long black hair pulled back and braided, revealing the most sensuous forehead Ben has ever seen. She has perfect teeth, except for one that tilts slightly backwards, set in a face that might not launch a thousand ships of Ilium, but that could certainly move a man to action—and distraction.

"No Coors?" Joe inquires sarcastically, referring to the beer.

The wispy-bearded guy laughs raucously. "Not on these premises," he says. "I don't allow right-wingers in my house."

Joe Coors, who owns the Coors brewery in Golden, is famous for his support of conservative causes and no friend of unions. As a point of pride, liberals never drink his beer.

The meeting begins with an appeal from Esperanza Morales to support the striking miners in Hanover, New Mexico.

"My husband and hundreds of others have been striking since October. They can hardly feed body and soul. Some of those poor devils used to work for three or four dollars a day. They had a real hard time of it. Their bodies show it. It breaks one's heart to see some of them. Why is it bosses consider working people as nothing but hands and don't care what happens to them? If our men are out of a job and pick up a newspaper to seek work, they go to the page where it says 'hands wanted.' If they're delayed and come to work late, the boss informs them he has all the hands that he needs. It isn't the mother's son, or sister's brother, or Mr. So-and-So that the boss wants, but a good, swift pair of hands, and, if they're used up, he finds others. The men don't count at all."

She stops just long enough to sip from a glass of water.

"All our people want is what Anglo miners in the district already receive: that they be paid for all the time they spend underground, not just at the ore face. Coal miners call it 'portal-to-portal' pay. We call it 'collar-to-collar' pay. We are also asking for six paid holidays and a contract without a 'no-strike' clause. The zinc company has refused all our demands, and instead has offered to raise wages five-cents an hour—*if* we agree to an increase in the workweek of eight hours. They say that it is a take-it-or-leave-it offer."

Joe, scarlet-faced, leaps to his feet and cries, "Tell them to go fuck themselves, if you'll pardon my Irish."

Though not in Joe's colorful language, others speak with equal force in support of the New Mexico strike. Esperanza says that the miners need food, water, money, and transportation to get into town so that they don't have to buy from the company store.

"If you have nothing else," says Esperanza, "lend us your moral support. Even if we lose, it's winter wheat that we are sowing, and others will reap it."

Ben already sees his jalopy heading south.

As she bids us adieu—she has other groups to address—Ben walks across the room and takes her hands.

"My name is Ben Cohen. I will be there."

She studies his face. "I will remember."

And she does.

*　　*　　*　　*

On the drive back to Boulder, Marty suddenly exclaims: "Eldorado Ridge! You and Dana were bird watching."

Ben knows that Marty and Dana are bird-watchers, but is surprised to discover Joe Riley's interest. On more than one occasion, Ben has driven Dana and Marty to Eldorado Springs to tramp the hills together birding, hoping to see yellow tanagers, white-breasted nuthatches, lazuli buntings, and killdeers. Joe Riley, whom Ben met at a Marxist study group on campus, frequently scoffs at outdoor activities with the wry comment that when he can't see concrete he gets nervous. His avian pursuits seem out of character.

Joe ignores Marty's comment and suggests that they canvass their friends at school for contributions to help the three professors and Local 890. They agree that to raise money they could use a beautiful, well-spoken woman who can rouse the spirit of those with deep pockets, or even just raise the serpents in men. Clarissa comes to mind, but Ben's persuading her will, as one of CU's basketball players recently said, "prove a task in front of him that lies in the future."

He broaches the subject, and she demurs. "No, I'm not the right person. Anyway, what would I tell my parents?"

Abby leaps at the opportunity: "Hell, yes, let's get started. It sounds like a bitchin' thing to do."

They rent the Elks Club in Boulder Canyon and invite everyone they know, from Greek to GDI, to a speech and a dance. Tickets: five dollars a couple. They figure that if the conservative kids don't like what they hear, they can wait on the porch until the speaker has finished. The day of the event, cars line the canyon. The area resembles a mob scene. One of the "tainted" professors talks poignantly about what it feels like to defend your-self against ghosts. After he finishes, Abby follows. She wears a dress that leaves little to the imagination, and supplements the literalism with frequent bends at the waist that nearly cause her bosom to spill out of her braless bodice. The effect is electric. Ben has written a speech for her that she nearly gets right. But very few listen; they mostly gawk—and cheer. Ben and his friends raise almost fifteen-hundred dollars, which gladdens them all, but none more so than Abby, who immediately becomes a campus celebrity.

dark**matters**
LEVITT

Marty

Acting on a suggestion of Joe Riley's, we staged a lecture and girlie show to raise money for the professors threatened with dismissal. The very thought of a burlesque put Clarissa out of sorts, but Abby found it exciting. Baring all but nipples and hair, Abby wowed the crowd. Clarissa, clearly upstaged by her roommate, feigned delight but I knew she wanted to throttle Abby. Daring, after all, was *her* specialty. At some point in the evening, after the speeches and during the social dancing, Abby and Ben disappeared. Clarissa asked me if I knew where they'd gone. I checked outside. The DeSoto stood where we'd left it. I knew that the Elks Club had several rooms upstairs, but off limits according to the terms of the rental. Clarissa and I were perplexed, even worried, when Ben and Abby seemed to materialize out of the ether.

"I couldn't find you," said Clarissa anxiously. "Where did you go?"

"Out on the porch for a smoke. Some guy coming down the canyon blew a tire. We helped him."

Clarissa studied Abby, who neither spoke nor nodded to confirm what just had been said. Bubbly Abby would normally have been embellishing Ben's story with every silly detail. I therefore doubted its truth, and wondered whether Clarissa, like me, found her stillness disquieting. If she did, she never said. Rather she took Ben by the hand and they swept onto the dance floor, where, once again, to the oohs and aahs of the others, they glittered and glowed. Nothing pleased them quite so much, I think, as dancing before an admiring crowd. I watched for a few minutes and then made my way upstairs to poke around. Nothing looked amiss, and the rooms unexceptional: offices, a bathroom, and a guest room, with a bureau and bed.

darkmatters
LEVITT

The party slowly staggered to a conclusion, leaving quite a mess. We cleaned up as well as we could, drove to the top of Flagstaff mountain, and sat under one of the shelters. The night air on the mountain had a rawness to it, made worse by a cutting wind moaning in the pines and assaulting our refuge. While Abby went to find kindling—we had plenty of logs—Ben took an army jacket from his car and put it over Clarissa's shoulders. A pack of mule deer approached, sniffed our scent, and trotted off into the woods. Abby returned with an armful of pine cones and sticks. Without any paper, she built a lovely fire that elicited praise for her woodcraft.

"Didn't you guys ever go to camp?" she asked. "I went every summer . . . starting at six years old. That's where I learned."

Clarissa said that Lexington, although hot and steamy in the summer, kept her busy with debutante balls and horse races and riding.

"I used to wait all year to have Scout to myself. He was my favorite horse."

"Favorite?" I said. "Geez, how many did you have?"

"Oh, there were others, but Scout, a beautiful Appaloosa, followed me around like a dog. I loved him." She grew reflective. "When he died, I felt like I could never love another living thing as much as I had loved that animal."

"What about the horses you stable here in Boulder?" I asked.

"They're not much. Ask Ben. He rides them. He can tell you what nags they are."

Ben chortled. "What she calls a nag, I call a thoroughbred."

"Just wait till we get to Lexington. There you'll see some real thoroughbreds! My folks wouldn't let me bring such valuable horses out west. But you'll see . . ."

Observing the night sky, Ben remarked that he always felt strangely moved by starlight. The incandescence, he explained, impressed him less than the thought that the starlight conveyed a history: events that might have occurred shortly after the creation of the world. He talked about constellations long since dead, whose light was only now, billions of years later, just reaching us. He compared it to a miracle, to our going back in time and seeing history as it happened.

"Every point of light," I remarked, "has a meaning greater than itself."

Ignoring my kabbalistic comment, he said, "What if, through some rare device, we could see the Crusades or the Crucifixion? Wouldn't historians and church leaders be damned surprised?"

"The events might appear just as reported," Clarissa protested.

"I doubt it," said Ben. "And even if we could see them, we'd all see them differently, according to our own self-serving lights."

"Perhaps some day in the future," I mused, "a scientist will build a machine that can from afar capture the words we exchange here, so that one day others will know our thoughts."

"We already have the means to do that," said Clarissa. "It's called a book."

At the time, I regarded her comment as glib. But as I sit here trying to reconstruct time past, I see that Clarissa was right: lacking recordings and films, and having only a few precious photographs, I am dependent on words.

"What we can't see is the history that lies in all the dark places," said Ben. "Some people say there are holes in the sky, dark holes, that swallow everything within their gravitational pull. We have the same thing here. It's called hatred. It's called bigotry. Ignorance."

"Can't we talk about something that's fun?" Abby sighed. "I don't like all this heavy stuff." Turning to Ben, she gushed, "Just wait till you see Lexington, you'll love it. Clarissa took me at Thanksgiving. I thought there'd be nothing to see. But there is! Rolling green fields, white fences that run for miles, gorgeous horses . . . the town isn't so hot, but God, that countryside is *so* pretty. You have to see the golden stallion weathervane on the Fayette County Courthouse. It's really neat. It has something to do with racing, doesn't it, Clarissa?"

"It symbolizes the aristocratic position of horses in Lexington."

"And be sure to see the tobacco markets. The smells are so earthy. And the trotting track. What I wouldn't give to own one of those horses! Clarissa also took me to see the University of Kentucky. That's not nearly so neat, though, as the big old homes set back among the trees and shrubs, and the gorgeous lawns that seem to run on forever."

"I don't suppose the owners do their own gardening," said Ben, "or cooking, or horse grooming."

Clarissa, well aware of the drift of Ben's allusion, said nothing. She energetically poked the fire, eliciting a spray of sparks.

"God no!" cried Abby. "They have cooks, horse trainers, farm hands, servants, gardeners, and who knows what else."

"All Negroes, right?"

darkmatters
LEVITT

Missing Ben's point, Abby rushed on: "They're really nice people. They have their own churches—we went to one—and choirs and social gatherings. Don't they, Clarissa?"

"Yes," replied Clarissa offhandedly.

"Oh," exclaimed Abby, "I nearly forgot. We also saw the Whitney Farm. Can you imagine: it has nine-hundred acres and its own horse cemetery! All that greenery . . . it's really something else. You'll just love it!"

"I can't wait," said Ben unenthusiastically.

He wouldn't have to wait long. Spring break loomed in less than two weeks. Ben and Clarissa had bought train tickets to Lexington: he a sleeper, she a compartment. It didn't take a sage to combine the first word with the second and arrive at a new word: cohabitation.

Having no wish to return to Detroit and given the requirement that all dorm residents vacate their rooms for the holiday, I planned to stay with my sister, though the prospect of hearing her whine about money left me wishing I had another alternative. Ben said that if I could find a ride or hire a taxi (since I didn't drive), he'd leave me a key to the cabin, but that I shouldn't use it until Thursday. The first few days he had sublet it to a friend. When Clarissa asked who, he declined to say.

"It's a deep, dark secret," he jested unconvincingly.

Abby had a plane ticket for Boston, but hinted that she might not stay in Massachusetts the full time. We all talked about what we intended to do over the break. Clarissa and Abby had parties much on the mind. Ben said, with no little seriousness, that "he hoped his acquaintance with the Stanton family would grow into a friendship."

"Just behave," said Clarissa puckishly, "and it will."

"That's the trouble," replied Ben. "I find it hard to rearrange my mind for . . ."

Ben had just talked himself into trouble. How could he finish the sentence without insulting the Stantons or humiliating Clarissa?

"Yes?" said Clarissa, with cold clarity.

"To rearrange my mind for people who come from a culture so unlike my own. I'm not saying that one culture is better than another. They're just so different."

Clarissa had the good manners and grace to say, "My dear boy, you just saved your ass"—and gave Ben a great bear hug.

darkmatters LEVITT

Well into the night, Abby extinguished the fire and we made our way down the mountain. I didn't see her again until the Wednesday of spring break. Ben and Clarissa had left for Lexington on the previous Friday. As I had anticipated, Abby found Boston boring and for whatever reason decided not to visit Brian in Delaware. Instead, she returned early to Boulder. I took a bus to the station to meet her. She bounced off the train full of breathless concern for Clarissa, who had telephoned her daily, sometimes two and three times, to convey the melodrama unfolding in Lexington.

darkmatters LEVITT

Ben

For the Easter holiday, Ben and Clarissa take a train to Lexington. Trouble awaits them the day they arrive. At the station, Mrs. Stanton gives Clarissa a peck on the cheek and greets Ben coldly, alluding to her disapproval of the couple having dated in Cape May. She behaves peevishly and asks what accommodations Clarissa had on her journey. Ben says nothing and Clarissa tries to divert the conversation by commenting on the "awful food," and asking why Mr. Withers had not driven her to the station.

"I had to let him go," Mrs. Stanton replies indifferently.

"Why?"

"He changed churches, from the Episcopalians to the Baptists."

During the drive from the station, Mrs. Stanton returns to the subject of their traveling arrangements, but not satisfied with Clarissa's answer— "the usual"—becomes testy. At the house, she orders her husband to pour everyone drinks. He cordially greets Ben and asks him his pleasure.

"Bourbon and Seven Up, thank you."

Mrs. Stanton snaps, "There is no such thing!"

"There is where I come from."

"Well," she says archly, "you're in Lexington now, not Brooklyn or Boulder."

Mrs. Stanton has a natural talent for nastiness, and enunciates "Brooklyn and Boulder" as though they are the garbage dumps of the world.

She clearly takes great pride in holding forth from a grand house on a hill with a long gravel drive that curves down to the road. Red brick with chimneys at every corner and several bay windows, the house has two porches on each side, upstairs and downstairs. The living room is particularly splendid, with panelled walls and a stairway that leads to a gallery of books and a balcony overlook. It is in some ways reminiscent of the inside of a theatre, except for the huge wall paintings of battle scenes and old people, the Stantons' ancestors, Ben guesses.

The garden abounds with crocuses, pansies, and budding roses, and topiary bushes in the form of animals. White trellises support bright-colored clematis, and a pond covered with lilies separates two gazebos.

The Stantons have a cook, a seamstress, a gardener, and probably other servants as well. Mrs. Stanton is pure DAR. She lectures Ben about the pride and patriotism of the Daughters of the American Revolution. At dinner, she rings a little bell and a black cook brings the food. Of course, everyone dresses for dinner. Mr. Stanton stacks the plates in front of him and always cuts the meat at the table. While he places a modest slice on each plate, the cook stands next to him dishing out the vegetables. When all the plates are passed around, he says grace so magisterially that it sounds like a parliamentary speech.

Dinner conversation covers the town's well-to-do families: their peccadilloes, possessions, homes, furnishings, clothes, manners, parties; in other words, people and things but never anything resembling an idea. Ben thinks that being buried alive might be preferable to spending a month eating among the dead at their table.

He finds laughter absent, except for his own private chuckle when he thinks about the difference between dining in Jewish homes and this gentile house. In Jewish homes, as soon as the food hits the table, everyone attacks. Woe to the poor guest not skilled in the boarding-house reach. Everyone talks at the same time, and often with a full mouth. Disagreements are rife, with no quarter given. Once the food has been inhaled—eaten would be too delicate a word—politics takes over. Republicans are skewered as the party of Hoover and the Depression, and conservatives excoriated for wanting the rules enforced so that nobody can take their pile the way they got it. In this gentile home, no one eats until the food has been dispensed in an orderly fashion and grace said. That's why the food's always cold. No one reaches. Food is passed. You can't leave the table unless you excuse yourself, and the exit had better be for a damn good reason. The conversation is never offensive, though a few disparaging remarks about uppity people and races will not invite censure.

Clarissa warns Ben that her mother always touches the side of her nose when she wishes to indicate that someone is eating like a pig. Ben elicits this gesture from Mrs. Stanton several times, though he never lets on that he knows. At one meal, Mrs. Stanton chides Ben for eating too quickly. "Chew each piece of meat at least thirty times," she says. "Remember, don't just swallow, chew!"

That evening, Ben has the temerity to praise public schools, an institution the Stantons deem socialistic. An argument ensues, and Ben tells the Stantons that as products of private schools, they have neither the experience nor the income to appreciate the value of public education. His comments touch upon money, a subject that the Stantons regard as unmentionable, like sex. By the end of the evening, Mrs. Stanton is saying that young people should marry among their own kind.

Marty

We took a cab from the station to Abby's sorority house, and I invited her to have dinner with me at Ben's cabin. She offered to cook, as I knew she would. My culinary attempts would make a hog gag. I had the key to Ben's place, and thought that whoever had been using it would probably be gone by the evening. Abby drove. She had borrowed a swank MG sports car from one of her sisters. At the cabin, we discovered a fuchsia Cadillac parked outside and the front door slightly ajar. The instant I entered, I smelled a familiar cologne. I also smelled fraud. Inky Miller, seated alone at the living room card table, appeared startled. Spread out before him were piles of cash, as well as the C.U. basketball schedule and legal-size yellow pads with numbers and names for dozens of teams. Inky seeing me stare at the money and pads, quickly gathered them up explaining, "I'm crazy about basketball. A hobby of mine. I like to keep track of the games and the players."

Abby, standing behind me, began fidgeting, as if she wanted me to show Inky the door so that we could sit down to dinner. "Marty and me," she said ungrammatically, "we're planning a meal, private, you know, just the two of us."

"Would never think of interrupting. I'll be gone in a few minutes. Just have to pack up my clothes."

So this was the person who had sublet the cabin. But why would Ben rent to Inky?

"You and Ben palled around in Brooklyn—and Korea," I said, trying to pierce the veil of appearances and turn concealment into revelation.

Inky stopped in his tracks, between the kitchen and the bedroom. His expression told me something was greatly amiss.

darkmatters
LEVITT

"Yeah," he said without conviction, and went into the bedroom to pack.

"Don't ask him questions," whispered Abby, "or he'll be here all night."

When Inky reemerged, he held a leather valise and a matching brief-case. Abby had already started to boil water for pasta and chop some greens on the bread board.

"Yeah, Benny's quite a guy."

Inky intended to exit on that comment, but I wanted to know more. Glancing at Abby, I hoped she couldn't hear. She appeared absorbed in her cooking. Perhaps I could get away with one or two questions and then see him out.

"Tell me, Mr. Miller, how did you save Ben's life?"

"Call me Inky, everyone else does." He walked into the living room, put down his bags, and repeated, "Saved Ben's life."

"Yes, in Korea," I prompted.

"Oh, you mean when he got shot," he said lamely.

Undoubtedly Inky knew that Ben had been wounded, but seemed short on details. "Aw, it was nothin', believe me. Better we should talk about Brooklyn . . . and Newark."

"But Korea—"

"Forget Korea," Inky interrupted. "I don't like to think of sad things."

As if my mouth had a mind of its own, I blurted, "You never served, did you?"

"Whattya talkin' about? Sure I served. With Ben. We hung together for years . . . till a sniper's bullet sent him home. Wasn't I there?"

Ben, of course, had been wounded by shrapnel during an artillery exchange. Inky had lied. But not knowing how to pursue the subject any further, I gave him an opening to talk about what he did know, Brooklyn and Newark.

"So you and Ben met in Brooklyn?"

"Yeah, Sheepshead Bay. We went to the same high school. A real dump. I quit. He graduated. Benny's smart, real smart. You know what I mean? Him and me, we ran numbers for some guys on Surf Avenue. We was nothin' big in the outfit, just bag boys, you know, collectors. Sometimes, though, we had a lotta dough on us and it made a guy jittery, if you know what I mean. We palled around, you know, Coney and all that. He had a girl, Eileen. A real knockout. I had one, too, but she didn't have no puss like Eileen. We used to do it under the boardwalk. We'd bring blankets.

Sometimes after a rain, the goddamned sand was so cold that even with blankets you could feel the cold up your ass. So we let the dames lay on us."

Abby, now standing next to me, listened intently, with a paring knife in one hand and a carrot in the other. Ben was right: Inky liked to talk, and undoubtedly our rapt attention encouraged him to speak all the more.

"Sometimes we'd have a pickup in Newark . . . at a restaurant called the Diner or at a Portuguese joint in the Ironbound section. After gettin' the scratch, we usually stopped by South High School to shoot buckets with the colored kids. Off to the side, there was always a game or two of "Poison" going on. That's a game you play with a carom board and a little wooden doughnut-shaped thing that you shoot with a short stick. Benny liked to play, but he was rotten. This one guy, Fernicola, Butchie Fernicola, that was it, he used to take Ben to the cleaners. I told him, 'Benny,' I said, 'why dya bet against this guy. He's too good. He cleans you out every time.' On the way home to Brooklyn, Ben tells me to stop the car at a game store. He goes in and buys a carom board. Every night he practices shootin' Poison. He wouldn't even take Eileen to Coney to do it. He was obsessed. When that guy gets it in his head to do somethin', watch out. Well, one day we're back in Newark, doin' the usual. You know, baggin' the brass and goin' over to South. While I'm playin' horse for a nickel a shot, he's playin' Butchie Fernicola for a sawbuck a game. The money adds up in a hurry playing for them kind of stakes. Pretty soon, the place is hummin'. Dozens of kids are crowdin' around the board. Butchie's lost eight games and offered to play Ben for double or nothin'. That comes to a hundred and sixty greenbacks. I never heard of such stakes, except maybe with the big boys down at Surf Avenue. Well, they play and it's close. But Benny wins. And wouldn't you know it, Butchie ain't got the dough. He ain't a four-flusher, though. So he whips off this ruby ring he's wearin' and hands it to Ben. It was probably hot. That's the very same ring Ben wears to this day."

Abby shifted impatiently from one foot to the other. I suspected that the mention of theft left her uncomfortable.

"Now, don't go away, I ain't through with the story. After Ben wins the ring, I notice that one of the gym windows is open. So we hang around till everyone leaves and we climb in. It was like breakin' into a candy store, with basketballs and mitts and catcher's equipment and tennis rackets layin' around. I couldn't believe it. We grabbed what we could and we head for my car. Well, wouldn't you know it, Ben gets cold feet and says 'Let's take

darkmatters
LEVITT

it all back. It ain't right. It's a school.' Jesus, here we are out in the street, our arms full of stolen goods, and he wants to put it all back. He wants to break *back in*! I said 'Screw you!' But he turned around and tossed all his loot through the open window and scrammed. That was Benny, always big with the conscience.

"But the best bash of all came when I told him—we was in Long Island—that my cousin owned a boat and we could use it if we wanted. Well, I had no cousin with a boat. We drove over to the Sound and walked along the docks till I saw a skiff wid an outboard. It was a small job, maybe twenty feet long. Maybe less. We hopped into the boat and I get the motor going and we take off. Now in them days, real warships docked in those waters. God, what a blast! We steered around carriers and cruisers and battleships, until we heard a siren wailin'. Guess what? It was the Coast Guard searchin' for us. The guy who owned the boat had a day off and, just our luck, decided to sail his skiff that very morning. Naturally, when he found it missing he called the cops. Well, the Coast Guard caught up with us and attached a rope to our boat. They hauled us back to shore. The next thing you know, we're shoved into a squad car and taken off to the local jail. We spent the night there and got off only 'cause we had friends on Surf Avenue. God, them were the days!"

"And what do you do now?" asked Abby, in a tone of voice suggesting that Inky's highjacking days hadn't ended.

"I travel," he said. "You know, here, there, New York, Chicago, L.A. That sort of thing."

"You're a gambler, aren't you?" Abby said with a righteousness that would have earned the admiration of a pastor. Frankly, I would never have credited her with the insight or sobriety that at that moment she evinced.

Inky, struck dumb by the directness of Abby's accusation, coughed, blew his nose, cleared his throat, and took out a comb that he nervously ran through his hair.

"I'm an agent," he said. "A sports agent."

"For basketball players," Abby added. "College basketball players. But college players aren't pros. So how can you be their agent, unless you're fixing games?"

"Lady, you're barkin' up the wrong tree. I don't know what you're smokin' but it ain't a peace pipe." He picked up his belongings and, without another word, went out the door. I could hear the fuchsia Cadillac drive off.

"How did you know?" I asked Abby, amazed at her discovery.

She led me into the bedroom.

"See this?" she said, holding up an envelope. "It's marked 'Ben.'" Slicing it open with the paring knife, she removed two bills, each a hundred dollars. "I knew it as soon as we walked into the cabin."

"But you didn't see the money and pads on the card table."

"I certainly did. And once he mentioned basketball games, I put that together with what he said at the restaurant, and I knew. My brother plays basketball for Boston University. I've been hearing about fixing for almost two years. Who do you think taught Brian about point spreads and betting? I did! He's just too proud to say so."

Utterly out of my depth, I mumbled something about where the envelope came from and what Ben would say.

"I found it under the pillow of the lower bunk bed. We'll just put the money in another envelope and copy Ben's name."

"What in the hell," I found myself saying, "were you doing looking under Ben's pillow?"

"I smelled cinnamon and figured I'd find a sachet. Clarissa has a lot of them, but she always buys jasmine."

Pondering the implications of Abby's disclosures, I puzzled about the extent, if any, of Ben's involvement. "If Ben knew—"

"Marty, he has to."

"I don't believe it."

"Let me give you some advice, Marty, all of us have our bad side." With that cryptic statement, she suddenly picked up the telephone—the cabin's one modern convenience—and called Lexington, asking the operator to reverse the charges. "I'm cooking dinner for Marty in Ben's cabin. What? I took Botsy's car. Say, did you ever buy a sachet case with cinnamon? I didn't think so. Oh, nothing, it's just that I saw one today and thought you might like it."

A dangerous pause ensued, which saw Abby's face go from bright red to ashen.

"No wonder he told me not to meet him in Delaware."

When she got off the phone, she was contemplative, an unnatural state for her. Saying little at first, she gradually warmed to her subject: that to the amazement of the Stantons, Brian Hazelwood had flown to Lexington in a private plane owned by his father's company.

darkmatters
LEVITT

"Maybe Brian's doing some business for his dad," I said, hoping to assuage the insult.

"Business, my eye," she snapped, revealing her hurt. "Lexington is all horses and tobacco. Mr. Hazelwood works for a chemical company. Brian is there because of Clarissa!"

"Why do you think so?"

"Money attracts money." Again she grew reflective. "Perhaps I deserve it."

The indefiniteness of her statement left me in doubt. But I do attribute Abby's subsequent behavior in large part to that call.

"Marty," she said, "it's time for you to enter the world. Tonight, you and I are going to skip all the bases and head straight for home plate."

During the meal I could barely digest a single morsel. My penis suddenly became independent, rising and falling at will until I involuntarily came in my pants, leaving a conspicuous stain. When Abby saw it, she simply remarked that there was more where that came from, and that my "little accident" just proved my need to taste forbidden fruits. Fortunately for me, Abby saw no relationship between sex and marriage. The first she engaged in for pleasure, her own and her partner's. The second she regarded as a contract that involved property and wills, and a promise to behave discreetly for the sake of her husband. If she ever thought of children—and they never surfaced in any conversation I ever overheard—I imagine she thought of them as incidental goods that came with the estate.

That evening, for the first time in my life, I saw a woman undress, and decided that the female form was the most subtle and profound creation of God. She helped me disrobe, to use an old-fashioned word that accurately describes my state of mind at the time. Together, we lay side by side in the bunk bed, as she led my hand on an exploration of her bounteous body. By the time my hand had circumnavigated her globes, I had again issued forth. And again she said the well was not empty, and I would be all the more able to carry on now that I had lessened my load.

On finally entering her body, I could hear the engine in the pumphouse rhythmically thumping as it sucked river water into the cabin. In an instant I knew—and I say this as a confirmed believer and in the full knowledge that some will think me profane—that God was sex, and that I would reverentially worship at its altar for the rest of my life. As I lay there after the third coming, I could understand why people confused sex with love, and married in the belief that the feeling of flying would never end. The perfume of sex, the rose water of lovemaking, utterly intoxicated me. But as my tutor used to say, once the spell has passed, you wake up facing a person whom you have to talk to for all the days of your marriage. At the moment of climax, I truly thought sex would be enough to sustain Abby and me; but I must grudgingly admit, even given all that I owe her, outside of bed we were utterly unsuited for one another. The lovely Abby knew it also, and so when the day came that we parted, we left as friends, which we remain to this day.

darkmatters
LEVITT

Ben

Ben and Clarissa, of course, are housed in different bedrooms, Ben in the third floor guest quarters and Clarissa in her own room. But late at night they manage to meet. On one occasion, they nearly get caught. It is their own fault. They make too much noise.

"Those damn bed springs!" Clarissa mumbles.

The next morning her father cracks a joke about mice overhead, but her mother, a heavy sleeper, takes umbrage at the suggestion that her house is anything but immaculate.

Although Clarissa can understand why Ben chooses to speak well of her father, she can't understand why he calls her dad "that old rascal." On several occasions, Ben and Mr. Stanton go riding together and therein find common ground for mutual appreciation. Ben feels sorry for Mr. Stanton, who is cowed by his father, the real owner of the newspaper, and governed by his wife, the real law in the family. He proudly tells Ben that, "They may race 'the ponies' at Louisville, Santa Anita, New York, and Florida, but they breed them and rear them and train them at Lexington. Why," he says, "Fair Play, Man o' War, and War Admiral came from a horse called Lexington foaled in 1850 at the Meadows, a nearby estate." Mr. Stanton unabashedly loves horses and thoroughbred lore. Ben admires him for his passion—and also his genuine regard for the Negro cook, Eliza Samuels.

"Christ, is she beautiful!" Ben says to Clarissa with regard to Eliza's almond-shaped eyes and statuesque bearing.

"And don't think," Clarissa adds, "mother hasn't noticed. If not for her gourmet meals and spanking-clean kitchen, she would have been gone ages ago."

darkmatters
LEVITT

Mrs. Stanton, a woman aware of her station, prides herself in setting an elegant table—and on recounting the many suitors she turned away as a young woman. So great is her vanity that she reads from her old diaries.

"The effrontery of it," Clarissa says later, "right there in front of us *all*, even Brian!"

Ben can't understand why Clarissa has singled Brian out as special. Surely Mrs. Stanton's reading in front of him should be the greater embarrassment. Or does she already regard him as family and Brian as a stranger who has no right to private glimpses into her mother's past? By the end of the summer, Ben discovers he is wrong on both accounts.

Clarissa's outrage seems disproportionate to the offense. "How many times do I have to hear about Wayne Eddy and how he took mother on a paddlewheeler down the Mississippi? The man is a cretin! And Charles Vickory, who squired her to her first debutante ball? Or Reginald Grayworth—the man is a sot!—who arranged for mother and her family to see the Kentucky Derby from his box. Oh, and let us not forget the idiot who drove all the way from Huntington, West Virginia just to pay her court."

Presumably Mrs. Stanton feels a great need to impress upon others that she, too, was once young and desired. She surely isn't the first and certainly won't be the last.

"If I could, I would burn those damn diaries, with the names of all the young men and the places they took mother to."

Ben says he is sure that Mr. Stanton would gladly countenance such a bonfire of the vanities. He genuinely likes the old man, who can't get over how Ben sits a horse.

"I'll be damned, Ben, if you don't ride like a cowboy."

"A Cossack," he corrects.

"Whatever, you sure tickle me with all your hand and butt movements."

"Hell," Ben replies good-naturedly, "you ride like a statue."

"It's called English. You know that."

"Bloodless."

"No, dignified."

Ben drops the subject, fearing that Mr. Stanton's humor doesn't extend to his riding skills.

On Sunday morning, the Stanton household hums with activity. The family expects numerous guests. After church, the Stantons raise a flag at the house. That's to tell everyone—at least those who matter—that the house is now open for sherry and tea cakes. Ben informs the Stantons that he won't be joining them at church. Mrs. Stanton insists. Brian sincerely encourages him to attend. Finally, Ben agrees to go, out of politeness. They take two cars so that Brian can stop for flowers, which he insists on buying for the service.

The minister, understandably, makes points for the home team. He extols the virtues of Christianity, and takes it upon himself to say what things Jesus would and would not approve of, among them mixed marriages between Negroes and whites, and between gentiles and Jews. On the way home, Ben asks: "Wasn't Christ Jewish? Isn't he the centerpiece of most Christian homes? So right from the beginning people mixed faiths."

Mrs. Stanton orders her husband to stop the car. She says that she is not going to ride in the same vehicle with a heretic. But instead of her getting out, Ben does, followed by Clarissa. They grab a ride home with Brian. Mr. Stanton is ashamed. But Mrs. Stanton won't talk to them for the rest of the week.

At the Brooklyn *shul* Ben used to attend, the rabbi had counseled the boys not to marry non-Jews. He said his logic was simple. When couples share a culture and faith, there are two fewer reasons to argue. Proceeding from that premise, he said it follows that the more people have in common, the more likely they are to agree. "Reduce the arguments and increase the agreements," he liked to repeat, "and you have maybe not a sure thing but a good bet."

As Ben and Clarissa prepare to leave Lexington, her mother, who has found her voice, takes them aside. They are standing on the front porch. Mr. Stanton is riding his favorite horse, Stealth, around the paddock. Mrs. Stanton discloses that she received an anonymous letter (read: Ron Johnson) accusing Ben of having communist ties. She wants to know if the accusation is true. Emphatically denying the "libel," Ben readily admits he supports liberal causes. Mrs. Stanton announces that if they choose to wed, she will write the Episcopal Bishop of Kentucky and request that he forbid the marriage because Ben's "Jewish roots" and "Red sympathies" would make it a "miscegenation."

darkmatters LEVITT

Marty

On Ben and Clarissa's return, we rejoiced to have our friends back. Ben invited me to spend the Sunday in Eldorado Springs. He knew that I wanted to stay out of the dorm as long as possible. Clarissa picked me up in the DeSoto and we drove to the cabin, where Ben had prepared a breakfast of bagels with lox and onions. His mother had sent him a Passover gift, packed in dry ice, that included not only the above, but also white fish and chubs. After breakfast, we listened to opera, though I knew that Clarissa preferred musicals to Mozart, whose vocal works Ben particularly liked, as well as Donizetti's. I must have heard *Lucia* with him fifty times. With the sun casting the mountain pines in a blue-green light, the three of us walked into the canyon to admire the rock climbers scaling the vertical walls. You could see the chalk marks where they sought handholds in the crevices and cracks. The atmosphere at the bottom was festive, with the kibitzers conducting a running commentary on the progress of the climbers. Ben and Clarissa climbed an easy portion, perhaps thirty feet, and sat on a rock, waving to me. I yearned to join them, but given my fear of heights, I restricted myself to mountain trails. On our way back to the cabin, we stopped to fill the ten-gallon water jugs that we had left next to a pump fed by a natural spring. Oh, how sweet the taste!

Ben and Clarissa liked to read to one another. In the cabin, they often took turns reciting poems, or enacting the different roles in a play, or patiently wading through novels, alternating every few pages. It took them at least two months to finish *U.S.A.*, by John Dos Passos, a glorious work that sadly no one reads any more. This particular day they selected Edgar Allan Poe's "Annabel Lee," a poem that I always thought fit only for

darkmatters LEVITT

children. But as Ben began, I heard for the first time the rhythmic tides of the sea that give the poem its haunting melody.

"It was many and many a year ago,
In a kingdom by the sea,
That a maiden there lived whom you may know
By the name of Annabel Lee;
And this maiden she lived with no other thought
Than to love and be loved by me."

Clarissa read the second stanza. But as Ben read the third, a shudder ran through me when he came to the words:

"A wind blew out of a cloudy night
Chilling my Annabel Lee;
So that her highborn kinsmen came
And bore her away from me. . . ."

To escape my dark thoughts as much as to go birding, I spent the afternoon tramping around Eldorado Mountain, among the granite and sedimentary outcroppings. But Rocky Mountain pines are a far cry from the magnificent hardwood trees of New England. One summer, my father's sister invited me to spend a few weeks with her in Vermont. The splendor of those woods will linger in my memory until my dying day.

I brought along my binoculars and birding book. Nestled just below the peak stood a flat boulder. From this perch I scanned the trees and searched the vacant air across the plains hoping to see an avian cloud of snow geese. As the sun inched toward the mountain rim, I pointed my glasses south, to Coal Creek Peak. That I saw what I did was owing to the powerful magnification of my binoculars, which my father had bought from a retired naval officer. Dana and Joe Riley, each with their own pair of field glasses, had them trained to the east, on the construction taking place below on the plains, the Rocky Flats Arsenal. Next to them, supported by a tripod, rested a camera with a telegraphic lens. Every so often, Joe would step behind the camera, presumably to take a picture. Their purpose, frankly, escaped me.

About a week or two later, Colorado and Bradley played a Saturday afternoon game in the fieldhouse. According to Abby, who schooled me in basketball and kindled an interest that remains to this day, it promised to be a blowout, with Bradley predicted to win by twelve or more points. You have to remember that in the '50s, when there was no shot clock and players passed the ball for minutes on end, fifty and sixty points constituted a high-scoring game. To lose by ten or more was considered a slaughter. Ben gave me the ticket intended for Clarissa, who seemed to be coming down with stomach flu.

The fieldhouse, a narrow arena with an arched roof, seated more people at either end of the court than along the sides. We had tickets at midcourt, among the faculty, the regents, and the state representatives, who always had freebies to keep them well disposed to the university. In front of us sat Inky Miller and a peroxided blonde with a bouffant hairdo that smelled as if she had bathed in cinnamon bath oil. I whispered to Ben that she really stunk up the joint, and he mumbled that the tickets had come from Inky. I said no more, but between Inky's cologne and his moll's scent, the west stands of the Fieldhouse could have passed for a Turkish harem.

Bradley came out like a house on fire. They tore right into Colorado, running up a ten-point lead by the end of the first quarter. Inky seemed none too pleased. But in the second quarter, Bradley looked lethargic, and by the half led only by five. During the thirty minute break, Ben and I drifted out the south door and walked over to the football stadium. Standing there above the field, we saw some young kids playing soccer on the grass.

"Don't often see that," said Ben; "it's a European game. My father played it as a child. He used to love the game, or so he says. I never could get the hang of it. We'd kick the ball around in the street or in the sand at Coney, but I much preferred baseball."

"And Poison," I said.

Ben's eyes glazed, as though I had clipped him one on the jaw.

"How do you know about that?"

"Inky."

"Inky?" he said incredulously, "you must have seen him at the cabin."

"I did."

"What else did he tell you?"

"Nothing, really."

"Marty, I know Inky. He couldn't keep his trap shut even if you threatened to kill him."

"He talked about Brooklyn . . . and Newark."

"That's how you heard about my playing Poison."

"And your returning the athletic equipment to the gym."

"Christ, Inky will talk about anything. I suppose he told you we also spent a night in jail."

I shook my head yes.

"Did he also tell you what he was doing at my place?"

"No."

Ben stared at me, trying to decide, I think, whether to tell me about his ties to Inky.

"You don't owe me an explanation," I said. "But Abby knows he bets on the games. She says he's a fixer."

"How would she know *that*?"

From the field, one of the kids cried, "My goal," and another yelled back, "You cheated."

"She saw him sitting in front of a stack of bills and basketball names and numbers, and put two and two together with what he had said at the restaurant."

"I knew we shouldn't have gone into Roger's that night."

"Who is he, Ben?"

"A jerk."

"Why then let him stay at the cabin?"

"I wanted the rent—in advance—so that when I got to Lexington I wouldn't be sponging off of Clarissa."

It had long been my impression that Ben spent little on himself, and the rest on her. Not that she demanded luxury, she just took it for granted. He simply couldn't resist taking her to dinner, buying her books that he admired, treating her to movies, and purchasing the occasional sweater or scarf.

His impulse, though generous, had led him to accept money from a con man. Anxious about Ben's welfare, I observed, "If Inky's really a fixer, I wouldn't want to see you get involved."

Ben stood watching the children below. One of them, in trying to prevent a goal, became tangled in the net.

"He's been using my place on Wednesdays to meet players and make payoffs. I'm already in up to my eyeballs."

"And you let him . . ."

darkmatters
LEVITT

"For the dough. Clarissa's expensive."

That my closest friend in the world consorted with a fixer left me sick at heart. Every cell in my body screamed Ben was wrong; yet I couldn't reprove him. Standing there high above the field, I realized that if I had to choose between the law and a friend, I would take the latter. Such an admission, I admit, flies in the face of everything I ever learned from the rabbi—and espoused. But I knew that I could never inform. I think Ben knew as well, given what he said next:

"You haven't yelled at me, Marty. Silence, you know, gives consent."

I nodded.

When we entered the fieldhouse, it felt narrow as a coffin and dark as death.

The third quarter, Colorado and Bradley stayed on even terms. At the start of the fourth, Bradley led by six. Inky sat contentedly shaking his head, presumably because he had wagered that Bradley would win by fewer than twelve points. But five minutes from the end, two C.U. players fouled out. In the next three minutes, Bradley ran up a thirteen point lead. Inky, wild with worry, tore off his coat jacket and wrung it, as you would a towel. He yelled, he screamed, he taunted, he cajoled. With little more than two minutes left, a couple of Bradley players kept losing the ball while dribbling or passing, or they shot air balls. Each time, Colorado recovered it. Bradley's defense became porous as the two players in particular forgot that their hands were to be used in the service of blocking shots and bedeviling the shooter. They stood by and watched as C.U. players dribbled past them and made easy layups. With about a minute to go, the Bradley lead slipped to eight and their coach called a timeout. He benched the two erring players and sent in two others. I thought Inky would tear his seat from its moorings and hurl it at the coach. He booed and screamed: "Stall! Stall! Stall!"

"Why's he yelling stall?" I asked.

"Inky wants Bradley to keep passing the ball around so that the score remains under the twelve point spread."

A Bradley player fouled the Colorado center. But unlike today's game, which requires a team to take foul shots after it's been fouled a certain number of times, thus giving the fouling team a chance to recover the ball if the shooter should miss, the old rules directed that the ball had to be thrown in from out of bounds. Bradley, playing a press defense, covered the Colorado players so closely that the guy throwing in the ball couldn't find an open player and for taking too much time lost possession of it. The buzzer sounded and the basketball turned over to Bradley, which inbounded it to a guy at the top of the key who took two steps to his right and went up for a jumper. The ball swished through the cords. Bradley now led by eight. Downcourt Colorado came, but the dribbler lost the ball. Inky howled: "Stall! Stall! Stall!" But one of the two Bradley subs gave his Colorado counterpart a head fake, went under the basket, and hooked it back up—and in. Bradley now led by ten. Inky, who had by now dismembered his jacket, foolishly urged the Colorado team to score. The blatant contradiction of his wanting Bradley to stall and Colorado to score turned more than a few official heads and attracted the attention of a well-dressed gentleman in a grey suit who made his way down the row, touched Inky on the arm, displayed some sort of badge, and led him and Miss Cinnamon out of the fieldhouse.

As matters turned out, Bradley won by nine. Inky readily admitted that he had bet against the spread—no crime in that—but denied he'd bribed players. The basketball officials and police, having no tangible proof, could not detain him for his erratic fieldhouse behavior, and therefore released him. But Inky decided against remaining in Boulder, pulled up stakes, and moved to the southwest, an area that he told Ben was "ripe for the picking." In the coming weeks, Ben's bank account took a beating—and not just because of Inky's departure.

darkmatters
LEVITT

Ben

Morning nausea and vomiting finally drive Clarissa to see a doctor. His office, on North Broadway, located across the street from the hospital, has a waiting room full of patients. Clarissa wants to go by herself, but Ben insists on accompanying her. The physician, Dr. Cadamus, comes highly recommended from a social action group on campus. Clarissa, striking up a conversation with a young woman sitting next to her, learns that she works in the governor's office and that Dr. Cadamus treats the governor's wife and a number of other important women. It heartens Ben to know that Clarissa is seeing the best. The nurse ushers Clarissa into the doctor's private office, and Ben remains in the waiting room. Seconds later, the nurse summons him. Dr. Cadamus's kind words—"You're not the first . . . I quite understand your fears"—puts them both at ease. Sitting behind a fastidiously neat desk, with a pad and a gold-plated fountain pen, he unscrews the top, asks her questions, and takes notes. Clarissa explains her symptoms. By the time he has finished, he gives her some literature about birth control and recommends some tests. The nurse leads her away to take blood and urine samples. In Clarissa's absence, the doctor asks Ben why, if the tests are positive, they don't simply marry. Ben disingenuously explains that they both want to finish school and haven't the means to do both.

In Eldorado Springs, alone with Clarissa, he proposes they marry and she have the baby. They have had a similar conversation before—when she thought herself pregnant—and agreed that their youth made it impossible. This time, the discussion takes a different turn.

"A baby out of wedlock!" she exclaims. "My god, it would kill my parents."

"Even if we were married?"

"They'd know it was a shotgun wedding."

"Some people behave well in a crisis. Perhaps your parents—"

She interrupts. "Please! Bad enough that we're having sex and not married. But a bastard? That's what they'd call it, a bastard!"

The discussion dies on that note.

On the appointed date, Clarissa calls Dr. Cadamus's office, and the nurse says that the doctor wishes to see them both. A week has passed and her nausea has continued unabated. In the doctor's office, they learn what they had feared.

"Clarissa," he says, "you are pregnant."

"I want an abortion," Clarissa declares frantically. "Can you help us?"

But the doctor says that he never performs such procedures. Ben thinks about the woman Marty has occasionally mentioned, the one in Detroit, across the street from the family's store, but quickly dismisses that idea. Locking the door, Dr. Cadamus explains that he "has heard that there is a doctor nearby who performs abortions," but he can't be sure. In any case, if Clarissa wants to pursue it, she mustn't mention his name. As they leave the doctor's office, Ben insists on approaching the mysterious doctor alone, arguing that Clarissa has gone through enough.

The doctor has an office east of town, between Boulder and Louisville. Ben drives out through a heavy spring snow to see him. A jolly sort, the man sits fingering a glass porpoise on his desk while Ben explains the situation. The doctor at first just shakes his head. Ben says, "Name your price." The doctor wants to know who sent him. Ben refuses to say. The doctor allows that though he never performs the operation, he knows someone who did—until recently. "In the past, a number of us advised our patients to go to this man, but not to tell him who referred them. We didn't want the abortionist to know that we were sending him patients. So we warned the women not to say who referred them. But this guy had a gimmick. Instead of asking who sent them, he'd ask, 'Who diagnosed your pregnancy?' Most women just answered the question truthfully. I can't blame them. It all sounds innocent enough. But unbeknownst to us, the man foolishly recorded the names of all the doctors referring women to him. When the police raided his abortion practice, they seized the referral book and found my name. It cost me a small fortune to retain my medical license. I simply can't help." Ben thanks him and starts for the door.

The doctor asks: "Aren't you forgetting something?" Ben has no idea what he means. "You owe me fifteen dollars—for the consultation." Ben contemplates reducing the number of doctors in the world by one.

Calling on two more docs and being rebuffed, Ben turns to Joe Riley for help. Ben figures that with all of Joe's union connections, he can surely find someone who has assisted the miners. Joe tells him that when it comes to abortions, the miners can be as conservative as the Republicans; but he confides that his sister, who lives in Los Angeles, has recently undergone such a procedure. He will call her. He does, and she agrees to make all the arrangements. Until she gets back to Joe, a week passes. It is a Sunday. She tells him the cost will be three hundred dollars, and the time is set for Saturday night, in six days. Not wanting Clarissa to endure this ordeal by herself, Ben says he will make the trip with her. At first she objects, arguing that he can't leave his teaching and grading, and that Abby can accompany her. After all, Abby knows the city, having spent a year at Hollywood High School while her father worked for the Sierra Plastics Company. Finally, she agrees that Ben would be the better companion. Clarissa goes to the sorority housemother, Mrs. Crandon, and explains that she has to attend a wedding in Los Angeles and that she will be gone until Sunday. Mrs. C., an elderly woman of the old school, thinks Clarissa entirely too wild and does not take kindly to a girl one-third her age having her way. But all her attempts to restrain Miss Stanton have proved fruitless. Clarissa simply runs circles around her. On one occasion, Clarissa cowed her by threatening to write the governing board of alumnae and charge Mrs. Crandon with "senility." So the old woman contents herself with warning Clarissa sternly not to overstay her leave.

Ben buys two tickets for a Thursday night flight. From Sunday to Thursday, Ben and Clarissa are inseparable. Mostly they reminisce, so as not to think of the impending procedure. Prior to their departure, Ben sleeps hardly at all. A low-grade nausea becomes his constant companion, as well as the thought that if Clarissa dies he will lose the bewitching woman he loves. Death, that most terrible of absences, should it come, will bring to both families untold misery. He finds solace in remembering the summer they spent in Cape May.

Her family had rented a large house in the old, established part of the town. He roomed near the hotels and amusement park, and worked at the Chalfont restaurant as a waiter. Clarissa, sunburned and sleek in her bright new body, spent her days playing tennis and lying on the beach, where the college boys crowded her with their attentions. At night, some young man from one of the Ivy schools would call at the house and drive her away in his roadster to the pier, where they would dance to the music of a big band. She had "crushes" and occasionally her heart skipped a beat, but none of the young men swept her off her feet, except the one she had run into at the Smith library, who had sought work in Cape May just to be near her.

The first time that she and her family dined at the Chalfont, Ben saw her wearing an aureole of Giottoesque gold, and interpreted it as an epiphany dedicated to his earthly delight. He served the madonna and her family. She wore a white dress, with spaghetti straps. Her bronze skin, lavishly laved in oil, shone like burnished brass. He couldn't take his eyes off her, and she knew it. That evening, she used every guileful move to let him see all that she could, in modesty, bare. But what he remembered most was what he saw in the darkness of her eyes: a den of wild things and the promise of love learned through acts of endless wonder.

He persuaded the manager to let him leave work early so that he could accompany her home, a gesture that pleased her and annoyed her parents, who never returned to the Chalfont. They followed the boardwalk to the end, walked along the beach, and, upon reaching the naval installation on the eastern point, hailed a cab. The Stantons left them sitting on the wrap-around porch of the Queen Anne house that the family had rented. They sat and talked until almost morning. Although her parents had occasionally allowed her to stay out past midnight, she had never seen the morning sun reflected in the sea as a million slivers of opalescent light. The great sphere, a bright simulacrum of God, reminded her that she would be young once only, so she leaned her head against Ben's shoulder and invited him to enter the orbit of her shining life.

On his days off from work, they rented one of the colorful tents that stretched along the beach; and there they lay for hours side by side in the sand talking, keenly exchanging biographies and eating each other with their eyes. They told stories about family and friends, Lexington and Brooklyn, church and shul, privilege and want, desire and sadness. They spoke in words and in silence. They laughed and looked long and longingly at one another. He taught her how to body surf: how to ride a wave and the instant to duck it. She taught him tennis. He taught her handstands. She taught him dance steps. He introduced her to a culture where people showed fondness through physical contact, like hugging and pinching cheeks. She opened the curtains on a southern society where good upper-class gentiles behaved with reserve and self-control, and regarded touching as an immigrant lack of manners. His family thought a hug preferable to a handshake. Her family, when embraced, stiffened their backs and recoiled as if surprised by a snake. Ben called such people corpses; Clarissa said they were merely exhibiting good breeding.

During his free evenings, they played miniature golf and skeet ball, at which Ben excelled and won numerous stuffed animals, dolls, cheap plates, carving knives, and silverware, all of which they gave to the local Salvation Army, except for a stuffed giraffe that she kept. As they walked on the boardwalk or stopped for hot chocolate sundaes on the pier, her admirers would greet her and give Ben a long critical stare. He knew that Clarissa allowed him to court her only because her wildness led her to slum. He set his heart on proving to her that romance with a poor Russian Jew could bring her all of pleasure's toys.

He challenged her imaginative mind, which she had previously used only in impish ways. Instead of people and events, he talked to her about ideas. Often, he read to her from Elizabethan poetry and quoted Thomas Campion: "Never love unless you can/Bear with all the faults of man." He read Pushkin to her in Russian. Though she understood not a word, the sounds charmed her. The high school and college boys she knew talked about beer and bashes. Ben talked about civil rights and socialism; he expatiated on the first amendment and labor unions. She had never heard such talk either at home or at school or on a date. Ben's oddness captivated her, and his mind intoxicated her.

One night in July, near the lighthouse, on the grass that slopes to the sea, they made love, a consummation they both wanted, but one that she feared. With their background and experiences so different, she worried that his family would reject her as a *shiksa*, and hers would resent him as a sheenie who had ravished their daughter. She therefore swore to keep their affair secret. Ben, for his part, never imparted a word.

On the day of departure, the four friends take a cab to Stapleton Airport. Ben walks hand in hand with Clarissa down the concourse to the gate. As they enter the plane, she turns and waves to Abby and Marty. When they land in L.A., Joe's sister, Mary, meets them. Ben pays for the parking and, noticing that the gas gauge reads empty, insists on buying Mary a full tank.

darkmatters
LEVITT

Mary drives over Sepulveda Blvd. to the Valley, where she lives in a small pink bungalow in Van Nuys. She has three small kids and an out-of-work husband, a pipe fitter. Over a chile dinner, she explains that "three was enough, which was why I had it done."

"Aren't you Catholic?" says Clarissa.

"And Jesus is Jewish," answers Mary.

"How," inquires Clarissa, glancing around furtively as if the room might be bugged, "did you find a doctor who would do it?"

"She—"

"She?"

"Dolores."

"What's her last name?"

"I have no idea. She won't say."

"Why?"

"For her own safety."

"I interrupted you. I'm sorry. You were explaining how you found her."

"A part-time actress lives next door. She had it done. She says most of them are butchers. Soon as you pay them, they vanish. But Dolores is different. She does a lot of the actresses. I got no complaints. She did a clean job on me, though at the time I worried plenty."

Ben puzzles over the absence of the woman's last name, and concludes that the secrecy is in Clarissa's best interests. If anyone should ever question her, she can honestly plead no more knowledge than a first name. Given that abortion is illegal, Ben can well understand why anyone engaged in the procedure would go to such lengths to conceal her identity. He can also understand why women are willing to pay princely sums to have the operation done by someone who knows her business. The alternative is often death.

Friday, while Ben plays with Mary's three little ones, Clarissa, nervous as a treed fox, and needing to discharge her tension, cleans Mary's house, which is a foot deep in dust. The part-time actress from next door drops by and chats, though Mary hasn't told her why Ben and Clarissa are there.

"Just call me Goldie," she says, chewing on a wad of gum, which she cracks incessantly. "You friends of Mary's? Me and her are great friends. We do things together when her old man's willing to take care of the kids. Ever go to the Santa Monica pier? I just love the pier. You know . . . the sea and the salt air and everything."

Clarissa, reticent at first, slowly leads Goldie into the subject by asking her if film directors ever try to "get her on the casting couch."

Goldie, an attractive blonde wearing stiletto high heels and, in Ben's estimation, too much lipstick and mascara, laughs raucously.

"You ain't kiddin'. They're all oversexed. And they ain't always careful. I oughta know."

"What happens then?"

"You have it done."

"Does it hurt?"

"Just for a day or two. I've had four of 'em. All different. The first was the worst, but I blame myself 'cause I didn't find the right person. Now I know where to go. You need someone? I got a name, if you do."

Clarissa shakes her head. "No, we're just visiting from out of town."

"Well," she says, as she cracks her gum, "good talkin' to ya. Gotta run."

She leaves. Clarissa looks ill. Ben can guess the reason. She has to be thinking: "Am I that kind of girl?" Ben consoles her by reminding her that Mary comes from a good family. Not everyone in her situation is a Goldie.

"Right," Clarissa replies tersely.

Saturday morning they walk over to Van Nuys park and watch the young children playing ball, until Clarissa can't stand it any longer.

"We should have gone to the movies," she says. "A comedy."

Clarissa, as directed, eats nothing Saturday evening. Around seven they leave the house. It has begun to rain. Mary drives them over Beverly Glen to Sunset Blvd. and turns east, dropping them off across the street from Ciro's. They wait about ten minutes until a skinny white woman with yellow teeth driving a two-tone Ford pulls up at the curb. By this time it is pouring and the sewers have begun to flood, unable to handle the sudden downpour.

"You Clarissa?"

"Yes."

"Get in."

"I'd like my boyfriend to go along too."

"Nobody said nothin' about two people. Dolores ain't gonna like it, but it's her business not mine."

They clamber into the back seat, covered with movie magazines and old newspapers, as well as some brown paper bags. The car continues east on Sunset to La Brea, where the woman turns right. Trying to break the ice, Ben cracks:

"Is this the reading matter you put in the waiting room?"

"The magazines are for the girls. The papers keep the seat from gettin' bloody. And the bags got towels for mopping up afterward, 'cause sometimes you gotta throw things away, if you get what I mean."

Clarissa and Ben painfully understand.

Somewhere around Pico and La Brea, the woman eases off the gas pedal. Her wipers can barely keep pace with the rain. She rolls down the window and peers out. Even she is having a hard time finding her way in the storm-darkened streets. "It has to be this one," she says pointing. At the end of the street, Ben can see two or three tacky, run-down houses and a ramshackle hotel, with a light in the lobby. The paint, peeling off the stucco, has left but three letters, H-O-T, which Clarissa finds apt, though she never says why. As they exit the car, the woman takes a few paper bags. Dashing through the rain, they go in and read the "guest board." Sure enough one of the names says "Dolores." Room eight, first floor. They find it at the back of the hotel and knock. A voice asks, "Who's there?" The driver says, "Open up, Dolores, it's me, Cookie." Dolores opens the door. Standing there is an enormous black woman.

She mutters to Ben, "Who are you?"

Cookie says, "Her boyfriend."

"I don't like this! It just doubles the chance of trouble."

"If I add another hundred will you let him stay?"

Dolores peers down the hall and agrees reluctantly. Closing the door, she locks it and tells Clarissa to put the money behind the toilet between the water tank and the wall. Clarissa takes out the envelope that Ben has given her with three hundred dollars, adds an additional hundred, and stuffs the bills in the envelope. She goes in the bathroom. When she returns, Cookie ducks in to check on the money. Reappearing she shakes her head yes.

Dolores resembles a powdered geisha. She has dyed red hair and too much makeup. Her long bright-red fingernails look woefully out of place. She has on a garish kimono, a bright yellow print with purple jungle leaves, and high-heeled floppy shoes, decorated with silver and gold sequins. As she walks, her shoes clatter.

The seedy room smells of iodine and rubbing alcohol. Two windows, covered with black shades, face an alley. The room has twin beds separated by a nightstand with a soiled doily. A bureau, missing a drawer, supports a mirror. A stool has been placed at the end of one bed. The light bulb in the ceiling fixture having burned out, a floor lamp provides the only light. A rocker stands by itself in a corner. Over each bed hangs a framed picture, one of Betty Grable, another of Harry James. Dolores points to the rocking chair and tells Clarissa to relax. Ben and Cookie sit on one bed, while Dolores settles her huge frame on the corner of the other, causing the mattress to sag to the floor.

"I'm Dolores," she says, and explains how the operation will proceed. She asks Clarissa if she has any questions. Clarissa says no. Talking about herself, Dolores remarks that she is fifty-five and used to work as a nurse, but Ben thinks her older and doubts that she has ever had any medical training. She puts on the nightstand some kind of medical kit. Telling Clarissa to take off her underwear and lie down on the mattress, really just a thin pad covered with a threadbare sheet, Dolores places the stool at the foot of the bed, shaves Clarissa, and then applies some kind of foaming disinfectant. Ben is terrified that the instruments she uses aren't being adequately sterilized. She just reaches into a bag, takes out objects with her bare hands, and dips them in a solution of iodine and rubbing alcohol. Ben asks if she shouldn't be wearing rubber gloves. She ignores him. But Clarissa doesn't seem to care. She just wants to get it over with. Cookie removes the shade from the floor lamp and trains the light on Clarissa's pudendum, with the cord trailing across the bed. Ben guesses that Dolores is using a catheter. She inserts something, but her large body blocks out his view. Clarissa lets out a howl.

"Listen, honey, if you're gonna make noise, I can't do this thing. I don't want the manager—or anyone else—knockin' on the door."

"The pain is awful."

"That's 'cause you got a bad infection. That's why! Who you been hangin' out with?"

Clarissa glares at Ben, who can easily read her thoughts.

Dolores applies silver nitrate to the infected area and continues with the procedure. Clarissa buries her face in the pillow to muffle her screams. But even with her face covered, Clarissa can't completely suppress her anguished sobs.

As Ben watches her lying there lacerated with pain, her face drenched with tears, he wishes that he could assume her torment. He repeatedly swallows and breathes deeply to overcome his nausea and keep his insides from spilling out. He blames himself for not using a contraceptive and depending on Clarissa's diaphragm. He also regrets his wanton behavior and swears that in the future he will devote himself to Clarissa. Why, why, why, he wants to cry. That she should be subjected to this! He will make it up to her, somehow. But for now, the important thing is her safety.

In a minute or two, it is over. Cookie removes towels from the paper bag, which Dolores uses to stanch the bleeding.

"Did you leave the catheter inside? . . . because the pain is still awful."

Dolores doesn't answer. Instead she instructs them to stay overnight "until something happens." She asks them if they have eaten supper. Clarissa says no. Dolores opens the bureau and removes an immersion coil. She fills two cups with water and takes from her purse a couple of tea bags. When the water boils in the first cup, she hands it to her patient. Ignoring Cookie and Ben, she keeps the second cup for herself. The hot liquid eases Clarissa's cramping. As Dolores relaxes over her tea, she grows talkative, mostly about her hair-raising experiences. Ben would prefer that she remain silent. Her tales don't inspire much confidence. He is glad that she has waited until after the abortion to start yakking. She describes a girl with collapsed veins. He doesn't quite know what she means, but it sounds serious, especially since the girl had to be rushed to the hospital. Ben feels sure that Dolores didn't go in with her, but Clarissa doesn't ask for details. She tells them other stories of "nearly losing a patient," usually from a hemorrhage, and of women who came to her dirty or diseased. Hearing her, Ben worries about the poorly sterilized instruments, and imagines what diseases Clarissa's immediate predecessor might have had. Clarissa's face maps her worry, and Dolores, seeing it, says that she has never lost a patient. Comparing her own skills to others, she mentions women who had either bled to death or died from overwhelming infections. One woman, she confides, had suffered a torn vaginal tract where the abortionist had used a coat hanger to enter the uterus in order to rupture the amniotic sac. "I would never do something like that," she says. "So you needn't worry, honey."

The tea and horror stories over, she recommends that Clarissa get some sleep and promises to bring them both breakfast in the morning. She gives Clarissa a slop jar and tells her to use it if she has to get up in the night. "But you be sure, honey, you don't turn the light on. If the hall bulb is out— just peek at the bottom of your door and you can tell—it means the police are checking the building and we've pulled the fuses and left so this floor of the hotel will look like it ain't being used. Of course, if we have to pull the fuses, you won't be able to turn the light on even if you want to. But don't be frightened. Cookie and me, like I said, we'll be back in the morning to give you folks breakfast."

Ben retires fully clothed, hoping Clarissa will sleep and that she won't wake up in the night to find it all dark. Sometime around two, Clarissa's cramps worsen. Ben towels the sweat from her face and holds her hand. Finally she aborts. Clarissa bleeds badly, but does not hemorrhage. Around three-thirty in the morning, Dolores wakes them up and says, "We have to get outta here. There's a police car outside. They're searchin' for drugs." Clarissa, barely able to stand, asks Ben to help her dress. As Dolores prepares to bundle the bloody sheets and towels under the bed, someone knocks at the door and shouts, "Police, open up!"

"Back into bed, honey," Dolores orders, "and start coughin'." She spreads the bloodied towels on Clarissa's lap and under her chin. Opening the door, she politely says: "Officer, she's almost a goner. She's near the end and will soon be with her maker."

"Whatta you talking about?" barks the officer.

"Tuberculosis. The final stages."

With that cue, Clarissa starts coughing, but instead of blood issuing from her lungs it starts flowing from between her legs, staining the sheet.

"She's bleeding internally," cries Dolores. "We have to get her out of here and to a hospital, lickety-split."

The officer, a good Joe, gently carries Clarissa to the squad car. Ben notices on the way out of the hotel that the name card "Dolores" has been removed from the board in the lobby. In its place there is nothing. Dolores has them call ahead to a gynecologist she knows, Dr. Gabriel, who arrives at the hospital right on their heels. He somehow manages to suppress the truth of the situation, patches up Clarissa, gives her some antibiotics to take over the next few days, and kindly drives the two women to Mary's house, which Clarissa likens to being delivered by the angel Gabriel into the hands of Florence Nightingale. Mary puts Clarissa to bed. By Sunday afternoon, the pain has gone. Mary hasn't misled them. Dolores knows her business.

That evening, she eats nothing and passes the time listening to Mary's records of Nat King Cole, until she can reach Abby to relate all the sordid details. Abby passes on the story to Marty, including the pain Clarissa endured because of the infection. The next day, Monday, she requests that they go to a movie. She can't stand the thought of hanging around the house with Mary's children at home. At seven o'clock, they board a plane for Denver. On the way back, Clarissa repeats several times, "Was it a boy or a girl, I wonder." Ben doesn't know how to console her, except to squeeze her hand and assure her that "There will be others."

Abby and Marty meet them at the gate. Clarissa leans on Ben as they walk to the parking structure, with the other two lagging behind. On the drive home, Clarissa and Abby sit in the back. As Clarissa relates her harrowing experience in L.A., Abby illogically observes: "You know, I've noticed that people in the abortion business and people who belong to communist cells both never use their last names. That ought to tell you something."

Ben thinks that the sooner both groups come out of the dark, the better off the country will be.

Marty

While Ben and Clarissa were gone, I tried to convince myself I loved Abby. But on the drive from the airport as soon as she started chattering, I knew that I was, in the gangster expression, "thinking with my dick." Speaking of such lowly matters, I found shortly after my friends' departure that I had developed a bad itch and went to see a urologist, where I learned that I had a yeast-related infection. My medical knowledge, though thin, encompassed enough to know that the infection had not originated with me. I therefore told Abby.

She frowned. "Maybe I better have a check up, 'cause I've been having some burning myself."

On the drive home, Clarissa talked about all the class work she'd missed, in particular calculus, which had been giving her trouble. Ben and I offered to help. Abby said that she couldn't understand why a university had any requirements. "They're such a bore!" For some reason that inane comment temporarily ended all conversation. In the silence, I began to worry about the web of infection.

As we reached the city limits and passed the stables, Ben remarked how much he longed to get back in the saddle again and ride along the foothills. Clarissa said that given her recent experience if he intended that statement as a pun, it showed bad taste. He apologized, disclaiming any attempt at humor. But I found Clarissa's comment telling. The abortion had tempered her views about sex.

Back at the sorority, the house mother questioned Abby. I have always been guided in my life by the unshakable belief that one should always keep his own counsel. How often are felons discovered because they yapped?

darkmatters LEVITT

How often do lovers confide in a "best friend" who spills the beans? My motto is: say nothing and you will have nothing to regret. Though sworn to secrecy, Abby—wishing to dissuade the housemother from reporting Clarissa's overlong stay—told Mrs. Crandon some cock-and-bull story. But the old woman wormed the truth out of her. Mrs. Crandon, usually tight-lipped, could barely suppress her shock. I have little doubt it was she who gabbed. Let me retract that last statement. Abby violated a trust. Mrs. Crandon used that violation for her own purposes. Never having commanded Clarissa's respect, she now had the means to settle old scores.

As we left the sorority house, I invited Ben to have a beer at the Timber Tavern. We drove east on Arapahoe and pulled into the lot. We found a booth and ordered two draft beers. The blaring jukebox, as always, made conversation difficult. A fellow wearing cowboy boots and a ten-gallon hat stood feeding the box nickels. As Teresa Brewer wailed *The Tennessee Waltz*, Ben and I sipped our 3.2 Buds.

"What's up, Marty? Beer halls have never been your thing."

I have always preferred candor to indirection. It saves time. When my boss starts complaining about lost letters, I always cut to the chase: "You want me to write another report to the postmaster." Then Mr. Henker comes clean and I am spared having to hear some lame excuse for his own laxity. In that spirit, I directly asked Ben where he and Abby had disappeared the night of the fundraiser.

A pained expression clouded his face. "You're not in love with her, are you?"

"Hardly."

"Why do you ask?"

"I'll explain in a minute."

"I could, of course, say it's none of your business."

"You could."

Staring at me, as if to confirm some truth that lay hidden behind my visage, he said: "You mean it; you're not in love with her? Because I know that you and Abby . . ."

Undoubtedly she had told Clarissa, who told Ben. Discreetness apparently was impossible for some people.

"I enjoy her company, but I could never love her. Trust me."

"All right, I'll tell you exactly what happened, but you must never breathe a word of it."

I swore that I wouldn't, and yet here I am indiscreetly putting it all down on paper. So what does that make me, a liar, a hypocrite, a betrayer of friends? I hope not. Besides, time has passed.

"After she danced and let all the boys get a gander at her bouncing bounty, we asked for additional donations. The guys—and even the girls—gave generously. I told her what a great job she had done. She was beaming. You could see she really enjoyed performing and exhibiting herself. 'Can I speak to you,' she said, and took me aside. I thought she wanted to talk about Brian, because she had remarked earlier that he wouldn't be coming. My guess seemed right when she said, 'You know, he doesn't approve of this fundraiser and is mad as hell at me for taking part.' 'I owe you,' I said. 'Yes!' She then asked me to accompany her upstairs. I had no idea what she wanted, though it did cross my mind that perhaps she wanted a cut of the proceeds. Frankly, the woman's a complete mystery to me. Again I told her that she had given us a great performance and, to be polite, I asked what I could give her. With those great calf eyes of her, she stared at me and said, 'You!' and led me off to the bedroom."

Suspicions confirmed. I now knew the identity of Typhoid Mary.

darkmatters
LEVITT

Ben

As the 8 a.m. bell in Old Main summons students to class, a great many have no idea for whom the bell tolls, having at an earlier hour set out for spring skiing, or having simply remained in bed, or having found breakfast with friends preferable to one with *The Autocrat of the Breakfast-Table*. The world seems oblivious to both sound and sense. The faculty and staff, ordered to the theatre, await their turn to mount the stage to sign the loyalty oath in the presence of a self-satisfied Doleman and a seated notary public. Having to sign in front of hundreds gives the proceedings the feel of a public execution. Professor Fine, absent from the ceremony, has been told that he will not be reappointed. According to reliable sources, he would have been hired by Western Reserve University if Stoneham had not asked friends there to quash the appointment. Jobless and broke, Fine goes to work for a chemist at Columbia Presbyterian Hospital, on an hourly basis. Judson Meyer, refusing to go gently into the night, eventually gets a meeting with the prez, who orders him to tell the gumshoes what they want to know or be fired. Behind the scenes, Professors Ermine, Klein, and Mackison press Stoneham to reappoint Judson. But Rodney stalls and Judson's status remains uncertain until he has little or no opportunity to find another teaching post. Several months later, the president, citing a confidential FBI report that he says damns Meyer, refuses to renew his contract. The report is immediately secreted in a safe-deposit box. Leonard Condor keeps his job only because Rodney, who had originally hired him, feels that if he dismisses Condor his own reputation will suffer. Ben and others vow to continue the fight. In an effort to publicize their cause, Ben offers to write an article for the *National Guardian*, a progressive news weekly that the government has condemned

darkmatters LEVITT

as left wing. The paper accepts his offer, the beginning of his modest career as a journalist.

Although the struggle for academic freedom at C.U. occupies a great deal of his time, he has also agreed, at Joe Riley's urging, to do what he can to help Mine, Mill and Smelter Workers, Local 890. On a bright May morning, while the campus morally sleeps, he and Joe post fliers for the union. The posters read:

Since October 17, ninety-two families have been on strike against the Hyperion Zinc Company, at their leading mine and mill in Hanover, New Mexico. Years of inferior working conditions and company slave-driving led the workers last fall to press for a New Deal. But Hyperion offered only the routine raise, and refused to discuss contract improvements already in force at other nearby mines.

FROM NOW ON THE SUCCESS OF OUR STRIKE DEPENDS ON YOU!

Although we are by no means ready to quit, money is running short. The wolf-like finance companies are closing in on us. The landlords are getting loud about five months back rent. Our credit drops every day.

As you know, it costs real money to feed 500 people, to keep them warm, to buy medicine, gasoline, to retread a tire now and then just to keep rolling, and to make furniture payments so that our striking brothers won't have their property taken away. We're living on a shoestring.

Hyperion Zinc is trying to start a "BACK TO WORK" movement. Even as we write, our strike lines are endangered. The company won't be able to get scabs in the district, but they'll try to bring them in from outside.

So please, friends, back us up. Send us help, either money or men to picket. Please join our ranks.

Signed: Clifford Jensen

That same day, Clarissa, Abby, and their sorority sisters compose invitations to the May formal. To Marty's surprise, Abby invites him. She and Brian have argued over Abby's participation in the fundraiser and her "loose" (or, as Clarissa calls it, *louche*) behavior. Unless Abby has told him, Ben has no idea how Brian could be privy to her intimate life. Besides, Abby has long suspected that Brian has eyes for Clarissa and not her—and told him so. When he says, "At least she's got some class," Abby tells him to take a long walk off a short pier.

As the women employ themselves writing invitations, Ben receives a peremptory call from Farkus Doleman's secretary directing him to come to the office at five o' clock. Thinking he will be reprimanded for posting the Mine-Mill posters, he calls Joe Riley to ask if he too has been cited. Joe says that he has not. Doleman's secretary tells him to wait. Ben studies the framed photographs on the wall: faces of the many stiffs who once presided over CU. In the main, it is an undistinguished lot. Doleman's voice crackles over the intercom: "Send in Mr. Cohen."

Several chairs surround a long table. Besides Doleman, he is greeted by two other men, thirtyish and well-dressed, sporting crew cuts and wing-tip shoes. Doleman introduces them as "consultants to the university," though he never mentions their names. They all shake hands. The chair at the head of the table has been reserved for Ben, who can see that his presence exacerbates Doleman's moroseness.

"You seem determined to court trouble."

"You mean the fliers?"

"What fliers?"

"Never mind."

"Ah, even more trouble?"

Ben is reminded of the Jewish joke in which a mother sends her kid off to school with a slap behind the head. The kid asks why she hit him, and the mother replies, "That's for all the trouble you'll be getting into that I won't know about."

One of the consultants leans over the table. "You have a friend, Joe Riley." As Ben takes the full measure of the question, the man continues. "He's part of a Trotsky cell that's headquartered in Mexico. His parents, too. They often travel back and forth as couriers. We have reason to believe that Joe has passed classified information, in particular, photographs, to his parents, who in turn have passed them to subversive elements."

Ben knows that Marty has seen Joe and Dana taking pictures of the Rocky Flats Arsenal; Marty had expressed bewilderment at what they could possibly want with such shots. Clarissa also knows, a fact that worries Ben, because if contacted she will probably be more forthcoming than he plans to be.

"I know very little about Joe's personal life. I've never even met his parents."

The first man leans back in his chair as the second takes over. Ben mentally labels them tweedledum and tweedledee.

"Dana Reháková," Dee reads from a manila folder, "a Czech national whose parents are high up in the Communist Party." He bites his lip. "You share an office with her."

"Yes."

"Have you ever seen her do anything out of the ordinary?"

"No."

"I gather she likes to hike."

"So do a great many other students."

"She's here on a diplomatic passport."

Ben is annoyed by the cat and mouse game. "I've never seen her behave undiplomatically."

"We have," Dum shoots back.

"Did she eat her salad with the wrong fork?"

"Mr. Cohen, are you aware that she and Joe Riley are lovers?"

Ben is amazed. He has never even seen them together. Collecting his thoughts, he asks wryly, "Did you catch them in the act?"

"No, but we bugged a room in the Wayne Hotel where they meet."

The Wayne Hotel is on Pearl Street. One of the few hotels in the city, it serves tasteless meals and has dingy rooms. Ben can't imagine how they knew which room to bug, so he asks.

"We followed them to the hotel on several occasions. The last few times, we instructed the manager to give them the same room, the one that we rigged."

"Maybe they knew it and sighed loudly for your benefit."

"Don't be a smart aleck."

Dee studies the folder with the intensity of a monk poring over papyrus. "Why do you suppose a Stalinist would make common cause with a Trotskyite?"

"I know little about his activities and less about hers. What's their crime? What have they done?"

"We thought you could tell us."

"In other words, you have nothing on them. This is just a fishing expedition."

"We keep you and other Americans safe by keeping tabs on people like them."

"Hey, who the hell are you?"

Doleman answers. "FBI."

"So you're the two shits who've been cruising campus spying on people. Fuck off!"

Ben gets up to leave.

"Unless you're planning to drop out of school immediately," Doleman says cryptically, "I would suggest you sit down."

Ben remains standing. "I'm on the G.I. Bill and, as far as I know, have some rights."

"You refused to sign the oath of loyalty. The university can dismiss you for cause."

"Forget it! I resign my teaching assistantship. Correct me if I'm wrong, but students don't have to sign the oath. I am no longer an employee of this dump, and therefore at liberty to finish my studies. I will tell my department first thing in the morning."

Doleman and the FBI agents look crestfallen.

Ben starts for the door, and Dum says, "Five hundred a month if you'll report anything that strikes you as unusual."

"*And*," Doleman adds, "you can keep your assistantship. We will even supplement it." The agents nod approvingly, as if Doleman has just aided and succored his country.

It dawns on Ben that he has no idea what in particular the FBI is trying to discover. To learn their intentions, he resumes his seat and remarks, "If you already know they're shacking up, why do you need me?"

"We want to know more," Dee says, smiling vacantly.

"Like what?"

"Like what they do on their mountain hikes. And this Reháková broad . . . we know very little about her except that she bought an expensive camera with a telegraphic lens."

"She and Joe are bird watchers. I don't think you can toss her out of the country for taking pictures of eagles."

"If that's all she's doing, fine. But if they're up to something else, it's our job to know. Otherwise—"

Dum completes the thought. "Otherwise if we ask her to leave, it looks fishy. Besides, her father's well-liked in some Washington circles, if you know what we mean."

Ben laughs, which puts his inquisitors out of sorts. "If you were running a spy operation would you be telling your agents why you wanted certain information? If Dana's spying for her country—and I can't believe that she is—I seriously doubt she's been briefed on her government's plans. We know how communist cells work, one never tells the other a thing."

"You're pretty knowledgeable about cells," Dum says caustically. Dee weighs in, as if they have Ben on the ropes. "You want to tell us what else you know about the inner workings of spy groups?"

"I get all my information from *Time* magazine. You ought to try it. The Luce family has all the dope."

"So you won't help," Doleman growls.

"Unaccustomed as I am to spying on friends, I find the assignment worthy only of scum."

"If you ever had a moment's privacy, forget it!" Dee warns. "From now on, we're going to watch you like a hawk."

"Now *there*," Ben mocks, "is an original turn of phrase."

Reaching for the intercom, Doleman calls his secretary, who has had to stay after hours. "You can clean out your office desk immediately! No, not you, Miss Simpson. I was talking to Mr. Cohen. Please inform the registrar's office and the scholarship office to terminate Mr. Cohen's financial aid. You needn't tell his department chairman why he will no longer be teaching. Mr. Cohen has volunteered himself for that patriotic duty."

"I hope you bite your tongue, Mr. Doleman, and die of the poison."

As Ben leaves, he hears one agent say, "Can't you expel him?" and the other, "If my kid ever talked to me that way . . . "

Marty

The formal, planned for Saturday night, was black-tie. On Pearl Street, Ben and I rented tuxes from a seedy store, and they looked it.

Clarissa, now recovered, never uttered another word about the trip to L.A., nor did Ben. Until the night of the formal, I figured the whole thing had blown over.

The large living room in the sorority house had been cleared of furniture and the rugs temporarily stored in the basement. Chinese lanterns, affixed to the chandeliers, cast the room in a pastel glow, and transparent boxes on posts resembled apples of gold in silver frames.

Abby insisted on trying to teach me to dance. We stood off to one side as she plotted a pattern of steps that I clumsily followed. The practice over, she led me on to the dance floor, where Brian Hazelwood, in the company of Sarah Chandler, a stockbroker's daughter, swept past us in his tailored tux and remarked:

"Practice makes perfect."

A minute later, I tripped over Abby's feet and fell to the floor. Brian exuded friendly concern, as he extended a hand to me. It seemed churlish of me not to be more appreciative, but I disliked the man and therefore said curtly:

"No thanks. I'll be all right."

Brian danced off in dervish-like turns and twists that made me glad to see Ben and Clarissa outshine him and his date.

I made a few more vain attempts to put one foot in front of the other and decided to retire to the portable bar, next to the stairs, where a white-coated attendant served an alcohol punch. Some of the boys, who had

darkmatters
LEVITT

brought bottles that had been discreetly stored out of sight, would sidle up to the bar and say:

"A snort from the Wild Turkey," or ask "for a slug of the Johnny Walker Black Label."

I had the impression that these guys cared less about enjoying a first-rate booze than they did about impressing their girlfriends. As they sipped the contraband, they would extol its virtues as beyond compare. I have often noticed, and wondered why, men who aspire to machismo or suaveness, which in some ways are opposites, both use liquor to reinforce their images.

While Abby and I sipped our punch, Ron Johnson, who had, like the other hashers, been invited to the dance, stepped up to the bar with a mousy gal on his arm. Sporting a flat-top haircut that made me think it had been measured with a micrometer, he looked older than his age, owing I think to his straw-colored hair beginning to grey. He had a light stubble beneath his chin that he had missed with his razor. He rubbed the spot, and I remarked:

"You're so fair, it must be hard to see where to shave."

"Yeah, not like you and your friend."

Of course he meant Ben. Both of us had black hair, though my beard was thicker. Sometimes I shaved twice a day because I didn't like the bristly feel.

"I knew a couple of Jews in the service. They had black hair, too. I guess it's a racial thing."

Had I been quicker on the draw, I would have told him that color came from genes, and religion from belief, but he turned away and asked for his Jack Daniels, which he liberally guzzled. Shortly, Brian joined him at the bar, where they began to get seriously drunk, causing their dates to drift off to the dining room, leaving the boys behind. By the end of the evening, Ron and Brian, reinforced with Dutch courage, took turns breaking in to dance with Clarissa, who had asked Ben not to make a scene by objecting. As Ben and I watched both men trying to paw her, Brian, the better dancer by far, got the upper hand. Ron slithered back to the bar, drunk and disconsolate.

"Some friend!" he said, referring to Brian. "Speaking of friends," he slurred, turning to Ben, "I hear you got one in L.A."

"What does that mean?"

"Just what I said."

"I don't know what you're talking about."

"You don't, eh? Well, either you or Mrs. Crandon's a liar."

Ben wanted to square off and deck Ron with one to the kisser. But I grabbed his arm and reminded him:

"Now is not the time . . . not here in the sorority house. For Christ's sake, it's the May formal!"

Without a word, Ben left me standing there and reclaimed his date, pushing Brian aside. Too wobbly to stand up to what he took as an insult, Brian muttered some obscenities and staggered back to his in the dining room.

Ben and Clarissa finished the night wowing the crowd with both familiar steps and eccentric dancing. At one point, their feet shuffled rapidly back and forth in a jazz number reminiscent of Ed Lowry's imitation of the legendary Joe Frisco. Ron and Brian sourly watched, while their dates, well aware of playing second fiddle to the woman in the white crepe de Chine dress, twiddled their thumbs.

darkmatters
LEVITT

Ben

Dana, absent when Ben cleans out his desk, waits for him outside of Zumbrat's class.

"I heard," she says, and insists that she has to talk to him. They walk silently to the Glen Miller Memorial Center and find a table in the corner of the student grill.

"What you didn't hear," whispers Ben, "is that the FBI knows all about you and Joe."

Dana expostulates, arguing against charges that Ben hasn't made. "I have no sympathy for that man Trotsky. He disrupt the whole movement. Split us apart. My family stays, how do you say, in the mainstream . . . so do I."

She continues to talk about the Stalin-Trotsky breakup, but never mentions Joe Riley. Ben doesn't know whether to admire her sexual discreetness or condemn her bad political judgment. Even if her part in the photographic expeditions was to abet the ruling Communist Party in Czechoslovakia, she should have known that consorting with a Trotskyite would invite the wrath of both sides of the divide.

"How the hell did you ever hook up with Joe?"

"He came to me. He said we both socialists, both for the underdog. I know he is dedicated to Trotskyites. Frankly, I thought to our cause I could convert him. I introduced him to people. We have a consulate in Denver. He said he liked the Czech government, and he, well, I shouldn't tell you, he admire me."

The jukebox blares. Ben finds himself shouting over the music. He goes to the box, inserts a nickel, and hits "No play," which will earn him three minutes of silence, courtesy of a blank record installed at the request of the

darkmatters
LEVITT

faculty. "On the other side of the room," he whispers, "are two crew-cut guys in dark suits sitting under the mural. They're FBI." She looks. They make no attempt to disguise their surveillance of Dana and him.

In their Marxist study group, Joe has often spoken passionately and affectionately about Leon Trotsky. Like Trotsky, Joe scorns home-grown socialist movements, and more than once has hinted that Trotsky cells are alive and well in eastern and central Europe. But why the photographs? The Trotskyites have neither the numbers nor the interest to pursue sabotage in the United States. Stalin, not America, is their principal enemy. Ben asks Dana.

She answers simply: "He was helping me." Her candor leaves him speechless. "Do you know there what they build? A plant to make for atomic bombs plutonium triggers. Don't you think the socialist world has a right to know a great much about this place of death? At us those bombs will be shooting. Self-preservation is a, how do you say, a moral imperative. Else why do governments spy, especially yours and mine?"

"Coffee?" he mumbles, trying to buy time to think through what she has just said. Standing at the counter, he tries to reconcile Joe's politics with hers but, unable to do so, concludes that sex trumps ideology. He would like to test his hypothesis but doesn't know how to broach the question with Dana.

As he puts the tray on the table, which includes a glazed doughnut, she reaches for her wallet.

"I pay. Remember, you're fired now."

He jokes. "Maybe I can get a job with your people."

She doesn't smile. "You serious?"

"No."

"Maybe I ask why not."

"Politics and the personal don't mix."

"It sounds you speak from experience."

"You'd know better than me."

"I know nothing," she says and sips her coffee.

His attempt to find out about her and Joe has misfired. He is in fact slightly embarrassed by his awkward attempt to learn about their liaison.

"You love Clarissa only?"

Her question startles him. Is she asking him whether he has other girlfriends? He decides to reveal as little as possible and put the ball back in her court

"Yes. Do you love Joe?"

She pauses.

"I love more my country."

"If you loved them both equally and had to choose, which one would it be?"

"Do you want that I should be sentimental or honest?"

"I have my answer."

Ben points to the glazed doughnut. "It's for you."

She grimaces. "Like your white breads, terrible it tastes."

"Yeah," Ben says, "food for goyim." She doesn't comprehend. "Are you and Joe through?"

"I'd wish your question comes from an interest in me."

"It does . . . in a way."

She smiles mischievously. "One month school ends. Even whether I return in September, I don't think I'll see him again. He graduates and for Mine-Mill union is working and maybe going to law school."

"Funny looking guy, isn't he?" The words come unheeded. They are meant not cruelly but fondly.

"The first time he asks me out, I didn't want to go. I didn't think I'll like him. Those thick glasses . . . his milky skin. But he's different, like you."

He leans across the table and whispers. "Be careful, they've bugged the Wayne Hotel."

As they leave, Dana takes the uneaten doughnut. At the table of the G-men, she pauses and hands them the doughnut and says in perfect English, "Any friend of Ben's is a friend of mine."

The red-faced gumshoes stare at it, at her, at each other. Their befuddlement amuses Dana. She smiles sweetly and they exit.

Ben is impressed. Her political savvy and maturity put her leagues ahead of American coeds, most of whom suffer from arrested development. He mentally compares her to Clarissa, to Dana's advantage. Outside the Memorial Center, she lights a cigarette. In the May air he can smell lilacs mixed with the smell of her smoke.

They have engagements in opposite directions. Ben's parting words are: "Those stinking weeds are going to kill you. Put it out!" The next day, the university expels her, and the State Department confiscates her passport for spying. She has been denounced. Her expulsion makes Ben want to find out who's pulling Stoneham's strings. With the end of the semester in sight, he decides to remain in Boulder to work with a group called the Liberty Committee, dedicated to the principles of free speech and assembly. The committee, a combination of faculty and students, agrees to spend the summer, or as long as it takes, working to see the two professors reunited with the university community. Ben and Joe argue, the latter contending that Judson Meyer's and Stanley Fine's cases have no chance of reversal.

"How the hell do you know?"

"Christ, man, just look around. You're in Colorado, not Massachusetts. This is no-neck country."

They have stopped on the bridge over Varsity Pond. Ben notices several turtles sunning themselves on a log, and thinks of his father. "We can't quit now. We're seeking a court order to release the FBI report. Then we'll know the names of the stoolies."

"Give it up."

"Sorry, Joe, I won't walk away from this fight. Two men ruined. Where the hell's your head?"

Joe picks up a stone and splashes it near the log. One turtle slides off, the others remain unmoved.

"Ben, if you think the FBI's going to let some court blow their cover, you are badly mistaken. These guys are the courts—and the government! Wise up."

"I can't believe you'd just have me leave . . . turn my back on the principles we've been fighting for."

"You were a soldier, not me. Aren't there times where you have to retreat and fight somewhere else?"

"And where would that be?"

"Hanover, New Mexico."

darkmatters
LEVITT

Marty

Joe urged Ben, Clarissa, and me to join him on the picket line at Hyperion Zinc. Clarissa said that although protesting appealed to her, she really had her heart set on spending the summer in Lexington riding. When she asked if she could combine both in New Mexico, Joe replied tartly:

"Not likely!"

I dithered, having no stomach for trouble.

It looked as if Joe Riley would be making the trip by himself, until a Denver court ruled that the secret FBI report could not be opened without the approval of the university's Board of Regents. Ben, knowing those zombies could not be raised from the dead, grudgingly agreed to make the trip. (To this day the report remains sealed.) As soon as Abby heard about Ben, she also volunteered. Clarissa declared that if Abby had the guts to go, she did as well. The last to decide, I reluctantly agreed. We had reached the end of May and the scent of late-blooming lilacs still sweetened the air. I remember thinking that Hanover would not be breeding lilacs out of mine tailings. The five of us, although unfamiliar with living conditions in New Mexico, visited the Army-Navy store and blindly bought second-hand camping equipment. Around the first of June, after I had moved my belongings to my sister's house, and Clarissa and Abby had packed their winter clothes in trunks that they stored in the sorority-house basement, we gassed up the DeSoto and headed south, with no more idea of what we would find than David Livingstone had on leaving Scotland for Africa.

We stopped in Colorado Springs to admire the Garden of the Gods, then continued through Pueblo, Trinidad, and Walsenburg. Crossing the

darkmatters
LEVITT

mountains, we went from Alpine terrain to high desert country. We turned west to Taos, camping in a gorge along the Rio Grande, where we watched teenage boys trapping muskrats, whose fur they sold in town for a pittance. During the drive, Clarissa pored over a Spanish grammar, which she said had much in common with French. She suggested we learn a few phrases as a gesture of respect for the local culture. Abby wanted to know the dirty words, but Clarissa's book omitted the juicy diction. To this day, I can still recall two of the expressions we memorized—"*Más vale doblarse que quebrarse*" (It is better to bow than to be broken) and "*Dónde hay gana hay maña*" (Where there is a will there is a way)—though upon arriving in Hanover, we would discover that the local dialect did not always correspond to the "pure" Spanish found in Clarissa's book.

That night I had my first experience of camping, which Ben extolled and I abhorred. My sleeping bag felt as if it had been filled with rocks; the food that we cooked over a kerosene stove tasted like gasoline mixed with sand; and worst of all, the cesspit that each of us dug to defecate in was disgusting. In my estimation the greatest invention of the modern world is indoor plumbing. I kept thinking that it took the Jews two thousand years to find their way out of the desert. Why return to it voluntarily?

The moon silvering the river and hills seemed an odd juxtaposition. But my distaste for roughing it eclipsed the romance of the night sky. Chatting around the glowing embers of our campfire, we talked mostly about family. I asked Joe about his, but he was not really forthcoming.

"They work for the Mine-Mill office in Denver."

"What in particular?"

"The union has political interests. They run the international office."

I had no idea what he meant, but I decided not to pursue the subject. Abby, always garrulous, regaled us with stories about the silliness of her three younger sisters. Her brother, I gathered, issued from the same mold as she, wild and carefree.

"My parents argue about who's to blame for the younger ones being such dips. Mother always portrays her family as sober and serious. Regular church-goers . . . no swearing allowed, otherwise you had your mouth washed out with soap. Father admits that his daddy raised hell, but complains that since mother's at home each day with the girls, she should put them on the straight and narrow. They have already given up on me and my brother. But they hope to shape up the others."

darkmatters LEVITT

Clarissa, an only child, reflected on the fun she might have had with a brother or sister.

"We could have gone riding together or swimming in the pond behind the dogwoods. Actually, my mother didn't want any children. She said they would ruin her figure. She was right."

All of us laughed, except Clarissa.

"What about your family, Marty?" Joe asked. "You're working class," which to him meant everything good.

"Poverty ain't pretty," I said, deliberately affecting a colloquial style. "I come from a family where grammar's a hit and miss affair and malaprops the norm. My mother often says, 'I am filled with humidity,' if you see what I mean. She came from Poland, my father from Lithuania. English pronunciation has always eluded them. They mostly communicate in Yiddish. Whatever their failings, they're good people at heart."

Joe grew contemplative. "You know what I remember most as a kid? My first pair of eyeglasses. I could never see, but we didn't have any money. When I got the glasses I thought I had been born into a new world. That's what a government should do for its citizens. Enable them to see."

"You know what I remember," said the irrepressible Abby, "my first pair of skis."

"A rich kid."

"Compared to you, yes."

Clarissa volunteered that her fondest youthful memory revolved around her fifth birthday. She received a colt from her father.

"Marty," said Joe ironically, "I don't suppose your folks gave you a horse, right?"

"Don't laugh, but what vividly lingers with me is the particular scent of my rabbi's hands. To my own amazement, I still miss it."

Ben remarked that for most people, the memories of childhood are stronger than convictions.

"Revolutionaries, even those who came from privileged homes, always have stories to tell about youthful pain."

"Don't get started!" Clarissa exclaimed good-naturedly, no doubt wishing to keep Ben from talking about politics.

Obviously annoyed, he answered her sarcastically, "We wouldn't want to mention anything serious. Let's just be cheerful."

An irritated Clarissa, who never took kindly to any rebukes, snapped: "Right!"

Ben looked at her dismissively. "I see. A little patience, a few adjustments, and in two shakes Ben will fit in perfectly."

"You *could* try."

"Heaven forbid that I should express views that are not consonant with the rest of the smiling crowd. That sounds like Stoneham's world."

"What's so terrible about fitting in?"

"Did you ever hear of Mr. Challah, the baker from Chelm?" he asked rhetorically. "He had a bad limp. When he walked, people said he looked like he had one foot on the road and one in a ditch. He rarely left his village because children would laugh at him and imitate his awkward gait. So he went to a famous doctor in Byelostok and said, 'Doctor, can you make me like everyone else? I want that as I go from one place to the next to sell my bread, people won't stare and make fun of me.' The doctor examined the baker and stroked his chin. 'Mr. Challah, I have discovered the source of your trouble. Your left leg appears to be shorter than your right. But since it is impossible to stretch your left leg, I advise you to have it removed.' The baker, understandably shocked at first, refused to let the doctor cut off his leg. But the more he thought about it, the more he agreed with the doctor: better to stand on one leg and be normal than to stand on two legs and be abnormal. So he let the doctor amputate his leg. But it didn't help. Now people joked about the fool on crutches who cut off his leg to be well balanced. Downcast, he took his crutches and boarded a train for Lublin to see another well-known doctor. 'Doctor,' the baker said, 'can you make me fit in; can you make me look like others?' The doctor examined him and rubbed the side of his nose. 'Mr. Challah, I have discovered the source of your trouble. You are unbalanced. You have one leg instead of two. But since it is impossible to grow a new leg, I advise you to let me chop off the remaining one.' Horror-stricken, Mr. Challah refused. But the more he thought about it, the more he agreed with the doctor: better to be legless and well-balanced than to walk with crutches and be lopsided. So he let the doctor amputate. But it didn't help. In fact, he found himself worse off, because now he was confined to a wheelchair, and people grew red in the face with laughter at the thought of the idiot who had cut off his legs to appear normal. Sadly, he wheeled himself to the station and took a train to Warsaw to see the most famous doctor of all. 'Doctor,' he said, 'can you make me inconspicuous; can you make me look like others?' The doctor examined the baker and scratched his head. 'Mr. Challah, I have discovered the source of your trouble. You are top heavy. You have a head and two arms but no legs to go with your body. But since it is impossible to grow new legs, I advise that you amputate either your arms or your head.' You know what, by the time Mr. Challah got through rearranging himself, there was nothing left."

Suddenly, Abby let out a yelp. At first, we thought she was expressing high spirits or reacting to Ben's story. But she pointed to her leg and exclaimed.

"I've been bitten by a tick!"

Joe immediately lit a cigarette and held the burning end just above the puncture.

"They usually back out to escape the heat," he said. "It's important that the head not break off. If it does, there's a problem."

Slowly the creature emerged from Abby's leg, and Joe ground it underfoot. No, camping had no place in my life.

darkmatters LEVITT

Ben

They pitch their tents along the Rio Grande and tell stories, but the beauty of the evening is marred. Abby discovers a tick bite, and Ben and Clarissa quarrel. A line of poetry runs through his head: "He didn't want her to get away, and now she's there all day." The next morning, they fold their pup tents, pack up their gear, and drive south passing through Albuquerque and Truth or Consequences to Caballos. Abby insists they stop for a beer. The temperature hovers around a hundred. The cafe has one fan that turns so slowly, it must be powered by a squirrel in a cage. A man sits at an adjoining table with a fly swatter. Every time he nails an insect, he flicks it on the floor. Marty remarks that a summer in Detroit is beginning to have its attractions. As they crunch through the hot gravel parking lot to the car, Ben feels hammered by the heat from above and below. They leave the main highway and shortly pass through the old gold mining town of Hillsboro, where they stop for another beer at a rundown bar. The detritus of past mining operations litters the area. They check the car radiator and continue into the mountains. At the lower elevations they see basalt rocks with prickly pear growing out of the rock like a rash. They pass stands of cottonwood, aspens, junipers, and scrub oaks, locust, spruce. The rolling road takes them upward past mesas, small gorges, stunning needle rock formations, and sheer cliffs of pink sedimentary stone. The air smells of ponderosa pines and piñon-juniper trees, living in easy camaraderie like old friends. They pass over narrow erector-set bridges and cattle guards until they reach Emory Pass at the top of the Black Range. By now the car is laboring and the radiator steaming. They stand at the top of the mountain reading the historical marker and looking across the valleys below them as the long shadows of late afternoon fall over the hills. On their descent, they see to their left small talus scree runs, yucca trees, yellow chamiso plants, and the first evidence of mining—piles of tailings. The little information they have, outside of political fliers and notices bearing on the strike, comes from a road map with some incidental information. The Spanish who explored this region noted that the indigenous population used copper taken from the nearby outcroppings. Sinking shafts into the hills, the Spanish extracted enough copper to send back to Chihuahua one thousand mules each loaded with three hundred and fifty pounds of rich ore. The rolling hills leading to Hanover are dotted with small diggings and an enormous open pit, the Santa Rita del Cobre copper mine.

Ben will soon learn that summers here proceed straight from the hot days of June to the rains of July and that the rarefied air at six thousand feet makes breathing difficult. His first impressions of Hanover never alter: a dry, windy, desolate place, dotted with prickly pear, cactus, and yucca; rutted dirt roads leading from the highway to dead ends; a land where poorly clothed people with stained and missing teeth live in shacks and plant scraggly backyards with beans, chiles, and corn. Where drinking water comes from a well, four-and-a-half miles away, carried in every conceivable kind of receptacle. Where overalls are more patches than denim. Where a man of wealth would not stable his horse in some of the company-owned houses, with their corrugated roofs and insufferable heat. Where many have been evicted and pawned their possessions, and still have nowhere else to go, nor a penny in their pockets. At every turning he hears the ancient cry: where is money? Houses want paint and stucco buildings plaster. A wooden structure, sporting a great false front, badly needs a hammer and nails to put the boards back in place. A few one-story housing units brought from the Deming Air Force base after the Second Word War sag from fatigue. A Catholic church stands below a hill topped with a tall, black conveyor belt, a symbol to him of money over ministry. Tired women alternate hanging up clothes with tending four, five, and six children. Exhausted miners, their faces lined with the crucifixion of toil, trudge down the road, peeling off at their houses. It takes Hanover to teach him the true function of money: to vouchsafe escape from the debilitating labors of the poor.

The Mine-Mill office, which they soon find, welcomes them warmly. Ben explains that they have come to Hanover to help the strikers, and that they need only a patch of suitable ground to pitch their tents. As they soon learn, only Anglos have plumbing; so they settle in the backyard of a house with a privy. Marty says that an outhouse seems like the height of luxury compared to a cesspit. The next day they walk around, seeing for themselves Hyperion's world: separate payroll lines for Mexican-Americans, as well as segregated washrooms, toilets, and housing. That evening, they meander a mile to the picket line. It blocks State Road 180 that runs north to the town of Fierro. The road, which cuts through Hyperion's property, passes between the company's offices and shops, and ducks underneath the black conveyor that links the mill and the loading dock. Railroad tracks run alongside the highway, but Mine-Mill makes no attempt to impede trains because the railroad unions, in support of the strikers, have refused to transport any of Hyperion's ore. As darkness descends, the strikers light a fire in a large metal oil barrel. "Only in desert climates," says Ben, "do you spend the day escaping the heat and the night trying to keep warm." Marty replies that he can understand why this part of the country has such a sparse population. A guitar suddenly materializes, and the pickets strike up a song.

Levántate Delgadina
Ponte tu vestido de seda
Para que vayas a misa
A la ciudad de Morella

The singing gives way to some raunchy jokes and ruminations about which kind of woman will and which won't. The men also talk about their children and the bleak future ahead of them unless the miners prevail in the strike. Around midnight, the others head back to their backyard campsite. In truth, they have little in common with the pickets, whose culture is so different from their own. Clarissa and Abby, in particular, feel out of place among the mostly male pickets. Ben stays behind, listening and learning to fit in better—and hoping to gain their confidence so that he can talk about labor and politics.

On Thursday, June 7, two things of importance occur: their move and a newspaper notice. The Mexican-American community finds them shelter, and they exchange their campsite for houses. Joe Riley kips in a storage area at the back of a union office; Clarissa and Abby lodge with the Jacinto family, who have two breathtakingly beautiful daughters, ages three and four; and Ben and Marty move in with the Bejel family, next door to the childless Esperanza Morales and her husband, Luis. In the morning, Ben catches sight of Esperanza, who is in her small garden hanging wet clothes on the sagging line. She looks up and smiles.

"You kept your promise."

They will speak often across the fence that separates the two houses, but always in Luis's absence.

For Marty and Ben, despite moving indoors, the physical conditions (except for the roofs over their heads) remain virtually unchanged: no electricity, no plumbing, no tubs, no easy access to drinking water; in their place, privies, rain barrels, and kerosene lamps. Marty and Ben, though, have one great advantage: the food of Rosita Bejel. The first person to arise in the morning, she cooks on a wood stove with juniper logs, which fill the house with their forest incense, and puts on a pot of beans and some corn that she simmers for almost an hour. Later, she grinds the corn and makes tortillas for breakfast; she also makes flour tortillas that she serves at lunch. For the dinner meal, Ben and Marty usually buy some kind of meat, which she will slowly cook over juniper embers. The leftovers, never wasted, become part of the next day's meal. If they have to be gone for any length of time, she packs them taquitos of eggs, meat and sauce, and beans, or some combination.

More important than their having found lodging is the appearance of a full-page notice in the *Silver City Daily Press* announcing the reopening of the Hyperion mine in four days, on Monday, June 11. With pickets blocking the road, the notice can mean only one thing: the company plans to force its way through the strikers and into the mine. A community on strike is one waging war. Rumors of impending skirmishes run rampant. According to the grapevine, Hyperion has agreed to shoulder the cost for twenty-four additional men if the sheriff and district attorney guarantee that armed deputies will escort the strikebreakers through the picket lines.

The miners find this report particularly galling because they helped elect the sheriff, Leonard Goleiter, the only Republican official in the county. Goleiter represented himself as a friend of the union. Mine-Mill swung its membership behind him, even though he came from a political party inimical to labor, and enabled him to win by a mere three votes. Following the election, Local 890 trumpeted its political clout, but now union workers begin to realize that in the soft-spoken and retiring

Leonard Goleiter they have brought onstage a puppet of Hyperion and its business supporters.

Ben drives the hilly road into Silver City to learn what he can about the rumor. This will be the first of many trips that takes him from the narrow vale of Hanover into the wide valley, where the city huddles surrounded by forested mountains. Marty accompanies him because, he says, his *nebbish* appearance will allay any suspicions. The old part of town, built in Victorian style, has high curbs because the San Vincente Arroyo, a block away, periodically floods. Their first stop is the Palace Hotel. In the small, narrow lobby they encounter four desiccated men enveloped in cigarette smoke and disinclined to venture beyond monosyllables. Continuing down Bullard Street, they stop at a number of stores but meet with only modest success, because the shopkeepers, like the men in the hotel, are reluctant to talk about the strike. Stopping at a drugstore, they ask the owner, who has the manners of a gila monster, what he thinks of "what's happening over at Hanover."

"I hope you're not here in these parts to help those commie miners. We oughta ship them all back to Russia—or Mexico, where most of them come from."

Ben seethes. "Where did you come from?"

"Huh?"

"The name in the front window of your drugstore looks foreign."

"My family come from Germany . . . Bavaria."

"I bet the Mexican-Americans have been here longer than you have."

"What are you, a communist rabble-rouser or maybe a draft dodger?"

Ben laughs at the leap in logic from ancestry to communism.

"Mr. Sturmer, ever hear of Korea?" asks Ben, addressing the man by the name displayed in the window. In full, the sign reads: Leopold Sturmer, druggist, Bachelor of Science.

"Korea! Who hasn't? And what particularly fries my ass is that them spics up at the mine are helping the enemy by cutting down on the zinc production. Jesus, there's a national emergency and they're sittin' on their asses. If we had a governor with any balls, he'd send in the National Guard."

"I fought in Korea," Ben says, removing an official card from his wallet that indicates his service and his having been awarded the purple heart.

"How do I know it's real?"

"You don't," replies Ben, a retort that leaves the druggist nonplussed.

"I'd like some aspirin and condoms," says Ben.

Sturmer gives Ben a nasty glance and retreats into the back room. We patiently wait. He returns and hands Ben the aspirin. As he slides the box of condoms across the counter he says sarcastically: "I didn't know spic women used them . . . they got so many kids."

"Too bad your parents didn't use one the night you were conceived," Ben shoots back.

Sturmer, in the grip of a paroxysm, literally foams at the mouth. If he could have, he would have reached under the counter, removed a gun, and opened fire.

Nonchalantly, Ben pays for the items and leaves. Out on the street, he tells Marty to glance over his shoulder and take a gander through the store window. "He's on the phone, isn't he?"

Sure enough, the pharmacist has the wall-phone receiver to his ear, yapping away.

"Let's get over to the sheriff's office," Ben says. "We might as well go right to the source."

They trudge up a hill to the County Courthouse, where Ben, preferring boldness to bashfulness, tells the fellow behind the counter that in his capacity as a war veteran, he has come to volunteer for the special police squad the sheriff is recruiting.

"Thanks, mister, but we got all the men we need. We swore 'em all in yesterday." Having let the cat out of the bag, he apparently regrets doing so because he immediately corrects himself. "You *are* talking about the auxiliary police we plan to use on the Fourth of July?"

"No," replies Ben, "the extra deputies to be used at the mine."

"Let me get the sheriff," the man blurts, rising from his swivel chair.

"Save yourself the trouble. Apparently you have all the men you will need."

On the drive back to Hanover, Marty observes that the miners had better beef up their pickets. Fortunately for Mine-Mill, Hyperion's full-page notice gives the union time to mobilize men from other mines in the district. For three days—Friday through Sunday—the roads into Hanover teem with cars and trucks of every description bearing miners intent on "holding the line." Sheriff Goleiter has declared that in the public interest, the road being blocked by Mine-Mill pickets has to be cleared. The union contends that since Hyperion helped finance the road it is not public, and points to a highway sign that reads: "Private Road, Pass At Your Own Risk." Goleiter dismisses the union's contention. Hyperion management, delighted with his ruling, recruits scabs to open the mine.

The five friends have come to Hanover intent on joining the picket line, but once they realize that the police intend to smash it, and that they run the very real risk of getting shot, they retreat into other union work. Mine-Mill has organized the strike force into six basic committees: legal and police, publicity, negotiating, recreation, relief, and soliciting. The friends all choose different paths, at least initially. Marty picks publicity, Ben, soliciting, Clarissa, relief, Abby, recreation, and Joe, perhaps because of his parents' connections, undercover work. But all those activities come later; first comes "confrontational Monday."

darkmatters
LEVITT

An Excerpt From Ben's First Newspaper Article

Dateline: Monday, June 11, Hanover, New Mexico. This morning, Mine-Mill Local 890 had dozens of men on the picket line at Hyperion Zinc. Grant County Sheriff Leonard Goleiter showed up with deputies carrying sidearms and shotguns. As at least a hundred other men and women watched from the hillside, the deputies slowly walked toward the line, with shotguns cradled in their arms. Behind them followed a group of ten or twelve scabs. About fifty feet from the pickets, Goleiter told them to make way for his men and for "honest working people who have no mind to make trouble." The pickets said nothing until Goleiter moved his group closer, but then began taunting the deputies as "hired guns," the scabs as "goons," and Goleiter as a "company man." Goleiter ordered the arrest of one taunter after another, until the count stood at eleven men and one middle-aged woman. But every time Goleiter removed a picket, another person left the hillside to take his place. At ten a.m., the sheriff ordered his people back to their cars. Not a single scab got through the line.

Dateline: Tuesday, June 12, Hanover, New Mexico. Hyperion persuaded District Judge Marshall M. Animut to grant a temporary injunction restraining Mine-Mill, Local 890, from preventing workers' entry to the mine. The pickets, however, remained unmoved, crying in Spanish, 'They shall not pass.' Women and children joined the line, but the injunction had changed the strikers' mood. The picketers knew that if they obeyed the law, scabs would replace them; if they broke the law, they would be jailed and the strike would be lost.

darkmatters LEVITT

Ben

Esperanza warns Ben that "the front office," where Joe works, seems to be losing its resolve. "You can see the effects on the picket line." Men begin to mutter "What's the use" and "It's a lost cause." But a man who looks worn and aged, though probably no older than forty, urges on the others. "I have spent most of my life underground . . . eight-and-a-half hours a day. The company says no paid leave, no extra for being a miner or mucker, no running water. I say they can run me down with their cars, or shoot me, or put me in jail. Make us pay a fine, ha, that's a good one; you can't get blood out of sand. My grandfather used to say, *'Quién adelante no mira altrás se queda.'* He was right. We cannot go back. Brothers, we must stick together. *Viva la huelga!*"

"But how?" another picket replies. "But how?"

That evening, the women's auxiliary, a fancy name for Local 890's social group, holds an open meeting. Ben and his friends dutifully attend. A radical idea surfaces. Whether it actually originates with the women or one of the men, as is later suggested, is immaterial. The idea: have the women take the place of the men. The injunction forbids union members from picketing but it says nothing about non-union members. The women contend that if they take over the line, other non-union members will come from afar to swell their ranks. The next afternoon, at the Fierro cafe, a union hangout, the miners argue back and forth, rehashing their reasons for opposing or supporting the idea. They finally agree that the decision must rest with the entire membership of Local 890. A meeting is called. As the miners enter the union hall, a large number of wives tag along.

darkmatters
LEVIT

Open only to members, the meeting would have come down to Ben and the others as a farrago of fragmentary anecdotes had not Joe Riley somehow obtained a copy of the minutes in English. Even with these, they have only the outlines of the proceedings. In Joe's cubby-hole office, he reads the translated notes.

Every seat taken. People standing two- and three-deep in the aisles. The temperature in the building . . . easily above a hundred degrees. Issue: should the women picket or shouldn't they?

In support of one side or the other, the C.U. friends frequently interrupt Joe.

A number of men shout. The women remain silent.

Ben murmurs. "I can hear my mother saying, 'Women don't yell—at least not in public,' and my father attesting to the truth of that statement."

Although Ben and Marty agree with the majority of miners, who adamantly oppose women doing a man's work, Clarissa, Abby, and Joe support the women.

"It's a machismo thing," says Clarissa. "The men say they'd be laughingstocks. But that's a crock."

Abby agrees. "God forbid they should have to wash dishes and mind the kids. They say it's unmanly."

Joe, always doctrinaire, argues: "In the working world of the future there will be no distinctions between men and women, except perhaps for a few types of jobs." He lights a cigarette.

"You're flying in the face of their culture," says Ben. "Calling it machismo or anything else still comes to the same thing for these men: losing face. Every day—in the jobs they're assigned, in their wage packets, in the places they piss—they're humiliated. And you want them to give up their last shred of self-respect, their masculinity."

"You're hopelessly bourgeois," says Joe.

Ben mentions that he has heard miners say they'd rather lose the strike than have to change shitty diapers. But his remark only incites the others.

Clarissa leads the charge. "Yes, I heard the Mendoza brothers say the men would be hiding behind their women's skirts. Well, better to hide behind a skirt than to kiss someone's ass." In high dudgeon, she turns to Joe. "Give me a cigarette, will you?"

"But you don't smoke."

"I'm smoking now!"

darkmatters
LEVITT

She awkwardly lights the cigarette, inhales, coughs, and inhales again.

"Hyperion knows this community," Marty says, "they know the culture. You can bet that if the women start picketing, the company will figure the men have caved in and they can push the women around. They'll show them no more respect than—"

Clarissa interrupts. "No more respect," she ironically says, "than what they currently receive? They get *nothing* now!"

"Just imagine," Abby gushes, "how good the women will feel supporting the men."

Ben skeptically shakes his head. "Yes, and just imagine what the reversal in roles will do to them."

"The issue is not roles but class," Joe chides. "The women and men are all working class. The sooner they realize that management is the enemy, not wives or husbands, the greater their chance of success in this strike."

Joe continues reading. *Rafael Gallego: I tell you, it's our job, not theirs. I would never let my wife do my work. Letting women man the line is a sign of disunity. Pablo Marcos: And what will we do if they hit our women? What then? Won't we defend them? So we might as well just picket ourselves, and the hell with Taft-Hartley.*

Abby looks blank. "What's Taft-Hartley?"

Ben explains. "It's a complicated law. But essentially it means heavy fines and maybe a long jail sentence if the union doesn't let the scabs through."

"All the more reason," says Abby, "to let the women picket. They're not union members. And from the little I've seen, some of those gals could command respect from a drill sergeant. Hell, the family Clarissa and I moved in with . . . the mother chops wood, carries it inside, makes the fire, does the cooking, raises the kids, milks the goats, feeds the chickens, and weeds the garden."

"All the more reason," says Ben, "for her not having to picket as well."

"Ben," complains Joe disgustedly, "I thought you believed in socialist principles. You sound like a Victorian headmaster."

Joe quotes from the minutes. *Victor Neruda: The law has no rival. The union has rules, the state has rules, the country has rules. What excuse can we give if we become lawbreakers? What reason? Hyperion already tells everybody that we're communists and blocking the war effort. They say that because of us soldiers are dying in Korea, that even the CIO kicked us out because we're too radical. If we defy this injunction, they'll accuse us of trying to create a riot in*

Hanover and overthrow the laws of the country. Let us show them that we are caballeros!

Joe hoarsely and badly out of tune sings some lines from a Pete Seeger song.

Now, boys, you've come to the hardest time;
The boss will try to bust your picket line;
He'll call out the police and the national guard,
They'll tell you it's a crime to have a union card.
They'll raid your meeting, and hit you on the head,
They'll call everyone of you a doggone red.

"Get a voice!" Abby moans.
Undeterred, Joe croaks another of Pete's songs.

Oh, the banks are made of marble
With a guard at every door
And the vaults are filled with silver
That the miners sweated for.

"Spare us," says Clarissa. "You sound like—"
Joe quits singing and in his monotone voice resumes reading.
Some men leave. Some call for a vote. Some want the women disqualified from voting. Reason: they are not officially union members. A motion: adjourn the meeting and reconvene as a general conclave. Passes. Roderigo Castro: I move that we let the women picket in our place. Chairman: Those in favor of the motion raise their right hand. Most of the women support the motion. About half the men vote yes. Discord. Some miners accuse others of having no respect for themselves. A number of men change their votes. People boo. The tellers have to restart the count. Eventually, Del Pino asks: All those opposed? The tellers count again. Del Pino tallies and announces: Yes 93, no 85.

After leaving Joe's office, Ben and Marty head home down the dusty road. They overhear a number of arguments between husbands and wives, who have taken refuge outdoors to escape the heat of their tin-roofed shacks. One man claims that the vote has been sinful. "Ask the priest! When women and men change places, it's the devil's doing." From the Bejel house, they can hear Esperanza and Luis Morales arguing. His words bite through

darkmatters
LEVITT

the darkness. "It's too dangerous! What kind of man would I be if I let you do this thing?" The next morning they learn that Luis has left for Mexico, to stay with his family. Mrs. Bejel says, "It's not the first time. He'll cool off and come back."

On only a few hours sleep, most of the women have started to picket, including Esperanza Morales. The men perform the chores and tend those children who do not accompany their mothers. Sheriff Goleiter, completely surprised by the switch in pickets, drives up to the line, glances around, and does nothing. He seems utterly baffled, and leaves the scene. But some scabs, who decide to test the resolve of the women, find them as unyielding as the men. Punched and stoned, the scabs retreat bleeding, and Silver City magistrate Arthur Hangerman hands down six arrest warrants charging women with assault and battery. As part of the publicity committee, Marty writes letters and fliers calling on the world to witness the treatment of miners and their wives in Hanover, New Mexico. Hyperion, intent on neutralizing the bad publicity generated by the strike, runs full-page newspaper ads decrying the lawlessness of the union and condemning Local 890 for putting women and children in harm's way. The company claims that as a public service it will pursue every means to open the road.

At 6 p.m. they huddle around the radio to hear how KOB, Albuquerque, represents the day's events.

KOB Radio

"This evening's news is brought to you by Hanson Buick, the king of auto sales, and Halo shampoo. Hanson, located at Central and 8th, has new cars and used cars, all at the best prices in town. Tired of taking the bus, weary of walking? No need to envy your neighbors. We can put you behind the wheel of a car for as little as fifty dollars a month. Our salesmen are waiting to serve you. Open six days a week, we're here from seven to seven. Hanson Buick . . . the name to remember in cars. And now for the news with Robert Van Meter."

"Good evening! The strike in Hanover continues. Today, Sheriff Goleiter and dozens of deputies tried to clear the road to the Hyperion mine. Meeting fierce resistance, he warned the pickets they were violating the law. His remarks, greeted with insults and taunts, led to numerous arrests. According to our reporter at the scene, Carlos Mesa, the number of arrested rapidly grew until forty-five women, seventeen children, and one infant had been taken into custody. Bail was subsequently set at fifty dollars a person."

"Hanson Buick and Halo shampoo are bringing you the news— Hanson, the trusted Buick dealership of Albuquerque for twenty-three years. Credit poor, money short? You needn't worry. Hanson is always ready to deal. In addition to new cars, we have used ones in tip-top condition for as little as two hundred dollars. Come see us and drive away in a Buick for only thirty-five dollars down and fifteen dollars a month. Is your hair droopy and dull? Do you wish it were radiant and buoyant? Just pick up a bottle of Halo, the shampoo that puts the shine back in your hair. Now back to Robert Van Meter."

"As the deputies led those arrested to the police cars, other women scrambled down the hillside to take their place. Faced with overwhelming odds and clearly frustrated, the Sheriff and his deputies decided, for the first time, to resort to force. Our reporter's microphone, though positioned some distance off, was able to capture the following. What you hear is Sheriff Goleiter shouting into a bullhorn, his words nearly drowned out by the protesting pickets."

"If you don't clear the road, I'm gonna have to use tear gas."

"The Sheriff's warning, however, went unheeded, leading him to shout a second time."

"Did you hear me or are you deaf?"

"Halo, everybody, Halo;

Halo is the shampoo

That glorifies your hair;

So Halo, everybody, Halo . . ."

Ben

Turning off the radio in disgust, Ben sees Joe at the door.

"Good day's work, don't you think?"

Ben wonders whether Joe is referring to the women taunting the sheriff with suggestions that he and his deputies might have more success if they went home and bullied their wives and kids, or to the tear gas attack. Infuriated, one deputy had pulled the pin from a tear gas canister and hurled it at the women. A cloud of noxious gas had sent them scrambling to escape its effects.

"When the CS clouded the road," said Joe, "I thought for a sec the pickets had all disappeared."

"Damn lucky the wind was blowing from the southeast. It blew that shit right back in their faces."

"Didn't stop Goleiter from trying again—with the same result."

"Where you been? I haven't seen you for days."

Joe ignores the question. "What a jackass that Goleiter is, ordering his deputies to break through the line. Did he think the men on the hillside would wave pompoms and cheer? 'No les dejan!' 'No les dejan!' He'll be remembering those words the rest of his life." Joe lights a cigarette. As he exhales, an image crosses Ben's mind: a corpse blowing smoke. "Who the hell would have believed the women would go hand-to-hand with the deputies? But once the men appealed to their wives, Christ, they fought like banshees."

"Yeah, it reminded me of fire fights in Korea, where you couldn't see the enemy through the dust. In the blizzard of gas and confusion, we could barely make out who was doing the punching, scratching, and screaming."

darkmatters
LEVITT

From Ben's Articles

Dateline: Monday, June 18, Hanover, New Mexico. . . . Seething at being outwitted by women, the sheriff ordered his men to drive two carloads of scabs through the pickets. The first slowly rolled forward, reached the line, and pushed forward. The second tried to outflank the women by maneuvering along the shoulder between the road and the tracks. But the women bunched themselves in front of the cars and dared the drivers to run them down. Both cars ground to a halt, then turned and retreated.

The sheriff drove the arrested women to the county courthouse. But the jail is designed for no more than twenty-four people; the rest had to be lodged in a local hotel. Local 890 immediately started churning out press releases to be sent to every part of the country. As this goes to press, reporters are booking flights to Albuquerque and El Paso, where they will have to board busses for Silver City. Sheriff Goleiter asked the state government for help. But Governor Edwin Mechem, sensitive to the Mexican-American vote, advised consultation and patience. The sheriff agreed to release some of the women and, in particular, the mother with a six-week-old infant—if they promised not to return to the strike line. But those involved in publicizing the strike urged the women to remain in jail as long as they could hold out, and the women rejected Goleiter's offer.

Dateline: Monday evening, June 18, Hanover, New Mexico. Grant County Sheriff Leonard Goleiter, pressed on one side by Mine/Mill Local 890 and on the other by Hyperion Zinc, summoned the union leaders to talk. He disclosed that Hyperion's management, already featured in radio reports, newspapers, and in magazine stories, including ones by *Time* and *Life*, wanted to avoid further adverse publicity stemming from the jailings.

darkmatters
LEVITT

But Hyperion is still refusing to grant any of the union's demands. For now, the women of Local 890 remain in the jailhouse.

Dateline: Sunday, June 24, Hanover, New Mexico. Today, the U.S. Labor Department offered to arbitrate between Hyperion Zinc and Mine/Mill Local 890. But Hyperion rejected the offer, arguing that the presence of a third party would make negotiations all the more difficult. Hyperion said it wanted to deal directly with the union, and declared that it would not bargain as long as the mine remained closed. Clifford Jensen, speaking for Mine/Mill Local 890, responded that without a new contract picketing would continue. In response, Hyperion has launched an ongoing war of words: radio spots and newspaper ads accusing the union of having been duped by communists, creating a national shortage of zinc that is adversely affecting the war effort, and holding views that are not consonant with a free market economy.

Ben

To counteract Hyperion's publicity campaign, Ben and Marty agree to leaflet Silver City businesses, while Joe writes press releases for the political office. Clarissa assists with the relief work, distributing clothes and food donated by people sympathetic to the plight of the strikers. Although feeling feverish, Abby helps tend children. Occasionally the five join the men on the hillside keeping vigil over the women pickets, but "standing around," as Abby calls it, taxes them more than working; and, as she colorfully points out, "the worst kind of standing around is minding children, which is like cleaning up rabbit droppings." In the evenings, they take meals with their host families or frequent the Fierro cafe. Later, Ben and Clarissa often continue up the river road, past the well, and into the hills to make love on a Navajo blanket.

For several days, Ben and Marty go from shop to shop handing out fliers explaining the union's position. Frankly, Ben thinks the explanations can use more detail, but the Local inclines to purple phrases like: "How can you turn a blind eye to the barbaric treatment of American workers?" Ben tells Joe that if the fliers actually gave examples of "barbaric treatment," they would be much more effective. But Joe says that people want headlines, not details. One afternoon, a car pulls up and two men jump out, both with crew cuts. Flashing a badge, one of them asks:

"You got a permit to distribute these things?"

Ben takes the badge and studies it. "Since when," he inquires, "did the FBI start caring about fliers?"

"We don't like people spreading communist propaganda."

"So you're here to protect the people."

"That's right."

As this exchange takes place, Leopold Sturmer comes up behind Ben with a baseball bat and hits him a glancing blow on the back of the head. Ben feels himself falling to the ground like a marionette whose strings have been suddenly cut, and hears Marty scream.

"Arrest this Nazi! Did you see what he did! Don't just stand there!"

The two FBI agents climb back in the car and drive off, without a word. A crowd quickly gathers and someone summons the sheriff. Marty explains to Goleiter what happened and who hit Ben. His reply:

"That's the risk you run handing out commie literature."

A friendly shopkeeper calls for an ambulance, which takes Ben and Marty to the hospital. The doctor diagnoses a concussion, made worse by Ben's recent head wound. A local ambulance chaser shows up in Ben's room and asks him if he wants to sue for damages. Ben dismisses him with the comment:

"I'll settle this matter myself—to my own satisfaction."

Leopold Sturmer voluntarily turns himself into the sheriff's office and admits his offense, for which the judge fines him one dollar.

Clarissa insists that they have to take a break from the strike and allow Ben time to recover. She suggests a dude ranch south of Las Cruces not far from Mexico, along the Rio Grande, and generously offers to pay all their expenses. Joe, nevertheless, stays behind. The ranch covers several hundred acres and caters to wealthy easterners. Ben, in no condition to ride horses, spends most of his time visiting pueblos along the river. He finds enchantment in the spinning potters' wheels and the flying fingers of the rug makers. Occasionally he takes a turn at trying to bring shape out of the formless clay. The Indians laugh at his awkwardness. On returning from his outings, he always brings Clarissa a handsome pot or rug. She asks why he won't let her join him. Ben has no answer except to say that they imbue him with a solitary spiritual peace. Clarissa knows that the blow has left him with blurred sight and with headaches, which respond to herbal treatments that he receives at the pueblos. She wishes that he wished for her presence.

Marty

Ben's injury provided us with a good excuse to get away from the ceaseless ferment of the strike. Clarissa footed the bill, but even that freebie couldn't dislodge Joe Riley, who growled that he had "no time for gallivanting." Of late, it seemed the strikers' every move was anticipated by Hyperion Zinc. For three days running the FBI showed up to ask questions. Joe said that someone had to tell the gumshoes "to shove it up their ass." He reasoned that as an Anglo, he was safe from their threats.

In the large guest hall of the hacienda, leather chairs, redolent of tanned hides, provided unparalleled leisure for reading. Although I took the occasion to lose myself in a book, I was not unobservant of the work and workers required to run a large ranch. The men groomed the horses and led parties over the dusty trails. They also kept the bunkhouses in good condition, and brought provisions from town. The women did all the rest: cooking and cleaning, making beds and changing sheets, washing the laundry by hand. As well, they raised and doctored their children, fashioned and repaired their own clothes, prepared for religious holidays, and organized the festive dances held every weekend. I remain convinced that the pueblos and dances restored Ben to health, or at least got him over the hump. Every night the guests gathered in the meeting room at long communal tables where they ate beef and pork tamales, with ice cream and coffee. Dinner done, violins and guitars played, and a "dancing master" led the guests in folk dances, mostly of European origin: forms of the schottische, varsoviana, polka, two-step, quadrille, waltz, and a dance, set to the music of "Coming Through the Rye," called *Vals del Ceteño*. The one weekend we spent at the ranch, Ben reluctantly agreed to dance with Clarissa. Still feeling weak, he proved a quick

darkmatters
LEVIT

study, outshining all but the dancing master, who, once Ben called it quits, teamed with Clarissa and entertained all those who chose to stay up until two in the morning. Around one, I took a break from the festivities to admire the night sky and enjoy the cool, tonic air. Strolling among the bunks, I noticed that the laundry shed door stood slightly ajar. As I approached, I heard gasps and peeked in. The moon cast just enough light through the window that I could see Myra, a petite and perky Anglo housemaid with a come-hither smile, leaning over a scrubbing tub while a man with his pants around his ankles probed her from behind. Voyeurism, I suppose, has its appeal, but not for me. What froze me to the spot was the man's identity.

"I have to get back," she said, "I'll be missed."

"*Me arrastra, me arrastra!*"

Committing those words to memory, I discovered their meaning the next day: "No one can do it as I can."

"Oh, Luis," she sighed.

I had never seen people making love for real. (I don't count the occasional blue movie shown at a stag party.) Frankly, I felt no vicarious pleasure, only dismay, as I stood there watching in the flesh—no pun intended— Luis Morales, Esperanza's husband.

I knew perfectly well that indiscretion invites harm, but I failed to heed my own maxim. I told Ben what I'd seen.

Not long after our return to Hanover, two events proved fateful. Esperanza began taking her meals with the Bejels, bringing her into daily contact with Ben and me.

Then an opinion piece appeared in the *Daily Press*, written by the editor, Mr. Creely, snidely dismissing the union's assertion that Hyperion discriminated against Mexican-American workers: "If you have a dark skin, belong to a minority religious, political, or racial group, look no further for an excuse for your ill success." A few days later, adding salt to the wound, he contended that "Mexico, of course, is poverty stricken because its early settlers lost their identity in a mestizo melting-pot that lowered the general level of culture to a point little above that of the swarming aborigines." Joe Riley and other union officials tried to force their way into the editor's office to express their outrage, but he had anticipated or been warned of their action and surrounded himself with men from the sheriff's department. This was not the first time that one of our plans had been thwarted.

"I swear," Joe fumed, "there's a fucking fink in our midst."

darkmatters LEVITT

"How can we find him?" Ben asked.

"Small chance. The one thing the FBI doesn't screw up is giving their informers a convincing cover."

I envied Joe's knowledge of the dark side of government, which I assumed he'd learned from his parents.

With the *Silver City Daily Press* supporting Hyperion, the company again refused mediation. On Thursday, July 5, with the wet and cloudy season at hand, the union offered to accept a contract modeled on any other in the district. No one wanted to spend days picketing in the rain. But the company said that the union had nothing new to offer and, yet again, tried to break the strikers' line with injunctions, hired guns, and scabs. For the next few weeks, the sheriff and his men showed up daily, provoking confrontations that grew increasingly violent. Scabs, paid a half-day's wages for trying to breach the line, ran into a fury of women who drove them off with rocks and with chili powder thrown in their eyes. In reply, police officers clubbed the women with truncheons and rammed the line with their cars, injuring two women, one of them seriously. The union immediately brought suit, but the Justice of the Peace ruled that Local 890 had precipitated the riots by blocking the road. Case dismissed.

Joe Riley and his action group came up with the idea of a petition. We would ask local businessmen to sign a statement supporting the strike. The logic was simple: if Hyperion saw the community siding with the union, the company would withdraw from the fray. That strategy, however, foundered on the rock of public indifference and the open hostility of the *Silver City Daily Press*. I must say that soliciting signatures for our petitions proved a sobering experience. Clarissa, the most successful, used all her feminine wiles to persuade businessmen to support us. Abby, listless and wan, collected no more than a dozen. My petition had fewer than ten, and Ben's about the same. Whenever someone refused to sign, Ben inevitably got embroiled in an argument; and because he knew more about labor history and law than his adversaries, he merely made them all the more intransigent by exposing their ignorance. One man, a lawyer, felt particularly insulted to have this "commie" best him in matters bearing on law.

"What's your name?" he asked.

"Ben Cohen. What's yours?"

"Warren Dudley . . . and I'm a graduate of the University of Texas law school."

"Well, Mr. Dudley, I think they taught you too much about Texas law and not enough about real law."

During this exchange, Clarissa had sidled up to Ben and continued the conversation. Mr. Dudley obviously found her charming. Though he refused to sign, by the end of their talk he did want to know her name and address. I suppose she should have ignored the request, but she politely answered:

"Clarissa Stanton, from Lexington, Kentucky."

"Stanton!" he exclaimed, "from Lexington, Kentucky! I used to date your mother, if her name is Roberta."

"It is."

"Imagine that! I used to drive four hours from Huntington, West Virginia just to spend an evening with her. Who would believe . . ."

Ben and Clarissa laughed hysterically, unable to stop. Poor Mr. Dudley, having no idea what had occasioned this seizure, brushed an imaginary speck off his jacket and straightened his tie, undoubtedly convinced that his attire had somehow caused the commotion. Eventually Clarissa managed an abbreviated goodbye and she and Ben, still doubled over, staggered away, leaving Mr. Dudley to ponder what he had done.

The petitions having proved ineffective, the union again sought relief from the courts. But before the court ruled against the union, as it subsequently did, we had a major worry on our hands. Abby's condition worsened. Seeing a doctor, she learned that she had tick fever. The Silver City hospital said that her immune system could be seriously impaired and that she needed to be moved to a better-equipped medical institution. Since Abby's family had just left for Europe, Clarissa insisted on their returning immediately to Lexington.

The next day, Ben drove them to the bus station. As the two prepared to board a Greyhound for El Paso, where they would take a plane to Kentucky, we all hugged. I whispered "thank you" to Abby, and Ben clung to Clarissa as if he feared she'd never return. After the bus pulled away, he stood in the middle of the road watching, until it had passed completely from sight.

darkmatters
LEVITT

From Ben's Articles

The 19th amendment to the constitution gave women the vote. It didn't happen without a struggle. Thousands of men thought women frivolous and feckless.

In Hanover the women had voted to picket in place of the men. Mothers and sisters had persuaded the men to behave contrary to one of their strongest cultural beliefs: virility demands female submission. But under the duress of having to assume the domestic responsibilities that their women previously discharged, the men began to grumble about their masculinity and honor, to which the women repeatedly answered:

"We must stick together. Otherwise, Hyperion will exploit our discontents."

Just as American men could not conceive giving women the power of the ballot box, and just as the miners of Local 890 resent their women wearing the pants, so too does Hyperion regard the women pickets as a standing reproach to its power. Make no mistake: power is the issue. Hyperion wants everyone to know who holds the reins, who gives the orders, who makes the rules. Bad enough that the miners have been opposing the company; but ever since women took over the line the situation has become even worse. The company, at a loss to explain the unbending will of the women, feels humiliated and therefore has put all its public relations behind the charge that the strike is a conspiracy by agents of a subversive foreign power.

Marty

On a Monday, we learned that a forest fire had broken out to the north of us, near Pinos Altos. I took the conflagration as a sign. Sure enough, the next morning Joe Riley barged into the Bejel house to announce that the government had cited his parents for contempt of court for refusing to answer questions about their political affiliations. I remember the day because by Thursday, Hyperion, quoting an FBI report, had trained its sights on Joe, calling him a Red. His mother wrote him a note: "Fight the good fight."

Friday night, over dinner with the Bejels, Esperanza suggested to Ben that in light of his injury, he leave off his current work and help her write a radio script for station KSIL that would speak to the charge of communist infiltration of the union. He reluctantly agreed, but only after she had backed him into a corner.

"What good will a play do?" Ben asked. "You're dealing with a lot of bums who can't even fathom Walt Disney."

"Who can?"

"I don't follow."

"It has no point. We'll write something with a punch."

"Like what?"

"Like children crying from hunger. Like parents who can't pay their rent. Like miners dying from the lung disease. That's what."

With pronounced irony Ben remarked, "And you think those swine care? They'd step over a starving child rather than stop to help."

Leaning over the table, her eyes blazing, she said, "My point exactly! That's the very thing we're going to tell the world."

Ben mumbled, "They have no shame."

darkmatters
LEVITT

"No, but some of their customers do."

Whenever Esperanza put her rapier-like intelligence in the service of her temper and her hatred of poverty, the blood would rush to her face, making the gold of her skin glow with the heat of her passion. Yes, she declared, they would go together to talk to KSIL. At first the station manager refused to air any further union material—unless the union could restore his lost revenues. He claimed that local businesses, opposed to the union, were cancelling their advertising. In a marvelous twist of irony, Mr. Sturmer, the druggist, paid for most of the program. Ben called on him in the company of a union lawyer, who spelled out the costs of a personal injury suit. Whether or not Ben could have won the case, Sturmer had enough grey matter to know that his legal fees would exceed the cost of a radio play. So he wrote out a check, albeit grudgingly.

"I told you," Ben chuckled, "I'd settle the matter to my own satisfaction," adding, "You can be sure that our radio script will make very clear who our principal sponsor is."

The script did not come easily. I should have known from the smoke and ash in the air that passions were stirring. A forest fire in the Gila Cliff Dwellings National Monument, a short distance away, had blackened the sky. For good reason the kabbalists teach that nature has its corollary in man. Ben and Esperanza first argued over whether to tackle the communist charge head on, then clashed over whether the script should be a straightforward account of the miners' plight—their hunger and evictions—or a radio play that exposed the stupidity and insensitivity of Hyperion Zinc. Sitting at the Bejels' dining room table, they frequently disagreed, each testing the strength of the other, as they finally defined the issue in terms of their aiming for the heart or the head. Esperanza held out for a serious script that would detail the agony of the workers. Ben contended that a satire would gain them more adherents than tears.

"Once people laugh at Hyperion," said Ben, "the game is up. They can't keep playing the communist card."

Esperanza answered impatiently, "We have to grab them in the gut."

"Feeling is like a piano note," he said. "It's a decaying sound that can't be sustained. Comedy is like a violin. The sound lingers for the length of the bow."

"I never had music lessons," snapped Esperanza, who deeply resented her lack of opportunities. "Believe me, if you get arty, you're going to bomb. Theories don't work unless they're driven by hunger."

Ben turned to me for support.

"I prefer satire."

"You don't know the people in these parts. You're just a couple of Anglo college boys. Start getting 'whitey' with them and they'll turn off the radio."

"Laughter is universal," said Ben.

"So too are tears," rebutted Esperanza. "And many of us around here have shed them."

"I don't need lessons in tears," said Ben sharply.

Around and around they went, for hours, snapping and growling and shouting, until I thought the script would never get written. Days passed. The union office grew impatient. Then Esperanza said that she had to check on the safety of her grandmother, who lived in Pinos Altos. Ben angrily objected.

"We're needed here—to finish the script. I don't want to go from the frying pan into the fire. The sky will be raining soot and the town choked with smoke."

Obviously concerned about her grandmother's welfare, she said, "Perhaps I ought to bring my abuela here. I guess I wasn't thinking. Our constant haggling has made me nervioso. Besides, Luis might return in my absence."

"Not this weekend, he won't," Ben blurted.

I could see in her eyes that she saw in Ben's a forbidden knowledge; and yet she never asked him how he knew. Fixing his face in her gaze, she decisively said: "If you drive me to my abuela's, you can cover the fire for your magazine—*and* I'll show you some of her old-world Jewish relics. On her wall, for example, she has a blanket with a little star of David woven into one of the patterns. Although she's as Catholic as I am, she goes to Mass on Saturday and always bakes bread on Friday night. I once asked her why, and she said because her mother and grandmother did. Don't you find that strange?"

"She sounds like a *marrano*," I said.

Ben looked puzzled. "Aren't those the ones who prayed in secret?"

"Spanish Jews who converted to Catholicism to save their lives but practiced Judaism in the privacy of their homes."

My rabbinic tutor had pointed out the irony that the same year that Columbus discovered America, Ferdinand and Isabella discovered their need for Jewish property and money. Those Jews not expelled or burned converted. But many of the converts remained secretly true to their faith. Some of them even accompanied Spanish expeditions to the New World, and stayed behind. Rumors abounded that at one time New Mexico had been home to numerous marranos. Although Catholicism eventually eclipsed their Jewish faith, they had retained some of the old customs, like worshipping on Saturday. Hearing my spiel, Ben jumped up and declared:

"I'll drive you to Pinos Altos. It could make good copy."

"May I ask one thing more?"

"What's that?"

"If I drive off with you and don't return for several days, people will gossip. Can I meet you in Silver City? I know it's out of the way, but I have to stop at the drugstore."

"I'll pick you up on Market Street, in front of Warren Dudley's law office."

Butting into Ben's business, I said, "Where the hell you gonna stay in a town overrun with fire fighters?"

"I can rough it. The smoke jumpers have a camp. I'll take a sleeping bag and a tent."

"My abuela will insist that you stay at her house."

"I'd rather camp."

Esperanza just shrugged and muttered, "*Baboso*."

During their absence, I grabbed a ride into Silver City to distribute fliers and to see *Grounds for Marriage*, with Van Johnson and Kathryn Grayson. Now I remember nothing about the film, but only the call I made afterward to Lexington to inquire about Abby's health. The pay phone voraciously devoured my change (a long-distance call used to cost a ton of money). I had to keep feeding it nickels and dimes, which I had stacked in a pile that shrunk to nothing in less than three minutes. A maid came to the phone; she passed it on to Mrs. Stanton, who finally gave it to Abby. By this time at least a minute had passed, so I had to talk fast.

"Are you all right?" I asked. "What did the doctor say? How's Clarissa?"

Abby's voice had lost all its bounce. She sounded exhausted. "I've been running a fever. The doctor keeps telling me it will take time. I sleep a lot. Clarissa's okay. She goes riding practically every morning. Guess what? Brian Hazelwood's here. He arrived just today."

"How long is he staying?" I enquired, dubious of his motives and resentful of his money.

"I don't know. He says as long as it takes for me to recover."

"Oh, he's there to see you!"

"I called and told him about the tick fever. He came immediately."

"Sweet guy," I said insincerely.

"Yeah."

"Where's he staying?"

"Here at the house. Mrs. Stanton's crazy about him."

"I'm running out of change."

"I'll write."

"So will I."

"Call again if you can. By the way, how's Ben?"

The operator cut us off.

Ben

Margarita Perez lives on a dusty, rutted street with four other houses. Her bungalow has a sagging, paintless porch and a rusted metal fence that circles the property. As they pull up, she is throwing pails of water on the roof because hot cinders from the forest fire carry on the wind. The sky, darkened by ash and smoke clouds, brings to mind a Bosch painting of the world's end. The scent of burning juniper and pine permeate the air. Esperanza introduces her abuela to Ben, who offers to continue watering the roof. Mrs. Perez hands him the pail and points out the backyard pump. She and her niece enter the house. Ben can detect in the lined face of the old woman a worry and has the impression that Mrs. Perez wants to speak to Esperanza about her showing up in Pinos Altos accompanied not by her husband, but by a strange man. While he waters the desiccated shingles, the two women talk. At last, they emerge and invite him to join them. Mrs. Perez hurries into the kitchen, and Esperanza sets the small dining-room table, spread with a white-linen tablecloth.

The two-bedroom house suffers from clutter. Every flat surface holds a knickknack, including a tarnished brass nameplate that says "Peretz." A small fireplace in the living room faces a battered puffy couch and two reed-bottomed chairs. The mantlepiece holds a menorah, a seven-branched candelabrum, a traditional symbol of Judaism. Next to it stands a ceramic madonna and child. Over the fireplace hangs a faded wall blanket with Indian designs. Ben surmises from its threadbare, faded condition that it is very old. In the lower left corner of the rug, he sees a Magen David, the six-pointed star of David, used for decorative and magical purposes in ancient times by Jews and non-Jews, and in

darkmatters
LEVITT

the Middle Ages by Christians. He and Esperanza have arrived on a Friday. He can smell bread baking in the oven. The house reminds him of his parents'.

That evening, as they sit for dinner, which includes a freshly baked challah, Mrs. Perez lights candles and speaks of attending Mass the next day, on the Sabbath. Fascinated by the Jewish objects in the house and the traditions she observes, Ben asks her about the nameplate. He remarks that Ferdinand and Isabella, the very monarchs who expelled the Jews from Spain, had for many years relied on a prominent Sephardic family, called "Peretz," as their counselors.

"A long time ago," says the old woman, "our family name was Peretz. Someone changed it."

"Tell me, why do you attend Mass on Saturday, and light candles on Friday night?"

"The same reason I make the braided bread. My parents did, and their parents too."

"The rug and the menorah?" Ben asks, but sees that Mrs. Perez is uncomprehending. "Woven into the rug is a Jewish star," he explains, "and the candelabrum over the fireplace, it's part of Jewish culture."

The old woman smiles and says simply, "I'm Catholic."

"A marrano."

"What's that?"

His explanation leaves her unpersuaded. "You must be wrong. I know others who go to church on Saturday."

Ben leaves the subject, but not without observing that the table is devoid of butter, no doubt because the main course is chicken. While Esperanza does the dishes, Mrs. Perez questions him indirectly about his friendship with her niece.

"You have a wife?"

"No."

"A girlfriend?"

"She lives in Kentucky."

"It's good to have someone. You have met Luis?"

"Yes."

"He is a good man, even though he sometimes, like all warm-blooded-men, admires a pretty leg. Esperanza understands."

Ben, not wishing to cause the old woman any discomfort, sides with her.

darkmatters
LEVITT

"I don't know him well. But if Esperanza married him, he must be a fine man."

"He is. Why," she begins to inquire, but falters.

Ben comes to her aid. "Why is she travelling with me? She needed a way of getting to Pinos Altos, and when she told me about your house, I wanted to see it for myself. Things like the menorah and the rug. I'm an anthropologist of sorts."

"What's that?"

"Someone interested in old cultures."

She looks confused but doesn't ask for further details. Excusing herself, she retreats outside and again douses the roof with water. In her absence, Ben talks to Esperanza about the fusion of two ancient Spanish cultures.

"You know, don't you, that at one time—before Ferdinand and Isabella destroyed their country—there existed a third great culture, the Moorish. They taught the world mathematics and medicine. Once the Inquisition got done, the priesthood plunged Spain into abysmal darkness. So much for religion."

Esperanza bridles at the suggestion that her faith could have anything to do with backwardness. Ben suggests that a good history of Spain might serve her well.

"Sometimes," replies Esperanza, "I despise your snobbishness."

"Just because you haven't had my advantages doesn't make my advantages contemptible. That's how anti-intellectuals behave."

She seethes. Ben leaves the house and walks down the road to the main street. Passing the Buckhorn Saloon and Opera, he arrives at the small fort where the firefighters have camped. Fort Webster, which was originally the Santa Rita del Cobre Fort and Trading Post, has long been unused, except for emergencies like the current one. He climbs a primitive ladder to the ramp that runs around the fort's inner wall, which provides a good viewing spot to see the distant blaze. The fire-heated air is oppressive. He muses about the absences that weigh people down. In matters of learning, to lift that burden takes a Herculean effort.

When Ben returns to the house he announces that he will camp with the fire fighters. But Mrs. Perez won't hear of his sleeping out-of-doors, arguing that the smoky air will infect his lungs and give him bronchitis. That night, Esperanza takes the guest room, and Ben the adipose couch. Finding it too lumpy and short, he retreats to his car and returns with a sleeping bag, which he spreads on the floor. During the night, he awakens

darkmatters LEVITT

to footsteps and sees peering down at him Esperanza. She kneels, and he pulls her close. She trembles in his arms.

"I want to know more," she whispers. "Forgive me my darkness."

She kisses him on the lips. He tries to detain her, but she immediately withdraws and returns to her room.

The next day they follow the winding road for several miles through the dark, tree-shaded Gila forest, until they reach the firelines. They have brought with them several loaves of bread and homemade jam for the crews who are feverishly trying to contain the blaze that rages out of control.

"I wish you had stayed," he murmurs.

"It would have been dangerous—and disrespectful to my abuela."

"And Luis?"

She doesn't reply.

darkmatters
LEVITT

Marty

Ben and Esperanza's return marked a change in their behavior toward one other. Although still testy at times and quick to feel slighted, Esperanza had come back with a look of soft contentment. She lovingly told stories of her abuela, who had stubbornly refused to leave because she insisted on feeding the fire fighters. For his part, Ben, who had in fact stayed in the house, returned convinced that Esperanza's grandmother came from a Jewish tradition.

Mixing his faiths, he exclaimed, "For Christ's sake, she has a menorah on her mantelpiece!"

From the day they returned, he treated Esperanza like an exciting new gravity. He stayed close to her physically and would brush her arm with his, or let his hand fall across hers, or outside in the wind stand close enough for her hair to blow in his face. She always smiled but never responded in kind. I felt as if they had made an affectionate peace, though his feelings clearly exceeded hers.

What transpired between Ben and Esperanza I could piece together only imperfectly from the discussion she and I had shortly after their return. Ben had gone to Silver City to purchase a typewriter ribbon and carbon paper. Local 890's old carbons had been used so often they were covered with indecipherable runes and no longer left an impression. Esperanza, taking advantage of his absence, said that she needed to talk to me. We sat in her house, a rough wooden frame structure owned by Hyperion. A single bookcase in the corner caught my attention. Readers always want to know what books others enjoy. Perusing the titles, I saw prayer books, collected poems in Spanish, and also some novels in translation: *Madame Bovary*, *Anna Karenina*, and *The Grapes of Wrath*.

"They're mine," she said, "I like to see the world through writers' eyes."

The house was decorated with rugs of her own making and pots thrown by Luis. A blend of earth colors and bright lemon yellows and pinks gave the pots and the house a soft glow. I praised Luis's handiwork, and she told me he had learned to work with clay in Mexico and in the pueblos outside Albuquerque. "He wanted to be a potter. But the mines paid more." What she said next caught me completely off guard. "You know something about Luis, don't you? Otherwise Ben wouldn't have made the comment about his not returning. Am I right?"

The rabbi's words rang in my ears: "*Der emes iz der bester lign.*" Truth is the safest lie. Ignoring his sage advice, I tried evasion in the hope that once she saw where the subject led, she would drop it.

"We saw him from a distance at the dude ranch."

"Why didn't you speak to him?"

"He looked occupied."

"You might have mistaken Luis for someone else."

"True."

"He's suspicious of Anglos—men, not women. How well did you know him?"

"Really only by sight. The few times we met on the road, we said hello. Nothing more."

"Yet you say you recognized him."

"His face, yes."

"Well, certainly not his back! What a strange reply. How was he dressed?"

"I can't really say."

"What was he doing?"

"Standing."

"Marty, answer my questions!"

"He was standing over a wash basin."

"You must have seen somebody else. Luis never stood over a wash basin in his life!"

"Maybe you're right. Perhaps it was another fellow."

"Then why did Ben say what he did?"

"You'd have to ask him."

"I did . . . and he wouldn't explain."

"What more can I tell you?"

"You and Ben are keeping something from me. And I think I know why. Luis likes to chase after skirts. He always has and he always will. You probably saw him with another woman. I'm right, aren't I?"

"Yes, he was with another woman. But she could have been his aunt or cousin or niece. I have no way of knowing. We didn't speak."

Esperanza turned away, lost in thought. A moment later, she said simply: "Ben loves Clarissa, doesn't he?"

"I suppose."

"Marty, tell me!"

"You've seen them together. Draw your own conclusions."

"I'm asking you because I don't understand his behavior. I just spent two days with him, and he made no attempt to hide his feelings."

That admission told me more than I wanted to know. Ben had twice tried to reach Clarissa by phone. I neglected to warn him that Mrs. Stanton was screening all calls. Both times, she had refused to summon her daughter. Lacking easy access to a telephone, Ben had to resort to letters. But he reasoned, probably correctly, that if Mrs. Stanton intercepted his calls, she would probably find a way to interfere with the mail.

Esperanza started to talk about the fire. "We stood behind the lines and watched as the blaze jumped from treetop to treetop. The heat . . . the copper-faced men with their hoses . . . it all reminded me of something that happened a long time ago. Certain memories you suppress because they're so painful. My father died in a plant explosion . . . in Mexico. A chemical plant. By the time my mother and I arrived at the gate, ambulances were removing the dead, some headless, some without limbs. But what I saw and forgot and suddenly remembered—there in the Gila forest—were the torsos of men whose skin had bubbled and burst from the heat. Some bodies still blazed, fueled by their own fatty tissue."

I could smell in my imagination the burning flesh of the death camps and could see my Catholic friends eating the wafer that had miraculously become the flesh of the Christ. Why, I puzzled, do we devour our neighbors and our gods?

"Is she rich?"

"Who?"

"Clarissa."

"Yes."

"Is she Jewish?"

"Esperanza," I exclaimed, "you're Catholic, married, and committed for life. Why ask these questions?"

"Because he makes me wonder."

"About what?"

"Him."

"Don't!"

"He has doubts."

"About?"

"Marrying Clarissa."

"She's a rebel. She insists on being her own person, but also wants to fit in. Ben knows. Believe me, if she has to choose between being bored her whole life and marrying Ben, she'll choose the latter."

"But will he?"

In the proceeding quiet, I knew she was pondering the heft of their conversations. Ben and Esperanza, I gathered, had spent much of their time talking. Words, our poets teach us, may be an aphrodisiac, but they also make us vulnerable. Only fools lower the mask to anyone other than a loved one. As my mother used to say, "Don't wear your heart on your sleeve—unless you're prepared to get hurt." Esperanza and Ben had obviously told each other things that only confidantes reveal. With each question that she asked me, she progressively bared her feelings, unaware that questions disclose more about us than the answers we give. By the end of our tête-à-tête, I realized that the woods were indeed ablaze.

Returning with the carbons, Ben traced his ideas for a radio script.

"The situation I have in mind," he explained, "is based on a radio play that I heard some time ago in London. It was called *The First Draft*."

"You were in London?" said Esperanza enviously.

"My one R and R during my stay in Korea."

"R and R?"

"Rest and recuperation. I flew in a transport to Heathrow."

"Did you see Piccadilly Circus?"

"Mostly I lay in bed listening to the radio. One night, a play was just starting. So I listened."

He expanded on how he intended to adapt it, and waggishly added that all their disagreements about what to write constituted an on-going first draft.

Esperanza shyly admitted to composing verses that she felt lost their immediacy the longer she worked on them. "There's something to be said for inspiration . . . for capturing the moment of feeling. First drafts often convey more passion than rewrites."

Ben neither quarreled nor agreed with her statement, observing only that most great literary works went through numerous changes and took years to finish, "like Joyce's *Ulysses*."

"I never read it," Esperanza remarked coldly, again exhibiting her resentment at having been left out of what she referred to as the "college circle."

For all his belief in rewrites, he behaved no better than she. Every time they showed me a draft of the play, and I suggested a change, the two of them whined like kids being toilet trained. They wanted to poop on the paper and have me say how much I enjoyed the smell. I refused, and they grew short-tempered. But I persisted, until they began to see for themselves that their work improved with each revision.

"What if after all these rewrites, the script is still lousy?" asked Ben.

I smiled. "You can trash it or do it again."

"*No mas!*" exclaimed Esperanza.

"Well, once you agree on the final draft, and the radio broadcasts it, you no longer have any control over the script."

Ben smirked. "That sounds like you're not convinced."

"My rabbi used to say that no work is ever perfect and therefore no work is ever really done. If you say 'That's it!,' all that remains is for your audience to render a judgment. Did you ever decide on a title?"

"*Dark Matters*," they said, and headed for the radio station.

*   *   *   *

Announcer: Local 890 of the Mine, Mill, and Smelters Union, owing to the generosity of local tradespeople, especially Sturmer Drugstore, brings you in the form of a play its view of Hyperion's adamant opposition to any improvement in the working standards of Mexican-American workers in Grant County.

(A FEW PHRASES FROM "OL' MAN RIVER," FOLLOWED BY AN INTERCOM BUZZING)

The script told the story of two families: Vera and Miguel Costanza, who worked for Hyperion and belonged to Local 890, and Colette and Hiram Hyatt. To counter the charges that communists have infiltrated the union and resorted to terror, the Costanzas laboriously draft a letter to Hyperion's management, namely, Hiram Hyatt. In turn, he and his wife painfully arrive at the decision to complain to the governor about the strikers in their midst. The comic flavor can be seen in the following passage.

> *HYATT: (DESPERATE) Colette, we have to do something!*
> *COLETTE: Call your mother.*
> *HYATT: What good will that do?*
> *COLETTE: She'll know if they're terrorists. It takes one to know one.*

Both families find that their letters demand more of them than they had expected, and in the end the Hyatts fear that they have badly compromised themselves by putting into print a wrong interpretation.

Dozens of us sat in a circle on the floor of the Bejel house, with the radio in the middle, like a sacred altar, as we listened to the play. Ben seemed satisfied with their work, Esperanza less so—until the room resounded with cries of "*Sí!*" and "*Vamos!*" But what the good citizens of Silver City thought took a few days to discover. In the meantime three FBI men drove into town to confiscate Joe Riley's passport, which he refused to relinquish. J. Edgar's boys said that Joe had crossed into Mexico, where he met with a Trotskyite group, and that they had the photos to prove it. We all knew that Joe dropped out of sight from time to time, but his serving as a courier between Hanover and Hermosillo, Mexico, seemed utterly mad. After a heated exchange of words, the Feds left, with Joe none the worse for telling them to arrest J. Edgar Hoover for crapping up America. But just in case we were needed, Ben and I hung around town for two days. Finally we went into Silver City, and received heartening news. The few college students who had heard the play liked it. Also, local businessmen and professionals had in the main responded well, finding the comic tone inoffensive. The humor had elicited laughter from people as disparate as garage mechanics and doctors; and just as Ben had hoped, people listened closely because, as one student said, "I didn't want to miss the next laugh." Hyperion Zinc certainly heard every word. The play so incensed their bigwigs that they bought air time to decry "the unfair portrayal of Hyperion's management." In particular, the company denounced the idea that the wife of their general manager would have any sympathy for the strikers. She was, they said, "opposed to the unreasonable demands of the strikers and a fervent anti-communist." Without intending to do so, they made her out to be worse than Salome, and in the process beheaded themselves. The governor, privy to Hyperion's complaints, urged the company to mediate with Local 890. Though his words went unheeded—Hyperion refused to budge—the union had been heard in the statehouse.

But all that came later. In the Bejel house, at the play's conclusion, the moment belonged to the authors. Esperanza gave Ben a smile that bespoke a previously undisclosed rapture. A great many of us saw it, and some mentioned it afterward, commenting that if word filtered back to Luis all hell would break loose.

darkmatters
LEVITT

Ben

The next day, Ben receives a letter from Clarissa, addressed to the Mine-Mill office, Hanover, New Mexico. Since it touches upon Abby, Ben shares it with Marty. Seriously ill, Abby sleeps a good deal of the time. Specialists have been called. With Abby in bed, Clarissa occupies herself riding. For want of a companion, she has decided to teach Brian Hazelwood how to sit a horse. Mrs. Stanton apparently enjoys comparing Brian to Ben, attributing to the former a wealth of virtues, and to the latter numerous defects. Clarissa, clearly annoyed, says that were it not for Abby's condition, she would immediately return to New Mexico. Her anger comes right off the page. She wants out! To her dismay, her mother keeps hinting broadly that she should marry, and that the right man is at hand. She asks Ben to write to her in care of a friend. For a short while they use that address to correspond, until Mrs. Stanton discovers the underground railroad and derails it.

About the same time, Marty receives a disquieting letter from Abby. Although able to leave her bed a few hours each day, she has been advised by her doctor to remain in Lexington until she regains her full strength. School, fortunately, doesn't start until late September. But she feels that the longer she stays with the Stantons, the greater becomes her indebtedness, which Mrs. Stanton seems to want her to discharge by disapproving of Ben. By now, Abby realizes that Brian cares little for her other than as a friend. He has his heart set on Clarissa, a fact that Abby, in her good-natured manner, accepts. When Mrs. Stanton and Clarissa fight, which they do often, the mother looks to Abby for support. Pleading weakness, Abby confines herself to her room and leaves only for meals.

She cannot, in good conscience, support Mrs. Stanton. But Abby's letter makes quite clear that "where's there's smoke, there's fire."

darkmatters
LEVITT

From Ben's Articles

Dateline: Thursday, August 23, Hanover, New Mexico. Shortly before 7:00 a.m., Grant County Sheriff Leonard Goleiter and ten deputies, eight of them armed, drove up to the Hyperion picket line in two cars and a truck. The sheriff got out and walked up to the women. Insults were exchanged, and violence ensued.

The sheriff clambered into his car, facing the picket line, and the driver gunned his engine. Watching strikers, advancing from the hillside, yanked open the hood and tore the wiring from the spark plugs. The men in the other vehicles were surrounded by strikers and pelted with stones. During a momentary lull the crowd surged forward, shoving the car backwards into the truck, whose driver then drove it straight into the line, injuring three women. The strikers descended in droves on the driver, who reached into the glove compartment, removed a .45 pistol, and fired it five times. One of the bullets ricocheted off a rock, hitting a miner, Hector Torres, in the leg. Mr. Torres, a Korean war veteran, had just returned from the front.

Sheriff Goleiter ordered his men to have their weapons at the ready to retreat into the mine for safety. He then took the truck back to Silver City for reinforcements. By the time he returned, his men had holed up in company offices with their guns trained on the crowd. Within hours, a general strike was declared in all the nearby mining camps, and miners arrived at Hanover to cordon off the company offices.

Dateline: Monday, August 27, Hanover, New Mexico. Grant County Sheriff Leonard Goleiter today appealed to New Mexico Governor Edwin Mechem, to send troopers as reinforcements to break the strike at the Hyperion mine. The governor said he would send his own man to evaluate

darkmatters LEVITT

the situation. Finally, a local businessman, Sherwood Davis, who had the goodwill of the miners and the trust of Hyperion, persuaded the miners to let the sheriff's men leave. A phalanx of policemen escorted them off the property and back to Silver City.

Dateline: Wednesday, September 5, Hanover New Mexico. The Hyperion strike appears to have reached a stalemate. The mining community in this state, to show its solidarity with local 890 and their dismay over 'The Bloody 23rd,' has gone on a statewide walkout. Hyperion has fought back with a full-page ad in the *Daily Press* charging Local 890 with inciting mob rule and anarchy, and contending that Mine-Mill's role in the strike is part of a Soviet plot to gain control of the American labor movement. The ad touches a nerve, especially with local merchants, who are weary of the strike and fearful of communism. Without paychecks, the miners have quit buying.

The merchants, unable to meet bills for rents, inventory, advertising, and payroll, want the strike settled. But at this time, neither side is changing its position.

Ben

With the strike at an impasse, the friends decide to take off a few days to explore the caves of the Gila National Monument. Unlike the miners, Ben and Marty have a little money to burn, a state of affairs that conspicuously sets them apart. It takes Ben some heavy lifting to persuade Esperanza to join Marty and him. They meet her outside of town, drive north, and stay at Dawson "Doc" Campbell's 320-acre Hot Springs Ranch, where he runs a guide service for guests. The accommodations, designed for outdoorsmen and hikers, are sparse but comfortable: twin beds, with a nightstand between them, a wardrobe closet with two bottom drawers, and a twig chair. One bathroom, with a cracked porcelain tub and claw feet, serves the entire floor. Ben and Marty room together, Esperanza alone. Dinner, a communal affair, introduces them not only to a nature photographer, Glenn Irwin, a UNM archaeologist, Morty Sloane, and a couple from New York City, the Guralnicks, but also to dishes Marty and Ben have never eaten: venison and rattlesnake meat.

Marty remarks, "What my rabbi would have said about such a diet, I dare not consider."

After the meal, they sit around a large fireplace and listen to Doc talk about the history of the cliff dwellings, as rain pelts the roof and the occasional drop escapes through the chimney and hisses in the embers. August and September, rainy months in the park, have put an end to the fires. Doc promises to supply them with ponchos.

"To reach the cliff dwellings," he says, eagerly anticipating hiking in country he loves, "we pass through some heavily wooded narrow canyons, where you'll probably see mule deer and, if we're lucky, some pronghorn antelope. The elk and bighorn sheep are pretty shy." He holds up some photos that Glenn Irwin has taken of sparrow hawks and golden eagles, remarking that although the fire has driven away a lot of wildlife, they might catch a glimpse of a few birds near the streams, like black phoebes and killdeers. "If we're lucky," he says, "maybe we'll even see a New Mexico whitetail, a really interesting bird. All of them are female and parthenogenetic, which means they need no mate to reproduce."

Having just eaten rattlesnake, one of the guests asks about their presence in the canyon.

"Oh, they're in there, but you probably won't see any of 'em. They don't like folks. You're more likely to see some harmless gopher snakes."

Doc explains that the cliff dwellings—ruins of Indian dwellings cut into the volcanic rock below the mesa at 5,600 feet—date from the thirteenth and fourteenth centuries. Sheltered in six caves, the mud-and-stone architecture has escaped the erosion of wind and water. The ruins, he says, range from archaic overhang rock shelters and small alcoves to pit houses and pueblos. Doc suggests they turn in early because the hike will be arduous, particularly with the paths soggy from rain. Marty stays behind so that Ben and Esperanza can walk to their rooms without him tagging along.

In the hallway, Ben studies the framed photographs of the TJ Ruin, a pueblo that overlooks the Gila River valley and stands apart from the cliff dwellings. One photograph, labeled "polo field," leads him to speculate whether the Indians played lacrosse or a similar game. Did they, like other people, use sports to express their hidden selves?

The next day, they hike past burned areas and troop along the river through willow and wild grapes and into stands of cottonwood, sycamore, and walnut. As they start their ascent, the vegetation changes, until they reach the canyon slopes, forested with piñon, prickly pear, yucca, and oaks. Warned not to move any stones or remove any shards, they explore the caves and overhangs, and revel in the view from the heights. The sheer cliffs afforded the Indians protection, and the valley below and the mesa above undoubtedly served as their cornucopia. In Hanover, the miners have no such natural resources, dependent for their survival on the goodwill of others. Surely, there must have been a moment when those who moved from barter to wage labor must have thought the exchange not worth the money. Ben shares that thought with Esperanza, as they drift into one of the cave dwellings.

Marty

Somehow we temporarily became separated. By the time I found Ben and Esperanza, slants of light had broken through the rain clouds, dappling the canyon walls. The old ruin, lit only by shadow, invited reflection about the people who had lived and prayed here. Esperanza, versed in the religious rites of the Indians and their spirit worship, speculated on the source of their faith.

"The seasons and death, which in some ways are the same thing, fueled their beliefs. They tried to chant into life great harvests and bring back the spirits of their dead."

Ben used a Yiddish expression that means, "It will do as much good as giving a dead man an enema."

Esperanza asked for a translation. I rendered one, and she soberly remarked that "religious ceremony imposes order on a chaotic, meaningless world."

"Religious belief," replied Ben, "has no more substance than the shadows of Indian fires cast on these walls."

Esperanza, a good Catholic, objected.

"Jesus lived *in the flesh*," she said emphatically, "and died for our sins! His spirit lives on."

I was reminded that a number of medieval kabbalists embraced Christianity because they too believed that a man's essence is spiritual and his body only a cloak.

"That he lived," said Ben, "we have proof. He's mentioned in a few of the historical records. Fact! But that he died for our sins and lives in the spirit we have no way of proving. Faith! We call faith "faith" because we

darkmatters
LEVITT

don't have the facts, and therefore in their absence we substitute belief. But you would never let a surgeon remove a section of your intestines because he had faith that your gut needed surgery. You would demand proof—facts—and if he couldn't produce them, you'd tell him what he could do with his knife. So why put your trust in religious faith, which is lacking in fact? And don't tell me about Pascal's wager."

Esperanza, clearly feeling out of her depth, used the allusion to vent her frustration.

"I don't know this Pascal; I didn't go to college. Some of us couldn't afford it. But I do know that not all truths can be seen. For example, the cross that hangs on my church wall, fact! has a truth behind it, faith!"

"What truth?"

"The love of one for another."

"Then why the sword? Why the slaying of infidels, heretics, Muslims, and Jews?"

"There will always be people who misapply the message."

"So according to you, truth and faith are synonymous."

"I have faith that what I believe in is true."

Growing exasperated, Ben said, "But you can't prove it, Esperanza!"

"Can love be proved? Or honor?"

"No, they're abstractions. We recognize them from the actions they inspire."

"And yet a thousand material acts of love or honor do not guarantee that a person won't lie or cheat in the future."

"Right! Under certain circumstances, the most craven coward might behave courageously, or the courageous man like a coward. Which is why predicting behavior is so difficult. There are no guarantees."

"We have the proof of the Bible."

"Written years after the events it describes."

"But you can't deny that the ideas in the Bible have lived on. Fact!"

"They have lived on. Fact! But are they true?"

"Ideas have a life of their own. They're more real than facts. Isn't that what the strike is about, an idea called justice or fairness?"

"It's about the materiality of wages, of paid leaves, and of the right to strike."

If Plato could have eavesdropped and seen the shadows on the walls, he would have smiled, though at the time I didn't know Plato from Pluto. I

darkmatters LEVITT

did, however, interpret the shadows as a kabbalistic symbol reflecting the mystery of God and the universe. As the sun streamed through the vanishing rain clouds, brightly illumining the cliffs and dwellings, I suggested we leave the cave and enter the light. Friends, I thought, they will always be, but never more, the one a devout Catholic, the other a skeptical Jew.

The next morning I awoke prepared for another day of touring, only to discover that Ben had already risen and left the ranch. I tried Esperanza's room. No one answered. The cook said that they had left together at least an hour earlier. I returned to my room and, looking around, found at the foot of my bed a note that I had inadvertently obscured with the covers. It said simply: "Marty, E. and I have gone for a walk in the woods. We'll be back in time for the tour. Ben."

Ben

Ben has long known that his love of women is likely to make marriage to Clarissa—or anyone else—a sincere pretense. Even as a child, he enjoyed the company of girls. In Carmel, the farmer down the road had three sons and two daughters. With the boys he played baseball, with the girls, jump rope and hop scotch, and on more than one occasion took part in their make-believe games of doll house. As he grew older, he discovered that above all he liked women's society—the fineness of their companionship, their faithfulness, their audacity. The gentleness of women appealed to him more than the competitiveness of men, who were always trying to show how far they could piss and how tough they could act. He found such expressions of masculinity tiresome, and therefore took for his close friends mostly girls. They always seemed understanding, eager to listen and cooperate rather than obstruct. In his teens, he discovered sex and was forever caught, addicted to its musky smell and the gentle touch of feminine fingers in forbidden places.

He relished the moment of love when women mumbled like a troubled fountain. He also revelled in the aesthetic pleasure women gave him. Their long hair and their excited eyes made him want to live lodged between a woman's breasts. He especially favored slim, swan-necked, full-bosomed women, lovely in their bones. But the most exciting women of all were those who also had lively minds. Like golden strings finely tuned, they made incomparable liquid sounds when played upon with a lover's touch.

The first time he saw Esperanza, he knew that she would stay in memory. Unlike Clarissa, who could afford to be willful, confident that her family connections would always see her through scrapes, Esperanza had little, and yet exhibited genuine courage, willing to sacrifice her few modest possessions to see the miners treated fairly.

Now as they walk along the rain-wetted path, and smell the fragrant earth, her silence intensifies his wanton thoughts and gives her a special grace. He believes—without any proof, any evidence—that if they were to become lovers, she would be the death of boredom. Leading her through the tall grass, he stops at a mossy spot not far from the river. They stand looking at each other. She smiles. He asks if he can undress her. She agrees. As he slowly removes her clothes and her bracelets, she tells him the history of each. Lovely in her nakedness, she kneels and waits for him to become Adam to her Eve. She teases him, and he enjoys it, not entering her until he has played all the chords on her sensuous body, and tasted her tongue and the liquor that miraculously flows from her vaginal lips.

darkmatters
LEVITT

Marty

The day shone clear as rain drops. I meandered down one of the paths to smell the damp woods and nearly stepped on a quail and her chicks that blended in with the plants. A great blue heron circled overhead and disappeared. Then the largest fowls of all came down the path: Ben and Esperanza. Her hair, which she normally wore in a braid, hung loosely about her shoulders. Showing no embarrassment and making no attempt to hide their feelings for one another, they cleaved so tightly that I knew they had consecrated their unbridgeable differences by transubstantiating the idea into flesh.

Returning to Hanover late at night, we found a Western Union telegram, addressed to us both, lying ominously on the dining room table. Ben lit a kerosene lamp, opened the letter, and blanched.

"Well, what does it say?" I asked impatiently, harboring fond thoughts of Abby and hoping her condition had continued to improve.

"Come immediately! The situation has taken a turn for the worse. Love, Abby."

"Darn!" I exclaimed, fickle as a sail in the wind, one second worried about Abby, the next wishing to wring her neck. "She doesn't even have the presence of mind to tell us what's up. Is she dying? Is Clarissa all right? Christ, you'd have to be a mind reader to know what the damned telegram means. But that's Abby! I guess I should try to reach her."

Given the hour and the time difference between New Mexico and Kentucky, I waited till morning; by then the post office had opened, and we had a good idea of why Abby had wired. Mrs. Fernandez, an old woman with a bent back and a salacious turn of mind, sorted and distributed the

darkmatters
LEVITT

mail. She handed Ben a letter from, of all people, Mrs. Roberta C. Stanton. The postmistress said that it had arrived on Friday, the day we had left.

"Maybe the mother . . . she want you!" said Mrs. Fernandez with a wink and twist of her hips.

The miners had either heard about, met, or seen Clarissa Stanton. In fact, they called her "Ben's woman." So it came as no surprise to hear the postmistress crack jokes about Clarissa's mom.

Ben devoured the letter and painfully remarked, "Yes, indeed, Mrs. Stanton wants me—out of the picture."

Perhaps in some cases it would be better if our communications miscarried. The letter, which eventually came to me as the executor of Ben's estate, lies before me now as a reminder that in our words can be read the soul's dark cottage.

darkmatters
LEVITT

Mrs. Stanton

September 10, 1952
Dear Mr. Cohen,

Having approached the bishop and been rebuffed, I have decided to take matters into my own hands and to address you directly. Lest you wonder, Clarissa has no knowledge of my writing this letter. Although I am well aware of the French proverb—Il faut laver son linge sale en famille—I think it necessary to speak openly not only about the sordidness that has recently come to my attention, but also about my daughter's conduct and character, as well as your own.

From someone in Boulder, I have learned of Clarissa's abortion. From an old friend in Silver City, I have heard about your left-wing activities and your "friendship" with a Mexican-American woman. I conclude from this information that you are a felon, against whom I could bring charges, but won't because I don't wish to implicate my daughter in the "back-street operation." I must also conclude that you don't love Clarissa enough to share a child with her, and that you exploited her merely for what you could get. Your sexual plundering is equalled in evil only by your political opinions. I'm not sure which I abhor more. But I am sure that such a person would be abhorrent to me as a son-in-law.

Yes, I know what you are thinking: that I am a DAR fossil, a relic. Samuel Johnson can say that patriotism is the last refuge of a scoundrel, but frankly I am proud of my patriotism and love of country. Unlike you, I do not harbor thoughts of revolution. I live in the greatest country in the world. If you think you don't, try the Soviet Union for a while. The experience will bring you to your senses—if you survive it!

What neither you nor my daughter could ever survive would be a marriage to one another. She is a passionate girl who lets her feelings overrule her mind. Although she appears to be open to all possibilities— the wilder the better, it would seem—she abandons them at the first hurdle. Her taste for adventure outruns her discipline. She is also willful, as I am; she must have her way and therefore will never be happy married to a man of strong character. Yes, I grant you that: you know your mind and you readily say what's on it. Clarissa will eventually resent being eclipsed. Her only talents that you cannot aspire to are her social graces. In every other regard, from what I could see during your stay at our house, you will have the upper hand. Clarissa needs to marry a man she can dominate, a man who will praise her frailties and cherish her modest accomplishments. You are too "european" to indulge her every whim.

If you think you can change her, I would advise you against it. She does not like to face problems. If she did, she would long ago have recognized that her father and I spoiled her terribly, with the result that she is fundamentally immature and selfish. (I told you I would be direct.) Clarissa desperately wants to grow up but won't do what it takes. She remains a child, running from responsibility. Being an adult means building a life from clay, not dreams. Most marriages involve repetition and boredom. Clarissa would never put her head in that harness. She wants to be pampered. Any task that fails to bring immediate pleasure or praise, she abandons. Except for horseback riding and some silly kinds of dancing, she has quit every other endeavor: piano lessons, art classes, French lessons, the swimming team, tennis, ice skating, ballet. The single-mindedness that I saw you exhibit during your visit here makes you utterly unsuitable for her.

Believe me, I am doing you a favor when I tell you that Clarissa will not make a good wife. She will be a disappointment to you; and you will be a torment to her because you will disapprove of her aimlessness.

Her father and I would prefer that she not return to Boulder. She is twenty years old and has already spent more time in college than most girls her age. It is time that she marries. Whatever her sins, we love her deeply and hope to make a good match for her here.

Trusting that you will accept this letter as a candid expression of a mother's concerns, I will not take kindly to any continued interest you show in my daughter.

Sincerely yours,
Roberta C. Stanton

darkmatters
LEVITT

Marty

Estranged by Esperanza's catholicism and Clarissa's mother, Ben found himself in love with two women, but prevented from marrying either. Although he and Esperanza were political and amorous soulmates, he often remarked that he could not free himself of Clarissa's attractions, the memory of which haunted his days. Torn, Ben wanted to drive to Lexington but was unwilling to give up the cause—and Esperanza—in Hanover.

Trying to find some impartial means of deciding, I said, "Let's ask Joe if we're needed. If he says yes, we stay. Fair enough?"

Ben reluctantly agreed, no doubt wondering whether the uncertainty in Hanover was preferable to the one in Lexington. At the union office, we found Joe seated at his desk amid a blizzard of papers hunting-and-pecking on his Remington relic. We pulled up two folding chairs and sat down. Ben explained that a delicate matter had come up, and asked if his absence would cause Local 890 any hardship.

"If you want my candid opinion," said Joe, lighting a cigarette, "there's nothing more that can be done on the ground. The fight is now going to be fought in the courts."

"That'll take dough. I can help raise it."

"Mine, Mill will shoulder the expense."

"I'll be back. It has to do with Clarissa. Normally—"

Joe interrupted. "Go! But take my advice," he scoffed, with a wave of his hand. "Women! They'll put you in the pussy trap every time. Just look at Luis."

Ben and I, utterly nonplussed, exchanged glances.

"What do you know about him?" Ben asked suspiciously.

darkmatters
LEVITT

"Never mind. His name just popped into my head." Joe shuffled some papers and kept his head down, refusing to make eye contact with us. "Well, like I said," he remarked to no one in particular, "we'll be holed up in court. There's really nothing you can do for the next couple of weeks. We know Hyperion's strategy, and they probably know ours. It's a standoff. Writing a few leaflets or letters won't help us now." He turned back to the papers on his desk.

On the side of a filing cabinet that abutted his desk, Joe had hung a handsome framed reproduction of a painting called "Garantías." As I stared, he remarked:

"It comes from Mexico. Nice, eh? You know who painted the original?" Ben interrupted.

"Joe, tell me about those FBI photographs of you in Mexico."

"Did you see them yourself? How do you know they didn't superimpose a picture of me on a Mexican background?"

"Did they?"

Joe opened the bottom drawer of his battered desk. I expected him to remove some document proving his innocence; but instead he removed a bottle of cheap Scotch, took a swig, and offered us the bottle, which we declined. Drawing deeply on his cigarette, he trailed the smoke out of his mouth as he spoke. "Better I tell you than some fink. We have important contacts in Mexico. We needed a go-between . . . a native. We knew that Luis had a girlfriend in Hermosillo. Sweeties cost money. We approached him about being a mule . . . carrying messages between here and there. He agreed. I accompanied him so that he could get the hang of things. Sometime during that period, the FBI snapped the pictures."

"He also has a girlfriend south of here, at a hacienda," I added.

"That's his business!" snapped Joe, suddenly unfriendly.

"Who's the 'we' you keep talking about?"

Joe extinguished his cigarette and lit another. "Really now, Ben, you can't be serious," he said, exhaling a plume of smoke through his nose.

Ben sat a moment, reached over and opened the bottom drawer of Joe's desk, swigged his cheap whiskey, handed Joe the bottle, and said, "I believe in Mine-Mill's cause . . . don't fuck it up with your Trotsky politics."

Joe glared out of rageful eyes.

"Is that how you got the minutes to the closed meeting—from one of your own operatives in the union?"

"If we can make common cause with our brothers across the border," said Joe, returning the bottle to the drawer, "we'll have the start of a North-American movement."

"For Chrissake, Joe," Ben fumed, "can't we just feed our friends here without you thinking in terms of a continental revolution!"

"There's strength in numbers."

"You don't care a shit for the individual. All you care about are the marching masses."

"If you mean some will die—" Joe broke off and stared at Ben blankly, as if his meaning was self-evident.

Ben leaned on the desk and snapped: "That's where you and I part company. I'm not prepared to sacrifice the few for the many."

Joe snuffed out his cigarette and lit another. "The blood of the few fertilizes the fields of plenty."

"That's what Mussolini said. You would have been right at home among the thugs."

Narrowing his eyes, Joe hissed, "Two of my uncles died in Spain fighting Franco and the fascists."

"Then you should know better," replied Ben.

I sat there remembering how Joe had often upbraided Ben for not being radical enough, and decided that Ben was now paying him back. Although Ben refrained from trotting out his own family credentials, the conversation felt as much personal as theoretical.

"I think it's best that you leave," said Joe. "Like I told you, we're entering a new phase of the struggle."

Ben took hold of Joe's over-flowing ashtray. For an instant I worried he would do something impetuous, but he just emptied it into a wastepaper basket, with the cryptic comment, "Don't grind up people's bones to make bread," and went out the door.

I wanly said goodbye and followed behind. As we walked back to the Bejel house, Ben uttered only one word: *govnaw*, which in Russian means shit.

Gathering our belongings and packing the car took less than an hour. The Bejels hastily summoned friends and neighbors for a farewell get-together. Esperanza, refusing to participate in the public parting, asked Ben to see her later so that they could take leave of each other in their own quiet way. But first we celebrated with the Bejels and other friends, eating and drinking, reminiscing, and swearing oaths of eternal loyalty.

darkmatters LEVITT

Ben

Ben agonizes about leaving Hanover for Lexington. How can he walk away from a fight he believes in and from Esperanza? Shouldn't he wait to see what develops? He rationalizes that the strike is at an impasse and will continue indefinitely. Esperanza, he keeps reminding himself, is married, not only to Luis but also to religious ideas that he would find a constant irritant. And Lexington augurs an obligatory scene, one that all the previous acts in the play have led up to. Though he has no legal claims on Clarissa, they have shared the greatest intimacies and sadnesses, have bonded their different petrols to form a single element that, even if unstable, contains their fractious love. The occasion calls for a conclusion, one way or another.

His parting with Joe convinces him that Joe has been using the strike for his own purposes. He doubts that he and Joe will ever be close again, and walks away troubled about the seeming impossibility of a revolution that embraces justice for all.

The miners, with very little notice, throw Marty and Ben a farewell party. Esperanza stays away. Ben goes next door and finds her telling her beads. She is sitting at the kitchen table, in front of a small wooden *santo*: an image of the Madonna with a votary candle. She is speaking Spanish. Ben watches. He knows that she has heard him enter the house. Without greeting him, she goes to a drawer and removes a small silver crucifix strung on an old shoelace. Wordlessly, she places the string around his neck and buries her face in his chest. He can feel the sobs convulsing her body. Taking her face in his hands, he looks into her pooling eyes and wipes the tears as they flow down her cheeks. He moves his mouth towards her,

dark matters **LEVITT**

intending to kiss her gently, but she seizes him and pulls his head down to hers and devours his lips and tongue.

Pulling him to the floor, she embraces him so tightly that he thinks of a winding sheet. She intends nothing sexual; she chastely holds him to her, reversing their positions. This time she holds his head against her breast. He can smell the lavender she laves herself with and knows that if he doesn't extricate himself, they will make love. The Bejels expect him, and the Morales's house is wide open. If they lock the door and pull down the shades, everyone will know. Suspicions are one thing, proof another.

Several minutes go by; he says he must leave. She whimpers and bites her lower lip, all the time intensely studying his face. The feverish moment passes. She stands and straightens her dress.

"Buy a nice chain for the cross."

"I will," he says, squeezing her hands.

She hangs back as he returns to the Bejel house.

darkmatters
LEVITT

Marty

As he left Esperanza, I caught a glimpse of her face, swollen from crying.

"Let's go," he mumbled and gave me a nudge. "It's time. There's no more to be said." Bidding friends farewell, Ben and I had to push through the tide of guests.

In the car, we sat for a spell while well-wishers leaned through the open windows and continued to pump our hands. As the car began moving, Ben saw me glance back.

"She won't come out. She doesn't want to be seen."

The old DeSoto moved down the road and people waved. It struck me that though we had tried to help, the vast money and power of Hyperion would finally defeat the miners in court. Only the triumph of the women at the end mitigated our sadness. Looking into the side-view mirror, I saw Esperanza emerge from her house. She stood erect, her black hair loose, swirling around her face in the wind. Just before we passed out of sight, she slowly raised her right arm and waved adios.

Among Ben's personal papers, along with Mrs. Stanton's letter, I found this note from Esperanza, sent to Ben's Brooklyn address and dated the same day that we had left Hanover. "If God in His goodness gives me a child, I want you to return to drink from my nursing breasts. Then I'll always be part of you, not just a memory."

darkmatters LEVITT

Ben

The drive to Lexington takes them through Texas, where one town introduces itself with a sign spanning the road. "We have the blackest soil and the whitest people." Although hungry, Marty and Ben agree that they'll starve rather than eat there. On the eastern side of town, a brass plaque mounted in stone thanks visitors for stopping. They stop, but not as the town fathers had hoped. Ben urinates on the sign, and they continue. Passing through Oklahoma and Arkansas, they drive well into the night, stopping at Memphis. The next day they drive to Nashville and north to Lexington, arriving about three. Checking them into a flea-bag motel, Ben uses the outdoor phone booth and telephones the Stanton house. Fortunately, Clarissa answers. He tells her that they have just rented a flop in a dive in downtown Lexington, and she explains that if Brian were not occupying the last free room, the one over the garage, he and Marty could have stayed there. She says that the house looks like an infirmary.

"Abby's still weak. Brian's derrière is killing him; a horse threw him. And Daddy is using a cane because of his lumbago."

The Stanton house has indeed become a caravansary for the sick, both physically and mentally.

As they make their way to "the house on the hill," Ben points out the natural beauty and historical landmarks. The rolling green countryside, home to horses that shine in the sun, had so impressed itself upon Ben on his first trip to Lexington that he now brings the car to a halt to admire the verdant land. On their arrival, Clarissa bolts from the house and throws herself into Ben's arms.

darkmatters
LEVITT

"Did you miss me? Did you miss me?" she cries. "Because I have been *desolée* without you."

Whether or not she realizes it, the French diction undercuts her sincerity. Straining for a continental effect, she says, "*Estoy encantando de que estis aqum.*" Even her tone of voice, slightly lacquered, wants candor. Taking Ben by the hand, she skips toward the front door, just as Abby emerges, dressed in a pink robe and plaid slippers. Through tears she says simply, "You're here!"

After affectionate hugs and kisses, they enter the foyer, with its ceramic stand for umbrellas and walking sticks. But before they proceed any further, Ben stops.

"What's the matter?" asks Clarissa.

"Does your mother know?"

"That you're coming? Yes."

"I don't want to set her off."

"Pshaw!" she replies affectedly, with a toss of her head. "Mother wouldn't dare! To the contrary, she's anxious to see you."

This last statement rings false, an impression that Abby confirms when she whispers to Marty that Clarissa and her mother have struck a deal: Mrs. Stanton will treat Ben politely if Clarissa agrees to keep an open mind about his serious failings.

True to her bargain, Mrs. Stanton greets them warmly.

"You'll stay for dinner, of course," says Mrs. Stanton. "We have a lovely roast and baked potatoes. Clarissa, you see to the wine."

Turning on her heels, Mrs. Stanton vanishes down the hall.

Clarissa remarks a little too cutely, "I hate pot-roasty. But tomorrow we'll eat at the club. They serve the most divine brunches. There's to be a reception for the Wellingtons, who have just returned from their honeymoon. Melinda Farnsworth, who married Richard Wellington, went to boarding school with me. We're the same age, and she's already married. I guess I'm just destined to remain an old maid. If you'd like to join me in the wine cellar, Ben, we could be utterly indecent."

Ben never likes seeing her posture, and therefore declines, causing Clarissa to go off in a funk.

Ben has the feeling someone is missing, and realizes that Brian has yet to appear. Turning to Abby, Ben asks, "Where's Brian?"

Mr. Stanton, hobbling down the long, carpeted stairway that gracefully sweeps to the upper story, answers Ben's question. "He's gone to the airport to fetch his father."

"Sore butt and all," Abby interjects.

"Well, you're not going to stand here in the hall, are you? Let's have a drink. I'm Alden Stanton," he says, extending his hand to Marty. "You always slouch, young man?"

He catches Marty by surprise. "Well . . . yes . . . I guess so." Rallying, Marty replies, "As a matter of fact, as a child my parents sent me to a woman to take posture lessons."

"Ben, how are you?" he says, having lost interest in Marty.

"Pretty well, sir."

"I heard you had a nasty blow to the head?"

"My sight goes blurry from time to time."

"Did you see a doctor?"

"I didn't."

"You can see ours. I'll arrange it."

"It can wait till I'm home."

"I'd feel better if you checked it out."

darkmatters
LEVITT

Marty

Ben had warned me that our reception in the Stanton house would be hostile. But nothing could have been further from the truth. Mrs. Stanton greeted us politely, and her husband seemed genuinely glad to see Ben, embracing him warmly. Mr. Stanton's friendliness made him both attractive and pitiable. He sounded truly anxious about Ben's health, and it struck me as touching and sad that Ben wasn't more concerned about his concern. I suppose Ben had his guard up. But apparently Mr. Stanton failed to notice and began reminiscing about their having gone riding together.

"This damn lumbago," he growled. "It keeps me grounded. Just as soon as I'm feeling fit, the two of us will saddle up and ride a few miles. What do you say to that?"

Ben weakly smiled. "Yeah, that would be nice."

The den, furnished in leather chairs and a couch, and hung with pictures of horses, had the feel of an elegant, private club at a track. A few items, however, appeared out of place: a large wooden rocking horse, at least four feet high, a handsome mahogany table, with toy soldiers in Union and Rebel uniforms facing one another, and, next to the table, a map on an easel depicting the Battle of Shiloh. I gravitated toward the table, which upon closer inspection I discovered had a colored battlefield engraved into its surface.

"A new hobby," said Mr. Stanton. "Since I've been housebound with this damn pain in my lower back, I've been reading some military history and decided to recreate the moves in that infernal but wonderful battle."

"Who won?" I asked stupidly.

"The South, of course," replied Mr. Stanton.

"I apologize. I know very little about the Civil War."

He scowled. "You mean the War of Northern Aggression."

I dropped the subject, but Ben foolishly pursued it until Mr. Stanton proclaimed:

"You can change the law but you can't change my heart. No black man is my equal."

"Not even Frederick Douglass? Not Paul Robeson?"

"The first comes from mixed blood and the second's a damned red!"

With Mr. Stanton in no mood to be gainsaid, Ben eased his way out of the incipient tangle by saying: "I really don't think you feel that way about Negroes. I see the way you treat Eliza Samuels. She's one of the family."

"She lives in the carriage house. And furthermore she's not black, she's a high yaller."

I thought: what the hell is that? Ben told me later.

Suddenly changing his mood, Mr. Stanton exclaimed, "All this talking has worked me into a sweat. It's post time. Call out your drinks and I'll mix them."

Ben, I noted, did not ask for a bourbon and Seven Up, but rather a shot of Scotch. Abby requested a Coke, and I took a beer.

"I see, Ben, we're the only serious drinkers around here," Mr. Stanton teased, as he poured himself three fingers of rye over ice. "Here's mud in your eye!"

As he tossed his head back and swallowed his drink, Abby tugged at my elbow and nodded that I should follow her to the other side of the room. "Just want to show Marty the Stanton family photographs," Abby explained. Mr. Stanton looked pleased.

Out of their hearing, Abby whispered, "Brian's buying her."

"Clarissa?"

"No, Mrs. Stanton."

"I don't follow."

"Waterford crystal. Bone china. Gorham silver. Presents, he said, for her generosity."

I couldn't help but chuckle.

"Almost 24,000 killed," Mr. Stanton's voice boomed, "is no laughing matter."

"Maybe he really has a yen for her mother."

"A sacrilege, really. All that killing around the wilderness church of Shiloh."

"I hate to say it but Clarissa, for all her attempts to be different, wants the same thing as her mother."

"Waterford crystal?"

"No, money!"

"The Yankees had their backsides kicked good," said Mr. Stanton, "but at no little cost to the Confederate forces. Which only proves that in war, just as much as in life, everything has its price."

Abby, no radical herself, sounded sincerely disturbed by Clarissa's acquiescence. "She goes along just to get along."

"Stoneham's ghost," I murmured. "Views that are not consonant with those of the majority are unwelcome."

"What?"

"Never mind."

Abby's S.O.S. letter issued from her worry that Clarissa would not be able to withstand her mother's blandishments on behalf of Brian. She truly had Ben's interest at heart. Whether she resented Brian's having jettisoned her for Clarissa, and having done so right under her nose, I couldn't tell. Her motivation, however, interested me less than her information. Clarissa had tried to escape her mother's influence by leaving Lexington for places like Boulder and Hanover, as she herself often repeated. But Abby had discovered that once out of Ben's orbit and under the Stanton roof, she let the spell of summer magic—river rides, country clubs, horses, and gelt—turn her head. For all her desire to be independent, the Stanton vaccination had taken. Call it protective coloration, call it respect for her family, call it a love of luxury, the apple had fallen not far from the tree. At least, that's how Abby represented the situation.

"There's something else I have to tell you," she whispered.

"What's that?"

"My bedroom window faces the carriage house. I could swear . . . though I'm not sure . . ."

"If you're not sure how can you swear?"

"Let me finish and you'll understand why."

"I'm listening."

"Mr. Stanton . . . at least it looks like him . . . he sneaks into the carriage house some nights."

I just stared at Abby, who emphatically nodded several times.

Next to the family photographs on the wall hung a handsomely framed genealogical tree. Mrs. Stanton traced her family back to some English village called Belstone. In 1710, her forebears had landed in Virginia. I ungenerously wondered if they had fled England to escape punishment for thievery. Mr. Stanton's paternal line had come to America from England in the 19th century, the same period that his mother's line had come from Germany. I pondered my own beginnings and knew only that my grandmother's father had been a scribe in Poland, copying the Torah by hand in a fine calligraphy. Whenever I peer at his picture, which hangs in my study, I see not only a bearded man dressed in a prayer shawl and yarmulke, but also a worn scrivener—and the hardness of repetitive labors. Come to think of it, he too had a slouch.

After drinks, we listened to Mr. Stanton relishing every detail of that long-ago killing field. "The country is undulating table-land. The bluffs rise to the height of one hundred and fifty feet above the alluvial. As you can see from my model, three principal streams and numerous tributaries run through the area occupied by the army; also a number of deep ravines intersect, making it the worst possible battleground." His description would undoubtedly have continued had not a stunningly beautiful black woman entered the room and announced that dinner would shortly be served.

"Just give me a minute, Eliza," said Mr. Stanton, and continued. "Did I tell you about the rivers?" he asked rhetorically. "Well, the principal streams are Lick Creek, which empties into the Tennessee, and Owl Creek, which rises near the source of Lick Creek and flows southeast, encircling the battlefield, and feeds into Snake Creek."

From afar, a dinner bell rang.

"We'll get back to this later," said Mr. Stanton, a promise that I hoped he would break.

We marched into the dining room, where the table glittered with wealth. Abby whispered, "I told you so," a statement that I took to mean that the settings had been purchased by Brian. Mr. Stanton sat at one end of the table and his wife at the other. Ben and I flanked Mrs. Stanton, so the arrangement was boy-girl, with Abby on my right and Clarissa on Ben's left. So, had I not excused myself between courses to use the bathroom, I would not have seen what I did. Stopping before reentering the dining-room to check that my fly was buttoned, I could see everyone at the table, though they couldn't see me. Eliza, standing next to Mr. Stanton, leaned over to clear Abby's plate. He ran his hand up Eliza's leg and under her skirt, causing her to buck ever so slightly, but she never uttered a word. I waited till she had left the room before I resumed my place at the table. Mrs. Stanton began talking about "good stock." At first, I thought she meant animals, but it quickly became apparent that she had people in mind.

"The Hoffmeisters recently returned from Vienna, where their son Benedict married into a very prominent family, the Franks. This noon, Sally Schmidt called to say that the Lebens' daughter Judith plans to marry Arthur Wessell. That attachment ought to be worth millions. But the shocking news involves Dr. Lippensuck!"

"Mother, please!" Clarissa appealed. "Our guests have no idea who these people are and care less."

"Well," Mrs. Stanton indignantly replied, "you and Abby should care. He's our family physician. How many times has he seen Abby? Five? Six?"

Clarissa sighed.

"To continue," she said, making no attempt to hide her annoyance, "the good doctor was found in compromising circumstances with one of the nurses."

"What's that mean?" asked Abby.

"*That!*" said Mrs. Stanton censoriously, "cannot be discussed in polite company. The only thing that can be said for Dr. Lippensuck is that at least he chose a *white* nurse."

I stole a glance at Mr. Stanton, but he never moved a muscle.

Irrepressible Abby cried, "The old buzzard . . . I didn't think he had it in him. Well, hip-hip for him."

"Abigail," Mrs. Stanton said starchly, "in this part of the country we do not encourage that kind of behavior, at least not in my family. Men are beastly enough, without being encouraged."

I marveled that Mrs. Stanton had even broached the subject, given her sense of propriety, and couldn't help speculating whether the Stantons had had conjugal relations since the birth of Clarissa. To hear her talk, you might have concluded that they made love only once.

"A number of Bricknells"—I took that to be Mrs. Stanton's maiden name—"studied theology at Yale and Princeton. They returned to the south and border states to spread the gospel."

Ben stared at his plate.

"Their wives were Christian saints."

"Mother," said Clarissa, "not now, some other time."

"I know of no subject more important than family," Mrs. Stanton scolded.

Trying to ingratiate myself with Clarissa's mom, I paraphrased the Kabbalah. "We are all part of the same family, with our roots in the spiritual world."

Instead of gaining her favor, I unintentionally invited the subject of religion.

"I want to read something to you." She went to the sideboard and returned with a scrapbook. "While sorting through some family papers, I came across this obituary. When my great grandmother Lily Mae died, December 26, 1889, of what they called in those days brain fever, here's what the local paper had to say. 'She became a Christian in her childhood and leaves a record for zeal for her Savior unsurpassed. She found no time for earthly pleasures, but took great delight in God's house. Some two weeks before her death, she had a vision of Heaven and her parents there and firmly believed she was called to go. No reasoning or pleading with her could change her view in the least. She made all her plans, even to her funeral arrangements. She constantly hummed "Tis So Sweet to Trust in Jesus." When those at her bedside sang "Jesus, Lover of My Soul," even in her delirium, she could sing the alto. And when her voice gave out, she pointed to her heart and then to Heaven, with a sweet smile on her face.' That's the sort of stock that *I* come from!"

The statement had the feel of a challenge. Certainly I knew better than to take the field against a Christian saint, and hoped that Ben shared my feelings. Apparently he did, because he said nothing. But Mrs. Stanton now used my comment as a means to introduce the subject of bloodlines. Pursing her lips in a thin smile, she said to Ben, "And from whence come your people? What are their roots?"

Ben had already told her in their first war of words that Jesus was Jewish, so what would he do for an encore?

"Mrs. Stanton," he said softly, "you have an admirable family."

"They descend from Robert the Bruce!" she added with evident pleasure.

"Let me tell you about another admirable family. Their name is Perez, and they go back to fifteenth-century Spain, where they held an important place in the Jewish community. Forced to become Catholics, they practiced their faith in secret, for hundreds of years, until they thought of

darkmatters
LEVITT

themselves as Catholics, though they still observed Jewish customs. Such people are called marranos. I met one in New Mexico . . . a friend of mine's grandmother. So when you ask me where my people come from, I have to answer that they come from the Bible and also from Spain and New Mexico. My guess is that most everyone has a trace of Jewish blood in his veins."

Mrs. Stanton, drawing herself up in her chair, raised her chin and uttered a snide comment that festered for the rest of our days in Lexington. "You undoubtedly heard that rubbish from your Mex!"

Ben

At dinner, their first night in Lexington, Mrs. Stanton dredges up her family history. Her motives seem transparent. She doesn't think Ben has the pedigree to marry her daughter. But Ben has the feeling that Mrs. Stanton is working up to some disclosure. He tries to avoid any disagreements, but when she persists on talking about lineage, he tells the table about the Perez family and their Jewish antecedents in Spain. Mrs. Stanton leans back in her chair and straightens her back. Ben can sense the coming whirlwind. It strikes, though from an unexpected quarter. She alludes to Esperanza as Ben's "Mexican lady friend." Ben's first reaction, strangely, is not to defend himself, but to ponder who could have told her. To escape from the oppressive conversation, he leaves the table. Clarissa follows him out into the garden. They sit in one of the gazebos, surrounded by a profusion of yellow, red, blue, and pink flowers, an intoxicating bouquet so different from the miasma found in the Stanton dining room.

"Ben, I am so sorry. Mother promised me she'd behave. I don't know where in the world she got the idea that you . . . in fact, I don't even know who she's talking about. Can you tell me?"

"Never mind."

"But I do mind."

"Gossip, that's all."

"You make it sound as if there is someone else."

"Have I asked you about Brian? People have a right to their lives."

"Ask me. I'll tell you anything you want to know. Have I been sleeping with him, no! Now, who is this so-called Mexican lady friend?"

Her dark eyes radiate a desire to know. She takes Ben's hand. "You can tell me."

"There's nothing to tell."

"I won't be angry. We've been through a great deal together. We shouldn't have secrets."

"It could be any number of women."

"Women, plural? I don't understand."

"We worked with the women pickets. I was friendly with a great many of them, as you know."

"But apparently with one more than the others."

"Well, I did collaborate on a script with Esperanza Morales, but I wrote you about that."

Clarissa's eyes, though dark, mysteriously illuminate her face. Ben has often thought they radiate a devilish glow that he finds immensely attractive. In her pensive moments, her eyes shine all the brighter, as if an internal furnace is heating her thoughts.

"Have you ever made love to her?"

"That's an indiscreet question."

"When does it become discreet, when we're married?"

Ben thinks of Ben Franklin's line, "Honesty is the best policy," well aware of Franklin's meaning: bad policy, though sometimes necessary, rests on dissimulation.

Clarissa impatiently says, "I'm afraid I have my answer."

"No, you don't."

"Every gigolo, every skirt chaser, would like to take cover under the defense of discreetness. Why do you persist in being so secretive? I hate it, because your silence makes me think you have something to hide—and then I think terrible things."

Ben remembers that Inky once blabbed to some of the fellows that Ben and Eileen had been making love under the Coney Island boardwalk. In no time, everyone knew, including Eileen's parents. The hurt felt not only by Eileen but also by her mother and father taught him that silence never betrays. Feeling her eyes boring in on him, he says that he's tired and that his head hurts. Neither excuse is true, but he finds it hard to escape her burning glance, and to turn away would be an admission of guilt.

"I'll just go back to the motel for a while."

darkmatters
LEVITT

"You can't simply leave," she says. "Mother would be insulted. Your absence would just provide her with an excuse to berate you."

Ben dryly laughs. "If I stay or leave she dislikes me. At least at a distance, I don't have to hear her."

"She's not all bad, you know. She does care for me."

"Yes, I know. I'm not good enough for you . . . and maybe she's right."

"That's crap! I won't hear you say such a thing."

Taking Ben by the arm, she leads him back to the house. He loves it when her willfulness is exercised on his behalf, but resents it when she uses it in the service of herself. Perhaps, then, he is the selfish one, and not she?

Marty

After Ben left, we all sat dumbly until Mr. Stanton reminded us that the menu included a delicious dessert. But before it could be served, Clarissa excused herself and went to find him. During their absence, I asked Abby about her health, having had little opportunity till now. She looked drawn and thin.

"The tick fever put my system into a state of collapse. My eyes couldn't focus and my head swam. All from a goddamned bug!"

"Please, Abigail! The use of bad language shows a want of vocabulary."

I could only shake my head in amusement. The old lady embodied all the Victorian values, but you had to give her credit for being able to turn a phrase. If my postal colleagues could use words as she did, I'd die from verbal richness. She certainly had her own way of speaking.

Abby took Mrs. Stanton's criticisms in good spirit. She neither argued with her nor complained. I could see why. Underlying the old lady's snobbery stood certain truths that in a different context would be hard to deny. Family *did* matter; so too does upbringing. Differences invite comparison, and Mrs. Stanton came from a family steeped in tradition, whereas Ben and I were virtually just off the boat.

The door opened and Ben and Clarissa returned. Mr. Stanton teased him into a smile.

"I knew you'd be back when you heard we were having homemade chocolate syrup over vanilla ice cream. Eliza's specialty."

"It's true. I can't keep away from chocolate."

"Me, too," said Mr. Stanton. Had he intended his reply to be ironic?

Mrs. Stanton said nothing for a minute or two. But clearly she had a burr in her saddle. She alluded to Ben's and my having worked with

darkmatters
LEVITT

women strikers in a tone of "and we all know what that means!"

Clarissa sharply rebuked her mother. "I don't want to hear any more about Mexican lady friends. Besides, I don't believe a word of it!" But Clarissa didn't have to wait overlong to discover what was gnawing at her mother, because Mrs. Stanton soon showed her hand.

As we finished our ice cream, Brian and his father, Willard Hazelwood, returned from the airport. Mrs. Stanton used the occasion of their entrance to wax enthusiastic.

"Oh, Brian, you're such a brave soldier to meet your father's plane and bring the good gentleman here, given your injury and pain. Mr. Hazelwood, so nice to meet you!"

Once we had all shaken hands and introduced ourselves, Brian handed Mrs. Stanton a gift-wrapped box. "A further token of my family's esteem and gratitude," he said, and encouraged her to open it in front of her guests.

Having arrived empty-handed, Ben and I looked like cheapskates. When the present turned out to be an antique Paul Revere silver bowl, we looked like double pikers. Needless to say, Mrs. Stanton thanked Brian with love moans and madrigals.

"You sweet boy! Kindness and consideration are your middle names. You are a true son of the South. My own flesh and blood have never treated me better."

Her orgasm spent, she invited the two men to join us for dessert. Mr. Hazelwood, who asked us to call him Willard, had arrived wearing a panama suit and hat, with a pale blue tie. A tall, thin man, he had a bald streak that he covered by combing his hair back to front and side to side. Except for that amusing peculiarity, his appearance was unexceptional, though he did constantly fidget with his wire-rimmed glasses, as if he couldn't quite get the focus right. A studious and well-spoken fellow, he differed from his son in every regard. Brian, dressed in blue cotton slacks, loafers, and a yellow sports shirt, acted like his usual fatuous self. Mrs. Stanton insisted that he sit on a pillow and sent Eliza to fetch one. He remarked, "All the comforts of home," a statement that led me to wonder who cushioned his ass in Delaware.

The dessert finished, Mr. Stanton suggested that the gentlemen take their coffee and brandy in the den, where he could smoke a "pure Habana in peace." The women remained at the table. Pouring us each a brandy, he passed around a cigar box filled with the most aromatic cigars I've ever sniffed. Messrs. Stanton and Hazelwood lit up, immediately befogging the room. Proudly showing Willard the table and toy soldiers, Mr. Stanton couldn't resist a few logistical comments. "The Confederates' greatest mistake lay in driving Grant toward the river instead of away from it."

Mr. Stanton's voice droned on, but I stopped listening as I sipped my brandy. While the two men took their ease in the leather parlor chairs, we exchanged airy remarks about the weather and the hotshot Kentucky basketball team and the ponies, until Ben asked Willard the name of the chemical company he represented.

"D and P Chemical."

"Isn't that the company that did business with I.G. Farben, the infamous gas-chamber people?"

Emily Post would not advise you to ask such a question if you're desirous of comporting yourself well in company. Every time I traveled with Ben, he bowled over some guy with a show-stopping question. I say "guy" because he behaved differently with women. Although he would argue with anyone, he loved the company of women and would push them, as he often remarked, "only to the point of seriousness." I knew what he meant: that most women had been taught to defer to men and therefore feigned vacuity by larding their discourse with silliness. He believed that they had equally good minds and should use them. My own experience has taught me that in matters of reading, women are far more serious than men, who often regard novels and poetry as fit only for sissies. Since women do most of the child rearing, their affection for literature is probably a blessing in disguise.

Ben's question ended the social patter, as Mr. Hazelwood explained his position.

"I joined the company at the end of the war. They had already severed their contacts with Farben. But you're right to mention it. Those were bleak days." He sipped his brandy. "We should never have been helping the Nazis' war effort. Mussolini, on the other hand, is a horse of a different color."

"Really?" said Mr. Stanton, now genuinely interested in the conversation. "I always lumped him and Hitler together."

"Most people do, but it's a misreading of the times."

Ben narrowed his sights for the kill.

"Surely," he said, "you don't condone the gassing of thousands of Ethiopians and the aerial bombing of those poor people?!"

"Ethiopia," replied Willard, "was Mussolini's one great blunder. He loathed Hitler, you know, but had to turn to him because of the debacle in Ethiopia. That proved the turning point. Even his mistress had warned him against his African adventure."

"How do you know that?" Ben asked civilly but skeptically.

"During the thirties, I worked for OAS in Rome, stationed in the American embassy. Margherita Sarfatti, Mussolini's mistress, and Jewish I might add, took money from us for certain information."

"Hearst paid her—and Mussolini as well," said Ben, "for writing a lot of crap in his crappy newspapers."

"True, but you know that she fled Italy for South America when Hitler forced Mussolini to introduce race laws. My point is simply that Mussolini had no stomach for gassing political opponents or Jews or anyone else. He wanted a well-run state and abridged some liberties to get it."

"You sound as if you admire the man," Ben said, his tone of voice clearly staking out his own anti-position.

"His form of fascism, syndicalism, had a great many adherents in America."

I couldn't help but notice that Mr. Hazelwood had not cast his reply in the first person.

"Sure," said Ben, "they saw it as a way to suppress the labor unions."

"Well, you must admit, Mussolini eliminated strikes and made the trains run on time."

"Yes, but what about the price in concentration camps and political murders?"

"The king supported him."

"Victor Emmanuel . . . that jackass!"

"You apparently know quite a lot about Italy."

"I took a course in modern Italian history and one in philosophy that covered fascism."

"Have you ever thought of taking the foreign service exam? That's how I got started."

"Spying is not my cup of tea."

"I worked as a diplomat, not a spy," said Mr. Hazelwood, slightly miffed.

"My apologies," said Ben, seeing Willard's discomfort. "I gather, though, that you served as the American government's go-between with Sarfatti."

"Smart fellow. Yes, I did."

"What was she like?" Mr. Stanton blurted out, hoping no doubt for some lurid details.

Brian seemed preoccupied with his own thoughts, but the rest of us genuinely wanted to hear Mr. Stanton's revelations.

"La Sarfatti, as most everyone called her, came from a noble Jewish family in Venice. As a young woman she married an older man, a lawyer, and had two children. She and her husband met Mussolini through their membership in the Socialist Party. The First World War changed everything. Mussolini, badly wounded, turned nationalist and then fascist. La Sarfatti's seventeen-year-old son died on the Austrian front, a personal loss so bitter to her that she exchanged her internationalist views for nationalist ones. Mussolini admired La Sarfatti's cultural polish and political ideas. He made common cause with her and her husband, who defended Mussolini in court more than once. Before long, Mussolini and La Sarfatti became lovers."

"What the hell did her husband say?" Mr. Stanton asked.

"He turned a blind eye to the affair."

"Did they correspond?" Ben inquired.

"Strange that you should ask. Their letters, presumed to have been deposited in a safe-deposit box in Milan, have never been found. I tried. And let me assure you, I had every investigative vehicle available to me."

Sitting there, it dawned on me that if Mr. Hazelwood knew everyone in the spook trade, he could easily find out about Ben and Joe Riley. "What brings you to Lexington?" I cordially asked.

"Brian," he said simply.

darkmatters LEVITT

Ben

Mr. Hazelwood arrives from the airport looking like the government's man in Havana. His palm-beach suit makes Ben think of salt water, cigars, gambling tables, and backroom deals. His voice sounds like a well-oiled piston, driving a formidable machine. He can sense the political animal in Mr. Hazelwood working on several levels. As he pours out doses of banana oil, he is also unsheathing a knife, just in case language fails and violence becomes a last resort. A true diplomat, he works both sides of the road, deploring fascism and praising its author. Ben shivers. He feels uncomfortable in the presence of people whose behavior he cannot anticipate, people who serve causes that become their own owing not to conviction, but to the paycheck at the end of the day. Mr. Hazelwood's presence in Lexington bodes ill. Why would the father of an unsuccessful suitor show up in the house of the sought-after woman with her intended present? Ben thinks of an aerial bombardment seen at a distance—bright flashes and muted sounds—and realizes that such an image aptly describes Mr. Hazelwood's voice.

The following day, they have brunch at the country club, a lavish layout with at least a dozen clay tennis courts, an Olympic-sized swimming pool, including an area roped off for children, dressing rooms, a clubhouse, and a restaurant. They prevail upon Abby to join them, even though she still has intermittent bouts of low fever. Clarissa wears a polished cotton full-pleated white dress, Abby a yellow one with a pinched waist that accentuates her bosom. To get to the club requires two cars. Mr. Stanton drives the Lincoln and Brian their second car, a Packard. Ben offers to drive, but Mrs. Stanton insists that she will entrust her car only to "young Mr. Hazelwood." The club, on the outskirts of town, has views of rolling hills

darkmatters
LEVITT

and whitewashed barns and fences. They sit poolside under a striped green and white umbrella not quite large enough to cover Abby and Ben. Ben insists that she pull her chair into the shade; and to make room, he slides his backwards into the sun. Mr. Stanton says he'll have them set up another. Ben volunteers to get it himself, but Mrs. Stanton observes: "That's what we pay the help for." The umbrella, however, never arrives, and she quickly becomes absorbed in the chin wagging that passes for conversation. The gossip flies, from Mrs. Stanton's explaining why she had exhumed the casket of her previous maid—she wasn't going to have any person who worked for her buried in a pauper's grave—until it finally lands on Lindbergh. His 1927 solo flight has for many years captured the imagination of Mr. Hazelwood, who extols Lindbergh's daring and hazards an amusing idea.

"Lindbergh, of course, was not the first to fly the Atlantic, but rather the first to fly solo. Supposing," he said, "a jewel thief or bootlegger had preceded Lindbergh. How would we know? The person would have been unable to make his flight public."

"Isn't that the point of any clandestine operation?" Ben says. "Not to be caught?"

"Sounds like some people I've heard of," Mrs. Stanton remarks enigmatically.

"Nowadays we would know," said Mr. Hazelwood. "Radar and all that."

"The larger question," says Ben, "is how do we know anything?"

"It's too hot for philosophy," Clarissa moans.

"I agree," Abby gasps, fanning herself with the brunch menu.

Mr. Hazelwood, though, takes up the question. "I left the foreign service and enrolled in law school because a friend of mine, an accountant, had been falsely convicted of a crime he didn't commit: forgery. His employer, later jailed for embezzlement, finally confessed to the crime."

Every time Mr. Hazelwood speaks, Ben has the same impression: whether he agrees with him or not, he doesn't have to violate his mind to understand the man's comments. He cannot say the same for the Stantons and Brian. Ben can see why Mr. Hazelwood would make a successful lawyer. He has the gift of being able to lull an audience into consent. How, Ben puzzles, did he sire a dope like Brian? It isn't until the story drifts to the abduction and death of the Lindbergh son, and in turn Mr. Hazelwood's own personal losses, does it all come clear.

darkmatters LEVITT

"My first wife died in childbirth," he says. "The baby girl died as well. When I married Brian's mother, I adopted Brian because his father was deceased."

"Cancer," Brian says automatically.

"I certainly hope it doesn't run in the family," Mrs. Stanton blurts out, not realizing, as usual, the effect of her snobbery and, in this case, obtuseness. Ben mentally compares Mrs. Stanton to Yumi's mother, a peasant woman, and Esperanza's abuela. Both had doubts about Ben, but both comported themselves with dignity. Although Mrs. Stanton would deny it, just beneath the veneer of her social graces lies a vicious vulgarity.

"Well, my mother's all right," replies Brian.

"I'm famished," Clarissa says.

Mrs. Stanton snaps her fingers in the direction of a waiter. "These darkies," she whines, "they're all lazy. Can't get an hour's work out of them."

A Negro waiter, decked out in a white linen jacket with black pants, an outfit that has to be hot as hell, comes running and asks for their orders. Marty, suffering from a hangover, requests cream of wheat and a muffin, but Mrs. Stanton brazenly objects, "You don't want *that*," and directs the waiter to bring him a steak covered with two eggs "sunny side up." Mr. Stanton adds: "And a Bloody Mary."

Marty

The brandy from the previous night had left me woozy. Trying to order a sensible breakfast, I was overruled by Mrs. Stanton. When her husband prescribed vodka and tomato juice to cure my nausea, I should have said no, but to be polite I foolishly drank it.

With brunch over, Abby invited me to join her at the tennis courts—to observe, not to play. She wanted to watch a singles match between two girls whom, she scoffed, "I could cream if I weren't so weak." We sat on a wooden bench in the small grandstand next to the courts, under the suffocating heat of a metal awning. At first, Abby provided a running commentary on the subtleties of the game and the failings of the two girls. Then she got down to business.

"We really haven't had a minute to talk," she said. "Remember what I told you yesterday? Well, there's more."

"What do you mean?"

"Just before I wrote you, Clarissa and Brian took a steamboat trip on the Ohio river. I didn't go 'cause of my fever. After she got back, she had only good things to say about that goofball and kept apologizing to me. So I asked her why she was apologizing, and she said, 'Well, you used to go with him. And now . . .' She must have felt she had said too much, 'cause she stopped and just asked me if my fever had gone down. But she couldn't resist talking about the trip: the paddle wheel, the meals, the fun, and all."

"So you think—"

"They're not screwing, if that's what you're thinking. But she's falling for that jerk. Anything I say will sound like sour grapes. So I just drop comments now and then about how great Ben is."

"He doesn't belong here. He's like a fish out of water."

"Well, he's definitely in foreign territory. But I couldn't just sit by and not warn him."

"Why did Mr. Hazelwood come?"

"Your guess is as good as mine."

"He told me he came to see Brian . . . I guess because of his fall."

"A sore butt!" howled Abby. "Get serious!"

"Then why?"

"Nobody's talking."

My head hurting and eyes swimming, and Abby looking none too good herself, we migrated back to the party and accompanied them to the air-conditioned clubhouse, where I fell into a parlor chair. Ben kindly brought me a cool compress that I placed over my eyes. In the distance, I could hear voices, most of them unfamiliar. But feeling as I did, I just sat there darkly catching tidbits of conversation.

"Roberta says he's a communist."

"You're kidding!"

"She says he comes from Communist Russia."

"And Clarissa?"

"Indeed! If she were *my* daughter . . ."

The voices faded, to be supplanted by two new ones.

"Rich as blazes, I hear."

"Well, corporate lawyers do make good money."

"Not that good. I'm told he inherited a fortune."

"His son's got it made."

"In spades."

I then heard a cacophony of sounds. Eventually I figured out that the Wellingtons had arrived, eliciting claps and shouts. Shortly, two women drifted into my hearing.

"Where on the French Riviera?"

"Nice."

"You mean nice."

They laughed and moved on. A man and a woman excited my attention, but I thought it best to keep my eyes shut.

"That's his friend. The one sleeping in the chair. Drunk, no doubt."

"You're sure?"

"Charles, I've known Roberta for years! She said it would happen only over her dead body."

"But Clarissa *does* have a mind of her own."

"Roberta gets what Roberta wants—one way or another."

"Yes, I suppose so."

"When she wanted the pastor thrown out of St. John's, she never ceased till he finally asked for a transfer. She can be ruthless."

"This'll be interesting."

Once the two had moved off, I removed the compress and opened my eyes. But to my disappointment, the couple had faded into the milling party celebrating the newlyweds' return. Looking around, I could see Abby stretched out in a chair with an ottoman, and Brian perched on a bar stool knocking back mint juleps. The Stantons and Mr. Hazelwood sat on a sofa, deep in conversation. But Ben and Clarissa had faded from view. I didn't see them again until we walked to the cars, where I found them seated under an oak, red-faced, though I felt certain not from the heat. Their forced smiles belied their actual feelings. Ben told me later that they had been "having it out."

The Stantons and Mr. Hazelwood drove off in the Lincoln. Brian climbed behind the wheel of the Packard. Abby and I sat in front, Ben and Clarissa in back. Brian, trying to fit the key into the ignition, began to sing drunkenly: "Ninety-nine bottles of beer on the wall/Ninety-nine bottles of beer/Take one down and pass it around/Ninety-eight bottles of beer on the wall." Ben said that he'd drive; Brian loudly proclaimed his sobriety. As we weaved out of the parking lot, I prayed that a policeman would stop us and ticket the numbskull. But according to Mr. Stanton, the country club had an arrangement with the local constabulary to stay away, lest the cops inhibit business by picking up all the drunks who wheeled onto the highway. The two-lane road posed a problem for Brian that he solved by straddling the highway and the shoulder. We could hear pebbles hitting the underside of the fenders as the car lurched along and Brian bellowed, "Eighty-four bottles of beer on the wall/Eighty-four bottles of beer. . . ." Ben and I grew restive, but Clarissa thought Brian's condition a hoot. She repeatedly cracked jokes at his expense that he found hilariously funny. If she married this bum, I thought, she'd always have an appreciative audience—and the upper hand. But Clarissa, I told myself, had too lively a mind to shackle herself to a dunce. A short distance from the city limit, Brian hit a soft patch of shoulder. The car, traveling about thirty miles an hour, veered to the right, scooted through a shallow gully, broke through a whitewashed fence, and stopped in a field. My head hit the front windshield and Abby's the dash. Brian used the steering wheel to break the impact and came away unscathed. Clarissa and Ben, thrown up against the front seats, each sprained a wrist from trying to cushion the blow. My forehead bled from a cut, and Abby subsequently developed a black eye. We all clambered out of the car, outraged at Brian's reckless behavior. I tripped on an octagonal hubcap, with a red P at the center. Clarissa, who had gone from jester to Job, stood cupping her cheeks, wanting to know why this accident had happened to us. She called Brian an idiot and some unmentionable expletives, and lapsed into silence. The mashed right fender prevented the Packard from moving. Removing a tire iron from the trunk, Ben tried to bend the fender into a usable shape, but the pain in his wrist made it difficult for him to exert much leverage. Brian, sprawled on the grass, kept saying that he wanted a drink. Although several cars had passed without stopping, perhaps because we made no effort to flag them, one pulled over when Clarissa and Abby waved. Ben volunteered to stay behind with Brian, and I accompanied the two women, for safety's sake, into town. Now gun shy, I sat in the back with Abby, Clarissa in front. The man who picked us up introduced himself as Jackson Payne, horse trainer. From Clarissa's questions I gathered she knew nothing about him.

"Emerald Stables," he said. "Me and my son, we work together there. You kids go to college?"

"Yes," replied Clarissa, "the University of Colorado."

"My boy, he's smart. Some hotsie-totsie college outside Chicago 'cepted him once. But it come down to a choice 'tween fixin' the roof on the house or payin' for him."

I could imagine Ben asking him: would you rather have a leaky roof or a leaky brain? But lacking Ben's nerve, I hazarded a softer word. "I sure hope the roof lasts as long as a college education."

In the rear-view mirror, I could see Judson's puzzled expression. Without much conviction, he said, "Me, too."

He pulled into "Herb's Garage," a greasy one-story building facing the railroad tracks and a billboard with an advertising jingle: "Seven-Up will quench your thirst/Among the drinks it's always first./Diners dressed in suits or turban/Mix it up with southern bourbon." On one side of the garage stood three rows of abandoned, rusted cars, some dating from the thirties; on the other side, a cafe exhibited a blinking sign: "Eats."

Herb, rubbing the grease off his hands with a red rag, explained that he had promised Mr. Buchanan he'd have his car ready in an hour.

"I have no idea who Mr. Buchanan is," said Clarissa, "but I'll give you ten dollars for the ride out and back, plus whatever it takes to get our car going again. What do you think?"

He didn't think long, because he threw the rag aside and said, "Hop into the truck," and off we went down the road.

Brian, asleep in the grass, never woke up all through the repair, even though Mr. Payne used a sledge hammer to bend the fender into an approximation of its former self. He also changed the flat, since the fender had punctured the tire. Clarissa slipped him two tens, and he tipped an imaginary hat and drove off. We helped Brian into the back seat and Ben took the wheel, slowly driving the car back to the house on the hill. Mrs. Stanton, standing out front, with her arms crossed in front of her, as if waiting to do battle, wanted to know "what in blazes" had kept us. Before we had a chance to explain, she concluded that Ben had been driving the car. The evidence seemed undeniable: she saw Ben seated at the wheel, Brian snoozing, and the car's grille and fender badly bent. It all added up. Ben had asked to drive; she had said no. Brian had too much to drink, so Ben drove.

"I thought," she said sternly, "that I made myself painfully clear when I asked Brian to take charge of the Packard. In case you missed my point, I didn't want you to."

Clarissa tried to set her mother straight, but Roberta waved her off and trooped into the house. "What's the diff," said Clarissa airily, "let her believe what she wants. We know the truth."

Hauling Brian out of the back seat, we got him onto his feet and marched him inside, where he soaked his head under a faucet of cold water. While the others cleaned up, I washed the blood off my forehead, which had grown a lump the size of a walnut. The cut itself was minor, but the booze, the sun, and the blow led to a Siserean headache. Mrs. Stanton invited everyone into the living room and insisted I join the party, even though I asked to be excused.

"We're going to look at some home movies," she said.

Honesty had little purchase in Mrs. Stanton's life. Had I had my wits about me I might have guessed that she intended to orchestrate a psychodrama.

Some people, I've noticed, cannot live without a crisis. Of the three great human traps—boredom, vice, and poverty—Mrs. Stanton, wealthy and strait-laced, had only the first to overcome. She did it by manufacturing "scenes," which gave her vicarious orgasms. Her face brightened and her eyes glowed as she fomented trouble. It all began slowly, with a question.

"Willard," she asked, "if I may be so bold, what exactly do you do for D and P Chemical?"

A blinding pain in both temples led me to bury myself in a chair. Although a floor fan stood wheezing in the corner, it felt as if the air in the house had been rationed. Breathing came hard and my eyes began playing tricks. On one wall, the vertically striped wallpaper was slipping sideways into horizontals, and on another curling and retracting, like the children's toy that shoots out a tongue if breath is applied and rolls back if the air is withdrawn. Surely, I prayed, I'm not having a seizure. The people on the couch—Abby, Ben, and Clarissa—were momentarily bereft of their bodies, as their heads floated free. Messrs. Stanton and Hazelwood, seated in the matching chairs in front of the fireplace, shrunk to the size of pygmies. Brian, stretched out on a love seat, faded in and out of the fabric. And Mrs. Stanton, standing with her arm resting on the mantel, pointed a finger as long as a broomstick.

The chimera came and went fleetingly, but I knew that for me it signalled an ictus.

"I work on fraud cases," said Mr. Hazelwood. "D and P has a great many imitators who infringe on our patents. They do it clandestinely, usually overseas. But we have agents who keep us abreast of these pirates."

Mr. Stanton flushed with excitement. "Do you know anything about the commies stealing our atomic secrets?"

"No, but I have friends who probably do."

"One A-bomb would put an end to Stalin and wrap up the Korean war in a day," Mr. Stanton opined.

"We're not here to talk about Stalin or Korea," said Mrs. Stanton, implying she had scripted this assembly.

But once Mr. Stanton had introduced the topic of Korea, Ben couldn't help piping up. "And how, sir, do you propose to keep American soldiers safe from radiation? A-bombs are not precise instruments. They spew death for hundreds of miles, maybe even thousands."

"I said we were not here to talk about such . . . things."

Clarissa stood up.

"And where are you going?" her mother asked.

"Ben and I have a conversation to finish," she replied, pulling his arm. But as he started to rise from the couch, Mrs. Stanton said, "You can both sit still. We're here for a reason."

Ben

As the party retreats from poolside to the air conditioning of the country club, Ben waits at the front door for Marty and Abby. He can see in the yellow of Marty's eyes an incipient illness. Finding a towel, Ben soaks it in cold water and makes a compress that he gives to Marty, who has sunk into a chair.

"I'll sit here with you."

"No, go mix or Mrs. Stanton will have something else to hold against you."

Ben listens to the revelers making silly jokes about honeymoons and sex and, after sizing up the bridal party, decides that he would rather take a vow of silence than have to share their company. As he moves away from the fringes of the crowd, Clarissa joins him.

"What do you think of my old classmate?"

"I'd rather not say."

"You are an intellectual snob."

"And you are a social one."

Clarissa's eyes tell Ben that she is in a warring mood. She mutely stares at him a moment and then says that "she's been thinking some about Mexican lady friends." He knows that she picks these words to anger him. He replies:

"You and your mother seem to share a vocabulary."

"Not here," she snaps. "Outside."

He follows her through the parking lot to the shade of an oak, which has a circular bench affixed to it. Fingering an acorn, he listens as she berates him.

"You never make the slightest attempt to be pleasant. Does it ever occur to you that most of the world doesn't share your opinions? You act as if you're trying to show up my friends and family as fools, and their values as stupid. If you find them so hateful, why do you love me?"

Her question, an admission that she is similar to them, has never before required an answer. He has always taken as a matter of faith that beauty has no ebb and sex eclipses all doubts. But his recent "adultery" has caused him to doubt this equation.

"I originally thought that your side of the tracks had a certain charm. But I've discovered that for all its civility it harbors a gutter bigotry."

"And your side of the tracks?"

He peels the acorn and exposes the kernel.

"Suspicious of gentiles and clannish."

"I see! You're above it all. Not a member of my side or yours."

"Remember? I vote Socialist."

"Crap!"

Her ill-tempered response cuts to the quick. For all their differences, he has from their first date felt bound to her like a tutor to a promising student. But what does that feeling betoken? Love, solicitude, a fascination with the rich? He wonders how anyone can parse an emotion.

"You asked me how I could love you. I didn't really give you an answer. Let me try. Yes, I feel as if I want to reform your smug society. And I'm well aware that I do it in the least effective way: by alienating the very people I would like to change. I admit that I enjoy showing them that their received opinions proceed from habit, not honesty. But you sounded susceptible to change, so I convinced myself that you would have it all: money, culture, sophistication, tolerance, a critical habit of mind. All things that I admire, perhaps because of my own deficiencies. And what did you do? As soon as you returned to Lexington, you reverted to type."

"I see. You were Pygmalion and I your Galatea."

"Not a bad way of describing it. Yes."

"Did it ever occur to you that once you had taught me to think for myself—and you were the one, Ben, I admit it—I might choose to reclaim part of my previous life? Not all, but some."

They hear familiar voices and the sound of shoes on gravel. The others arrive. Clarissa and Ben fall into a conspicuous silence. Brian can barely stand up, but Mrs. Stanton refuses to notice. Given her infatuation with him and her dislike of Ben, she insists that Brian drive the Packard. Ben mulls over the idea of hitchhiking back to the house, but decides that that would recall his and Clarissa's leaving the Stanton car after church and returning home with Brian Hazelwood—with all its recriminations. He desperately wants to continue his conversation with Clarissa. Even in disagreement, he takes vast pleasure in her spirited intelligence.

darkmatters
LEVITT

Marty

Clarissa impatiently asked her mother which reason perforce required their presence.

"I told you: a home movie."

"It's too hot."

"Brian," Mrs. Stanton directed, "Eliza has an ice cooler in the kitchen with cold drinks. It's too heavy for her. Would you kindly put it over there on the coffee table. And tell her to bring the tea sandwiches as well."

Brian left.

"Sweet young man," said Mrs. Stanton, and proceeded to pull down the shades, explaining that it would cool off the room.

Brian returned with the cooler and trivets to support it. Spreading out small serving tables, Eliza set them with plates and glasses; she then distributed the tea sandwiches, made from white bread without crusts and small pieces of sliced liver. Cut into triangles, the sandwiches, lacking mayonnaise or mustard, tasted like raw dough laced not with cold liver, but with cold lizard. The drinks—root beer, orange, and cream soda—had been cooled to a point shy of freezing. The chilled bottle felt good in the hand. I held mine to my forehead, finding relief in the coldness.

"I designed the snack myself," said Mrs. Stanton, an admission that explained the absence of Eliza's inimitable cooking. "People don't eat enough liver. And be sure to chew it well. Mastication helps digestion."

Why the goyim eschew breads with hard crusts has always remained a mystery to me. I presume they have teeth; I presume they have taste buds. So why serve bread fit for an infant?

"I repeat, Mother, it's too hot for movies."

darkmatters
LEVITT

"Nonsense! It will keep our minds off the weather."

She directed her husband to set up the projector, which stood boxed on a table. As he attached the reels, inexplicably Mr. Hazelwood stepped up to the machine and removed from his pocket a small roll of film that Mr. Stanton threaded into the maze of geared wheels.

"Roberta's idea, not mine," said Mr. Stanton apologetically. "I have no idea what this is all about."

Mrs. Stanton removed a small painting from a wall next to the fireplace, and turned off the lights. In the darkness, the projector bulb cast a large square of illumination, and the film started to roll.

I think most of us had expected to see a home movie of the Stanton family, with clips of Clarissa as a baby. Instead, we saw a car, bearing New York license plates, slowly moving down a city street in a residential neighborhood. It pulled up in front of a bungalow with a porch. As the camera panned the house, you could see the number affixed to the door: 172. Immediately I felt relieved: the numbers equalled one, a particularly good kabbalistic sign. Seven plus two plus one come to ten; but since ten is a compound and not an individual numeral, we drop the zero and it comes to one. Ben, however, seemed out of sorts, restlessly crossing and recrossing his legs. The car remained standing, double-parked, until a man in an overcoat and a hat descended the front steps. He carried an envelope. On reaching the car, he waited for the driver to roll down the window. Only then could you tell that the car also held a second man, who leaned across his companion and handed the man in the overcoat a paper bag in exchange for the envelope. The driver and the man in the coat shook hands, and the car pulled away. As the man returned to the house, he paused on a porch step, tipped back his hat, and peered into the bag. Inky Miller! Here the clip ended. With the projector suddenly turned off, the room plunged into darkness.

Until light was restored, a brief silence ensued. How did Mrs. Stanton know about Inky Miller? Abby shot me a glance. Would she spill the beans? I needn't have worried. Like a loyal sport, she said nothing.

Mr. Hazelwood spoke first. "A basketball fixer," he remarked dryly, without adding a name.

"What the hell's that?" sputtered Mr. Stanton.

Clarissa, no doubt sensing something badly amiss, said to Mr. Hazelwood: "I fail to understand the point of this."

Though the rest of his face remained completely impassive, a slight smile played at the corners of his mouth. "Since Brian and you are so friendly, I thought it a good idea to look into the background of your friends. What you've just seen is an FBI film of a basketball fixer—Inky Miller—turning over the names of players susceptible to bribes, and the gamblers paying him off. He would still be fixing basketball games had he not been apprehended. When questioned, he implicated your friend Ben here."

I don't believe it!" snapped Clarissa.

"Not for being in on the fixes," said Mr. Hazelwood, "but for providing him with a safe house from which to conduct his nefarious negotiations. A place, I believe, in a town called Eldorado Springs. I suspect that you know it."

Clarissa, frowning, turned to Ben. "What's he mean?"

"Inky asked me if he could rent my house for a few hours a week. I needed the money, so I let him."

Clarissa raised her voice, making no effort to disguise her anxiety. "So *that's* the friend who sublet your cabin!"

Ben cracked his knuckles. "A big mouth, yes. A basketball fixer, I wouldn't know."

"He is and says that you knew," said Mr. Hazelwood.

"If he's a felon, as you say, why believe him and not me?"

A pall fell over the room. The heat, heavy as hate, became suffocating. Only our labored breathing could be heard.

At last, Clarissa broke the spell. "So?"

"So there's more," said Mrs. Stanton, again nodding in Mr. Hazelwood's direction.

"Your friend here," he said, seeming to take a malicious delight in repeating the word *here*, "travels in dangerous circles. His comrade Joe Riley—"

"My comrade as well!" interrupted Clarissa.

"That's what troubles me," replied Mr. Hazelwood. "I used the word comrade for a reason. Joe and his parents belong to a Trotsky cell, with contacts in the Mine-Mill union and in Mexico."

"That's news to me," said Ben.

"Is it? You've been observed by the FBI attending meetings of Trotsky cell members."

"They were social gatherings to protest working conditions for Mexican-American miners."

"For a clever man like you not to notice whom you had climbed into bed with I find hard to believe. And speaking of climbing into bed, I might as well add that my investigations have also turned up troubling information about your morals. Normally, I would say your personal habits are no business of mine. But since you apparently have designs on Clarissa, a young woman who matters a great deal to Brian, I can't remain silent."

"You ought to join Senator McCarthy's legal team. Baseless charges are right up your alley."

"In Hanover, after Clarissa and Abby had left, you bestowed your affections on another woman, Esperanza Morales, an occasional speaker for labor causes."

"Bullshit!" Ben shouted.

Mrs. Stanton objected sharply. "I won't hear such language!"

"Her work on behalf of the union is public knowledge. You don't think the government's without friends in Local 890, do you?"

"No, quite the contrary."

"You, Marty, and Esperanza stayed at Dawson 'Doc' Campbell's ranch."

"As tourists. Marty and I bunked together. We all hiked up to the cave dwellings shortly before we left for Lexington."

Mrs. Stanton, exuding a bogus sincerity, asked sweetly, "Do you always vacation with Mexican lady friends?"

"So *that's* what you meant!" exclaimed Clarissa. She turned to Ben. "Why didn't you just say so?"

"I should think the reason is obvious!" her mother said.

"What in the hell's wrong with a hike?" a bewildered Mr. Stanton inquired. "Or a ride? Frankly, this discussion is beyond me."

Although speaking to Clarissa, Ben stared at her mother. "I don't like hearing my friends defamed, and when they are, I go out of my way to protect them."

"You also accompanied Mrs. Morales to her grandmother's house," Mr. Hazelwood continued.

"She had no way of getting there. I simply drove her."

"And didn't return for several days."

I could see the lawyer's progressive disclosures slowly eroding Clarissa's confidence. Like water on sandstone, they quickly began to eat through the surface. Her body stiffened and a skepticism crept into her voice. "Perhaps," she said jauntily, a tone that bespoke her concern, "he was improving his Spanish."

Mr. Stanton, now visibly annoyed at the shadow boxing, cried out, "I repeat, what the hell's going on?"—a question that proved he had not been privy to his wife's machinations. "Can't we talk about horses or . . . or . . . Shiloh?"

"Or Los Angeles!" said Mrs. Stanton.

Clarissa turned white. Even her lustrous eyes lost their light. Although Mrs. Stanton had said in her letter to Ben that she had written it without telling Clarissa, he assumed that Mrs. Stanton had probably talked to her daughter about the abortion. Not so. Ben, Abby, and I suddenly realized that Clarissa had had no idea her mother knew her secret. She visibly gulped, took a drink from a now warm root beer, and sank back into the sofa, exuding defeat.

"What's so special about L.A.?" asked Brian. "I've been there. We stayed at the Ambassador Hotel. Danny Thomas performed in the Coconut Room, or whatever you call it. Geez, was he funny!"

"Brian," said Mrs. Stanton annoyed, "that's not what we're talking about!"

Mr. Stanton fanned himself with a newspaper and tried once again to discover the subject. "Then what *are* we talking about?"

Apparently Clarissa's mom had conspired with Brian's dad, though not with her husband or Brian, to advance Brian's chances with Clarissa, a scenario that would explain why Mr. Hazelwood had asked his government cronies to check into Ben's life and loves. By sinking Ben, they could launch Brian. But it appeared that she had kept from Mr. Hazelwood the abortion.

"What are we talking about?" repeated Mrs. Stanton rhetorically. "I think Clarissa and Ben know well enough." She looked at her daughter. "I trust I needn't continue."

Clarissa stood up and walked to her mother. "You disgust me!" she sneered.

Mrs. Stanton dropped her supercilious mask and for the first time I had a glimpse of the real woman. Her face, etched in pain, bespoke her devotion to her daughter. "Why, because I have only your best interests at heart? Because I want to keep you from making a terrible mistake? I admit that what I've done is underhanded, but to save my daughter from a disaster I would resort to any kind of extreme measures. Your father is the hugging and kissing type. I show my affection in other ways. As you can see, I am willing to risk losing you completely—in order to save you. If what I have done is wrong, blame my love."

She extended a hand to Clarissa, but her daughter failed to take it and left the room without uttering a word.

I too tried to stand, but my legs wouldn't support me. The heat, the alcohol, the blow to the forehead . . . I began to experience visual distortions, a harbinger for me of an epileptic episode. People contorted themselves into gruesome shapes or spoke strangely. Brian, lying down, had a beer bottle sticking out of his mouth. His father chided his "unseemly posture" and removed the bottle. Unplugged, Brian floated to the ceiling and announced that he'd forgotten to pack his topsiders and sailing cap. To console him, his father put a hundred dollar bill in a cash clip and tossed it to him.

"What are you doing up there?" I asked.

"Collecting my allowance."

Mr. Stanton, dressed in jodhpurs, mounted and wildly rode the rocking horse, while his wife assumed a serpentine shape. She wore no clothes, and had pancake-flat breasts, which didn't suit a snake. Slithering across the floor, she unhinged her mouth and swallowed a slab of raw liver. She then coiled and made a hissing sound that sounded like "chew," or perhaps it was "Jew."

The door opened and my rabbi entered, wearing a black and white prayer shawl and a blue yarmulke. I hailed him but my words went unheeded. Shaking a disapproving finger at Mr. Hazelwood, he turned the lawyer's chin, just as he used to twist mine, so they stood eye to eye. "To know a man well," he advised, "you must ride in the same wagon with him."

"This is a Christian country," Willard said, "not a place for disputatious men with sidelocks and prayer caps. In God we trust!"

"Trust what?" my rabbi replied, warming to the argument. "That God will sit silently through another Holocaust? That He will feed the poor and heal the lame? That He will put an end to religious wars? In *what* are you trusting? Tell me!"

"See what I mean? All you people do is dispute. As far as I'm concerned you—"

He never finished because my rabbi said, "A *goyisha kup*," flew around the room, and sailed out.

"He can't even speak English," Mr. Hazelwood mocked.

"Chew!" cried Mrs. Stanton.

Once again the door opened, admitting a stranger whose face streamed with blood. But as soon as he spoke, I recognized Joe Riley. Mrs. Stanton swallowed another liver and slid under a chair. Joe reached into his pocket and took out a Local 890 Mine-Mill union badge. Miraculously, it became an octagonal hubcap with a red P in the middle, which he threw in the air. We all watched as it circled the room several times, turned sharply, hit the fireplace, and fell to the floor. But Joe just shrugged fatalistically and said, "Some things we hold apart, like the secrets of the heart."

Ben

Again retreating from the oppressive Stanton house, Ben and Clarissa slowly proceed down the garden path, edged with nasturtiums and geraniums whose passionate colors mirror their mood. He can think of no other way to defend himself than to declare:

"Let's leave Lexington. I know a Justice of the Peace in Brooklyn who can marry us."

"You heard her. She *does* care!"

"So do I."

She pleads. "It may take time, but I'm sure I can bring her around. Once the Hazelwoods leave—"

"I can't wait."

"You've waited since that first day at Smith."

The rightness of Clarissa's statement gives him pause. In love with her since Massachusetts, he fruitlessly tried to find in the military surcease from her siren charms. But as he both hoped and feared, he was ineluctably drawn back to her.

"Staying won't work."

"It will if you give it time."

"Your mother has a mind of her own. Don't underestimate her will power, Clarissa. I may not like her, but I have a grudging respect for her steeliness."

"There are ways to get around her."

"Like?"

"Like making her see that you don't despise her religious beliefs and that she can make all the church preparations for our wedding."

Ben feels betrayed. He and Clarissa have frequently talked about how a marriage between them might proceed. She has never objected to his wish for a secular service. Is this her way of changing the contract?

"I thought we had agreed we'd keep it non denominational."

"You can see for yourself . . . I can't."

"We could just drive off."

"I would feel sneaky and dirty, like Los Angeles."

"After what has just taken place, I don't suppose your parents would agree to any kind of wedding."

"Not so long as you keep provoking mother."

Engaging Clarissa in a discussion about Mrs. Stanton and her values will, Ben decides, merely harden her in her resolve to side with her mother. So he introduces the subject of his competitor.

"Would you actually marry that creep?"

"Please, Ben, don't!"

"If you leave now, we can be husband and wife in three days."

"I can't. It's wrong. I want my family there, and my friends."

"I see," he says mordantly, "you want a gown and a veil, and an organ playing. You want invitations and a minister, and untold relatives and friends with armloads of gifts. Well, if that's the case, then you want Brian Hazelwood. Your mother certainly hopes you'll marry that cretin."

"Stop, Ben! I admit it: I want what every young woman wants. Don't you see that your eccentricities are driving me toward him?"

"I'm unlikely to change."

"Think what you're saying, Ben. You want me to be your Galatea, but you refuse to budge."

From the maid's quarters, they can just barely hear music. "You'll cry and cry and try to sleep/But sleep won't come . . ." Ben strains to hear the rest of the words, but loses them as he continues down the path.

Clarissa grabs his hand and stops him. "I'll make you a deal. We can be married by a rabbi *and* a minister. If my parents refuse to attend, so be it. But at least give them the chance. At least invite them. Just make this one concession, and I'll never let you down in the future. Come, we'll face mother together."

"She'll just start in where she left off."

"Then we'll ride out the storm together."

Staring into her magnificent eyes, brimming with tears, he reluctantly and irrationally agrees, knowing that what he accedes to now will lead to self-loathing later and what she swears to at the moment will undoubtedly change with her whims.

As they enter the living room, Brian is shamefully trumpeting his family's wealth: their house and cars and boat and Caribbean trips, but Clarissa pointedly ignores him and crosses to her mother, seated with crossed legs on the couch, and whispers into her ear.

Mrs. Stanton rises like a wraith. "You mustn't listen to him, dear. If he doesn't kill you with his wicked ideas, he'll kill you with his insane driving. Look what he did to our Packard!"

"Brian was driving the car, not Ben! I've told you ten times."

"What about the girl in New Mexico?"

Clarissa sinks down on the couch next to her mother with a pained expression that says, "Ben, just tell us all it's not true, and be done with it."

Mrs. Stanton, seeing her daughter's discomfort, exploits it. "Esperanza Morales is his Mex!"

Mr. Hazelwood studies his manicured nails.

Clarissa's eyes flash. Ben can see that she's hurt. "God, Mother, you really are desperate."

"My dearest one, I'm only to trying to keep you from danger. At least some young men I know don't make love to . . . revolutionaries."

"Clarissa," Ben intones, "we should've never returned. I think it's time to go—before matters get worse."

Desperately, Clarissa bullies her mother to show her the proof.

"Show me the evidence! How do you know?"

Mr. Hazelwood comes to the old lady's defense. "It hurts me to say, Clarissa, but your boyfriend couldn't wait till you got out of Hanover. The next day he was in the arms of Mrs. Morales. We have a sworn statement from an unimpeachable witness."

Oblivious to her surroundings, she turns to Ben and asks frenetically, "Is what he's saying about you and Esperanza true?"

Ben can hear the desperation in her voice. "No."

"Did you *ever* make love to her?"

"Please, Clarissa, this is neither the time nor the place."

"The hell with the others. Answer me!"

"I'll explain, but not here."

Suddenly, Clarissa grows calm, as if the emotional storm has subsided.

"On second thought, I'd rather not know. What galls me is not your infidelity, but that you've proven *her* right and me wrong."

A triumphant Mrs. Stanton squeezes her daughter's hand and condoles with her daughter. "I told you he was dangerous and couldn't be trusted."

At the height of the furor, Marty assumes a vacant expression and his eyelids begin twitching, obviously the result of a seizure. The others stand transfixed. Ben orders Mrs. Stanton to summon a doctor and, at Mr. Stanton's direction, moves Marty to the leather couch in the den. With Dr. Lippensuck having fallen into disrepute, a new doctor is called. He gives Marty a shot of phenobarbital, and insists on bed rest. Abby, Ben, and Clarissa hover nearby. Mr. and Mrs. Stanton remain in the background. Ben can tell from Mrs. Stanton's frown that the inn has no vacancies.

"Marty can stay in my room," Clarissa volunteers.

"And where will you sleep?" asks her mother. Her tone of voice expresses horror at the very thought that her daughter might sleep with Ben in a motel. "The Stantons *are* well known in Lexington!"

One can't be sure if she objects to the sex or the scandal. If asked, she would probably say both. But Ben suspects that the latter bothers her more.

"I'll sleep here on the couch," Clarissa says coldly. "Surely you have no objections to that?"

Before Mrs. Stanton can interrogate Ben, he assures her that he'll be returning to the motel just as soon as Marty awakes.

That evening, with Clarissa's giraffe peering down at him from a shelf, Marty, now fully recovered, speaks to Ben in Yiddish, recalling as a child hiding in the basement of their building during a race riot, and shivering from fright. Ben bids his friend goodnight and joins Clarissa in the den. He knows how much she loves flattery, and praises her for relinquishing her room. At first, they avoid talking about the awful events of the day. But slowly they meander into the byways of confession. Ben tells Clarissa about Esperanza and seeks absolution. She admits that she has allowed Brian liberties, though not the ultimate one. Ben asks, "What next?" Clarissa says that Ben exhausts her, and that she cannot envision a life lived with a rebel.

"Seeing you here makes me realize that I'd always be living on edge, always worrying that you'll go too far with your comments. I've seen it too often. Then I resent you, and want to side with your opponents."

Ben resorts to sarcasm. "Take up with Brian. He'll never embarrass you, just bore you to death."

darkmatters
LEVITT

"At least he fits in."

"Most dullards do. Living with him, you'll never have to engage an idea."

"Why do you revel in being different?"

"But you knew that about me. You even called your family ghastly, and I said your father wasn't a bad sort, just eccentric."

"Speaking of eccentric!"

"Did it ever occur to you that I find others odd and think of myself as perfectly normal?"

"That's what makes you so eccentric."

"If fitting in means accepting the status quo—"

Clarissa interrupts. "It's you who says that you can't enter the same stream twice. Nothing remains the same. And frankly after what Mr. Hazelwood said, things are different."

"I see." Ben's voice sounds a strident note. "I'm a bastard and your mother's an angel."

"No, she's a willful woman who often behaves cruelly. But she does love me, in her own way."

"And I don't love you?"

Clarissa bites her lip. "I didn't mean it that way."

"I'm not telling you to abandon her."

"But don't you see, Ben, to marry you *would* be to abandon her."

"Are you saying that if it comes to a choice between me and your mother, you'll take her?"

"No, I'm saying that I need more time . . . that I'm unsure. You must admit, you *are* a dangerous man. You have unconventional opinions, strong ones, which you like to argue about. You belong to radical groups. You have a weakness for women. You—and I probably shouldn't say this—often make me feel dumb. Not deliberately. But you *are* smarter than I am. Which sometimes bothers me. I like having my own way, and you won't let me. There, I've said it. I didn't think I ever would, but I have. If you want to criticize me, go ahead."

"You're far too intelligent to be satisfied with *things*. I guarantee: possessions won't make you happy. A new house has no substance."

"It does if you don't have one."

"We're talking about you, Clarissa, not some poor family on the other side of town. You'll always have a house and money to decorate it. What you lack is courage."

darkmatters
LEVITT

"Why, because I'm not just like you?"

"No, because you won't do what it takes to be more than a beautiful woman. Just remember, you have to spend the rest of your life living in your own head. So you'd better furnish it well. And the kind of furnishings I'm talking about won't be found in this home or Brian's."

"Sometimes you scare me, Ben."

"Ideas *are* scary. A chest of drawers is not. What made Stoneham behave as he did was his fear of ideas."

"Radical ones," she says critically, as if to suggest that such ideas deserve to be punished.

"If not for people thinking radical thoughts, we'd still be dying from the plague and living under a king. Serious ideas command our attention and demand comprehension. Acquiring possessions doesn't require much thought, just money."

"You're preaching."

"Yes."

"You make me feel inadequate."

Ben falls silent because he senses Clarissa fleeing the issue.

"I just hate it when you look at me that way. It's as if you're saying I'm an accomplice to stupidity. Maybe it's best that we not see each other until we meet back at school."

Ben feels the sting of her words but refuses to leave without first giving her a parting embrace.

The next day, Ben and Marty drive out of Lexington.

darkmatters LEVITT

Marty

Clarissa never returned to school. She and Brian married in early December, with a supporting cast of hundreds. I received an announcement, as did Ben, and sent a wire congratulating the couple. Mulling it over, Ben mailed Clarissa a handsome first edition of John Dos Passos's *U.S.A.* At the start of the fall term, I had returned to the dorm, with its guarantee of meals and clean linen. Ben kept his cabin in Eldorado Springs. Wedded to left-wing politics, he encouraged student activism and led several protests; he also worked as a part-time labor organizer, which occasionally brought him into contact with Esperanza Morales, now living in Silver City with her abuela and with an adopted son, and apart from her husband. On her infrequent trips to Colorado, they would meet in Denver and stay at a small downtown hotel, the Cimarron. Had her catholicism not prevented her from seeking a divorce, she and Ben I believe would have married. He dated frequently, including Abby, with whom I'm sure he was intimate; but I never again had the pleasure of her bed. Strangely, I felt relieved. Abby and I had resumed our friendship without the added burden of my hoping for sex.

The next three years passed quickly, as I moved toward a business degree and Ben completed a double M.A. in economics and history. At Commencement, an ambiguous word meaning both the conclusion of college and also a beginning, Ben and I received our diplomas from the hand of President Fuller, who had replaced Stoneham. My sister attended the graduation and said she hoped that I would be able to support myself. Ben joined Joe Riley working for the Mine-Mill union office in Denver. A year later, Joe enrolled in law school on the West Coast and Ben, thinking he

darkmatters
LEVITT

might like to teach reading to inner-city kids, matriculated at what he disparagingly called the Drek School of Education, where he endured, according to him, "the incubus of ignorance." We spoke often during this period, but I particularly remember him saying that a prerequisite for a certificate in education was the abdication of imagination and common sense. In his second year, he quit and went to work in Newark, New Jersey, as a reporter for *The Star-Ledger*, and subsequently supported himself freelancing.

Abby graduated from the University of Connecticut, where she met and married the scion of a wealthy Dutch family who made their money from diamond cutting and lived on Central Park East. She and her husband took up residence across the park in the Dakota apartments. From Abby I learned the little I knew about Clarissa, information that I faithfully passed on to Ben, who mourned her as one might a dead child. After honeymooning in Hawaii, she and Brian had settled in Delaware. Through his father, he had found work in the advertising department of D and P Chemical. They had a daughter, Tamara, whom they called Tammy. Apparently, Clarissa belonged to all the right clubs—yachting, tennis, and golf—and felt "profoundly unused," living a life of conspicuous consumption. Her boredom led her to Europe in the summer and to the Caribbean in the winter. She frequently flew to New York to see Abby, and invariably took a side trip to Newark to spend time with Ben. On one occasion, knowing that Clarissa had recently seen him, I telephoned to ask how the visit had gone. Discreet as ever, he would say only that she remained a beautiful woman but had become "terribly fitful."

From 1953 to 1969, Ben and I usually met in early January. His socialist principles had survived both Hungary and the death of his parents. "I'm a democratic socialist, not a Stalinist," he would periodically remind me, and cite the Scandinavian countries as a model of what he espoused, although "spoused," to coin a word, might be more accurate, given his love of politics. We would meet in San Francisco at the St. Francis or in New York at the Essex House. Joe Riley had started a legal practice in the Bay Area, and had made his peace with Ben. We occasionally joined him for dinner in Chinatown, until his murder in a courtroom, at the hands of a fanatic who hated Joe for defending young women accused of breaking the abortion law. In New York, we frequently dined with Abby, who always insisted on paying the tab. "My old man can afford it," she said, "whereas you two guys don't have a pot to piss in." Ben's fondness for

darkmatters
LEVITT

Abby continued unabated—how could one not love her?—even though he teased her about her millions. If the truth be known, Abby helped me out financially after my father's business had failed, and I drifted from one job to another. With her support and my shrink's, I finally stabilized my life and landed my current position at the post office, which enabled me, as of a year ago, to get off Abby's payroll.

In May 1969, Ben invited me to spend a fortnight with him in Prague. He had contracted with *The Star-Ledger* to cover the first anniversary of the Warsaw Pact Invasion. Knowing that I wanted to visit the Jewish cemetery, one of the most famous in Europe, he urged me to join him. I was well aware that he wanted to see for himself what had killed the Prague Spring, counterrevolutionaries or Russians or a combination of both. Socialists around the world invested Czechoslovakia with a symbolic importance. Here was a nation in the Soviet orbit that had evolved peacefully into a democratic one. Somewhere in Ben's ghostly heart he needed to believe that the country of his parents—the country that had toppled the hated Czar—could not be blind to the aspirations of others. Admittedly, Stalin had been a monster; but Khrushchev had denounced Stalinism and apologized for the Terror. The argument that the Russians hovered over the country like the sword of Damocles, threatening to liquidate independent-minded socialists, he called capitalist propaganda. Convinced that the west had misrepresented the state of affairs, he pointed to the fact that the liberal socialists in Prague had been quashed not only by all the Warsaw Pact countries, but also by once-progressive socialists in the Czech communist movement. He wanted to learn for himself why Husák, who had himself been imprisoned for failing to toe the party line, had betrayed three old friends and genuine reform-minded communists: Alexander Dubček, Colonel Ludvik Svoboda, and Frantisek Kriegel.

I cannot emphasize enough his hope to prove the world wrong. He was utterly persuaded that the real story had yet to be told.

Although I volunteered to make all the arrangements for visas and plane tickets, Ben having no head for travel details, I did so with some trepidation. My mother had been seriously ill, and my sister, staying with her in Detroit, made me promise I would keep in close contact, since we had not reserved any hotels in advance. Ben and I met in New York and flew to Milan, where we bought a used Fiat "bus," no larger than most American cars, and continued on to Venice, staying at the Albergo San Maurizio, just across the canal from the Accademia. Even before I unpacked, I called home to check on my mother. She appeared to be holding her own.

In our college days, Ben and I had both sworn that we'd never visit Austria or Germany. We wanted no part of those murderers, and we certainly didn't want to contribute to their financial well-being with our tourist dollars. But the way to Prague led through Austria. Sitting in the Piazza San Marco, we dawdled over a bottle of wine and a map, plotting our course so that we wouldn't have to spend much time among Jew-haters. Our discussion migrated to Mussolini and Margherita Sarfatti, two names which recalled that long-ago talk in Lexington with Mr. Hazelwood.

"He was a cultured man," Ben mused. "I don't suppose his son gives him much joy. Let's hope his granddaughter does."

I found this statement strange, as if it concealed more than it said. "She's a teenager now. Most teens are a handful," I offered in hopes of drawing him out.

"After her birth, Clarissa decided that motherhood didn't suit her. So she's hardly ever at home. First a nanny raised Tammy and now Brian's family. It's got to be hard on the kid."

"What the hell does Clarissa do in Europe every summer?" I asked, expecting him to say that she shops or takes a Cook's tour. But he left me speechless with an uncharacteristic glimpse into his personal life.

"Studies French at the *Alliance* in Paris . . . and spends one month with me in Greece."

Ben

Dear Abby keeps Ben current on Clarissa's complaints. Within a year of marriage, Clarissa writes to Abby lamenting her husband's mundane interests and her pointless life. Brian's vacuous table talk apparently affects their pillow talk. Just as she feared, she finds him boring, even in lovemaking. Abby, always irreverent, says that he can erect a penis but not much else. Aimlessness has led to a profound ennui that she tries to dispel with frequent trips abroad. She asks Abby, who has remained friendly with Ben, to serve as a go-between. At first Ben resists, but when Abby reminds him that the best revenge is generosity, he agrees. Two months go by and he hears nothing. Finally, Clarissa sends him a short note saying that she will be in New York City to see *Pagliacci* and would be terribly pleased if he would let her treat him to the opera and a post-performance dinner at her hotel, the Plaza.

They meet at the Met, on Broadway in the West Thirties. He arrives first. She pulls up in a cab. Her beauty and red velvet dress turn more than a few heads. In the lobby, they stand a moment awkwardly gazing at each other. She holds out her hands; he takes them. They embrace. Strangely, they don't speak until they have taken their seats, and even then their conversation proceeds haltingly. Nothing of substance is said until Pagliacci kills his faithless wife and her lover.

Ben whispers, "I don't want Brian getting the wrong idea."

Clarissa replies enigmatically, "Or the right one."

On the street, she starts to hail a cab but he says he'd rather walk. The evening air has been freshened by a light rain. In a short time, they reach 59th Street and Central Park. He can see in the leaves the first signs of autumn, and smell in the breeze the coming of winter. As they approach Fifth Avenue, they detour into the park and amble toward the Mall. In the distance stands the statue of Sir Walter Scott. Ben uses his handkerchief to wipe off the dampness from a bench along Literary Walk. They sit. The fountain in front of the Plaza Hotel glows in the play of the overhead lights. After an uncomfortable silence, Clarissa alludes to the opera.

"I don't think Brian could generate enough passion to kill a lover of mine—or me."

Ben wants to say that he knew all along how dissatisfied she would be, but embraces her instead. She softly cries.

"I lost my nerve . . . that's what happened. And you, what about you?"

Ben has had numerous flings but has yet to find someone who can satisfy his restless spirit or his taste for radical politics. "The dating game."

"But no one special?"

"No."

She smiles, clearly glad. "Not a day passes that I don't think, 'Where is Ben? What's he doing now?'"

"I think of you also."

"But not every day," she teases.

He chooses his words carefully, knowing that she might take them as a reproach rather than as a relief. "If what you are saying, Clarissa, is that you still want me—"

She spares him the pain of saying, as he'd planned, "you can't recover the past," by interjecting:

"I'd gladly leave him. Get a divorce. We can start over."

"Clarissa—"

Again she stops him. "There's only one impediment." She pauses and looks away. "I'm pregnant. But," she says in a steely manner, "I can get that fixed—if you'll have me."

Ben's head swims from desire and bitter memories of defeat. He has often thought that Clarissa did him a favor by marrying and freeing him from her temptress ways. He realizes that he can use Brian for his own selfish purposes. If Clarissa remains Brian's responsibility, Ben is at liberty to be her lover. He briefly relishes the thought, but forces himself to reply:

"Maybe this child will bring you and Brian closer."

"The truth is I'm a terrible mother. I can't stand kids."

"But . . ."

"It was an accident. Funny enough, Brian makes a wonderful father."

"Clarissa, have the baby. Then see what happens."

The rain returns and they walk across the street to the Plaza for dinner. Both of them seem disinclined to resume the subject broached in the park. They eat slowly and meditatively, with mute intervals between shreds of conversation. Mostly they reminisce. Consciously keeping the talk from touching upon his own personal life, Ben asks Clarissa about hers. Leaning on the table, her chin resting on her clasped hands, she talks to him about the years since they parted.

"I've been a vagabond . . . aimless. I now realize that I needed someone like you to give me direction."

"You would have resented my advice."

"Yes, but in fact it would have been good for me."

The discussion migrates to Clarissa's daughter and how little Clarissa is involved in her life. "She adores Brian and his parents. Perhaps if she had been yours, I'd feel differently."

At the end of the meal, Clarissa settles the check and sees him to the curb. The doorman steps into the street to hail Ben a cab.

"I guess we're even," she murmurs. "The first time, I said no. This time, you did."

Shortly after their rapprochement, Clarissa writes to say that she has had a miscarriage. Ben can guess the cause. He pens a note of condolence, but of course omits his suspicions. She replies immediately, initiating a regular correspondence that leads to their meeting whenever she comes to New York. She always follows the same schedule. Saturday morning, she takes the train to Newark. Ben meets her at Penn Station and drives to Milburn, where he has a two-bedroom apartment littered with books and newspapers. Clarissa always tidies up. They walk in Weequahic Park and occasionally take a rowboat out on the lake. After dinner, they invariably stop for a chocolate sundae at Grunings Ice Cream, in South Orange Village. She returns to New York the same day, on a late-evening train. Although Ben has more than once asked her to spend the night, their visits are always chaste—a penance, he believes, for his failure to respond to her offer of marriage.

Enjoying the benefits of being a free lance, Ben chooses to escape Newark's summer heat by spending August to mid-September on the Greek island of Thasos, a short distance from the picturesque city of Kavalla. He prefers to travel alone. Often friends, including Clarissa, ask where he spends his holidays. He prefers not to say, and if pressed will say only "Greece." On Thasos, he retreats to the mountain village of Panagia, where he stays in the house of Ariadne Toupoyannis. A widow, she warmly attends to his physical needs and also teaches him the rudiments of Greek. But Ben soon learns that in a foreign tongue he can utter only banalities. In 1960, he decides to try a different Greek island. Uncertain which one to select, he visits several. While enjoying the sandy beaches of Andros, he meets a young Dutch couple who tell him that Santorini is well worth a visit; but, short of time, he decides to save that trip for the following summer.

In early August 1961, the night before flying from New York to Athens, he dines with Abby and tells her *en passant* where he's headed. "I hear it gets pretty crowded. Have you made reservations?"

Perhaps because on Thasos he has standing accommodations, he has never written in advance. "I'll just try my luck."

From Piraeus, he sails to Santorini on a wheezing boat that smells of diesel fuel and sun lotion. Landing at the bottom of a towering cliff, he and the others ride mules up a winding trail. The narrow path terrifies most of the tourists, who lean toward the mountain, bright with white outcroppings of tufa. At the top, he finds himself on a flat plain in Santorini City— and without lodging. Told that the one large hotel has been booked for months, he stops in the restaurant for a snack and bumps into Clarissa. When he explains his plight, she invites him to share her room, expressing regret that her reservation expires the next day, at which time she plans to fly from Santorini to Athens.

"What are you doing here?" he inquires.

"Searching for you. Abby told me."

He doesn't know whether to believe her. "Your dishonesty is outrageous, but flattering nonetheless."

"Just so long as you're flattered."

That night, memory and desire unite them, and the next afternoon Ben accompanies her to the airport, where she cashes in her ticket and returns with him to Santorini City. Now both without any hotel reservations, they approach a cab driver who speaks English, and ask him if he knows a place to stay. He says "Please," gesturing toward his cab. As they speed into the moonless night, Ben can't see more than a few feet outside the taxi. Clarissa begins to worry that they are being shanghaied to some out-of-the-way place where they will be robbed and killed. Eventually, the cab comes to a stop and the driver exclaims, "We're here!" Ben and Clarissa can see absolutely nothing in the darkness. The driver leads the way, until they are standing outside the door of what appears to be a large house. Taking a key from his pocket, he opens the door. They follow him a few feet through an unlit hallway that smells of fresh plaster and raw wood. He enters a room, gropes around, and finds what has momentarily eluded him: a bulb hanging by a wire. The room, furnished with a chest of drawers, a chair, and twin beds, *sans* mattresses, feels utterly removed from this world. Ben asks what town they are in, and the driver says "Akro Tiri," a name that means nothing to them. Clarissa wants to know who owns the albergo. The driver proudly declares that he and his family have built it, apologizing for their having completed only this one bedroom and a bathroom at the end of the hall. He takes them through a side door into the garage, which holds dozens of mattresses, still in their plastic wrappers, stacked from floor to ceiling. They carry two of them into the bedroom. The driver says he has no linens, and requests they use the plastic for one night, and the next day purchase sheets and pillow cases in town. Ben inquires what the room costs. The driver shrugs, as if to say "who knows," wishes them a pleasant stay, and leaves. Stepping outside the hotel, they look around, but blackness has devoured the landscape. They cannot see even a light twinkling in some faraway farm. That night, the plastic mattress covers cause them to sweat profusely and sleep poorly in the summer heat.

At daylight, they step outside the front door and find a basket of fresh tomatoes and a loaf of newly baked bread. In one direction, the road undulates till it disappears; in the other, it leads to a taverna about fifty yards distant. Across the way, a field stretches to the far treeless hills. But nowhere can they see a single person. Eating the tomatoes and bread, they walk to the taverna, actually a house with an outdoor patio. The door, hung with strings of glass beads, opens into a small room that holds five tables and chairs. Beyond it stands the kitchen. Ben calls. An elderly woman and her fortyish daughter materialize and speak to them in Greek. Ben can understand just enough to discern that they are being asked what food they would like to eat. Ben tries to explain. The old woman motions for them to follow her into the kitchen. Ben and Clarissa point to a coffee pot and some eggs. For the next ten days, Ben and Clarissa take most of their meals at the taverna, which charges a pittance. During that time, they learn that

darkmatters LEVITT

Akro Tiri, located in the southern part of the island, houses a small archaeological dig, less than a mile away, along the road to the main beach. The town, perched on the backside of the hill that overlooks their "hotel," cannot be seen unless one continues down the road to a point several yards beyond the taverna. On the main street, they find a few shops, including one with linens, and a bakery, where the owner manages in broken English to identify himself as the person who had left the bread, and the woman who owns the fruit and vegetable stand as the source of the tomatoes. Ben and Clarissa regularly patronize their shops and quickly become known as the "Yankis."

Never having really lived together, Ben and Clarissa find this new experience comfortable. The metronomic beats of a shared life dictate their days: sweeping the albergo, changing the linens (a woman in town does the laundering), cleaning the bathroom, shopping for food, participating in village events. Clarissa's attention to the details of dressing and Ben's to his ocular migraines (owing to the head wound) become natural. The irony of a summer marriage is not lost on Ben, not now, not later. He and Clarissa can be married only on holiday, only in a place where neither of them has roots.

One morning, while Ben is sitting alone on the terrace of the taverna sipping a cup of coffee—Clarissa having remained behind to wash some clothes—a young woman, thirtyish, approaches him and in perfect English says, "You must be one of the Americans the locals are talking about. My name is Artemis Skouras, and several men in the town would like to introduce themselves to you. I teach English and French in the local school. If you don't mind, perhaps tomorrow you could spare an hour or two. I will bring the men here."

Ben agrees, and the next day holds court for the butcher, two fishermen, a retired soldier, an Albanian refugee, and the brother of the taxi cab driver. From each issues a boon. The butcher insists that Ben and Clarissa must attend a "festa" in the town square that features the slaughtering and roasting of a bull, followed by dancing. The fishermen disclose the location of a secluded beach, with black volcanic sand as fine as powder, known only to the townspeople. The retired soldier recounts the German occupation of Greece and tells him about a nearby monastery that often hid allied soldiers during the war. The Albanian describes the conditions of his country under the Stalinist regime of Enver Hoxha, persuading Ben for all time that whatever ills a revolution cures, when it no longer trusts the

darkmatters LEVITT

people, it has lost all legitimacy and forfeited its right to lead. The brother of the taxi cab driver invites him to his mother's house for coffee and cakes, where he and Clarissa, assisted by Artemis, enjoy the company of the leading lights of the community.

After two weeks nude bathing on the volcanic beach and dinners taken at the taverna, Ben and Clarissa fit right into the rhythms of the town, so much so that the mayor invites them to attend a party at his house, which stands high on a hill above the sea. A four-piece island folk orchestra plays the violi (violin), the lavouto (lute), the sandouri (hammered dulcimer), and the toumbeleki (hand drum). On the outdoor terrace, strung with colored lights among the vines in the overhead trellis, are arrayed innumerable dishes of food and several kinds of wine. At a dozen long tables, the guests eat sitting down, communal style. During dinner, the musicians play popular lachrymose songs, and later, folk music. The guests uninhibitedly dance for hours and introduce the Yankis to numerous steps—including the pyrrikheos, a pyrrhic dance described by Xenophon in the fourth century B.C.—that enable them to show off their splendid dancing skills. By the end of the party, at three or four in the morning, Ben and Clarissa have become local favorites. Every summer thereafter they return to Akro Tiri, where they feel wedded to the culture—and to each other.

darkmatters
LEVITT

Marty

As Ben and I packed our bags to leave Venice, he sheepishly apologized for not accompanying me back to the States. From Prague, he planned to fly to Milan and then Athens, where he and Clarissa would spend a few days en route to Santorini.

"Doesn't Brian get suspicious?"

"It's not my place to ask."

"One of these days, his sleuth of a father will have you in court for alienating the affections of his daughter-in-law."

Ben laughed. "Alienation's no longer a punishable crime, except in a political context."

"Ain't that the truth," I said colloquially for emphasis.

"When I'm alone with Clarissa, I've often thought that she remains married to Brian precisely because she can meet me each summer. Were I not there to provide some relief, I'm convinced she would leave him."

"And if she did?"

His answer surprised me. "She thinks we could be happily married. But it isn't true. She'll never really mature because she always seeks the easy way out. Her fecklessness would normally keep me away, but I admit that I'm still drawn to her beauty and those special moments when she actually employs her mind. She's really quite clever, you know. But because she's so out of practice, she finds it hard to sustain a serious thought." He then added off-handedly: "Besides, as I said, now that I'm around she'll never leave him. She has the best of both worlds, money and me. I may be dangerous, but as long as she can return to Brian, she's safe."

I found his explanation oppressively sad, because together, and at the top of their game, the parts exceeded the whole; and apart, they added up to a loss.

Driving toward Austria through northern Italy, we amused ourselves by trying to stump each other with arcane words, until we stopped to see the monument erected to La Sarfatti's son, Roberto, who had died here. Ben claimed that had he not lost his life, and had Mussolini not been so badly wounded in the same war, the modern history of Italy might look entirely different. The alpine landscape and the pervasive scent of pines reminded me of the Gila National Forest, leading me to ask Ben about Esperanza.

"Do you still stay in touch?"

"Yes."

"And?"

"And what? She's still married, though separated from Luis."

"I suppose if she divorced him—"

Ben interjected with a comment that still lingers. "My life might have been vastly different."

The second morning, in Lienz, we heard music outside our window: a funeral procession, complete with a brass band in Tyrolean dress and a horse-drawn hearse. I tucked my thumbs into the palms of my hands to ward off the evil. The third day, we crossed into Czechoslovakia, south of Susice. On both sides of the border, dark forests covered the landscape. Just inside Czechoslovakia, as far as the eye could see, stretched rolls of razor-studded barbed wire. The border guards greeted us coldly, ordering us out of the car. Marched inside, we had to undergo a body search, while the police virtually dismantled our bus. Finding nothing of a political nature, they stamped our passports and visas—and sternly warned that if we changed dollars for korunas (crowns) on the black market, we would be subject to a fine and imprisonment. Moreover, on our leaving the country, all our purchases would have to bear a receipt in korunas. Money could be changed only at official currency offices.

A Czech friend of mine, Jirí Nehnevajsa, whom Ben dismissed as an incorrigible nationalist, had said that dollars were the true Czech currency, buying escape from the country and supporting dissident groups. Dollars, he claimed, paid for clandestine printing presses and thereby bought trouble for the Husák government, which particularly feared demonstrations on the first anniversary of the Warsaw Pact invasion, August 21. The

darkmatters LEVITT

border guards had clearly been instructed to sniff out troublemakers whom they could bar from the country; but we seemed hardly the sort. Looking back now, I wish we had qualified, and Ben had flown down to Greece. But that's anticipating the blow.

Twenty miles into the country, we passed a prison work camp. Another omen, I thought, and again knuckled my thumbs. The flat countryside housed small farms surrounded by golden bales of rolled hay. We passed through a number of wretched villages and arrived in Pilsen around dinnertime. The tourist agency, pleading an absence of beds in the city, made reservations for us at a sports camp outside of town, and converted dollars into korunas. Ben changed five hundred and I six. Before leaving the city, we stopped for dinner at what had once been the grandest hotel in the town. The entire restaurant had only one waiter. It took almost an hour to be seated, another hour to be served, and over three to exit the dump. The cavernous room stood virtually silent, though every table was taken. The menu, four pages long and printed in four languages (Czech, German, French, and English), meant nothing. You could choose from one of two entrees, but only one dessert, ice cream. After we placed our orders, Ben went into the next room to the bar and returned with four Pilsen beers. The frothy ales made up for the execrable service and food. A piece of burned meat, swimming in grease, and cold, hard potatoes constituted the entree. While eating my ice cream, I felt a foreign object in my mouth and removed it, a small metal screw.

"It's probably an electronic bug," I said kiddingly, and held it up for the diners around us to see.

No one smiled.

"You'd better put it away," Ben advised soberly.

Dinner over, we took a long walk. Pilsen, known for its brewery, stank of hops. The sooty grey city had been badly neglected. The shop windows exhibited no more than three or four items, all covered with dust. Buildings and streets needed repair. The few people we saw shuffled along in a slouch. We stopped in a small park. Four old men sat wordlessly, dressed in shabby grey clothes. I had on a red polo shirt, and I remember thinking that my shirt provided the only touch of color in that dreary setting.

"This place is cheerless and hopeless," I said.

Ben didn't answer. I wouldn't have been surprised to learn that his thoughts concerned the so-called successes of communism.

Finally, when I urged, "Let's get out of here," even Ben, who scrutinized each building and street with the eye of a surveyor, had had enough.

We drove to the sports camp, only to discover that our room slept eight. All of us washed with cold water and bunked in narrow beds as hard as stone. In the morning, some health nut woke everyone at first light, directing us to congregate on the field for calisthenics. Although Ben and I stayed in bed, we could hear the barking directions of the counselor instructing the others.

On the morning of August 17, forgoing breakfast, we set out for Prague, passing well-groomed fields and a few farmers plowing with horses or an ancient tractor. A mile or two from the city, in a stand of woods, we saw at least fifty or sixty Russian tanks and hundreds of soldiers. Ben slowed the bus, but one of the soldiers waved us on. At the Prague city limits, Ben stopped at a tourist office responsible for making room reservations. Again told that housing was scarce, we discussed driving into the old town and taking our chances. But the pretty blonde woman in charge of the counter insisted that we had to book rooms through her office. She directed us to a place on one of the main arteries leading into the city: the Stop Motel. To this day, I find the name disconcertingly prescient.

The motel, prophylactically clean, smelled of disinfectant. We checked in and, as directed, left our passports with the woman at the desk. Ben took his bags upstairs, and I wired my family in Detroit, giving them my Prague address. The cell-like room had two cots, a three-drawer bureau, and a radio with only one station, which broadcast either speeches, inevitably followed by thunderous applause, or 1940s music. But the motel did have a bar that served cold Pilsen beer and also *slivovitz*, a potent plum brandy. By the end of our stay in Prague, we had become heavy users of both. In the lounge, we ran into a number of foreigners, mostly Italians, Aussies, and Brits. One sallow-faced fellow sitting alone in a corner turned out to be the state's official guide assigned to our motel; in other words, a security agent. Ben spotted him almost as soon as we walked in the door. At first, I took him for a dyspeptic drunk. But when Ben spoke to him in Russian, the fellow nearly leapt out of his baggy suit. Although amusing to see, the man's surprise should have warned us that any western foreigner speaking Russian would be considered a spy. He wanted to know where Ben had learned Russian and why his parents had left the socialist paradise of the Soviet Union for the U.S. Introducing himself as Mr. Stavický, he never once smiled, and clearly liked asking discomfiting questions. For example, he asked Ben whether he approved of Dubček's press laws. But Ben never had a chance to say more than a few words, because Mr. Stavický asked how a foreigner, like him, would even know about such things unless he had been prepared in advance.

"Who paid for your trip?"

"I did," said Ben.

"You're a journalist."

"How do you know that?"

"Your visa says so."

"But you've never seen my visa."

"No, but the woman at the desk has."

"I see."

Mr. Stavický opened his mouth slightly, as if to smile, but must have thought better of the impulse because he closed it. "*Do svidanya*," he said, and left the lounge.

That evening, we signed up at the motel desk for a tour of Hradĉany Castle and the Strahov Monastery, which houses the Museum of National Literature. In the morning, the bus arrived in front of our motel, and who should board with us but our friendly agent, Mr. Stavický. I noticed that he nodded toward the interpreter, a gesture devoid of subtlety for a man engaged in surveillance work. Mr. Stavický insisted on sitting behind Ben and me, so we deliberately changed our seats to the front. Following us down the aisle, he asked the couple behind us to move, and took their place. Ben foolishly mocked the man by saying loud enough for him to hear that at the castle, he knew just where to place the incendiaries and bombs. As the bus moved through the busy city streets, we heard for the first time the chant that would resound through our entire stay: Dubček, Svoboda! Dubček, Svoboda! Ben repeated the names, and the snitch behind us madly scribbled notes in a soiled little pad.

Even though the communist authorities had let the old architecture fall into a deplorable state, presumably as a result of terrible economic conditions, the buildings and monuments of Prague have few equals. What had been built since the end of World War II qualified as the ugliest structures I had ever seen. They too showed wear, not from neglect, but from shoddy workmanship. Ben and I disparagingly called the new buildings "Stalinist Modern," a phrase that elicited further notes from our ubiquitous agent.

Divided into four historic districts—Staré Mesto and Nové Mesto on the east bank of the Vltava river, and Hradĉany and Malá Strana on the west bank—the city had escaped widespread destruction during the war and still retained its Hapsburg character. As the bus pulled into Castle Square, the interpreter/guide, Mr. Horvath, stood up at the front and told us that we had to stay together as a group. If any of us strayed, we would immediately be led back to the bus, where we would have to remain until the others returned. Mr. Stavický remained in the bus, I suppose in the capacity of jailer, should anyone wander from the group. The Castle, the traditional home of the king, Mr. Horvath explained, now housed the Czech president and chancellery. As he led us into the Castle, Ben whispered that our group had a tail. Sure enough, a fellow with a battered fedora and tasteless tweed suit followed us from a distance. The tour guide took us through three different courtyards, one constructed as early as the sixteenth century, and showed us St. Vitus Cathedral and the great Gothic-style Vladislav Hall. Although one might have expected the reverse, he waxed lyrical when we stopped to see the oldest Romanesque church in Prague, the Basilica of St. George. Everyone behaved as ordered, walking in line and forming a semi-circle about Mr. Horvath as he spoke. But at the Strahov Monastery, Ben decided to bedevil our guide and our tail.

On our way back to the bus, he eased away from the group, hiding behind a pillar. When our official snoop noticed Ben's absence, he and the guide became frantic, the both of them gesticulating and talking madly. The guide ushered us onto the bus, while our bird dog scurried off to find Ben. In took Ben about fifteen minutes to appear, leisurely making his way toward the parking lot. The driver, the guide, and Mr. Stavický huddled; the guide then scurried off, presumably to find his companion.

"Where the hell did you go?" I whispered, wanting to hear the details before Mr. Stavický returned to his seat.

"Once our shadow walked past me, I shadowed him. He merely retraced the steps of our tour. But not finding me, he ducked into a kiosk to make a telephone call, and I snuck into the monastery library."

"Why did you do it . . . because they ordered us not to?"

"In junior high school, a kid by the name of Bobbie Greese tried to steal my bag lunch. A friend, Louie Russo, kicked his ass. Greese knew he could never take Louie in a fight, and he feared what Louie might do to him if he assaulted me. So he used to follow me at a distance, always with a knife

darkmatters
LEVITT

tucked away in the palm of his hand. I never forgot the experience. These snoops who follow us . . . they know they have the police behind them. That's their knife. I wouldn't be surprised if the army showed up."

The army never did, but several policemen came on the run. By this time, the guide had tracked down our shadow and told him that Ben could be found on the bus. The guide and the bird dog, after conferring with the police, boarded and asked Ben to answer some questions. The police, in the meantime, remained stationed outside.

"Ask!" said Ben calmly, implying that he intended to hold court from his seat.

"Come with us!" ordered the guide.

"No!" said Ben. "I'm staying put."

Again the authorities conferred. Finally, the guide returned and said that he needed to know where Ben had gone during his absence from the group.

"To the lavatory."

That reply threw the men into such confusion that the police reached for their walkie-talkies and babbled away. Finally, they signalled that the bus could proceed. The other tourists, none too happy with the delay, made some critical comments that prompted Ben to respond. "I don't like being followed. I want to know what the government's afraid of." Out came Mr. Stavický's pad and pencil, as he scribbled more notes.

Back at the hotel, Ben suggested we take the Fiat and find a tavern in town. "The Stop Motel probably has wiretaps everywhere," he said. So we drove to a small place not far from Wenceslas Square, taking some care to avoid being followed. At mid-afternoon, the bar, surprisingly full and quiet as a coffin, had only one vacant table. The patrons glanced at us quickly and then leaned over their drinks. We ordered slivovitz and beer. Knocking back his shot, Ben asked for another, which he put away with equal dispatch. The beer had a thick foam on it. Ben took a draught that, unbeknownst to him, left a thick white mustache on his upper lip. As he looked around the tavern, the other men broke into laughter, an explosive guffawing that sounded to me like people finding a release. We both chuckled as well when I told Ben what had caused the merriment. The ice broken, chatter broke out all over. Men previously hunched over their drinks now sat upright and garrulously spoke to their companions. I had never witnessed anything like it. The scene transformed itself from a funeral to a farce, with men pounding the table, holding up their glasses, singing songs, conspicuously belching, and deliberately imitating Ben by dipping their faces into their beers and coming up with foamy mustaches. The waiter, who knew a few words of English, came to our table and said:

"You make laugh . . . feel good . . . thank you."

Leaving the tavern, we entered the square, the place that began Ben's days of truth. Hundreds of students had gathered on the grounds of the National Museum, coalescing around the statue of an armored King Wenceslas on horseback, a popular destination of the dispossessed and the disenchanted. The square itself, a half-mile long and 180-feet wide, still served as the traditional gathering place for announcements and speeches. Here protesters gathered and laid wreaths; here people lit candles and celebrated open-air masses. The square, relatively free of protesters, buzzed with shoppers, creating a disconcerting juxtaposition of normality and unrest.

An eerie siren suddenly wailed, and from behind the National Museum hundreds of policemen with white helmets descended on the students, who waved arms and made fists. Their expletives, mostly incomprehensible to us, included two words we could understand: "Gestapo!" and "Fascist!" As the students dispersed, we retreated from the square, returning to our motel and an early night.

The next morning, August 19, we drove to the Jewish cemetery, which lies between the Old Town Square and the river. My tutor's greatest desire had been to see this famous burial ground, but God never granted his wish. Considered one of the most significant historical relics of Prague, the cemetery attracts thousands of visitors because of its ancient origin and the many important persons buried there, as well as the unique art of its tombstones. One cannot escape the impression of medievalism created by the scattering of the large variety of tombstones made of different materials, in a multitude of archaic styles and shapes. My rabbi had always spoken reverentially of Rabbi Loew, a scholar whose works fill fifteen volumes. The good man, interred here, died in 1609. With the help of a guidebook I found the pink marble tomb, adorned with a pine cone, a lion, and a wreath. The top of the tombstone was covered by pebbles, an honor Jews bestow upon extraordinary people. I picked up two from the path and did likewise, silently remembering my tutor.

For reasons lost to history, Rabbi Loew came to be associated with the Golem, a clay figure that comes to life. As I studied the gravestone, I had the feeling of being watched. Standing next to the cemetery wall was Mr.

Stavický. Ben walked over and spoke to him in Russian. He replied in kind. Turning to me, Ben said, "I asked Mr. Stavický if he's Jewish. He said yes. Then why, I said, do you work as a snoop for the hated Husák government?" Ben returned his gaze to our unwanted guest. "Repeat in English what you said, so my friend Marty can hear."

"If you mean," said Mr. Stavický , "why do I work for the communists—"

Ben interrupted. "Dubček is a democratic socialist. Husák is a puppet."

"I lived through the fascist period of the Vlajkists, and the German occupation of Czechoslovakia. The Nazis shipped my two daughters, Rebeka and Rachel, to Terezín, and also my wife. They died there. Rebeka painted beautifully, and Rachel played the violin. I joined the partisans, most of them communists. If not for them, we might still be living under a fascist government. The communists liberated us. I owe them a debt. Do I wish they'd live up to the ideals they proclaim? Of course. But at least no one goes hungry."

His candid admission still haunts me, because I often ask myself how all the idealistic communists must have felt when Lenin and his successors turned to terror to effect their so-called Bolshevik paradise. How great must have been the self-hatred among utopians when the revolution started murdering its own believers, and when the Russian leaders declared that anyone who disagreed with them or wished to leave Russia's paradise for the corruption and greed of the west must be a traitor or unbalanced, and was therefore shot or imprisoned in a mental institution. As the long, terrible night descended on eastern and central Europe, as the bullets of Stalinist firing squads tore through the flesh of the poets and priests, the dramatists and doctors, as governments became the preserve of apparatchiks and assassins, what could the idealists have been thinking? I suppose Mr. Stavický had answered Ben's question. But surely there comes a time when a debt requires no further payment.

"Why do you shadow us and not the others?" Ben asked.

"You speak Russian."

"I see, therefore I'm an American spy."

"Orders."

The three of us entered the Jewish museum adjacent to the cemetery.

"It was here," remarked Mr. Stavický, "that Hitler said Jewish history would end. He planned this museum as a monument to a dead race, one that he had extinguished."

The artifacts of a once flourishing people and the vibrancy of different Jewish communities now appeared under glass. I felt sick, but the worst lay ahead. In the next room, the walls had been covered with the letters and drawings of children in the concentration camps. Under each letter, the authorities had included translations in several languages. As I stood there reading the pleas and hopes for a better world, tears clouded my eyes and, no longer able to endure the pain in my heart, went outside.

Around noon, we all left the cemetery together, and Mr. Stavický actually joined us for a drink at a bar he recommended. Over beers, he and Ben talked mostly in whispered Russian, because the Czechs didn't take kindly to their occupiers. Sitting there, dark to their words, reminded me of those times my mother's sister would visit, and the two women would speak in Polish. I always felt obtuse and wondered why I couldn't understand. Even now, I think of language as a code that one learns to crack. From time to time, Ben would translate. Mostly they talked about family, but at one point Ben recoiled and became agitated, raising his voice.

"What's wrong?" I enquired.

"He warned me not to go to Wenceslas Square today, tomorrow, or the next day. He said there'd be worse trouble than I could imagine."

"Namely?"

"He won't tell me. That's why I got so annoyed."

Thursday, August 21, loomed in two days. We had come principally to satisfy Ben's curiosity regarding the occupation of Czechoslovakia, and to see whether reactionaries were provoking the demonstrations planned for the first anniversary of the Warsaw Pact invasion. I therefore knew that nothing could deter Ben from showing up in the square. Although we fully anticipated that soldiers would try to prevent any "counter-revolutionary" activities, as the government called them, the statement about "worse trouble" sounded ominous. Mr. Stavický leaned over and whispered to Ben.

"He says that the Czech police intend on Wednesday night to block off all the streets leading into the square. But he frankly admits that many of them will probably turn a blind eye because they sympathize with the protest."

"I'd still like to know what he meant about 'worse trouble.'"

"I guess we'll find out."

When we parted company, Mr. Stavický hopped on a streetcar and disappeared in the crowd. We returned to Wenceslas Square.

From Ben's First Prague Dispatch

Dateline: August 19, Prague. This morning, Gustav Husák warned that his government would repress any hostile demonstrations on the first anniversary of the Warsaw Pact Invasion. Nothing seemed amiss in Wenceslas Square, as shoppers and tourists filled the cafes and stores. But around 4 p.m., hundreds of students entered the square, some distributing small printed leaflets in the national colors, blue, white, and red.

Titled "Days of Shame, August 20–21," the leaflets reviewed the Warsaw Pact invasion and its aftermath, and sounded a call for peaceful protests. Slowly the crowds moved toward the statue of King Wenceslas, where several young people laid flowers at the foot of the monument. Immediately, armored cars poured out of the side streets and police tossed tear gas canisters into the crowd.

As the young men and women shouted "Gestapo!" and "*Ruská sviňe*" (Russian swine), heavily armed policemen kicked them and beat them on the head with truncheons. The protests went on for hours, fueled by an endless parade of people who came to lend their moral support. By 8 p.m., armored troop carriers arrived, chasing the demonstrators up and down the eight-block long square as onlookers on sidewalks and streetcar platforms sarcastically applauded, shouting "Democracy!" and "Shame!"

Marty

As soon as we could safely quit the square, we returned to our Fiat and drove back to the Stop Motel, where Ben immediately composed his dispatch for the *Star-Ledger*, and wired it courtesy of the London *Times* back to the States. That evening state radio and television included no mention of the disorders. After taking dinner at a nearby bistro, we moseyed through the new part of the city, constructed of ugly prefabricated cement slabs, already evidencing serious decay. The vast, dark, bleak buildings made me feel slightly nauseated, as if I had entered a dizzying maze that permitted no exit. Aimlessly walking the deserted streets, we turned a corner and stumbled upon a theatre, not the Laterna Magika, for which we held tickets on Friday night. Approaching it from the rear, we could hear people inside and saw an open stage door. Seeing no one, we entered and found ourselves standing alone in the wings of a puppet theatre. Two puppeteers sat above the stage, pulling strings. Our sight lines allowed us to see, at the same time, both the show and the showmen. The puppet masters, devoid of expression, manipulated the cords as if playing a harp. Their hands flew from one to another, dexterously unfolding a story in mime.

I can still remember the set and the action.

On one side of the raked stage, a low wall; on the other, a pile of rags. Upstage, four tables, each holding something different: food, clothing, a small stove, keys. A fat man in a tuxedo and high hat enters with a walking stick. Oversize dollar bills hang from his back pocket identifying him, I suppose, as a capitalist. He comes downstage and burps. The audience laughs. A poor bedraggled rag picker, wearing spectacles, enters and sorts through his wares. He finds a glossy remnant and offers to sell it to the capitalist. Fingering it, the capitalist pockets the cloth and pummels the rag picker with his cane. The rag picker falls to the ground; the capitalist puts one foot on the downed man and triumphantly raises his arms. A third man enters, dressed in a brown uniform and a cap sporting a red star. He punches the capitalist, a whack that sends him staggering across the stage until he reaches the wall, behind which he takes shelter and waves his cane in a threatening manner. The uniformed man, presumably a good Marxist soldier, lifts the rag picker to his feet and leads him to the various stations, not of the cross, but of the socialist paradise: to the tables holding food, clothing, a stove (heating), and a large set of keys, which I assume represent the way to a better life or the kingdom of plenty. All the while, the capitalist continues to wave his walking stick and gesticulate angrily.

The soldier exits, giving an excuse for the capitalist to summon the rag picker, who warily approaches the wall. Brandishing dollar bills in a come-ye-hither manner, the capitalist tries to lure the rag picker over the wall. But the poor man points to the tables, as if to say, I have all that I need. The capitalist throws the dollars over the wall and then removes from each of his pockets, in turn, an egg-sized gem stone, gold coins, and a miniature car. Given all these inducements, the rag picker climbs over the wall and follows the capitalist into the wings. For a brief spell, the stage remains empty, as patriotic music plays. The soldier returns, looks around, shakes his head in dismay, and exits.

Scene two opens with the rag picker slumped over a sewing machine. The capitalist enters and beats him with his stick. A pretty woman, immodestly dressed, enters, wiggles her hips, and leads the capitalist off stage. Shortly, she returns to lift the rag picker from the floor and lead him to a doorway with some Czech words written over the lintel. From the subsequent action, I take the words to mean the equivalent of Home Sweet Home. As the woman leads the man through the door, the set revolves, revealing the inside of a house. The rag picker embraces the woman. She holds out her hand. He drops into her palm the gem stone, which she stows in her bra. The rag picker sits down to dinner, and the woman holds out her hand. He puts in her palm the gold coins, which she stows in the same place. The rag picker opens a closet door and discovers a rich array of women's clothes. He pulls at his hair. She ignores him. He stamps his foot and shakes a reproving finger at the woman. She folds her arms across her breast and impassively watches until his tirade ends. Pointing to the clothes,

darkmatters LEVITT

she holds out her hand, as if to say, the bills on these clothes have come due. He hands her the oversized dollar bills. She walks to the door, opens it, points toward the street, and holds her palms up. The rag picker produces the miniature car and hands it to her. She takes it and leaves.

In scene three, a man arrives who removes all the furniture from the house, but not until he and the rag picker have wrestled over each lamp, couch, and chair.

In scene four, the rag picker is back at work in front of his sewing machine, suffering the beatings of the capitalist. Unable to stand his down-trodden situation any longer, the rag picker throws over his sewing machine, grabs the cane, and beats the capitalist, who runs off stage. The puppeteers lower the old tables, with their food, clothing, stove, and keys. The rag picker runs to them and clasps his hands in gratitude. Patriotic music plays. The soldier returns, leading a modestly dressed winsome young maid. To sentimental music, the rag picker and maid embrace and leave arm in arm, as the soldier points to the red star on his cap. Applause. Curtain. The puppeteers take a bow, and Ben and I exit.

So much for folk art in the Socialist Republic of Czechoslovakia. Marxist theorists had said that artists had to meet the people at their own level, and together they would rise. By 1969, the altitude hadn't risen much above the pits. But at least I knew that on Friday night we would enjoy the Czechs' best, the Laterna Magika.

On Wednesday, August 20, as we ate our breakfast, we studied a tour book. In particular, Ben and I wanted to see the sites associated with John Hus, a fifteenth-century professor-priest at Charles University. Influenced by John Wycliff, Hus had preached against the sale of papal indulgences. In November 1414, with the promise of safe passage, he had attended a church council at Constance, Germany, where a commission examined his theological beliefs, found them imbued with heretical Wycliffism, con-demned him, and, according to custom, turned him over to the civil author-ities, who burned him at the stake. Our favorite C.U. history professor, Charles Vandersee, had often praised Hus's courage.

We left the motel late in the morning and parked on a side street. Agreeing to meet at the Old Town Square, we took separate paths to throw off any possible tails, and caught up with each other in front of the Hus monument. A group of students were singing the Czech national anthem, *Kde domov můj* (Where Is My Home?). One of them offered to serve as our guide. Ben and I exchanged skeptical glances. Was this another surveillance agent? Whether the young man worked for the government, I'll never know, but he did give us a first-rate tour of Charles University and the haunts of Hus. At the end of the tour, Ben handed him five bucks, and we wandered back to the Old Town Square to gaze at the medieval astronomical clock. My family background and my fascination with the kabbalistic idea that behind all appearances lies a spiritual reality compelled me to marvel yet again at the ingenious morality play. The skeletal figure of Death rang his knell and turned his hourglass. Apostles marched past two windows above the clock face; a rooster flapped its wings and crowed. As the hour struck, a Turk standing next to Death knowingly shook his head.

"What do you see?"

At first, I didn't answer, mesmerized by the intricacy of the timepiece and the subtlety of the medieval mind. What better way to imbue the uneducated with religion than by means of an animated clock, which shows us the inevitability of death through the passing of time? "I see illiterate peasants standing here hundreds of years ago reading this symbolic story as clearly as they used to read the biblical scenes in stained-glass windows. Both served as picture books."

"At least you can say this much for religion: it inspired beautiful works of art."

"And gave people a reason to live."

"Don't you mean die?"

"I mean both."

Ben dropped the matter and we continued down one of the commercial streets. The few goods for sale looked shoddy and customers scarce. Money changers, though, flocked thick as flies. Any time we paused at a shop window, someone would sidle up to us and offer to change Czech currency for dollars at black market rates, which stood at five to ten times above the official rate of exchange. Sorely tempted, I reached for my wallet.

"Don't do it!" said Ben. "They'll put you away for three years. It's not worth the difference."

Failing to heed his own advice, he stopped in an art store and decided to buy a small pencil and crayon drawing on coarse paper, handsomely framed, that depicted Wenceslas Square at night, bounded at one end by the National Museum and the other by a street called At the Moat. With meticulous dots of color, the artist had captured the sense of excitement

darkmatters
LEVITT

that comes from a boulevard alive with shops open till late, restaurants, hotels, automobile headlights. The woman who owned the store said that the asking price "was negotiable." In Czech currency it came to about three hundred dollars.

"If you'll pay me in dollars and not crowns," she said in perfect English, "I'll give you the painting for one-third the price."

Ben said he wanted to think about it. We left the shop and walked around the city for several hours, ate lunch at a cafeteria, used the public lavatories, which had no toilet paper, and returned to the art store. Ben paid the woman in dollars and left with the painting, wrapped in brown paper, tucked under his arm.

"Why the hell did you tell me not to change money, and then you go and pay for a painting in dollars?"

"Three reasons. One, I wanted the painting, but not at her price. Two, I left the shop because I saw a man at the rear. Three, I wanted to decide if she could be trusted. I think she can."

"The people who stopped us on the street were alone."

"Yeah, and how do you know they weren't Husák plants?"

"Well, you can't be sure about her."

"She's not accosting strangers on the boulevard and offering to change money at black market rates. Her business is art, not currency."

"Did you get a receipt?"

He reached in his wallet and showed me a slip of paper. "It indicates that I bought the painting in Czech currency."

darkmatters
LEVITT

From Ben's Second Prague Dispatch

Dateline: August 20, Prague. Late this afternoon, Czech protesters again took to the streets. Smoke and the smell of burning rubber rose from Wenceslas Square. On Narodní, a major shopping street, three barricades had been erected with building material taken from a nearby construction project. A tractor had also been commandeered. The barricades, savagely assaulted by the police, eventually gave way, and vicious fighting spilled from Narodní and Na Príkope Streets into Wenceslas Square.

Students hurled cobblestones and rocks. Some clambered up a stationary troop carrier, apparently to reason with the crew. At least a dozen eight-wheel troop carriers moved from both sides of the National Museum to the upper end of the sloping square. Armored tank trucks arrived bearing four water cannons. When the water failed to disperse the crowds, the police and militias mounted a massive tear-gas charge.

People fled into the lobbies of the Yalta and Alcron hotels. Policemen and soldiers put on gas masks, and white-helmeted security police ran after demonstrators, swinging their rubber truncheons. Your reporter found refuge in the lobby of the Alcron, where a young man shoved into his hands a slip of paper, which a desk clerk translated.

The paper called for a protest the next day, the 21st, in Wenceslas Square, and issued guidelines.

Walk to work in groups.

Don't use municipal transport.

Boycott stores, restaurants, theatres, and movie houses.

darkmatters
LEVITT

Buy no newspapers.

Halt all work for five minutes at noon.

Wear black as a sign of mourning.

It concluded with the following plea: Friend, the government has violated the constitution by arresting participants in demonstrations against the occupation of Czechoslovakia. Protest tomorrow in Wenceslas Square. Long live freedom of speech, of the press, and assembly. Please reproduce and circulate.

Marty

That night we repaired to a second-floor restaurant that advertised itself as specializing in Italian food. My mother, who cooked every morsel to death, would have loved it. A small cloakroom, off the foyer, advised patrons in four languages to check their coats and jackets. We had a window seat overlooking the virtually car-free street. A talkative waiter served us. Unlike the Dutch, who learn numerous languages, the Czechs, if they have another language, usually speak German; our waiter, however, spoke English fluently. Having been born in Chicago, he told us that he came to Prague in 1948 with his parents, committed communists. At first, we chatted about the city and then, as we sipped a slivovitz, Ben asked him what he knew about the upcoming protests.

"What protests?" he said unconvincingly. Perhaps he thought that we worked for the Husák government, or perhaps he did. But Ben made no headway with him, even though everyone knew that the next day, August 21, would bring thousands into the streets. After we left the restaurant, Ben found in his coat pocket a slip of paper that read: "Beware the men in white helmets." We figured that the waiter had slipped the note into Ben's jacket, and that the cloakroom enabled Czech security agents to rifle through pockets in search of incriminating evidence they could use to extort information or money.

"When a government distrusts its own people," Ben mused, stuffing the note in his pocket, "that government has lost all legitimacy and forfeited its right to rule."

"The people no longer go hungry," I said ironically, aping Mr. Stavický.

"The bribe of bread can work for only so long. Once the people have filled their bellies with pork and potatoes, they want to taste the sweet-meats of freedom."

darkmatters
LEVITT

Ben's Last Prague Dispatch

Dateline: August 21, Prague. At the stroke of noon, blasts of horns from vehicles in the dense midtown traffic signalled the start of today's protest on the anniversary of the Warsaw Pact Invasion of Czechoslovakia. Public transport came to a standstill. Cars and cabs could barely inch their way through streets massed with people walking toward Wenceslas Square. At all the entrances to the square, the government had erected wooden barriers, but the crowd, growing like a tsunami, swept aside the roadblocks and the soldiers, who fled their posts to escape the crush.

At first, the demonstrators spoke little. Hundreds wept. Others softly sang, "Ať žije Dubček!" "Long Live Dubček!" followed by the national anthem, *Kde domov můj*. Shortly they began to shout "Long live Dubček!" "Long Live Smrkovsky!" "Long Live Kriegel!" "Traitor Husák!" Then they took up a rhythmic chant: "Dubček, Svoboda! Dubček, Svoboda!"

Your reporter stood there—halfway between the National Museum in front of him and the Old Town behind—waving his fist in the air and shouting, "Dubček, Svoboda!" The same incomprehensible force again began to move the crowd, this time forward, toward the museum. Two boys climbed on the large statue of St. Wenceslas and one of them raised his arms in a V. An ear-shattering roar of assent gave the authorities their cue.

From behind the museum streamed a phalanx of tanks, followed by policemen, soldiers, and the so-called people's militia, a private army of the Communist Party, all armed with rifles, batons, and tear gas. The tanks and soldiers slowly moved down the incline of the museum hill toward the square. From side streets leading into the square, trucks rolled up discharging more soldiers, and from the rooftops of the buildings lining the square, Czech policemen appeared. In no time, the troops had cordoned off the square. Hurling coins and cigarette butts in contempt at the helmeted militiamen, who advanced with metronomic precision, college-age young people chanted "Shame on the Soviets."

In the distance came the sound of helicopters. A minute later they swooped low overhead. Loudspeakers repeated the same message every few seconds. "Clear the square immediately! Clear the square immediately!" The mob hooted and whistled so loudly that they drowned out the message, and the authorities unleashed a tear gas attack. Canisters, trailing contrails of smoke, came out of the sky, dropped from the choppers and shot from the rooftops.

Our eyes smarted and teared, our noses ran, our heads ached. The elderly in the crowd quickly made for the side streets. When a canister lands, a moment or two passes before it discharges its full dose of gas. The young people, having tied handkerchiefs or scarves over their hands, picked up the red-hot canisters and flung them at the tanks and the soldiers advancing from every direction. Wherever one landed, the soldiers quickly broke ranks.

The day would have belonged to the protesters had the government not called in massive reinforcements. Soldiers beat anyone they could reach with their batons, hitting young men and women in the face and over the head with such force that blood sprang from them like geysers. On downed protesters, they used rifle butts. Students with broken arms and legs were thrown into army trucks and driven away. Water cannons knocked people off their feet and broke their noses. Forty minutes after the reinforcements weighed in, the square stood frighteningly empty, except for litter, clothing, pools of water, and the blood of Czech citizens advocating change.

Savage fighting continued throughout the city center and in the side streets and smaller squares for the rest of the day and into the night. At six in the evening, Russian tanks that had been parked in the woods outside Prague rumbled through the quiet suburbs, lumbered over the bridges, upending stones that had stood for hundreds of years, and prowled the heart of the city. Following the tanks came trucks bearing soldiers, who flooded into the side streets, where protesters had ignited old tires and in some cases blockaded the streets with overturned cars, garbage cans, and any refuse and rubble they could find.

As this report goes out, the fighting continues.

Marty

With a tank bearing down on us, we darted down a side street, turned into a second, a third, and kept running till our lungs nearly burst. At last we stopped to consult our city map, which told us that we had overshot our Fiat by at least half a mile. Cautiously we made our way back to it and drove to the motel along a road that took us past dozens of tanks and trucks heading into the Old City. All the fighting should have told me, a believer in omens, that ill fortune lay ahead. Checking for messages at the desk, I found a telegram from my sister: "Mother failing. Come right away." With the aid of the clerk at the desk, I changed my plane ticket and left Prague that same evening. Ben drove me to Ruzyne Airport. Stupidly, I asked what he would do with my ticket for the Laterna Magika. He said that he'd try to reach Dana Reháková. It took a moment for me to recall the name.

"I haven't thought of her in years."

"We exchange Christmas cards. I would have called her, but her family's out of favor with the current government. If her telephone is bugged, I could be making things worse."

"Contact her," I said, "she'll be delighted to hear from you."

Ben and I hugged. Had I known that this would be the last time I would ever see him alive, I like to think that I would have been moved to eloquence. My parting words now seem utterly insipid. "Have a good time in Greece."

Flying through Frankfort, London, and New York, I arrived in Detroit just in time to bury my mother. It took several days before I learned of Ben's death. The Czech authorities informed the American Embassy that there had been an accident, a fall, in which Ben had struck his head and died on the steps of a police station. The American Embassy treated the report skeptically, though in my opinion not nearly skeptically enough, and made some inquiries, which led them to me. I proposed that they sell the Fiat and send me the money, which I planned to use for Ben's funeral. As well, I urged them to continue investigating Ben's death. But as far as I could tell, their inquiries accomplished little or nothing. They did, however, fly the body and Ben's belongings back to New York. I arranged for the service and his burial in the Brooklyn cemetery next to his father and mother, who had passed away in the early sixties. Clarissa could not be reached: she had remained in Athens waiting for Ben. When he failed to show up, she repeatedly tried calling him and me. Receiving no answer, she guessed that something had gone terribly wrong and returned to the States. I had left a message with Brian that she call me, but never told him about Ben. Telephoning Esperanza, I had the same ill luck. A man said that she had just left for Mexico, but would return in ten days, at which time she would call. Abby joined me for a brief ceremony at the graveside. The only other people in attendance were two distant cousins of mine, whom I prevailed upon to drive over from Queens. Instead of a rabbi reciting prayers, I hired a cantor to sing. As well, I said a few words, nothing profound, just straight from the heart.

"I'd like to believe that Prague never happened, that it was just a dream. But we all know dreams aren't true. What lives on is the memory, and in mine I am talking to Ben: listening to classical music in Eldorado Springs; watching a few brave professors defend the rights of free speech; riding around in his old DeSoto; fighting the good fight in Hanover. I know that he will remain in my thoughts for all the days of my life."

A week passed before Clarissa reached me, and upon hearing the news sobbed inconsolably. Hardly able to speak, she whimpered:

"I suppose a divorce is inevitable now."

At the time, I thought her statement peculiarly self-serving. But after thinking about it, I decided she had merely said what Ben had thought all along. Her marriage was viable only because of her summers with him. On the pretext of having to tell their friends in Akro Tiri what had happened, she flew back to Greece, where I could imagine her visiting all the old spots that Ben had talked about: the taverna, the secret beach, the bread store, and of course the hotel they inaugurated. The few times that I've spoken to her since, we mostly reminisce about our college days and that summer in Hanover. Recently she told me that she had established two scholarships in Ben's name, one at the University of Colorado and one at the University of New Mexico. She did not divorce Brian, but continues to live as the most unmarried married person I have ever known.

Marty

My two-week vacation, courtesy of the post office, found me traveling to Prague. Haunted by Ben's death the year before, I felt compelled to find out what had happened. Having previously queried the FBI, Amnesty International, and the American Embassy in Prague—with little success—I wrote to the last-known address for Dana Reháková, in Prague, which I found among Ben's belongings. But my letter came back stamped "Person Unknown." In one way or another, I seemed unable to escape the durance vile of failed missives. During a telephone conversation with Clarissa, she mentioned that her father-in-law had been appointed as an under secretary to some political office in the Nixon administration. Writing to Mr. Hazelwood, in care of Clarissa, I asked him if he could locate an address for Dana Reháková and arrange to have a letter delivered to her in a diplomatic pouch. I hoped that if she replied, he could get the letter out of the country the same way mine got in. Fully expecting the old bird to turn me down, I was overjoyed to receive his offer of help. He penned a courtly note—"that given Clarissa's and your interest, I feel obliged to sedulously pursue this matter"—and ended with a personal touch, recalling "our pleasant meeting in Lexington."

In less than three weeks, a special-delivery packet reached me at home. It contained Mr. Hazelwood's business card, copies of his correspondence with the diplomatic corps, and a letter from Dana Reháková. She said that her family had recently been forced to leave Prague, briefly settled in Bratislava, and now lived not far from Senec, in the Carpathian mountains. Yes, she had met Ben. Yes, she knew how he died but admitted that her initial impulse was to say nothing, owing to the danger she could be visiting

darkmatters LEVITT

upon herself and her family. Having discussed the risks with her parents, she had decided, in the words of her father, that "it is one's moral duty to bear witness to crimes that governments try to hide." She would tell me the story in person, as I had suggested, and meet me in Bratislava. In my letter, I had offered to pay for her accommodations in the city, but she said that we would have more "opportunity" to talk if we stayed at her parents' house. I understood her words to mean that the Husák government had put her under surveillance, which indeed was the case.

In July, I flew from New York to Frankfort to Prague. Customs officers questioned me closely and appropriated a copy of *Playboy* magazine that included an article by Norman Mailer I wanted to show Dana. They also wanted to remove one of three pairs of Levis that I had packed, on the grounds that given the number I'd brought, I must be planning to sell a pair on the black market. Not long after arriving in Prague, I boarded a two-engine aircraft with ten other passengers and flew to Bratislava. A cab took me into the city and to the destination that Dana had indicated: the Town Theatre, an imposing yellow building with a jutting porch and four pillars. Standing under the porch, with my suitcase resting at my feet and a tote bag slung over my shoulder, I worried that I had misunderstood her message, because I found myself staring at streets devoid of both pedestrians and traffic. Five minutes went by and a Skoda, a Czech car, pulled up with Dana behind the wheel. I climbed in, tossing my suitcase in the back seat. She looked considerably older, much thinner and less attractive than I had remembered. Her face, mottled yellow and brown, suggested ill health. Once an impeccable dresser, she wore old jeans and a faded blouse that needed ironing. We sat briefly at the curb exchanging warm greetings, just enough time for me to reach into my tote bag and hand her a blue University of Colorado sweatshirt, which I had bought through the CU catalogue as a gift for her. She smelled of nicotine and the fingers of her left hand were badly stained. As we drove off, she lit up a Gaulois cigarette and whispered through a stream of smoke:

"I'm followed."

As she pulled away from the curb, a black car reeled out of a side street and fell in behind us. The government vehicle tailed us up and down hills and through the maze of streets that Dana took to show me the city. Not until we left Bratislava and started to climb into the mountains did our tail head in another direction.

Dana's spoken English had deteriorated from lack of use. She apologized and explained that she had been working as a book translator, rendering French into Czech.

"If we could talk in French . . ."

"Sorry," I said, "mine is hopeless. How about Yiddish?"

She just laughed.

"Tell me about Ben."

"Not now."

During the drive, I mostly gabbed about my own life, occasionally repeating or reorganizing a sentence that she had trouble understanding. She sounded inordinately interested in Clarissa, and why her marriage to Ben never took place. I attributed the failure to a clash of cultures, to which Dana responded:

"Class. In America even, you have class differences."

Not wishing to open the door to a discussion of Marxism, I nodded agreement and passed on to other small talk. The foothills had a certain sameness, farms and fields, cows and sheep, the occasional town, and at last the real Carpathians. Leaving the main highway, she wended her way down a dirt road through a forest of beech, ash, and chestnut until we arrived at a small lodge, with a handsome stone foundation. Constructed of split logs, the rustic building resembled a small hunting retreat, which in fact it had been in an earlier century. An open front porch faced a large pond.

"In my house speak only small things, it may be bugged," she said. The Rehák family greeted us warmly, apologizing for the cramped quarters. But I had no complaints, given that Dana moved into her parents' bedroom and I occupied hers. The most attractive aspects of the lodge, the large fireplace and the wall-to-wall bookcases, made me imagine cold winter days and the elderly Reháks reading the classics next to crackling logs. A hearty chicken dinner with dumplings left us all in a mood for a walk in the woods, the safest place to talk. Even though suffering from jet lag and wanting to learn about Ben, I tramped along, listening to the account of how Mr. Rehák had fallen from the communist pantheon. He said his crime was merely that he had supported the Prague Spring, the liberalization of the country. Exiled with Dubček to the countryside, he now lived out his days writing his memoirs and reading. Mrs. Reháková, a still-life painter of some note, worked in water colors. She complained not about the forced solitude but about the difficulty of finding good-quality paper for her art work.

As the couple talked, a quotation came to mind: men in exile feed on dreams. I wondered what dreams sustained them.

That night I slept for twelve hours, awakening around noon. Dana made me a breakfast of fried potatoes and sausage, a meal that would have made my rabbi grepse in his grave. For old time's sake, I washed down the food with a glass of Pilsen beer, whose tart flavor brought back memories of the previous summer. Refreshed, I took Dana's arm and we strolled to the pond. Oblivious to my surroundings, I had but one thought: to find out what happened to Ben. I knew that Dana's mind worked like flypaper. In Boulder, every buzzing item of gossip and politics stuck fast to her inexhaustible memory. We sat in two wicker chairs and I waited. Kabbalists believe that like unfathomable stretches of space, most people are dark matter. You never know what they're really thinking; and yet you can feel the gravitational pull. Whether that force emanates from prejudice or principle, faith or facts, you know that behind the surface lies a deeper, darker reality. Certainly that was true of Dana. I had the uncomfortable sense that she did not want to talk about Ben, even though she had told me to come. She lit a cigarette and began nibbling at the edges of what I took to be a much larger story talking about meeting him the day after I'd left.

"His call came to me a surprise. I was living still in Prague and only by luck home. My boss, he leave me go early. Why I say luck? It was terrible!"

"You mean his death?"

She ignored my question.

"We undecided if to use the theatre tickets. Maybe just go to dinner. Then Ben say we go to dinner and the Laterna Magika. I meet him. When I take trolley . . . everywhere . . . military escorts. How do you say?"

"I think you mean convoys."

"Yes, convoys. Frightening. Ben at Charles University wait for me. He come by car. The people in the streets, no one talked. They look *féroce*, everyone. But we I suppose do too."

She told me that Ben returned to the same restaurant at which we had eaten. He wanted to learn more from the chatty waiter.

"The man, he was gone. I thought good. There the food is *exécrable*. To a small bistro I take Ben. A mama and papa, as you say, own it. Near the university. We eat wiener schnitzel and sauerkraut, and beer and slivovitz. Ben, he described what happened. I listened and then painted more parts of the picture. Last year, you and Ben don't know about the article in

darkmatters
LEVITT

Tribuna. August 20. Oldřich Švestka, a Russophile, a former editor of *Rudé Pravo*, he accuse Dubček of lying. Švestka claim that Dubček know that invasion is imminent. Švestka lies. The Czech people were hating Švestka for the letter, which give them a big reason to make a riot."

Dana related the events in Wenceslas Square, and mentioned a scene that reminded me of one that I had witnessed myself, and that will never leave me. A young woman was struck with a baton on her cheek, parting the skin as if a zipper had been slowly opened, releasing a rush of blood down her pale pretty face. As Dana spoke, the image came back to me: the slow-motion zipper, the issue of blood, and the woman's horrified expression.

"Dinner over, we go the theatre. We see fighting on the little streets, battles. Students throwing stones . . . police shooting rockets, tear gas. It's small, the Laterna Magika. You know it?"

"No."

"They have, how you say, a mishymashy: sound and light, film projections, music, ballet, pantomime. They want to create a black theatre. Do you know what that mean? Strangeness. Bizarreness. We sit in wonderful tickets."

I remembered purchasing them from the agent in the motel for just a few dollars.

"In the third row, in the center. I can almost touch the stage. But every seat a good one in the Laterna Magika, because it so small. The curtain rise. We see an image of desert at twilight."

As she spoke, I closed my eyes to picture the fairy-tale skit in my mind. Two people, holding lanterns, slowly advance across the sands and materialize out of the screen as dancers, though the lanterns remain behind, frozen in the film. Sweeping across the stage, they move in perfect lockstep, turning their heads and moving their hands precisely at the same time. On the screen, a moon rises and an oasis appears and disappears in swirling sands. Out of the vortex, as if by magic, emerge two more dancers. Moving in perfect unity to the accompaniment of Dvořák's Third Symphony, the four dancers fade in and out of a semi-transparent mirror, suddenly coming to a foot-stomping halt. An enormous egg rolls out of the wings, and a clown breaks through the shell. He rolls pell-mell across the stage until he stops at the foot of the dancers. Pointing at them, he turns to face the audience.

"Slowly his mouth he twists and his face contorts. It's like he want to say, 'What fools!' Maybe, though, the audience they see a meaning different."

darkmatters
LEVITT

Dana bit her lip and lapsed into a reminiscence of other performances of the Laterna Magika.

"You didn't tell me to come this distance so that you could relate a dinner and skit."

"I like to see you. Old friend."

"And I'm glad to see you, as well. But I came because I thought you could give me some idea of how Ben died."

"Many died . . . from beatings, from bullets."

"He wasn't shot."

"No."

Close to the shore of the pond, a duck and five ducklings floated by, all in a line. The young ones observed a pecking order, never trying to jump the queue.

"What are you afraid of? We're outside. Nobody can hear us."

She began to pick at her nails and cuticles. One finger bled. She sucked on it. "My father, he would not, how do you say, go in lock step."

"Yes, I know. He supported Dubček."

She again tore at a finger, visibly straining to speak. "Something else," she mumbled reluctantly. "Trotsky."

"What about Trotsky?"

"My father, our family . . . we belong."

Although Ben and I had always thought the Rehák family were regular party members, their being Trotskyites did not come as a terrible surprise. It would certainly explain why the current government had exiled them, but there had to be more.

"I guess that's why you and Joe Riley—"

"Don't mention him," she said bitterly.

Her tone took me aback, but I was less interested in Joe than in Ben. "How could your being Trotskyites affect Ben?"

"To you, I will explain. I wanted to." She paused to light a fresh cigarette from the butt of the old. "The government wanted to make Ben's death hush-hush. They say if I talk, we all go to jail for being with Trotsky. But although better you know, it still means for my family danger. So what I tell you—"

"Not a word," I promised.

"Still it hurts to think about. The memories bring pain."

On that day, listening to her revelations, which she disclosed only vagrantly, all the while consuming cigarettes as greedily as food, I learned the cause of Ben's death, and began to put together this final chapter of the story, now reconstructed from Dana's imperfect English and rendered in my own cadences.

About a half hour into the show, the audience began to cough and wheeze. The retching and blowing of noses drowned out the performers. Their eyes began to smart terribly. Tear gas was seeping in under the front door. The manager ran on stage and declared the show over. He directed everyone to leave by a side door that an usher had opened. The back rows, with better access, exited first. Ben and Dana, among the last to leave the theatre, watched as the usher slammed the door behind them. They found themselves on a side street, under an arcade. One end had a locked metal gate, the kind that merchants use to shutter their stores. The other led into a street barred at the far end by a six-foot high barricade composed of old tires and two overturned cars. At the near end of the street, which had provided an escape for most of the theatre patrons, five or six young men had nearly completed another barricade.

"Let's leave from here," Dana said, "before it's too much late."

They started to run, but just as they reached the barricade, a truck rolled up and at least a dozen armed men leapt out, wearing white helmets. Finding themselves hemmed in with no exit, they and a few other stragglers ducked into an apartment building. The front doors, made of glass, enabled them to see out—and the soldiers to see in. They shoved their way past a number of trash cans and headed up the staircase. A young man, who had taken refuge with them, chose to hide among the trash cans. They urged him to join them upstairs, but he refused. Ben insisted that they could not leave him alone, and joined him kneeling behind the metal bins. Dana perched on a step just below the next floor, from which she could easily see Ben and the young man; but she had only a partial view of the street, which looked empty. For several minutes, no one said a word. Ben left his hiding place and stole a sideways glance through the glass doors.

Dana asked him: "What do you see?"

"Sh! The soldiers are sweeping the street."

At first, she misunderstood.

"Shoulder to shoulder, with rifles and bayonets crossed at their chests."

The young man, whom they naturally assumed couldn't speak English, whispered, "Are they entering any buildings?"

"Some, but not all."

Inexplicably, the kid decided to make a dash for it. Moving out from behind the bins, he peered through the glass doors, eased one of them open, and started running in the opposite direction.

"Shit!" said Ben, "he'll never make it."

Dana scampered down the stairs to peek out. Two members of the riot squad had overtaken the boy, knocking him to the ground and clubbing him with their rifle butts. Impulsively, Ben bolted out the door and tried to help. The other soldiers had by now reached their comrades. Ben stood encircled by uniforms. Dana left the building and quietly moved toward them, taking care to stand at a distance. Ben and one of the soldiers argued in Russian. During the dispute, the pummeling of the fallen man had come to a halt. But as he tried to rise from the ground, a militiaman stomped on his arm, causing him to scream. Ben gesticulated wildly and let loose a torrent of heated words. The man stood stone-faced, utterly unmoved. Turning to his companions, he said something. Two of them immediately took hold of Ben and started marching him back down the street, leaving behind the bloodied young man. Impulsively Dana shouted in Czech:

"Stop! Where are you going? He's an American citizen. He hasn't done anything."

The soldiers stopped and exchanged a few words. One of them came back for her, prodding her with the end of his rifle. Led past the barrier at the end of the street and shoved into a truck, they glanced back and saw the young man painfully rise to his feet. His forearm, the one the soldier had trampled, hung limply at an odd angle. The truck drove through streets eerily lit by fires and flares. Once they arrived at the main post office, the riot squad marched them inside. When Dana saw the savage beatings and ruthless interrogations taking place, Dante's inferno came to mind—and her mother and father. She believed she had entered a human abattoir.

Why do hateful governments use stadia and post offices to torture dissenters? Is it because these are places where people seek to connect, through loyalty or language? For me, the idea of the post office as a site of pain had a kabbalistic meaning: tyrants try to despoil the memory of these institutions to disconnect us.

Ushered into a small room next to the mail-sorting area, they sat at a table, with a guard standing sentinel at the door. Fearing that the room might be bugged, they said virtually nothing. Their watches and wallets having been taken, as well as Ben's jacket and belt, they had no idea of the time and felt the chill of the room—or was it fear?—enter their bones. They seemed to sit there for hours, but it may have been only minutes. At last, three men entered, two soldiers and a man in a dark rumpled suit, carrying a folder. The soldiers stood at attention behind Ben and Dana. The man seated himself across from them. Opening the folder, he studied the papers, saying nothing. Finally, he pursed his lips and, raising his eyes, said slowly:

"Miss Reháková, Dana Reháková. Your father is Milan, a disgraced member of the former government, exiled for counterrevolution and Trotskyism. I see we have a plot here."

Dana explained that Ben, a friend from college, had merely come to Prague on a visit.

"He has certainly picked an auspicious time."

"Only a coincidence," she said.

He forced a smile, disclosing a row of discolored teeth. Dana remembered thinking that they accounted for his foul-smelling breath.

Turning from Dana, he questioned Ben.

"Mr. Cohen, Benjamin Michael Cohen."

"Yes, and I want to know why we're here."

The man returned his gaze to the papers and adjusted his wire-rimmed glasses. Without answering Ben, he continued. "Mr. Cohen, you speak Russian. We in the socialist bloc know all about how America trains people like you to come here to disrupt our way of life. You are an agitator. A spy! Isn't that true?"

"False. I'm a journalist."

"You work for either the CIA or the Trotsky movement. Which?"

"Neither. I can assure you, I intend your country no harm."

"Whatever that means! You are here to write articles that will foment trouble against the socialist government of Czechoslovakia on the anniversary of our liberation by the Warsaw Pact countries, who saved us from the rightist counterrevolution of Dubček and Svoboda."

"I am here to see for myself what happened to socialism with a human face."

The man reached across the table and slapped Ben's cheek. "Don't insult the memory of those who died fighting fascism."

Exercising great self-control, Ben said with electric deliberateness: "My family left Russia because of what they had suffered under the Czar. Don't tell me about repression!"

darkmatters
LEVITT

Thumbing through the papers, the man observed: "Your family left *after* the revolution. Could it be they were White Russians?"

"My father fought the White Russians. If you like, I'll give you the details."

Abruptly turning to Dana, their inquisitor threatened: "You won't get away with it—you Trotskyites who are always conspiring!"

The man glared over his glasses at Ben. "You're a Jew. You should be sympathetic to our form of government. We do not allow religious hatred and sectarian warfare. We have done away with all such stupid superstitions."

Although the room where they had been taken stood some distance from where they had seen people being tortured, Dana could still hear the muffled cries of men and women being beaten with truncheons.

"I'd like to call the American Embassy."

The man spoke in Czech to the soldiers, sarcastically telling them that Ben wanted his mommy. The men laughed. From the folder, he removed a slip of paper and handed it to Ben. "Do you know this?"

Ben shook his head yes.

"Tell us," said the man, "what does it mean: beware the men in white helmets?"

"I started to write a poem, but couldn't finish it."

"In someone else's handwriting?" he said, holding up Ben's passport and pointing to his signature. "And how is it," he asked, "you could pay for your expenses in Pilsen and Prague and still have enough money to buy a painting worth three hundred dollars—when you converted only five hundred dollars?" He produced the receipt for the painting Ben bought. "Unless you paid for it in another currency or traded dollars on the black market for crowns, a state crime."

The police had obviously entered Ben's room in the Stop Motel, where Ben had left the painting. His wallet contained the receipts for the picture and for the money he exchanged in Pilsen. Dana tasted a rush of bile in her mouth, as she imagined the two of them standing trial in a hostile Czech court. Their inquisitor spread his fingers on the table and briefly studied them. Without looking up, he directed one of the soldiers to bring in the "other evidence," which turned out to be an old leather-bound book.

"After you left the tour at the castle, you stole into the library. While there, you put in this book a roll of microfilm."

He opened the volume. It had been hollowed out. Dana noticed the title on the spine, *Imitatio Christi*, by Thomas à Kempis.

"That's a lie, and you know it."

"See for yourself." He reached into his pocket and tossed Ben a roll of microfilm.

Ben instinctively caught it and said, "Never saw it before in my life," and handed it back.

The man smirked. "It has your fingerprints . . . now."

"You prick!"

"We have Mr. Stavický down the hall. He refuses to call you a spy, but we can shortly get him to do so. You can spare him *and* your girlfriend here—if you just sign a confession. It's up to you."

Ben paused. Dana anticipated an explosion, only to be utterly nonplussed by his reply.

"All right, I'll confess."

"Confess what?" Dana blurted. "We haven't done anything!"

"That's true," said Ben. "Dana doesn't know a thing about my activities. She's an innocent bystander. I used her for a cover."

"Mr. Cohen, we have already drawn up the confession. All you have to do is sign it. But if you wish to make a statement, the socialist state of Czechoslovakia guarantees you that right."

The man sent one of the soldiers for a recording secretary, a drably dressed woman, who took down in shorthand the confidential discussion.

A picture of self-satisfaction, the man folded his arms across his chest and said sardonically: "The floor is yours."

"Why this charnel house?" exclaimed Ben, waving his arms to indicate the surroundings. "Why the beatings and the tanks and the Russians? What was Dubček's crime? Or did cowards around him misrepresent what he hoped to achieve? Help me to understand. Then I'll confess."

The man signalled the woman to stop writing. His smirking face turned serious, as he bitterly reviewed the Dubček regime. "Under the guise of what he called socialism with a human face, he tried to reintroduce capitalism and bourgeois values. He tried to drive a wedge between us and the other Warsaw Pact countries. He tried to undermine the fraternal friendship between my country and the Soviet Union." His toxic feelings contorted his mouth, as he continued at a febrile pace. "Naturally, he had to be stopped. The contagion would have spread: to Poland, to Hungary,

East Germany, Rumania. Everything we accomplished . . . lost, and all because Dubček and Frantisek and the other worms wanted to cripple us with so-called western freedoms." He laughed sarcastically. "Some freedom! It is nothing more than the freedom to buy, buy, buy! Ach, all that western capitalism buys is an unbridgeable gulf between rich and poor. The wealthy grow fat by exploiting the workers and by picking clean the bones of the halt and the lame. If capitalism is so glorious, why does it worry about communism? Is it because you compare the differences between us and worry that some of our ways are better than yours? For all your complaints about our press being unfree, yours expresses only the opinions of the Democrats and Republicans, who are in fact one and the same. Voting rights? Most of your people don't vote!" He fumbled out of his pocket a crumpled pack of cigarettes. Quickly lighting one, he tossed the match on the floor. "I'll tell you why America sends spies into the socialist countries. The capitalists want more markets for their goods. Commercialism is all you people think about, never education or health or the arts. That's why you are here . . . to undermine our form of government and to introduce yours—for reasons of profit!" He inhaled deeply and blew the smoke out his nose. "There! Does that answer your question?"

When Dana related to me what their inquisitor had said, I must admit that I thought to myself, he was not far from the mark. Although the man had obviously been programmed to say what he did, had he separated the grain from the chaff, his argument might have raised some thorny issues.

"Yes," said Ben. "But what I don't understand is why there can't be different kinds of socialism, some conservative, some liberal."

"One is either free of cancer or not. Capitalism is a cancer. The least taint spreads and very soon kills the organism."

Ben shook his head. "I see."

"Now you will sign?"

"No, I will sign the statement I make, not the one you wrote."

"Will you admit that you spied?"

"Yes."

All smiles, the man leaned over the table and solicitously cooed. "I'm glad you've chosen to cooperate. You're wise to spare yourself and your girlfriend, and of course Mr. Stavický." With false bonhomie, he chortled: "Oh, how silly of me, I forgot to introduce myself. My name is Gajda, Imre

Gajda. Just make your statement, sign it, and you and Miss Reháková can leave." He motioned to the stenographer, who took down in shorthand Ben's words.

"At the age of eight," Ben began, radiating sincerity, "the CIA abducted me from my family and took me to a secret outpost in Virginia, where they trained me for ten years in languages, spying, electronics, espionage, and propaganda. That's how I learned Russian, not from my parents. At eighteen, they infiltrated me into the Mafia, so I could learn the ways of gangsterism. I spent a year in Sicily studying about money laundering, drug running, the white slave trade, and assassination."

Mr. Gajda appeared uncomfortable and shifted in his chair.

"I began my journey in Venice, having arrived on a Nautilus submarine that sailed under the north pole. My contact in Venice, an old woman by the name of Ghersani, owns the San Maurizio hotel. She supplied me with a Fiat bus bearing Milan license plates and gave me a briefcase with a thousand dollars worth of korunas. That explains the discrepancy between the amount of money I changed and the amount that I spent. When we drove across the border, your guards examined our vehicle and took us inside for a body search. But I said that I had to go poo-poo, and went to the bathroom. I stored the money, which I had put in a waterproof plastic bag, in the overhead water tank. After your people frisked us, I said that I had to poo-poo again, you know, diarrhea, and returned to the bathroom to get my money. In Prague, my contact is a doctor, Dr. Gustav Husák. You may know him. The day I disappeared at the castle, I stopped at his office, where he gave me a transcript of the meeting that took place between the Russians and Dubček, the meeting at which they forced him to capitulate and sign that dishonorable repudiation of the Prague Spring. Is there anything else you'd like to know?"

"Why do you wish to injure yourself—and your friends? All you have to do is sign a statement." He handed Ben a piece of paper, which he read and shoved across the table to Mr. Gajda.

"You'll be laughed at. Nobody will believe this bullshit."

Mr. Gajda leaned across the table and again slapped Ben on the cheek. Ben started to rise from his chair, but the soldiers restrained him.

"Had you struck me," said Mr. Gajda, "you would have caused your own death." He blew his nose in a dirty handkerchief. "Stavický and your girlfriend may leave. The Státni Bezpecnost (State Security) will consider

darkmatters
LEVITT

their cases later. But you are remanded to the People's Revolutionary Tribunal for trial and sentencing. Let them decide whether to hang you or send you to the wall," he chuckled, as if he had just amused himself greatly. "The court will even tell you in which order you and the other imperialist revanchists will die."

Taken to a police station, Ben remained there for three days. Dana tried to see him, but the security people refused her visiting rights. Acting from fear and frustration, she went to the American Embassy and reported Ben's arrest. (The embassy had told me there had been a "judicial proceeding.") The next day, the authorities put him on trial before a revolutionary tribunal. Ben had been assigned a lawyer who spoke English. No member of the American Embassy attended. Presumably a deal had been struck in advance. Dana suspected that the embassy had run a check on his background, turned up his left-wing sympathies, and decided not to intervene. Dana described the small courtroom as windowless and bare, except for some chairs and two tables. She sat with other friends of the arrested in a glass-enclosed balcony. Wall speakers carried the proceedings. Seated behind a long table, the judge and four other tribunal members, two men and two women, resembled zombies. All of them wore dark, rumpled clothes. As Dana pointed out, most apparatchiks, including those in the judicial system, had no more than a high school education and deeply resented the cultural privileges that had not been available to them. The judge began by accusing Ben of being a spy, presumably the point at issue.

"Our country is surrounded and besieged by your own. Everywhere we uncover underground stations and arms caches and anti-socialist forces. American troops are stationed in West Germany and Belgium. They train and send armed people in secret to Czech and Slovak areas illegally, as tourists and journalists. You are such a person. In place of arms to shoot us with and explosives to blow up our bridges, you have made common cause with the Trotskyites, notorious plotters against the socialist cause."

The lawyer, instead of defending Ben, asked for leniency. Dana assumed that this strategy had been crafted beforehand. He said that Ben regretted the riots that had wracked the country and could see now that revanchists had stage-managed the whole regrettable protest. When Ben asked for a translation of what his lawyer had said, the man replied in English:

"I told them that you regret any injury that your behavior might have caused others."

Dana knew that the trial was a charade because one of the women at the table knew English, and she said nothing as the lawyer rendered his dishonest translation.

Ben asked to speak, but the presiding judge said that that wouldn't be necessary. The others sat stone faced as the lawyer, in Ben's stead, apologized to the court and the people of Czechoslovakia for his having been misled into thinking that Dubček was right and Husák wrong. The English translation again came out distorted.

"I told the court," the lawyer said to Ben, "that as a journalist you know that no case is black and white. Rights and wrongs occur on both sides."

"Which rights and wrongs are you referring to?"

The lawyer replied enigmatically: "Violence is an abdication of reason."

"Tell that to Brezhnev!" Ben blurted, causing a commotion among his judges, and the lawyer to whisper frantically in Ben's ear.

"Please stand," said the presiding judge. The lawyer mumbled and Ben approached the table. Adjusting his glasses, the judge read from a prepared statement.

"The Czechoslovak Socialist Republic, the guarantor of the people's rights, has the responsibility to protect the state through its democratic laws and judicial proceedings. Anti-socialist activities are inimical to liberty and provide incontrovertible evidence that a guest of the nation who engages in such activities is unwelcome in this country. Although the Czechoslovak Socialist Republic has inscribed in its constitution that the free expression of political views is the very essence of a free society, and although membership in a dissenting group should not and must not divorce anyone from his fundamental rights under our laws, subversion cannot be countenanced.

"In my capacity as a judicial magistrate appointed by the Central Committee, I must uphold the well-being of the state. It is customary to say that a man's political views have no relationship to his place in our society. But political views that are not consonant with a free Socialist state, and are fundamentally destructive of our society, cannot be condoned. It is the responsibility of the people's courts to extirpate such views, because they would in the long run be ruinous to our country's institutions and freedoms. Though the holders of such views often talk about freedom of speech and assembly, they are in fact devoted to denying both. As I said at the start of this trial, Mr. Cohen, you are such a person. Your activities are incompatible with those of a journalist. For this reason, the court revokes your visa, and you are ordered to leave the Czechoslovak Socialist Republic within forty-eight hours."

A party of three hunters, cradling shotguns in their arms, came out of the woods.

"How do you say," she whispered, "outlaw hunters?"

"I think you mean poachers."

"Yes, that's it . . . maybe."

"What do they poach?"

"Bear and fox and sometime lynx."

She greeted them and invited them to sit. Removing their knapsacks, they lounged on a fallen log by the pond. For the first time, I let myself see the beauty of the surroundings. On the water, a canoeist's wake gently rocked the water lilies. The mountain air, full of golden pollen, magically dusted the trees. Across the pond, the hills swam in molten blue. The idyllic moment felt obscenely at odds with the state of the country. One of the men coughed. Exceedingly tall, he wore a suede jacket with arm tassels. His face looked chiseled, and his laconic speech complemented his appearance. A second man, who stuttered, spoke little. He had a shock of black hair that reached the bridge of his nose. I had the feeling that given his impediment, he hid under his hair. The third fellow, short and stocky, with a full curly beard, made up for the reticence of his companions. He and Dana chatted at length. She offered the men a cigarette, opening a new pack of Gauloises. Only the garrulous one accepted, and smoked it in silence. Snuffing out the butt, he removed from his knapsack a wild duck, which he insisted Dana take. She adamantly refused. As they faded into the woods, she repeated what had just transpired.

At first, she had remarked to them that the game wardens—or, she joshed, were they security agents?—seemed of late to be proliferating. They shrugged off her comment and said that hunting in the Carpathians was a way of life that stretched back to the dawn of time. It mattered not the nature of the government nor the person in power. The hunters observed an older law: tradition. But even so, they grumbled about government restrictions on their use of arms and the duration of the hunting season. The short, bearded man likened the government to a noxious weed, and expatiated with a pithy tale. He told her to think of a large lake with one small water lily growing in the middle of it, a water lily that each day

darkmatters
LEVIT

doubles in size. "Now," he asked, "if it takes the water lily one year to grow large enough to cover half the lake, how long will it take to cover the whole lake?" She had rashly said "another six months." The man accepted her offer of a cigarette, drew deeply, and exhaled both smoke and words together. "One day! If the water lily doubles in size each day, and it now covers half the lake, it will take only one day for it to cover the other half of the lake." The tall granite-featured fellow added: "That's why you either pluck the damn thing or keep it severely under check. And we did neither." The chatty one drew the moral: "That's how the communists took over." Dana made no reply, and the stutterer said, "true?" as if expecting her assent. But she gestured noncommittally, and the three men fell silent. Finally, they looked at each other, nodded, and faded into the forest.

"How come you didn't take the duck?"

"If they secret police, they accuse me of poaching."

"Secret police!" I exclaimed. "I thought they were poachers. Isn't that what you said?"

"I said 'maybe.' But when I mention security agents and they will not answer, I am suspicious. Even more I worry because they want me to say the government is like the water lily."

"You don't know for sure, though?"

"How can anyone know?"

I picked up a small branch and peeled off the bark. "If you can never trust another person . . ." I trailed off. In a world where it is impossible to know who can be trusted and who cannot, no person can ever confide in another, can ever love for fear of betrayal, can ever risk being loyal, lest it be used against him. Now I knew the true meaning of madness. Why should I even believe Dana? If she thought me an agent—or I thought her one—neither of us would believe the other. Truth was beyond reach. What, then, was I to make of what she said next?

According to Dana, the authorities released Ben the next day. She met him as he descended the steps of the local police station in the company of two white-helmeted security agents armed with submachine guns. Ben greeted her in Czech, having learned a few words from other inmates during his brief incarceration. She had a cab waiting at the curb. One of the agents gave Ben a shove toward the street and called him a fascist, but instead of ignoring the insult, Ben sneered *Ruská sviňe*. The agent went berserk. Raising his rifle, his eyes feral with rage, he struck Ben on the back of the head. For an instant, Ben remained upright, as his head, according to Dana's graphic description, burst miraculously into red bloom. Like a poppy in a sudden spring shower, it bent and drooped to one side. He pitched forward onto the sidewalk, unconscious.

Dana accompanied him in the cab to the hospital and translated. As the cab inched its way through the crowded streets, having no siren to clear the way, it passed sullen groups of roving young men and women. Two orderlies carried him on a stretcher to an elevator, which rose as slowly as a kite on a windless day. Placed in a drab ward with white metal beds and grey foot lockers for personal belongings, he remained on a gurney unattended for two hours. With every bed in the large ward taken, Ben had to wait until a cot could be wedged between a couple of beds. On one side of Ben, a patrician old man with a death-rattling cough sniffed pinches of snuff and spoke to Dana in French. The old gentleman felt that he deserved treatment commensurate with the splendor running in his blood, namely, a private room. On the other side of Ben lay a casualty of the street fighting, a student blinded by tear gas. His parents sat at his bedside, but neither he nor they ever spoke.

Once the doctor finally arrived and examined Ben, the place became a beehive of activity, as attendants shaved and swabbed his head, all the while mumbling in unsettling tones. An orderly brought back the gurney; the others gently lifted Ben off the cot, taking care to protect his head, and wheeled him away to surgery. During Ben's absence, Dana paced the cheerless waiting room, a faded green holding area with wooden chairs and bare walls. An old woman sat in a corner clandestinely telling her beads. A crumpled newspaper had been left on one of the chairs. Dana read it and, as expected, found a brief notice about counterrevolutionaries disturbing the peace of Wenceslas Square. It included no photos of the fierce fighting, but exhibited some morose bureaucrats who undoubtedly had been marshalled to condemn "outside agitators." Four hours elapsed before the surgeon emerged from the operating theatre, looking sallow and sober. He explained Ben's condition:

"I did my best. He might live. I can't say. The skull splintered—into the brain. I removed what I could. There was an old injury, a metal plate, in the same place where he struck his head."

At first Dana thought she'd misunderstood, and asked the doctor to repeat what he'd said.

"Where he struck his head, it was vulnerable from a previous injury."

"He didn't strike his head!" Dana cried. "He was clubbed by a soldier . . . with a rifle!"

The doctor smiled and touched her arm. "You are distraught, confused. The events of the last few days. Riots and tear gas will do that. It disorients one. Mr. Cohen fell and struck his head on the steps in front of the police station. It says so in the official report brought just a short time ago."

"They're liars!" Dana cried.

The doctor left her standing in the waiting room, where she remained throughout the night. Early the next morning, a nurse led her into a private room. Ben lay unconscious, with his head heavily bandaged. The day passed. That evening, an attendant brought her a cot and some linens. She slept in Ben's room, eating hospital food and never changing her clothes. On the third day, he briefly regained consciousness and struggled to smile. The corners of his mouth slightly twitched. He tried to lift a trembling hand, but it fell helplessly back on the bed. His speech came out in reverse. Instead of speaking as he exhaled, he enunciated words—imperfectly—as he inhaled. It sounded like a combination of gasping and talking.

"A favor . . . write Marty. Tell him . . . if you can."

"You'll tell him yourself," she said with false optimism. "It's all right. Everything will be all right."

He again tried to smile, but gave up the effort. With great difficulty, he began to talk about loss and being blessed by the love of two women. He meandered into a memory about a friend in Korea. From what Dana could gather, he and another soldier had been sent out in a snowstorm to scout an advanced position. As the storm worsened, Ben insisted they return to their camp. In the swirling clouds of snow, those strangely fascinating whiteouts, his companion had refused and told Ben to go back. His body was never found. But Ben wanted Dana to know that even in the tragic mystery that surrounded the man's final moments, his courage stood out.

"He died . . . so full of youth."

Ben lapsed in and out of consciousness. In his lucid periods, he tried to explain that stories, sadly, don't matter unless they happen to us. "What good is it for me," he said, "to tell you stories about friends who died in the war. They don't mean anything to you—and if not to you, why am I telling them?"

Dana said that as she sat bedside him holding his hand, she thought of what life might be like if we all knew in advance what was going to happen. Would we continue? She supposed that our not knowing made life bearable.

Ben regained consciousness one last time, late at night. Dana heard him stirring. Turning on the night light, she held his head in her arms.

"Ask Marty . . . if he knows the word 'carking.'"

He spelled it. A hateful darkness then came into his pale blue eyes and he died.

Dana's story left me numb. My mind wandered and I found myself thinking that at death's door, people were supposed to make memorable statements, like Henry James's final words, "So here it is at last, the distinguished thing." I wept, because my friend's final thoughts had been about me.

The Czech hospital listed the cause of death as a clot, but the postmortem that I insisted be done in the United States gave so many other causes I could only conclude that he died of life.

Before leaving the Carpathian mountain redoubt of the Rehák family, I asked Dana to write down on a piece of paper a sentence in Czech, and through her father's old comrades to find out the address of Imre Gajda. I hung around for three more days until word came back—via a hand-delivered note because no one trusted the post—that Mr. Gajda still lived at the same Prague address, which was enclosed. The last night, I asked Dana why she had reacted with such distaste when I had mentioned the name Joe Riley.

"You knew," she said, "we once lovers."

"Shall we go out on the porch?" I whispered, fearing that her comments, if overheard, might prove compromising.

"Not necessary."

She lit a cigarette and filled the room with the unmistakable odor of Gaulois smoke, which always makes me think of a French railroad station. Mr. and Mrs. Rehák had gone on a walk, leaving Dana and me to say our last goodbyes. A hickory log crackled on the grate, spitting flinders up the flue.

"I wanted in America to stay."

"You were, of course, spying."

"You knew and Ben knew only."

"We didn't turn you in."

"No, Joe Riley did."

"Joe? He was a dyed-in-the-wool communist."

"So you don't know?"

"A Trotskyite, like you."

She drew so greedily on her cigarette that I thought she'd diminish it by half with one breath.

"Joe," she laughed sardonically, as her face vanished momentarily in a haze of smoke, "he was FBI."

"Joe!" I exclaimed, utterly disbelieving.

"Still while my father is serving in the Dubček government, I am working in the security department. In the files, I find a dossier marked Joe Riley and a photograph. He was a double agent."

My first impulse—to declare that Dana had lost her mind—gave way to disconcerting memories. During our stay in New Mexico, it seemed that every time we devised some strategy for advancing the cause of the strike, the government knew in advance. We often said that we suspected a mole had insinuated himself into Local 890.

"He used communism as, how you say, a camouflage. When they tell me I must leave the country, I ask for reasons. What they tell me, Joe can only know."

"He's dead," I said, explaining how it happened.

"I hope he kill Joe by shooting off his balls."

That night I slept uneasily, tortured by dreams. The mind can endure only so many betrayals until it retreats, like a flower folding its petals at dusk. I dreamt about being a young child, standing on a wall. Our next door neighbor in Detroit, Harold Denholtz, told me to jump and he would catch me. As I jumped, he turned and walked away, laughing.

Early the next morning, after breakfast, I left two pairs of Levis with the Reháks and pressed a hundred dollars into Dana's hand, even though I knew that if found with foreign currency, she would be subject to imprisonment. But the money, if used cautiously, might one day get her out of a tight scrape. She scribbled directions telling me how to reach her by mail. Letters should be sent to a certain person in Munich, who periodically brought them over the border and distributed them to couriers for hand delivery. The dollars would be used for that purpose. She drove me to the train station in Bratislava. As Dana and I embraced in the parking lot, I could have sworn that a man across the street focused his camera and telegraphic lens on us. I'll never know. Admittedly, since the hunters had emerged from the woods, and Dana said they might have been security

darkmatters **LEVITT**

agents, I believed that everyone spied and that every room in the country was bugged. As I bought a ticket in the train station, the woman asked to see my passport, a request that reinforced my belief that the country swarmed with informants.

Arriving in Prague, I checked into a small hotel near the station, and noticed that the streets had been recently scrubbed. The thought crossed my mind that they stood for Czech history, which now claimed that Dubček was no socialist. I made it a point to take a circuitous route to the address that I clutched in my hand. Arriving at an ugly block of apartments built in "Stalinist Modern," I felt glad that Mr. Gajda lived in such a tasteless building. The elevator, as one might have expected from the looks of the place, didn't work. Mounting the stairs to the third floor, I stood outside apartment 312 asking myself what mad impulse had led me to this pass. Anger seeks an object—a person or place—that we can blame for our pain. But when the cause of our ire issues from an abstraction, or from a vast network of banal people acceding unthinkingly to the momentum of the moment, whom can we blame? I nearly turned and left. But hearing voices inside, I knocked at the door. A plain woman in a chintz dress answered. She leaned on a crutch, her right leg missing below the knee. She greeted me in Czech. Her thick yellow hair, the prettiest part of her, billowed slightly at the sides, and lyrical loops bound in a bun topped her head. I mentioned her husband's name. She peered at me apprehensively, no doubt because my accent marked me as a foreigner. She closed the door. Shortly, a most ordinary man peered out. Except for his badly scuffed shoes, he would have been as indistinguishable as air. I spoke to him in English, identifying myself as a dear friend of Ben Cohen, a name that clearly meant nothing to him. So I showed him a snapshot that I kept in my wallet. A faint movement of his head told me that he recognized Ben.

"What do you want?"

"You interrogated him."

"That's my job."

"He died in Prague. One of your security agents . . ."

"Thousands died in the war. Our Russian friends liberated us from the fascist monster."

It was then I realized that I had come to view the face of evil and to hear the sound of its voice. But what I saw and heard came to nothing grander than a guttered human flame struggling to keep burning. His tallow was nothing more than cheap platitudes. From my pocket I removed the slip of paper. He looked expectant. I paused. Behind him I could see his wife's careworn face. It crossed my mind that perhaps she feared I represented another form of the hateful knock on the door. I therefore pocketed the note and left. He called out to me, but I never turned, his utterance obscured by the voices of two elderly people shuffling up the stairs. All I could be sure of were the Talmudic words on the note: "Who can protest and does not is an accomplice."

At the end of the summer, I flew to El Paso and from there took a bus to Silver City. Esperanza met me at the station. When I had telephoned and said I wanted to see her, she immediately divined Ben's death, which I had never disclosed. But now that I knew the end of the story—assuming that Dana had told me the truth—I felt Esperanza should know.

"I wanted to tell you in person," I had said on the phone, "not this way."

"You still can," she had gently replied.

Beautiful as ever, she radiated delight at my visit. We took a cab to her house. Her abuela met us at the door. Their small, tidy bungalow had been decorated with some of the ceramic pots and rugs that adorned her old place in Hanover. I wondered if Luis had parted with them gladly and where he had gone; but I refrained from asking because I decided the day belonged to Ben. On a sideboard and end tables stood a profusion of framed photographs taken of the "Salt of the Earth" strike. A number of them included Ben; even I showed up in a couple. The rest of the pictures I guessed were of family, some charting the growth of her adopted son. The talk naturally gravitated toward Prague. She softly cried as I recounted the awful events.

Her abuela spoke to me in Spanish. The only word I could make out sounded like "lachrymose." I smiled and shrugged. "No yo hablo español."

She pointed with pride to the menorah on the mantelpiece and showed me the wall blanket with the Star of David. I could envision her medieval ancestors—bronze-skinned Spaniards and North Africans—outwardly observing the customs of Catholics and surreptitiously retreating into cellars to pray, hidden from the eyes of the Inquisition. It occurred to me that our secret lives, even if no more than private thoughts, mean more to us than all the daily routines that constitute a life. Esperanza returned with a tray of food and a pot of strong coffee. We ate and we talked, with Esperanza occasionally translating for her abuela, but keeping from her

darkmatters
LEVITT

what she told me about Luis. He had been arrested in Mexico for subversive activities and had cooperated with the police, subsequently becoming an informer and trafficking in the lucrative marijuana trade. Living in Laredo, he had surrounded himself with anglo whores and with horses. Although their religion forbade them to divorce, Luis had sought and received an annulment on the grounds of her abandonment.

"Your abandonment!" I exclaimed in disbelief.

"It's true. I lived apart from him for a year, in Mexico. He didn't know where."

"I don't understand."

A door slammed at the back of the house and a handsome young man came through the kitchen into the living room, carrying a mechanical apparatus that illustrates with balls of various sizes the relative motions and positions of the bodies in the solar system. For one magical moment, I sincerely believed that Ben Cohen had come back to life. The boy had Ben's high cheekbones, small mouth, and narrow face. Swarthy and dark haired, he also had his mother's radiance.

"My son, Benjamínito!"

We exchanged greetings and shook hands.

"Professor Shull let me bring this home. It's called an orrery," he said taking it into his bedroom.

"He's wild about astronomy. He even has a telescope mounted on the back porch. I wanted him to go to the university in Albuquerque, but he decided to stay here in Silver City. It's not a bad college. Small but caring."

I remained two nights, sleeping on the living room couch, just enough time to befriend Benjamínito and see in him the qualities I would wish to inculcate in a son, if God in His goodness granted me one. Even though I deplore those people who debase the coinage with unearned praise, I must say that the boy had imbibed the politeness of an older culture and had inherited his parents' unalloyed decency and combativeness. He also shared Ben's interest in philosophy and politics. Fittingly, he headed an active campus chapter of Amnesty International, whose services his father could have used.

While waiting for the cab to take me back to the station, I asked her why she had never told Ben that he had a son. "He would have been overjoyed."

"I had to hide it, my pregnancy. The shame . . . for Luis, my abuela, my community. So I stayed with a girlfriend in Mexico City, until the baby was

darkmatters LEVITT

three months old. When I came back, I said he'd been adopted." She reached for a photograph of Ben that she kept on a side table. Admiring it, she continued: "If Luis had known the truth, he would have said that I insulted his manhood, and would have wanted to kill the father. That's why I couldn't tell Ben."

"Does your abuela know?"

"I never told her. I said that I had a job in Mexico. But by now I'm sure she's guessed. He resembles his father. She would rather die, though, than utter a word."

My memory of Esperanza and Ben together led me to say wistfully: "If he had only known about the annulment, perhaps the two of you could have—"

She interposed. "That's for storybooks and romances. I'm a faithful daughter of the Church, even if I have sinned."

I said nothing further touching on the subject. The cab arrived, and Esperanza walked me to the curb.

"He's the spitting image of Ben," I said. "Same intensity also."

"Yes . . . both dark."

I misunderstood, imagining skin color. Esperanza, whose emotional radar system was so exquisite that it could detect a faulty synapse, smiled and said:

"Dark matters."

Shortly after arriving home, I contacted Clarissa, just then packing to leave for a Christmas in Paris. I asked her to give a Chanukah present to my godson.

"I didn't know you had one. Who is it?"

Wary of telling the truth, I lied. "Luis and Esperanza Morales's son."

She paused. "What's his name?"

Although I had anticipated this question, I still found it awkward to say: "Benjamínito . . . Benjamínito Morales."

Whatever Clarissa's thoughts—and I could sense in the silence her knowing—she didn't share them with me. To her everlasting credit, she rose to the occasion.

"I like the name. What's the gift?"

"A college scholarship . . . in honor of Ben."

"Done!" she said, and agreed to send a check to the office of financial services at the school.

I called Esperanza to tell her about the scholarship, but decided not to disclose the ruse I had used. Her response brought tears to my eyes.

"I will tell the priest to enter in the church registry that you are Benjamínito's belated godfather."

*　　*　　*　　*

Upon my return to the post office, I asked Mr. Henker if he would speak to the postmaster to expedite my application for a transfer from the Mail Recovery room. Evenings and every free moment I spent feverishly working on this manuscript.

In early December, I received the following reply.

Dear Mr. Bartleman,

Normally in the postal system, we say that a person's competence counts more than his team spirit. When we say this, we mean that our principal responsibility is to the public; even so, we would like to see our staff contribute to departmental morale. In a first-rate postal system, staffers exhibit a willingness "to step up to the plate." There is certainly a wide range of activities that properly fall within contributing to departmental morale. But unfortunately, there are today attitudes that are fundamentally unhelpful to our well-run institution, attitudes that are not consonant with our motto "Enlarger of the Common Life." If attitudes held by a postal employee are of this kind, then it becomes our obligation to concern ourselves about them, because in the long run they would undermine cooperation and be destructive of our system. The holders of such views often parade, whether they know it or not, under the banner of free choice, while in reality they are devoted to selfishness.

According to your supervisor, Werner Henker, you refuse to accommodate yourself to his requests. Although the rules of the workplace guarantee the free expression of one's views—a guarantee that is in fact the very air of a free society—those rules do not transcend the needs of the post office.

In light of what Mr. Henker has reported to me about your
uncooperative attitude, I must regretfully turn down your application for
a transfer to the passport department.

Sincerely yours,
Foster Bayard, Postmaster

*　　*　　*　　*　　*

One evening, a few days later, sitting in near darkness, with a bottle of Bordeaux Chateau Talbot, and listening to Beethoven's "Archduke" trio, I contemplated a future of repetitive labors. How, I worried, would I survive? A single candle, resting on my mother's antique hutch, the only piece of furniture that had come to me shortly after her death, illumined Ben's drawing, the one he had purchased in Prague and I had inherited: Wenceslas Square at night. In the flickering light, the dots of color darted in and out of the smoke, one moment visible, the next not. From my oblique angle of vision, I noticed for the first time that at the bottom of the frame the picture bulged slightly—and not just from the stretcher bars, which had left their own distinctive ridges. My curiosity piqued, I removed the brown-paper backing and found a small notecard tucked between the stretcher bar and the canvas. I had no memory of Ben asking about the painter or the provenance; perhaps the notecard contained both. Written in Czech, in a hand that resembled a child's scrawl, were the words

Kreslím, abych nemusela myslet na Terezín. Žiji ve vzpomínkách. Tam
jsem vždy šťastná, mám dost jídla a teplý kabát. Co dalšího by mohl
člověk chtít?

Dvanáctiletá Rebeka Stavická
koncentrační tabor, 2.21.44

Unwilling to wait until morning, I reached for the phone and called Josef Michl, a Czech colleague. Spelling the letters for him and describing the diacritical markings, I listened as he translated.

"I draw so I won't think of Terezín. I live in my memory. There I am always happy, with enough to eat and a warm coat. What more could anyone want?"

Rebeka Stavická, age 12
Concentration camp, February 10, 1944

Comprehension came slowly. Then tears trickled down my face. The children's drawings in the Jewish Museum came to mind, and I puzzled how this one had ended up in the hands of a private art dealer. Perhaps a guard or a survivor from the camp had smuggled it out. Whatever its history, I knew what I had to do. From Dana, I would learn Mr. Stavicky's address, and send him the drawing, so that he too could have the consolation of memory.

And as I sat there, with the note in my hand, I could see it all again, as if watching a movie: the professors in the university theatre, with a president driven by a warped sense of duty travestying academic freedom; Roger's Kitchen and four college kids devouring fried chicken and biscuits; the shelter on Flagstaff Mountain, as the light of a billion years rained down; the unbowed women and men of Local 890; the cabin in Eldorado Springs and the thump, thump, thump of the electrical pump pulling water from the river in accompaniment to my sexual initiation; Clarissa and Abby in their white and yellow dresses; Esperanza's shining forehead and radiant hair; Dana's nicotine-stained fingers; Lexington; Hanover; Prague. Especially Prague, the city of beauty and bane. Yes, I could see it all again; and as the past became present, I pondered the wilderness of this world and wondered about the crimes we commit in the service of impossible loyalties. Although Ben had willed me these pages, I couldn't help feeling that perhaps I had violated a trust. And yet I took comfort in thinking that Ben wanted me to remember him as a young Korean war vet singing the Hallelujah chorus in Brackett Hall. So when it's time to close the book, I can leave consoled by the story we shared, and smile at grief. What more could I possibly ask for?

darkmatters
LEVIT